A Broken Resilience

Rachel Mays

ISBN: 979-8-9872089-6-0

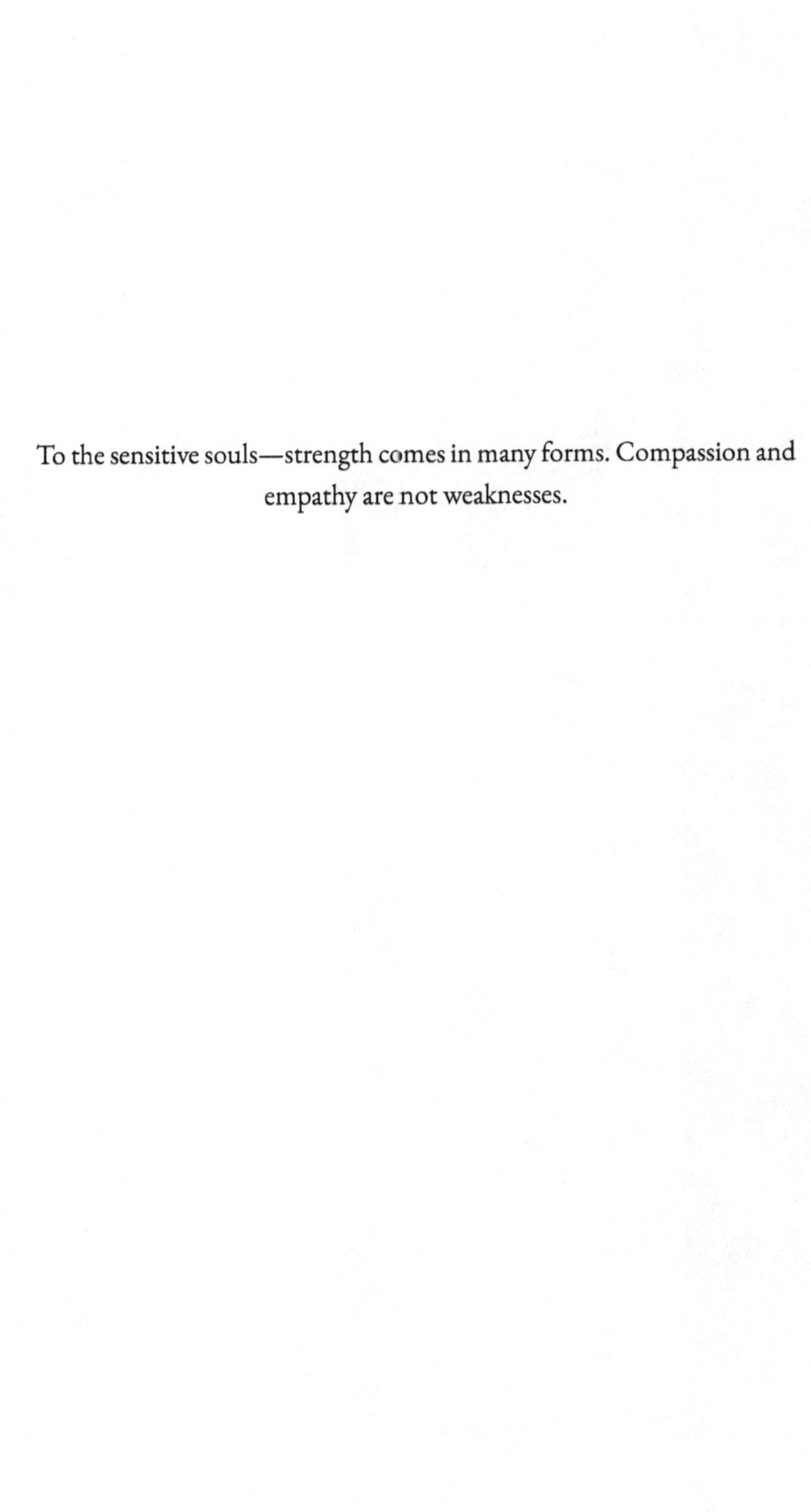

To the sensitive souls—strength comes in many forms. Compassion and empathy are not weaknesses.

Author's Note:

This story contains content that may not be suitable for all readers, including but not limited to, graphic depictions of and references to violence, death, depression, PTSD, and miscarriage. Please take care of your mental health!

Chapter One

GRACE

"Eli," Grace breathed, her voice soft in his ear.

Eli stirred, though his eyes remained closed.

She traced a hand along his hip bone, grazing the skin above his waistband until the smallest smile appeared on his face. "Eli..."

He sighed, and she was fairly certain he was waiting to see just how far she'd go to wake him from his slumber.

She toyed with the hem of his shorts, her fingertips drawing a path across his stomach. He shuddered, and her thighs rubbed together as she considered every depraved thing she wanted to do to him. And luckily, they had all day to do it.

His breath hitched when she cupped him over his thin sleepwear.

"I know you're awake, Eli."

A tortured moan rumbled in his throat as she began to massage his balls. "I don't know, Grace. It feels like I might still be dreaming. It's hard to tell."

With a soft laugh, Grace climbed on top of him, his rigid length easing the ache between her legs. It had been less than a week since Eli had declared his participation in the Rite. Would he grow tired of her invading his bed every evening and waking him up early every morning? By the grin growing on his face, she was certain it hadn't happened yet.

"You're insatiable."

"You know me so well."

At last, he opened his eyes, and she melted into him. No one had ever looked at her like that. Like she was more than a title. She knew deep in her soul that if she'd been just another girl from Berland, Eli would've looked at her exactly the same. Like she was precious. Like she was meant for him.

As she leaned in to kiss him, he drew her close, his arms tightening around her. That groan resurfaced when she rolled her hips against him.

His lips parted, and she had no trouble sliding her tongue over his. Her hips moved faster, and she gasped when the tip of his cock brushed her clit.

"Take these off," he said, gesturing toward her pajama shorts. She quickly removed them, as well as the matching top, and tossed them aside. When she moved to grab his shorts, he grabbed her wrists.

"Not yet."

Eli held her hips and pulled her forward, bring her closer to the headboard until she was kneeling over his face. Her heart skipped a beat as his hungry eyes met hers. Again, he grabbed her thighs and squeezed. He held her, suspended only inches above his mouth.

"Sit," he said, flicking his tongue out to tease her slit.

Grace's legs trembled, but she obeyed his command and lowered until she worried she wouldn't be able to hold herself up any longer.

Eli pressed his tongue flat against her pussy and made a swirling motion that had her whimpering. She grabbed the headboard to keep steady, but the things he was doing to her would inevitably cause her to combust.

She could feel it already—her skin turning blazing hot, her cunt dripping with arousal, her mind going hazy...

A needy moan escaped her lips as Eli plunged his tongue inside her. It was just enough to drive her mad with desire. When he hummed his approval, she squeezed her thighs against his cheeks.

"Eli, I need more."

He pulled away just long enough to respond. "You'll take whatever I give you, Grace."

She couldn't help but smile. It wasn't that long ago that Eli had seemed so reserved. She'd enjoyed teasing him, but now it seemed he'd learned a lesson or two in mixing pleasure with torture.

She ground her pussy against his face while he squeezed her ass. Peering over her shoulder, she found his erection taut against his shorts, and she could just make out the outline of the head through the thin fabric. If she wasn't mistaken, that dark spot was evidence of his arousal gathered at the tip.

Another swipe of his tongue across her clit had her gripping the wooden headboard with all her might. She looked down at him and watched as he greedily devoured her pussy. It was a magnificent sight to behold, and the view sent her tumbling over the edge. She let out a sigh of ecstasy and pulsed against his face. "Fuck, Eli."

She felt him smile beneath her, though he kept licking and sucking until the last of her tremors ceased. When she tried to pull away, he gripped her tighter, still running his tongue over her sensitive clit.

Grace threaded her fingers through his messy hair and pulled his head away. "Give me a second."

The intensity in Eli's dark eyes had her second guessing whether he could possibly restrain himself. But he conceded and loosened his grip.

She rolled off of him and fell to her side, propping her head up on her palm. Her heart was still hammering in her chest, her limbs heavy, when Eli turned to face her and ran a teasing finger up her leg.

As her eyes traveled down his body, they caught on the large bulge in his shorts. She reached to free him, but he caught her around the wrist again.

"It's your turn," she said. She was aching to wrap her fingers around his cock, to please him the way he had pleased her. "You're not going to let me touch you?"

Eli grinned. "Of course I want you to touch me. In fact, I'd prefer if you'd use me for your pleasure for the rest of your life."

A mixture of heat and longing swelled within her as his gaze roamed over her body. She was completely enamored by the way he studied her with lust-filled eyes and spoke to her like he was content to serve her—to give her everything—rather than take from her like everyone else seemed to do.

Eli didn't care about what he stood to gain by marrying her. He only cared about making her happy.

"You'll let me do whatever I want?"

He looked a little wary but nodded. "Anything."

"And if I want you to do something?"

"Just say the word."

Grace thought for a moment of all the filthy things she'd like to do with Eli. The list was extensive. Hopefully they'd have the rest of their lives to explore each other.

She pushed up to a kneeling position, and this time, as she reached for the waistband of his shorts, he didn't stop her. She tugged them down, pausing for him to lift his hips so she could slide them past his ass. When his cock sprung free, she inhaled sharply.

But she didn't touch him.

"Show me how you touch yourself."

Eli chuckled with amusement. "Yes, sweetheart."

Grace watched as Eli moved his hand down his chest, down until he reached the base of his cock and wrapped a hand around his thickening shaft. He sucked in a breath, and she pulled her bottom lip between her teeth.

She tried not to squirm—this was supposed to test his self-restraint, not hers—but the sight of him pumping his cock set her skin on fire. Watching with undivided attention, she slid her hand between her thighs and began to rub circles over her clit.

Noticing her movement, Eli's grin widened. "Does this turn you on, Grace?"

Quickening her pace, she nodded. "Show me more."

Eli stroked himself with more intensity, adding small thrusts with his hips. His breath turned ragged and frantic as he pushed himself closer to the edge.

When he groaned and his head rolled back, Grace commanded him, "Stop."

Eli gritted his teeth. A spark of lightning flashed in his eyes, but he dropped his hand immediately, clutching at the sheet beside him instead. "Fuck."

Grace's chuckle bordered on villainous.

The vein in Eli's neck pulsed, matching the highly visible vein in his cock. "Do you enjoy torturing me?"

Grace slid her fingers down further, feeling the gathering wetness between her shaky legs. As she withdrew her hand, she grazed that protruding vein, leaving a trail of her arousal up his shaft. "Maybe just a little bit."

Eli responded with a frustrated groan, his cock twitching at Grace's delicate touch. "Please."

"Please what?" she asked, brushing her fingertip over his sensitive head, painting him with her arousal.

"Stop taunting me." The way he gritted his teeth seemed painful, and only excited her more.

"But it's so fun."

"Grace..."

Although she was enjoying taking her time and driving him wild, it wouldn't be long before he snapped and flipped her on her back. He could easily take control and she didn't want to relinquish it. Slowly, she inched up his body, dragging her tongue along the center of his stomach until her knees rested beside his hips.

Reaching between her legs, she found his firm cock and wasted no time guiding him inside her. They both released a sigh in unison.

Eli tried to reach for her waist, but she pushed his hands away, keeping them at his sides.

"You said I could use you."

With a smile, Eli nodded. His eyes roamed her body—from her full red lips to her flushed chest to where his throbbing cock fit inside her.

It didn't take long for her to adjust to his size. Leaning forward, she placed her hands on his shoulders and began to rock her hips. Faster, and with more fervor, she ground against him, chasing that explosion of ecstasy she felt building in her core.

Using him...she didn't know why that idea excited her so much, but she'd always been taunted by wicked thoughts. Things that she could only put into action at Azalea's, but Eli was keen to fulfill every one of her desires.

In public, she had to be the pristine, perfect heiress of Berland. But here, in private with Eli, she was free to be herself. He would never judge her.

Her pace became frantic. She could hardly feel anything aside from the ravenous hunger inside her, and when Eli groaned with satisfaction, she happily toppled over the edge with him.

She wasn't sure how much time had passed when she came down from her high, cheek pressed against Eli's warm chest.

"Has your mom spoken to you?" he asked a few minutes later, stroking her hair. Ever since the moment Eli stood and declared his entrance to the Rite, Grace's mother had been even more irritable than usual. They'd hardly spoken aside from official business matters.

"No," she said quietly.

"I don't know why she's taking it out on you. I'm the one who defied her wishes."

"Yes, but she knows I'm happy you did." Grace smiled against his rising and falling chest. Even if her mother was angry with her, she wouldn't change a thing. Eli was the one for her. "She'll get over it eventually."

"Still, I'll never understand why she treats you the way she does."

Grace propped herself up so she could look into Eli's eyes. "I like it when you get all protective like this, but you don't need to worry about me. I can handle it."

He looked like he might argue, but he bit his tongue. Perhaps he realized that if he tried to intervene, he'd likely only make things worse.

A knock rapped against Eli's door and they both fell silent.

"Were you expecting company this morning?" Grace whispered.

Eli shook his head. "If we both stay quiet, maybe they'll go away."

Grace held her breath, hoping whoever it was would move along. She'd been looking forward to spending all day tangled in the sheets with Eli. Just one day off duty—that was all she wanted.

Someone knocked again, and this time a voice rang out, sounding muffled through the door. "I know you're in there, Eli. Stop ignoring me."

Eli sighed. "Damn it, Ali."

Grace reluctantly rolled off him and he rose out of bed, grabbing a pair of shorts as he headed for the door. Pulling the soft white sheets up to her chin, Grace waited patiently.

She heard the door swing open, and Eli greeted his friend. "Ali, what are you doing here?"

Ali was bursting with energy, speaking freely as she strode through the door. "You can't avoid me forever. I knew it. I *knew* it. I told you to get your head out of your ass and go after her, but you just had to wait till the last minute to declare yourself a suitor. So typical." She prodded Eli in the chest, still not noticing Grace hidden under the covers.

Grace chuckled softly. When she had first met Ali, she'd wondered if Eli might still be in love with her. How could he not be? She was beautiful, gentle, kind, poised—all the things Grace's mother wished for in a daughter. All the things Grace tried to be but could never live up to. Not to mention the two of them had a very long and complex history. How could Grace ever compete with that?

Watching the two of them now, it was clear there was a strong connection between them, but he didn't speak to Ali the way he spoke to Grace. He certainly didn't look at her the same either. Maybe there would always be an unbreakable bond, but seeing them interact as mere friends eased Grace's worries.

Ali moved further into the room, still rambling on. "You should've listened to me to begin with. You could've saved yourself—oh!"

Grace waved at Ali, who had finally spotted her in Eli's bed.

Ali clasped a hand over her mouth, glancing back and forth between them. "I'm sorry. I didn't mean to *interrupt*."

Grace laughed. "It's okay. We can't stay cooped up forever."

Even if she wanted to.

She gestured to the navy-blue shirt discarded on the floor. "Can you toss me that?"

Eli was quick to retrieve it and toss it in her direction. Both he and Ali turned away while Grace pulled it over her head. The button-up shirt belonged to Eli and was long enough to fall down to her upper thighs, but she kept her legs tucked beneath the blankets, just in case.

"Did you come here for a reason, Ali? Other than to yell at me?" Eli crossed his arms and looked as if he was seconds away from pushing Ali out the door so he could be left alone with Grace again.

Before she could respond, Grace chimed in, "Actually, I need to speak with you. I had planned on finding you later today, but if you're available now, we should get together. Nik and Sam as well."

Ali flashed a kind smile. "Sure. I'll go grab them and meet you in the dining hall?"

"Be there soon."

Eli walked Ali to the door and, once he closed it behind her, he turned to Grace. "What was that about?"

Grace slid out of bed and gathered her clothes. "Work arrangements," she said, slipping on her shoes and planting a kiss on his cheek.

He stared with a bewildered look on his face. "What happened to spending all day together in bed?"

"This won't take long. But if you want to climb back into bed, no one is stopping you." She headed toward the door, but when she reached the handle, she turned and winked at him. "Don't have too much fun without me."

Chapter Two

NIK

THE COMMOTION IN THE dining hall had already started to die down by the time Nik made his way with Ali and Sam beside him. He had just been about to go for a run when Ali burst through the door of their small home and insisted he come to the dining hall with her. He'd have to get his workout in later.

"Did she say what she wanted?" Sam asked, gathering fruit from the buffet onto his plate. After he'd selected a variety of berries, he added a dollop of creamy white yogurt.

Nik opted for the sizzling sausage links and potatoes, the savory scent making his stomach growl. Beside him, Ali grabbed a slice of buttered toast and a serving of some sort of breakfast casserole, primarily made of eggs and green herbs. Nik held her plate while she dug in her pocket for some money. "Nope. But if she wanted all of us together, it must be important."

The dining hall was nearly deserted, with only a handful of people scattered throughout the vast space. Crowds were already dispersing to go about their day, whether it be work or leisure, leaving behind empty seats. They chose an open table on the left side of the room, close to the entrance so they could see Grace when she appeared.

Nik's stomach growled again and this time, Sam's echoed. He took a hasty bite, not caring if the scalding potatoes burned the roof of his mouth.

Halfway through his second helping of sausages, Grace waltzed into the dining hall holding a notebook and pencil, looking casual in jeans, a silk tank top, and a beige cardigan. She spotted them immediately and took a seat next to Sam.

"Good morning," she said in a lyrical tone that irritated Nik for no reason. "I wanted to talk to you all today about open work positions. Since you've been here for a couple weeks and have had a moment to get adjusted, I thought it was time to discuss your options. I have some ideas picked out for you, but you may choose to go a different direction if you prefer."

Ali and Sam gave Grace their full attention while Nik gave a noncommittal nod. Whatever Grace had chosen for him, he was sure it would be fine. Now that he'd been given a fresh start, he had no idea what he wanted to do. Who he wanted to be. He'd never had a future full of possibilities, and now that he did, he wasn't sure what to do with it.

"I'll start with you, Sam," Grace said, turning in her seat to face him. "Theo said you have an interest in art?"

Sam's face betrayed a hint of surprise, hearing that Theo had shared such information with Grace, despite how true it was. He cleared his throat. "Yes, that's right."

She tapped the end of her pencil against her lips. "Unfortunately, most of our artistic positions are temporary—painting murals, designing landscapes, things like that. It's not a steady stream of work around here. But I'll let you know if any short-term positions open up. In the meantime, how do you feel about animals?"

"Animals?" Sam repeated with skepticism.

"Yes."

"I'd rather not be a butcher, if that's what you're thinking."

Grace let out a short burst of laughter. "Not at all. Our veterinarian's assistant had an accident and will need to be off her feet for a few months. Since she was the only assistant, we need a backup as soon as possible."

The tension across Sam's forehead relaxed almost instantaneously. "Oh, that does sound much better. Although I can't say I have much experience with that sort of thing."

Grace waved a hand. "Don't worry. Zoe is an excellent teacher. Folks around here are used to giving hands-on training. It comes with the territory."

Sam nodded, looking pleased with his new position. Nik couldn't explain it, but working with animals seemed like the perfect fit for him. Perhaps it was his aversion to interacting with humans.

Grace turned her attention back to the notebook in her hands, skimming down the page. "Nik, from what I've heard, you've spent your whole life as a guard."

Nik straightened in his seat. "That's right." Though he wasn't sure what he was made for anymore. He was tired of the violence and risking his life for people who didn't deserve it. All he wanted to do was live peacefully with Ali...and maybe have a few kids down the road.

"I was thinking with the recent uptick in rebellion activity paired with the fact that I'll be required to attend multiple public events throughout the Rite, that you might want to be my personal guard."

Nik drew in a breath, his shoulders going rigid. Out of the corner of his eye, he could see Ali staring, her lips pulled into a frown and her brown eyes full of compassion. She knew the toll it had taken on him during his last few months in Rysburg. Could he return to that life?

"I don't know…"

Grace's gaze flicked between the two of them, realizing she was missing something, though she couldn't possibly know his side of the story. She'd probably only heard Eli's description of Nik—a heartless brute who'd manipulated his friend and ex-lover. "Sorry. I assumed you'd want a position you were familiar with, but I can look for something else."

Beneath the table, his legs bounced restlessly. "What would I be responsible for?"

"I'd need someone at my side during ceremonies, parties, and each of the three rounds, of course. Someone to watch my back and prevent anything from happening. I doubt anything will, but it's better to be safe than sorry, I suppose."

Despite her lighthearted tone, Nik detected a subtle trace of anxiety when she spoke. She wasn't quite as self-assured as she let on.

Relief washed over him, realizing that he wouldn't be required to pillage or attack defenseless populations. He would only need to defend Grace when the situation called for it. Maybe he could handle that.

Nik scratched the stubble on his chin. "Can I think about it?"

"Sure," Grace responded. "That just leaves you, Ali."

It was Ali's turn to sit up straight. Her enthusiasm for being part of the community was undeniably charming. Nik briefly wondered what her life had looked like in Andus before his people had ruined it. She deserved to be happy, and it was partially his fault that her life had turned out this way. He shifted in his seat, unable to relax.

Grace continued, "With Gabriel accused of treason and after Nelson's death, our council is down two members. Since I will be taking over leadership duties soon, my mother has allowed me to fill one of those positions."

The conversation came to a halt and even the air felt stiff. There could only be one reason for Grace to bring up the council. Certainly, she didn't mean for Ali to fill that position...

"I want you to join the council."

Heavy silence fell again, only broken when Ali let out a small laugh. "Are you serious? I'm not qualified for that at all."

"The council's job is to weigh options and make recommendations, and I think you're perfectly qualified for that," Grace countered.

"I haven't even lived here an entire month. How could I possibly make decisions for the people in Berland?"

"That's exactly why I want you for the position. You've lived in several communities now and can bring fresh ideas to the table. You know first-hand what works and what doesn't. But really, I need someone I can trust. Someone who is on my side. Most of the council is loyal to my mother and I don't trust them."

Ali's cheeks flushed pink. "But you think you can trust me?"

"Absolutely. Eli has told me enough about you to know that you're selfless and innovative, two characteristics that would make an excellent resource." Reaching across the table, Grace grabbed Ali's hands. "So believe me when I say you are exactly the kind of person I want to join my council."

Ali blinked a few times, clearly still caught off guard by Grace's suggestion. But to Nik's surprise, she didn't immediately decline. She bit her bottom lip as she contemplated the offer, and then cleared her throat. "Can I also think about it?"

It may as well have been a 'yes.'

Grace dropped Ali's hands and leaned back from the table with a huge grin on her face. "Of course. Take a few days to think it over and I'll be in touch. And Sam, I'll let Zoe know that you're able to start right away."

She lightly brushed Sam's arm as she stood from the table, and their gazes followed her out of the hall before unleashing their thoughts in a torrent.

"I don't know how I feel—"

"They'd never accept me—"

"What other animals do they have aside from horses?"

Nik and Ali turned to Sam, whose cheeks brightened as his lip turned up into a sheepish grin. "You know what? I think I'll take a walk and let you two discuss things."

Once the two of them were alone, Ali twisted in her seat to face Nik.

"Are you nervous?" he asked, eyeing her lap where she was wringing her hands.

"A little."

"Tell me what you're thinking."

She brushed a hair behind her ear and took a deep breath. "Would you think I'm crazy if I said I wanted to do this?"

Nik's brows rose. He hadn't been expecting that.

"You don't think I can?"

"Not at all. I just didn't know you wanted that kind of responsibility. We haven't been here that long and you're ready to take on that big of a role? And what about Eamon and his rebels? They've already made attacks on Grace's mother. Ali, you could be putting yourself in danger by taking this position."

How was it possible that the job she'd been offered was somehow even more dangerous than the one Grace had selected for him? It was a twist he hadn't seen coming at all.

Ali's shoulders slumped. "You're right. I probably can't handle it."

Damn it.

"That's not what I meant. Of course you can handle it. You can do anything you want. I just didn't realize *this* is what you wanted."

The shadow on her face lessened a bit, and Nik breathed a sigh of relief. "I didn't know I did either until Grace offered it. I've always wanted to do something more meaningful than checking fish traps or planting crops. Maybe this is it. Maybe I could have a positive influence here."

Nik nodded. He had no doubt she'd succeed if it was what she truly wanted. Her empathy and compassion made her perfect for the job. "You should accept the position."

She smiled and brushed his cheek with her palm, planting a chaste kiss on his lips. "And what about you? You didn't seem thrilled at the idea of being Grace's bodyguard."

He let out a long sigh. "I don't know. I thought I left that life behind. I'm not proud of who I was or the things I had to do in Rysburg. You know that." He chanced a glance at her and recognized the sympathy in her eyes. "I don't want it to be like that again."

Ali took his hand and slid her fingers between his, giving him a small squeeze. "You're not a monster, Nik. It won't be the same. You'll be protecting someone, not harming them."

"But I might have to. If Grace is ever in danger, I would have to be that person again. What if I'm put in a position where I have to kill again?"

"I don't think you will, but *if* it happens, then it would be out of necessity."

Nik shook his head. "That's exactly what I told myself before. That I *had* to fight and pillage because it was for the good of Rysburg. That it was for our protection. But we were never at risk."

"It's not the same," Ali said.

Nik appreciated her defensiveness, but he wasn't sure he agreed. "Isn't it? We're all taught to think in black and white, but one person's savior is another's villain. Who ultimately gets to decide?"

Ali laid her head on Nik's shoulder. Her next words were soft. "The fact that you're even this concerned about taking the position shows that you're a decent human, Nik. You're the savior in my story."

Nik huffed a laugh. "You saved yourself, Ali."

"Maybe. But I don't think I would've fought as hard without you on the other side."

A weight seemed to press on Nik's shoulders and it wasn't Ali's head resting there. Her words made sense, but something still told him this was a bad idea.

"Are you scared?" Ali asked.

Nik shook his head. "Not of fighting. I can hold my own. I'm more scared of who I could become. I thought I had finally made it off this path, but now I'm right back where I started."

"I don't think you are. You've abandoned that path completely and now you're paving your own. One that's more honorable and righteous. But it's completely up to you, Nik. I'll support you no matter what you decide."

Maybe she was right. Unfortunately, the only way to know was by going through with it.

"Can you promise me one thing?" he asked.

"Anything."

"If at any point you think I'm headed in the wrong direction, will you be the one to set me straight?"

Her smile was so wide, it crinkled the corners of her eyes. "Of course, I will."

"Looks like I'm a guard once again."

Maybe this time, he wouldn't blindly follow corruption. Maybe this time, he could prove his worth.

Chapter Three

GRACE

Before Grace made it halfway down the hall leading to the council chamber, she could hear the heated debate. Fighting the urge to roll her eyes and turn back around, she steeled herself and prepared for the hours of arguments that awaited her.

It hadn't always been like this. Grace had begun attending council meetings at the age of fifteen. Back then, she'd only been required to sit through an hour or two of discussions before being dismissed. Her mother had wanted her to see firsthand how issues were resolved and how to efficiently navigate tough conversations and compromise for the betterment of Berland.

But over time, things had changed. If Grace had to pinpoint a specific moment in time, it was probably when Eamon had joined the council. Slowly, his toxic beliefs had spread to other members of the council until half the chamber was covered in his poison ivy.

His gripes varied from day to day and year to year. First, it was finances, then it was the number of outsiders Berland took in. Occasionally, he brought up disadvantageous trade agreements. Every single one of his complaints all led back to the same root issue—that once upon a time, his ancestor was bypassed as ruler in favor of a matriarch.

It didn't matter how many years had passed. There had always been someone in Eamon's lineage who had an issue with women in leadership, a belief he had now passed on to his son Trevor. The complaints Eamon brought up during council meetings were nothing more than flimsy evidence of her mother's inability to rule.

Grace wasn't even sure Eamon believed his own bullshit, but it had proven effective in gaining supporters for his cause. In fact, a few other members of the council were now Eamon's allies. Grace was surprised that so many had fallen for his lies and empty promises.

Lately, these council meetings had grown even more heated and tiring. It was all she could do to not stand up and walk out at any given moment, letting the so-called grownups carry on with their tantrums.

The room quieted as she entered the circular room filled with antique furniture and frowning faces. The room had two tiers. The upper level was the outermost circle, filled with shelves of old tomes and various odds and ends. A long table curved around the room with seats spaced evenly for each member. There was a single break in the arched table, where two steps led down to the lower level—an empty space for presentations and displays.

Grace looked each council member over as she made her way to her seat next to her mother's at the top of the arch.

There was Diane, the most reasonable of the council members by Grace's standards. She held the same beliefs as Grace—that much of the fear mongering was entirely unnecessary and unjustified. Nine out of ten times she sided with Grace, so Grace offered her a friendly smile as she passed.

Then there were the more neutral council members. The ones who mostly sat back and waited until either side had exhausted their arguments before they voiced their opinions. Some days, she adored them. Some days, they irritated her beyond belief.

Violet was the eldest, and recent survivor of the attack on Grace's mother. Her haunted blue eyes indicated she wasn't quite over that day. Nelson's loss had rattled them all, but even more so Violet since it could've easily been her.

Then there was Mason, a dark-skinned man twice Grace's age. Most council members were—another reason Grace was so intent on having Ali join. They needed more young people to represent the voices of Berland. He pushed up his thin-framed glasses and tipped his head to acknowledge Grace as she walked by.

Clayton, the man with a buzz cut and wooly sweater, sat next to Fox. Fox wasn't his actual name. It was Finn, but his blazing red hair had earned him the nickname when he was just a child. They were in their thirties, the youngest in the group, and the easiest to sway to Grace's side.

And then there were the *others*. Grace couldn't help but grimace as she studied them huddled together on one side of the room. Eamon, Trevor's father, was hunched over, speaking quietly to his best friend Walter. Then there was Maggie—a frail-looking woman whose voice reminded Grace of a snake. Every time she spoke, it was like she was hissing.

That left two positions open. One for her mother to fill, and one for Ali.

Side conversations picked up again as Grace took her seat next to her mother.

"Glad you could join us," her mother said quietly so the other council members couldn't hear.

Grace matched her cool tone. "Our meeting doesn't start for another fifteen minutes. It isn't my fault you all love to show up hours early. Don't we sit in this room long enough?"

Irritation practically radiated from her mother's body. She smoothed the wrinkles in her skirt, casting a pointed look at the fraying hem of Grace's pants. She didn't have to speak for Grace to understand her displeasure.

Grace had spent much of her life trying to live up to her mother's expectations, hoping she would see that Grace was capable of stepping into her leadership role. But now that she was an adult, she found herself less and less inclined to appease her mother.

She was under no obligation to rule as her mother would. Grace could rule however she saw fit.

Her mother stood, and the room fell quiet. "Hello, everyone. Now that we're all here, we can get started. Violet, if you'd like to start us off with updates."

Ellen sat back down as Violet cleared her throat.

One by one, the members of the council gave a quick report, occasionally interrupted by Ellen with suggestions or questions. Most of the concerns brought up lacked importance, and Grace struggled to feign interest.

Then it was Eamon's turn to speak.

His eyes met Grace's before he cleared his throat. "I've come up with a short list of candidates to fill the council vacancy—"

"That's not your responsibility," Grace said firmly. It was the Lady of Berland's responsibility, and her mother had already given her the power to fill one of the two positions.

Around her, the other council members stiffened. It was considered bad manners to speak out of turn like she just had, but Eamon was infuriating. He was a fool if he thought he could get away with inserting himself into *her* duties.

Ellen's voice was just over a whisper when she spoke. "There will be no more outbursts like that. Understood?"

Grace didn't dare look at her mother. She knew the look of disappointment she'd find there. But she also couldn't look across the room at Eamon. Despite how quietly her mother had spoken, she was sure the entire room had heard the soft lashing. She could easily picture the shit-eating grin Eamon was probably wearing at that moment.

Grace nodded.

"Good." Ellen raised her voice. "Carry on, Eamon."

"As I was saying, there are a few people I think would be ideal to fill the position. Owen is the Graysons' youngest son. He comes from a long line of Berlanders who have contributed greatly to this community through their businesses around town. Everyone loves Mr. Grayson's furniture shop, and what Sunday morning would be complete without a trip to Mrs. Grayson's tea shop?"

His pause for effect was filled with murmurs of agreement. Grace had to admit, even she liked to sit and drink tea there sometimes. It didn't change the fact that it wasn't Eamon's decision. She narrowed her eyes at him, but he was clearly emboldened by the council's interest.

"Owen is hardworking, and he knows the people. Knows what we all want to see in the future. Mr. Grayson has already confirmed that Owen can step down from his role in his father's business should he be offered a council position.

"The second candidate I hope you'll consider is Scott Montgomery. Some of you may recall his father used to be a council member before he stepped down for health reasons. Before that, his grandfather was also a council member. He comes from a long line of service to the community and was practically born for this role. I still recall the days when he used to tag along to meetings when he was just a few years old. Such a clever kid. We used to joke that he was the youngest member of the council."

Eamon finally looked toward Grace and smiled, knowing how much it would irritate her.

The eldest members of the council smiled and chuckled alongside Eamon, recalling some decades-old memories of a young Scott playing in this very room while they conducted business.

Apparently, nostalgia held a lot of persuasion.

"Thank you, Eamon," Ellen said. "We will consider these options."

Grace's head swiveled toward her mother. "May I?"

After her mother nodded, Grace addressed the room. "I've already decided on who I'd like to join the council. Pending her acceptance, Ali, the newcomer from Andus, will be joining us."

There were a few nervous glances and hushed whispers from the council members, but Grace was most interested in Eamon's reaction. She could tell even from across the room that he was grinding his teeth.

Good.

"That's outrageous," he said calmly. He knew better than to share his wrath in front of the council.

"What's outrageous is you thinking you have any say in the matter."

"You ungrateful—"

"That's enough," Ellen said, pressing two fingers to the space between her eyebrows. She moved them in circles, massaging the headache Grace knew was brewing.

Her mother looked more tired than usual, and even though Grace was confident in her decision to bring Ali into the council, she felt bad for causing her mother so much trouble. She didn't do things to be spiteful. It was what she truly believed was best for the people of Berland. Maybe one day her mother would see that.

"Apologies, Lady Ellen. I didn't mean to offend you or your daughter." Eamon's attempt at an apology was nauseating. "I merely wanted to express my *concern* that perhaps Miss Grace hasn't thought this through. If she gave it some more thought, she'd see that someone with more history here would be a better choice."

The insinuation that Grace hadn't given it enough thought, or that she wasn't taking it seriously made her shoulders tense. Undermining her authority and intelligence in front of the entire council was unacceptable. She opened her mouth to speak, but Ellen cut her off.

"Thank you, Eamon. Yes, I agree. My daughter and I will discuss this before any decisions are made. Let's keep the meeting moving forward. Walter, do you have anything to share with us?"

Just like that, Grace lost her opportunity to defend herself. She slumped in her chair as the meeting continued. Not only did her mother doubt her abilities, but she had belittled Grace in front of the council, making it difficult for her to be taken seriously.

What did she have to do for her mother to believe in her?

As the meeting finished, Grace collected her things, organizing them neatly in her bag. One by one, the council members filed out of the room until only Grace and her mother remained.

Ellen broke the silence with an exasperated sigh. "What are you trying to achieve, Grace?"

"What you've taught me since the day I was born—to look after our people and ensure their wellbeing. You can't honestly believe that Eamon can say the same."

"It doesn't matter. Eamon is a member of this council, whether you like it or not. You can't interrupt meetings and speak to him in that manner."

"But he can?" Grace hated that her voice was rising, but it was difficult to remain calm. Even though her mother seemed to do a fine job of it.

"No, he can't. That's why I also told him to be respectful."

"He doesn't know the meaning of the word," Grace muttered.

"What was that?"

"Nothing."

Her mother appraised her. "Let's talk about this council appointment of yours. When I told you to choose someone, I didn't think you'd be so reckless in your decision. There wasn't *anyone* else you could've chosen?"

Nerves rumbled in Grace's belly. "Are you revoking my ability to choose?"

"No. I wouldn't do that. I am hoping you will reconsider this foolishness. Really, Grace. Ali? What were you thinking?"

"I have my reasons."

"Explain them to me," her mother said, rubbing that space between her eyebrows again and making Grace feel like a nuisance. She had perfected that special talent by the time Grace had become a teenager.

"She'll add a fresh perspective, something this council is desperately in need of. And she cares about people."

"How would you know? You've only known her for a couple weeks."

It was hard to explain her faith in Eli and his friends. She'd always felt like she could read people better than anyone else. Something in the eyes gave away a person's true nature, and both Eli's and Ali's eyes had told Grace they were good people. "I just do, okay? Can't you trust me for once?"

Her mother dropped her hand from her face and peered at Grace with her full attention. If Grace were to read her mother's eyes now, they'd tell a story of disappointment and failed expectations. "I do trust you, Grace."

Those words were like a heavy weight on her chest, making it difficult to take a breath. She couldn't remember the last time her mother had any praise to give her. "Then trust me now."

Her mother paused for a moment, studying Grace for any cracks in her confidence. Grace put on her best show of unwavering conviction, straightening in her seat with her shoulders pulled back and her chin held high. An exact replica of the way her mother composed herself.

After a moment of tense silence, Ellen sighed and rose from her chair. "I can see you're as stubborn as ever. I guess we'll see what happens." She gently squeezed Grace's shoulder before slowly walking to the door. It was an unusual pace for her, as if her head was still bothering her.

"Are you okay?" Grace asked.

Ellen waved a hand over her shoulder. "Oh, yes. Just a migraine. I'm heading home to lie down for a bit. If anyone needs me, you know where to find me."

Grace gave her mother a few moments' head start before following her out of the council chamber and locking the door behind her. She had almost made it to the mountain's entry hall when she ran into Eamon and Walter.

As soon as they spotted her, their conversation ceased.

Grace looked between them. Although she would've liked to confront Eamon, it was probably better to ignore them entirely. She moved to step around them.

"I hope you aren't too upset with me, Miss Grace," Eamon said.

She turned to look at him but kept her lips closed. He didn't deserve her attention or her words.

His smile was sickening, and she did her best to keep her lip from curling upward. Turning on her heel, she continued down the hall.

Before she could reach the din of the entry hall, she heard Eamon speak to Walter, clearly intended for her ears. "The bitch already knows when to keep her mouth shut. Trevor will appreciate that in a wife."

Chapter Four

NIK

"ARE YOU ALMOST DONE?" Ali yelled over the sound of the shower. "I still need to wash my hair."

Nik scrubbed his skin with the angelfruit soap Ali had brought home, a small smile on his face. He usually opted for unscented, but he couldn't get enough of the divine aroma since Ali had used it. It immediately filled his head with images of Ali's soft, bare skin.

"I did say you could join me."

Her voice sounded closer as she moved from the bedroom to the bathroom. "And I told you that would make us even more late because you don't know how to keep your hands to yourself."

He chuckled. She was right. Showering separately was for the best if they hoped to be on time meeting Grace. Today was Ali's first day as a council member. She wouldn't be able to join the meetings right away, but there were a lot of orientation details she needed to go through with Grace. Nik wasn't sure of the specifics. He had zoned out once Ali let Grace know she'd accept the position and Grace began to drone on about "standards" and "procedures." But Ali was excited, so he was thrilled for her.

He rinsed his hair and turned the water off, stepping into the steamy bathroom to find Ali waiting. Before he could grab a dry towel to wrap around his waist, he caught her eyes trailing down his body, coming to a halt at his hips.

He tilted his head in amusement. "You said we'd be late."

Her big brown eyes shot up, and she cleared her throat. "I did. If you'll step out of the way, I can get my shower done and over with."

Nik stepped to the side, just enough for Ali to squeeze by, her body brushing against his front. She kept her eyes locked on his as she moved around him.

He'd never get used to this. Spending life with her, waking up next to her, building a family with her. He wouldn't take a single moment for granted.

She reached for the hem of her shirt, but before she could lift it over her head, Nik leaned in for a hungry kiss. Ali froze for a moment before pressing into him and opening her lips wide enough for him to slip his tongue inside her mouth. Her taste and the touch of her skin as she leaned against him made him moan with pleasure.

Before they could get too carried away, he pulled back.

"What was that for?" she asked, a little breathless.

"Because I love you."

Her grin was accompanied by a twinkle in her eyes. "I love you, too."

⁂

Ali and Nik held hands as they walked through the dark corridor that led to the entry hall. Even though she did her best to hide it, Nik could tell she was anxious. She walked a little faster than usual and was noticeably quiet while they wandered the hall.

"You're going to do great," he told her.

"Hmm? Oh, yes. Thank you."

"Relax. You have nothing to worry about. You can do anything you put your mind to. Grace was right to trust you."

That seemed to ease her nerves, and her shoulders slackened. When she was done for the day, he would massage those shoulders until her entire body was his to mold.

It didn't take long to spot Grace in the main entry chamber. Unfortunately, she was standing next to the tall, brown-haired bonehead that Ali called her best friend.

As if he could sense their approach, Eli turned around and waved at Ali before frowning at Nik. Nik narrowed his eyes in response.

The two of them had come to an understanding in recent weeks. They could be in the same room, but they'd never be friends. They'd get along for the sake of Ali, but deep down, Nik still wanted to knock him down and possibly knock out a tooth or two. He had no doubt the feeling was mutual.

Following Eli's gaze, Grace mimicked his greeting. "Good morning," she called, her voice cutting through the noise of the crowded chamber. It was always busiest during the first few hours of the day, when everyone was headed to work or to spend their leisure time by the lake or one of the many shops outdoors. Today was no exception.

Ali closed the distance with a few quick strides, dropping Nik's hand to hug both Eli and Grace. The latter didn't irritate him so much as the former did. Grace had never been in love with his girlfriend.

"Are you ready for today?" Grace asked.

Ali responded with an eager but nervous nod. "Definitely."

"Perfect. Then we'll be on our way."

"Before you do," Nik blurted. "I wanted to let you know that I've decided to take you up on your offer."

The decision to become a guard again had been on his mind all weekend, but in the end, he knew Ali was right and he should at least give it a shot before declining the position.

"You have? That's wonderful news." Grace glanced between Ali and Nik. Was she aware of the weight Ali's opinion held in his decision? "After I get Ali situated, I'll have to go over the details with you. How does tomorrow sound?"

He gave a quick nod. "That works for me."

"If you don't have anything else to do today, you could help Eli with his training. He was just telling me he was going to do some conditioning this morning to prepare for the first round of the Rite."

Eli groaned at the same time Nik sucked in a sharp breath. He'd rather roll around in horse shit than spend an entire day with Eli. And even worse, Ali wouldn't even be there as a buffer.

"That's not necessary," Eli said quickly. "I can handle it myself."

"Of course you can. But won't it be much more fun with someone to keep you company?" Grace asked.

Beside her, Ali was smirking. "I agree," she said. "You two should spend some time together. Maybe get to know one another a little better. Plus, Nik has had a ton of physical training to be a guard. He can give you pointers."

Nik glared at her, which only made her grin widen. She was clearly delighted at the torture she was inflicting. He'd make her pay for that later.

"Really, I don't need his help," Eli said.

"Yeah, and I was going to hang out with Sam," Nik lied.

"Sam's busy," Grace replied. "Today was his first day on the job, too."

"So it's settled then," Ali said cheerfully. "We'll see you two at lunch."

Nik sighed, knowing he couldn't get out of it. Technically, he could make a show of helping Eli and then bail once Ali and Grace were gone, but he wouldn't be able to live with her disappointment.

He shook his head before giving in. "I guess. We'll see you in a few hours."

Beside him, Eli ran a hand through his hair and released a long breath. Neither one of them was thrilled to be spending the day together. But neither was capable of displeasing their partners.

Together, Grace and Ali walked to the tunnel that led to the council chamber. Just before she disappeared from his sight, Ali turned and winked at him. Despite his annoyance, he couldn't help but smile.

"Are you done staring, or would you like to stand around all day waiting for her to return?"

Nik scoffed. "Says the guy who's literally putting his life at risk for another woman."

"Unlikely. Grace explained the rounds to me. They might be dangerous, but none of them are life threatening."

Nik raised an eyebrow. "Didn't someone just attack Lady Ellen? And one of the council members was killed? It doesn't matter how easy or hard the rounds are. Your life is at risk as long as you're attached to Grace."

Eli's brows furrowed, but he didn't bite back. He began to walk toward the mountain's exit, a brown bag slung over his back.

Nik trailed behind and prayed the day would pass quickly. "So what do you have planned for the day?"

"You don't *actually* have to come with me," Eli said. "I can cover for you with Grace and Ali. Go terrorize some townsfolk or whatever it is you do with your spare time."

"No way. I don't trust you not to sell me out. You'll make it seem like *I'm* the bad guy for leaving you to your own devices. I gave Ali my word and I meant it."

Eli rolled his eyes. "Fine. Figured I'd start with a run and then do as much body weight training as I can." He shrugged the bag on his shoulder and Nik heard what sounded like metal clanging inside. "Borrowed a few items from the research lab to use for weights as well."

"Remind me what the first round is."

"I'll show you," Eli said, and together they set off for a field on the outside of town.

❧ ☙

"What am I looking at?" Nik asked as they approached a large hole in the middle of the ground, wide enough to fit at least two houses. He couldn't tell how deep it was since it was full of reddish-brown mud.

"A mud pit."

Nik grimaced. "And the point is...?"

Eli dumped the bag on the ground and began stretching his legs, pulling his foot behind him until it touched his backside. "There will be eight medallions hidden in the mud. All sixteen of the suitors will be racing to find them first. Whoever finds one moves on to the next round while everyone else is eliminated."

"Perfect task for a pig," Nik muttered.

"I heard that," Eli said, switching to his other leg.

"And?"

Eli stomped off like a toddler throwing a tantrum.

"I thought you wanted my help?" Nik called after him.

Eli began to jog, ignoring Nik entirely. He could either sit and wait for Eli to finish his run or join him. The latter seemed like the better option. At least it would give him the chance to blow off some steam.

They followed a path through the field of tall, yellow grass and into the woods where the treetops protected them from the scorching sun, down along the glistening river, and back up a hill until they reached the mud pit again.

It couldn't have been more than thirty minutes, but Nik didn't think he could take one more second of stifling silence. The only sound he'd heard during the entire run was their jagged breathing and heavy feet. He collapsed to the ground and watched as Eli pulled out a bottle of water from his backpack.

"Do you have an extra one of those?" Nik asked, wiping the sweat above his lip. The sun only seemed to beat down harder the more he wished for clouds. In this field, nestled between two peaks, the wind was nonexistent.

Eli replaced the cap on his water and tossed it to Nik. "I didn't know I'd have company today. I only brought the one."

After quenching his thirst, Nik rose to his feet again. "What's next on the agenda?"

Eli propped himself up on in a plank position and began his first set of pushups. Nik watched, and although he'd love to find fault in Eli's form, he had to admit he was in semi-decent shape.

While Eli kept busy with his exercises, Nik took the opportunity to dig through his bag. Eli grunted when he heard Nik rustling through its contents, but he didn't move to stop him.

Inside, Nik found two nearly identical metallic cylinders. He pulled the first one out and tested the weight of it. Though it was only a foot long and a couple inches in diameter, it somehow weighed the same as one of the old wheelbarrows in Rysburg.

"What is this?" he asked.

Eli shot a quick glance over his shoulder. "Dunno," he grunted. "We haven't figured out the purpose of that piece yet. It's"—he paused as he pushed away from the ground—"from the junkyard in Jellico. They had a dozen of them in a variety of colors."

The one in Nik's hand was a shiny silver, while the one that remained in the bag was more copper in appearance. He rolled the object around in his hands before walking toward Eli and plopping it on his back.

Eli's arms almost gave out at the sudden increase in weight, but at the last moment, he was able to press back into a plank. "What the fuck?"

"I'm supposed to be helping you."

"You call that helping?"

Nik shrugged and made a gesture pointing in Eli's direction. "This thing you're doing right now doesn't seem like enough."

Eli slowly lowered to the ground and rolled to the side, the weight falling off his back. "Then what do *you* suggest?"

That was more like it. If Nik had to suffer through this day, then Eli should at least be interested in whatever advice he had to offer. He was *not* some nuisance tagging along like a lost puppy.

Nik peered at the pit of mud. Around the sides, the clay had begun to harden and crack in the heat of the sun, but the mud in the center glistened with moisture. "Functional training."

"Huh?"

"Exercises that mimic what you'll need to do during the first round. You need to get in the mud pit. Practice moving, finding your footing, identify the deeper or shallow parts of the pit...like a rehearsal."

Eli looked at the pool of mud with a disgusted expression. It came as no surprise to Nik that he wouldn't take this seriously.

"There's a reason we came here, right?" Nik asked, gesturing toward the pit. "If you'd rather fuck around with scraps of metal, be my guest.

But your time will be better spent working on those scrawny leg muscles by wading through the mud."

A fire lit in Eli's eyes at Nik's casual insult, but he didn't argue. Although Nik and Eli were about the same height, Nik probably sported an extra fifty pounds of muscle. He assumed everyone from Andus must've been on the slender side, but if Eli didn't want to get knocked around in the first round, he needed to bulk up a bit.

"Fine," Eli conceded. Rising to his feet, he reached behind his head and pulled his shirt off with one hand. "Let's do this."

A few hours later, Eli was covered in brown muck and panting from exertion. Nik had tossed a rock the size of his palm into the mud pit while Eli chased it. Over and over again.

Nik could've gotten in the pit with him to increase the difficulty by fighting him for the rock, but it was much more fun to watch as Eli trudged through the thick mud seeking the hidden object. Once or twice Eli stumbled and his face dipped below the surface of the pool. He used his shirt to clear the mud from his eyes before carrying on.

"See, that's what I mean," Nik said when Eli roamed too far to one side and his entire head disappeared beneath the surface. "Now you know to avoid that corner."

Eli climbed out of the pit, using his hands to feel his way forward. Nik grabbed Eli's shirt and brought it to him. Before wiping his face clean, Eli spat on the ground. "I've had enough for one day."

"Good thing. There isn't an inch of clean space on that shirt. If you dunked one more time, you'd have to go blind."

"Or you could lend me yours."

Nik smirked. "Not likely."

Slowly, Eli rose to his feet. He was clearly worn out despite only a few hours of training.

"Do you plan on training again tomorrow?" Nik asked, packing Eli's bag and slinging it over his shoulder. It was the least he could do, so the mud didn't transfer to all of Eli's belongings.

"Definitely. My boss has given me some time off to prepare for the Rite and I intend to make the most of it. Why? Are you going to keep me company again?"

"Depends on whether Grace needs me," Nik said. Grace had mentioned an orientation of sorts, but not whether he'd be expected to start right away.

Eli nodded. "Thank you, by the way."

"No need to thank me. I was practically forced into it by Grace and Ali."

"Not that. Although I do appreciate the help. Thank you for keeping Grace safe."

Nik furrowed his brow. "I'm surprised you approve of me becoming a guard again." His previous position as guard in Rysburg hadn't earned him any favors with Eli before.

Eli shrugged. "I may not like you, but I don't doubt your ability to protect someone."

Protect. It was the same word Ali had used to convince him he wasn't a villain. He didn't really need to embrace his role as guard...he needed to embrace his role as protector.

Chapter Five

ALI

Ali's first day of training ended with her returning to her room, weighed down by a stack of papers and a headache. Grace spoke so fast, it was hard to keep up sometimes. She had pointed out names of locations and people that all blended together in Ali's disorganized brain. By lunchtime, the symbols on the pages began to swirl together in an inky storm of despair and mockery.

Despite the lessons she'd begun in reading and writing, her skills were nowhere near where they should be for a job like this. If she didn't put in some extra work, the other council members would laugh in her face. What was Grace thinking?

She dumped the papers on the kitchen table and pushed back the frazzled bangs from her forehead. The responsible thing to do would be to begin reading one of these journals, manuals, or historical documents, but all she wanted to do was collapse into bed.

She took a deep breath and committed to reading at least *one* of the smaller journals before calling it quits for the day. Small steps.

Searching through the cabinets, she tried to find a snack to lessen the suffering of the work ahead of her. There was a mix of nuts and dried fruit that she liked to get from one of the shops in town, but Nik loved it just as much and had developed a habit of stealing it and hiding it from her so he could hoard it for himself.

The upper cupboards contained plates, cups, and various dried goods but not her favorite treat. The lower cupboards were equally disappointing, with only pots and pans to offer. Where had he hidden it? Next time, she'd have to hide her snacks first.

Sighing, she racked her brain, trying to figure out where he might've stashed it. Inside his bedside table drawer? No. Perhaps his dresser between his many folded shirts? Not there either. She checked the bathroom and what felt like every nook and cranny of their small apartment, including under the bed, before finally giving up.

She was still kneeling beside the bed when the door opened and Nik walked in, looking tan and sweaty from the summer heat. He paused at the threshold and tilted his head when he noticed her sitting on the floor. "What are you doing?"

She pointed at him and narrowed her eyes. "I *know* you took my snack mix. Where did you hide it?"

Laughter tore through him, and he moved toward her in a few fluid steps, pulling her up off the floor. He kissed her forehead and then leaned down to whisper in her ear. "You'll never find it."

Wrapping his arms around her waist, he tossed her onto the bed. As much as she wanted to pester him until he gave up his hiding place, all thoughts eddied from her head when he removed his shirt and exposed his defined abs. In a blink, her cravings changed course.

Nik crawled onto the bed and pinned her in place with the weight of his body. Her hands slid over his warm skin while he tucked a strand of hair behind her ear.

"You're in quite the mood today." Ali said, though she certainly wasn't complaining. She fought the urge to grind her hips against his. He'd have to work harder than that if he wanted her forgiveness for stealing her snacks.

Nik peppered kisses along her neck and slid his hands beneath her shirt. His thumb rubbed the underside of her breasts, inching closer to her hardened nipples. When he licked her neck just below her ear, the heat of his breath had her eyes rolling back in her head. "Being away from you all day has that effect on me."

She smiled, lacing her fingers through his hair and pulling his head up so she could press her lips against his. A taste so divine and addicting, she'd never get enough.

Wrapping her legs around his waist, she ground into him, eliciting a moan from deep in his chest. The vibrations sparked a fire inside her and she pulled him closer until there was no space left between them.

"I'm not the only one who seems to be in a mood," he said between ragged breaths.

"Just shut up and fuck me already."

Like an animal released from his cage, Nik clawed at her shirt, pulling it over her head and leaving her thin bralette in place. He yanked her pants down her legs without bothering to unbutton them. Then he was back at her stomach, kissing and running his lips over the thin black fabric of her panties.

Her back arched off the mattress when he felt his way between her thighs, seeking the spot that always left her gasping. She clutched his hair so hard she was sure it must've been painful, but he kept his head in place, still teasing her through that damn barrier she began to despise.

"Take them off," she panted.

She didn't need to ask twice. He hooked his fingers beneath the band and slid her underwear down her thighs, spreading her wide and settling between her legs.

His breath was hot on her cunt. She reached for his head again and sighed with relief when his tongue finally caressed her clit.

"Oh my god, Nik."

He hummed in approval before pushing one finger inside her, curling it around to stroke her inner walls. That sensation alone had her clenching her thighs around his head.

With careful precision, he built her pleasure until it was about to overflow. Then he pulled back and his hands dropped to unfasten his pants.

Ali made a noise of frustration.

"You're not going to come on my fingers, sweetheart. I want you to come on my cock."

Nik sucked his fingers into his mouth and then pressed them against her clit, swirling in a circular motion while simultaneously pushing the tip of his cock inside her.

Ali's toes curled, and she thrust her hips forward, needing more of his length to fill her and stretch her. Desperate for the friction, she rocked her hips against him, but he gripped her by the waist and slowly pulled out, then slammed back in.

Her eyes rolled back in her head. It was too much and not enough all at once.

"Nik," she pleaded.

Still, he moved at an agonizing pace, and she felt every inch of him as he slid in and out of her pussy.

"I love watching you like this. When you're so needy for me…"

"Please."

"Beg for me, sweetheart."

"Fuck. I need you, Nik."

With enough force to rattle the bed, he drove into her over and over again until she couldn't take any more. Her legs trembled as her pussy fluttered around his cock.

Catching her breath was a difficult task while Nik continued to thrust forward until he, too, came undone, spilling inside her.

He released a pleasured sigh and fell to the bed next to her. Wrapping an arm around her waist, he pulled her tight against his chest while she threw her leg over his hip.

There was something so comforting about the way he held her, the way his fingers trailed down her back and his lips curved in a contented smile. It made her forget everything she'd been stressed about before he came home. She couldn't hear the call of the papers left abandoned on the table over the sound of his heavy, sated breathing.

"How was your day?" he asked, drawing lazy circles on her back.

"It was...a lot." She smiled, recalling the way Grace had led her around the mountain, introducing her to important people whose names she'd already forgotten and pointing out locations she'd hadn't ventured into before—the council chamber, the office of the woman who oversaw Berland's finances, the room labeled "controls" written in bold red letters. By the end of the day, she didn't think her brain could handle any more information.

"Everything you hoped it would be?" He smiled in a mocking way that made her press a finger into his chest.

"All that and more." She chuckled. "Honestly though. It feels challenging, but in a good way. I'd always hoped that my life would be more meaningful than catching fish or weeding gardens. This seems like the perfect opportunity to make an impact. Grace introduced me to a few people, and they all seemed optimistic and welcome to the idea of me joining the council." Although Ali suspected that Grace had only introduced her to the people who would be accepting of her.

"I'm happy for you," Nik said. "I hope things continue to go well."

"Thanks. And what about you?" This time, it was her turn to smile. The thought of Nik and Eli spending a day together made her giggle maliciously. Did they talk? Did they argue the whole time?

Nik rolled his eyes. "It went exactly as you'd expect."

He shifted to lie on his back, seemingly done with the conversation, but Ali rolled on top of him.

"That's it? I want to know every detail. What did you guys do?"

"Ali..."

"Did you help him like I asked? Or were you an asshole?" She frowned, although she should've known throwing the two of them together without a buffer would lead to a high likelihood of violence.

"It was fine, Ali. We went for a run and then he practiced in the mud pit."

"And you weren't mean to him?"

Nik licked his lips and tried to hide a smirk. "Why do you assume I'm the mean one?"

"Because you are." She paused to kiss his tempting lips, then hugged his sides and rested her cheek on his chest. "But I love you anyway."

"Mm-hmm."

"So, are you going to help him again tomorrow?"

The irritation in his voice was unmistakable, though partially muffled by his hands as they swept over his face. Once he reappeared, he released a long sigh. "Maybe. I'm supposed to meet with Grace, but if there's time, I could probably work with him again."

"That's so sweet of you," she teased.

"It's not sweet. It's taking pity on a poor guy who desperately needs some guidance."

She doubted Eli was in that bad of shape. He'd always been lean and toned, but he also had a surprising amount of strength. "Well, thank god he has you. The first round of the Rite is coming up soon, isn't it?"

Nik nodded. "He's only got a couple weeks left to train. It's hard to believe we've already been here for a little over a month."

Ali smiled against his chest. Berland had turned out so much better than she could've hoped. Her top priority had been finding Eli, but they'd also found a home. A place they could build a life and be happy together. She was terrified that someone would wake her up and it would all be a dream. Nothing was ever this easy.

Something twisted in her stomach, and her mind drifted to the rebellion and their determination to disrupt her paradise. She quickly dismissed the unwelcome thought. She'd been through hell and back. A few entitled men wouldn't scare her off.

They'd been in Berland for a month with a lifetime to go.

A month.

Ali shot up in bed, still straddling Nik, who looked alarmed by her sudden movement.

"What's wrong?"

Maintaining a blank face, Ali swung her leg over Nik and hopped out of bed, stumbling over their discarded clothing on the floor. She forced herself to walk calmly to the bathroom and rummaged through the cabinets, searching for the reusable cup she used for her period and the small note she kept with it to keep track of her cycle.

One month? That couldn't be right.

She shoved a stack of clean washcloths out of her way.

Where was it?

"Is there something I can help you find?" Nik had left the bed and was now standing behind her, watching as she dug through the cabinet below the sink like a rabid animal.

There!

She snatched the cup and the note trapped underneath and checked the dates. It had been almost two months since her last period. She remembered it perfectly. She'd wondered that very day if there was something wrong with her. If there was a reason she hadn't gotten pregnant.

Upon their arrival in Berland, she'd meant to get a contraceptive from their medics but had never gotten around to it.

Leaning against the open cabinet door, she let out a small laugh. "Unbelievable."

"Ali, are you okay?"

She nodded before meeting his gaze. "Yes. I'm better than okay, actually."

Nik tilted his head, confusion and concern written all over his face.

She laughed again and covered her mouth. "I think I'm pregnant."

Chapter Six

ELI

THE SUN HADN'T YET risen when Eli left the mountain with a lantern in one hand and his tattered backpack thrown over his shoulder. He packed food, water, and a handful of coins from the lab that Luka said he could have. They were an old form of currency that held no value in Berland, but they made an excellent replica of the medallions that would be used during the first round of the Rite. Better to practice with the old coins than the stones Nik kept finding on the side of the mud pit.

He also packed an extra set of clothes. After the first day of training in the mud, he'd learned to bring along something to change into afterward. Nothing was more miserable than walking through town, covered in filth, and then washing the slimy mud from his body in the lake while crowds of children and their parents watched. One time rising from the water in his underwear and walking back to the mountain while avoiding the gazes of everyone he passed had been enough.

Something shifted in the woods beside him, hiding from either the sound of his footsteps or the light of his lamp. The nocturnal creatures were still awake, but they were nothing to be afraid of. If he could put up with Trevor, or Nik for that matter, he could fight off a raccoon.

The trail opened up to a clear night sky. The moonlight was just bright enough to make out the silhouette of the barn where the horses were kept, along with the fence that lined the expansive field. He spotted a few stallions—the ones that didn't get locked away by their owners before nightfall and were free to roam—but most were still tucked away in their stalls.

Eli had no doubt he was the first to visit this morning. He wanted to let Obsidian out before he had to meet Nik for training, which meant waking up before the rest of the mountain.

The wooden latch creaked open and Eli stepped inside the dark barn. He was greeted by silence only broken by the occasional sound of shifting hay and heavy breaths. As he made his way to Obsidian's stall, other horses began to turn in his direction, hoping they might be the lucky recipient of one of the apples he'd brought along.

"Sorry, buddy. Not today," he said quietly to the brown and white spotted horse who nudged the gate with its nose.

When he finally made it to the next-to-last stall, Obsidian was waiting patiently for him. He shook his head and prodded the ground with one hoof while Eli unlocked his gate.

Eli chuckled when Obsidian greeted him with a wet nuzzle. It was something he'd gotten used to over time, though the first time he'd pulled back in disgust.

The horse continued to shake his mane with delight while Eli filled his trough with water and food and tossed the snacks he'd brought with him into an empty basin.

"Don't eat them all at once," he said, taking a moment to brush through Obsidian's mane. "Sorry I can't stop by later. Work and training for this Rite has kept me pretty busy. Trust me, I'd love to spend all day with you, but right now I have other obligations."

Obsidian huffed his displeasure. Though he couldn't understand Eli's words, he felt that maybe the stallion *could* understand his body language. Like an extra sense that connected them on an intrinsic level.

After a few minutes, Eli led Obsidian out to the open field. The sun was beginning to rise, casting shades of pink, orange, and yellow over the pillowy clouds.

Obsidian pranced excitedly, waiting for Eli to set him free. As soon as he unclasped the lead, Obsidian bolted into the grassy meadow, running a perfect circle around Eli before slowing to a casual jog. His silky mane reflected the glow of the morning sun, and Eli watched in awe.

Such a beautiful creature.

He wished he could stay longer, but it wouldn't be long before the air turned humid and hot. The last thing he wanted to do was run in the sweltering heat.

⊱⋆⊰

Running solo was far more pleasant than running with Nik. For one, it was much quieter and Eli had time to clear his head and mentally prepare for the upcoming round. Grace had told him that mental preparation was just as important as physical and he had every intention of being in the best shape possible in both regards.

Second, he could run at his own pace. As much as Nik liked to torment Eli for his lack of muscular build, Eli was much faster than Nik, and running with him only slowed Eli down.

After their first week of training together, Eli made a point to get to their meeting spot early so he wouldn't have to run with Nik anymore. If Nik minded, he didn't say anything.

Eli was done with his run before the morning fog had fully lifted. Nik was waiting when he made it back to the mud pit, stretching his legs as if he might actually do something.

Eli huffed a laugh. Nik never took part in the training. He only barked at Eli and criticized everything he did. Still, Nik pushed Eli, and that was what he needed.

But Nik wasn't the only one waiting patiently. Sam sat on the ground beside him, using a band of fabric around his foot to pull and push against.

"Hey, Eli," Sam said as Eli approached.

"Good morning." He nodded his chin toward Sam's contraption. "What have you got there?"

"Zoe gave it to me. Apparently, they use it to help rehabilitate animal injuries. She thought it might help me as well."

"I thought your leg was all healed," Eli said. Ali had mentioned Sam's injury when she'd caught him up on their time apart, but he hadn't noticed Sam limping or showing any signs that his leg still troubled him.

"It is, mostly. I can do everyday tasks fairly easy. But I used to be a guard too, if you remember."

It was hard to forget. Although Sam had always been a more pleasant warden than Nik.

Sam flexed his foot and pressed against the band again. "I miss being able to train. I can't recall the last time I ran or did any strenuous activity. The last time I tried, my leg was sore for days after.

"Anyway, I mentioned it to Zoe one day, and she pulled this thing out of what looked like a box of trash. She showed me a few moves, and I thought I'd give it a try. Can't hurt, can it?" He smiled as the tension in the band eased and he rolled his ankle in circles, loosening the tendons. "So, what's on the agenda today?"

Eli gestured to the mud pit with a forced look of delight. "A swim in the clearest, most luxurious pool you could find, obviously."

Sam chuckled.

Nik shot them both a look. "You've only got a week until the first round. So if you're done chatting, we should get started."

We. As if he were an active participant in the daily training Eli had been enduring.

Eli dug in his bag for the spare coins he'd brought, handing them to Nik before removing his shirt and stripping down to an old pair of shorts.

The first hour proceeded much like all the days before. Eli closed his eyes and Nik tossed the coin into the pit. Once the coin fell beneath the surface, Eli began his search.

By now, he was familiar with the layout of the pool—the shallow areas that would be easiest to search and the deep areas he'd prefer to avoid. He even knew where a boulder three times the size of his head was located, after stubbing his toe on it in one unfortunate search. Finding the hidden coins became quicker with every try.

And moving through the mud? He no longer gave it a second thought. After their relentless training, it felt as natural as walking on the ground. He hardly noticed the way his thighs strained to wade through the thick muck.

After finding the hidden coins a dozen times, Eli climbed out of the pit to grab a drink of water. Removing the lid, he drained half his canteen in a few large gulps. As he replaced it in his backpack, he couldn't help but notice Sam staring at him out of the corner of his eye.

"What?"

Sam shrugged.

Eli sighed. Playing guessing games was the last thing he wanted to do. He placed one hand on his hip and waved the other, gesturing for Sam to hit him with the truth. "What is it? You've clearly got something to say."

"Well, it's just that...the pit isn't going to be empty when you're competing in the first round, correct?"

"Right..."

He squinted at the pit. "It's going to be a lot harder."

Nik inched closer to eavesdrop on their conversation. "Is your break almost over?"

Eli resisted the urge to shove him in the mud.

If Sam wasn't going to share his thoughts, it was time to get back to work.

Eli took a moment to stretch out his arms and, just as he was ready to hop back in, Sam spoke up.

"Nik should get in, too."

"What?" Eli and Nik said almost in unison.

Sam pointed at Eli. "He needs resistance. Someone to fight off. During the first round, he'll have men coming at him from every direction, fighting to find those medallions. He should be practicing that, too."

He did have a point.

"Why don't you jump in, then?" Eli asked.

Sam wiggled his ankle. "I don't think that's a good idea."

Nik grumbled, and Eli ground his teeth. Neither of them was inclined to heed Sam's suggestion. Perhaps there was someone else Eli could ask. Theo, maybe? Some of the other men trained later in the afternoon. Could he wait for them?

"Forget I said anything," Sam conceded. "It was just a thought."

Fuck.

"You're right. I do need someone in there to challenge me." Eli turned to Nik. "Your entire philosophy for training was centered on functionality. Well...this is the next step."

Nik's head fell back, clearly searching the sky for someone, *anyone,* to step in. An angel or some other figure to fall from heaven and save him the trouble of getting in the pit with Eli. No one did.

He sighed. "Fine. I'll do it."

With his signature disgruntled frown, Nik removed his clothes until he was left in nothing but navy briefs.

When Eli raised a brow, Nik shrugged. "What? No one told me I'd be jumping in a pile of filth today."

Eli kept his mouth shut.

They both scrambled into the muck, waiting for Sam to toss a coin in. When he gave them the call to begin, Eli darted in one direction while Nik darted straight toward him.

It didn't take more than three steps for Nik to wrap his arms around Eli, pulling them both into the mud. Eli had enough sense to close his mouth and breath out his nose before he went under. When he resurfaced, he sputtered and did his best to wipe the mud from his face. Though his eyes stung, he blinked quickly, aware that he wouldn't have much time during the actual competition.

He started toward the center again but immediately felt the weight of Nik on his back. This time he managed to stay above the surface, but it was difficult to move with an extra body hanging off him. He clawed at Nik's arms and swung back and forth, hoping to knock him loose, but Nik's grip stayed firm.

Nik pulled on his arm, and Eli wobbled. Maybe Nick was larger and stronger than Eli, but he was clumsy as hell.

"Fight me," Nik grumbled.

Gladly, Eli thought. He jammed his elbow behind him, knocking the wind out of Nik. He heard him cough and sputter, but he was already making his escape. If he could put a few steps between them, it would make his search much easier.

But his freedom was short-lived. He felt around with his hands and feet for the smooth coin, but seconds later, Nik was shoving him over. Eli sent a frustrated slap of mud at Nik's head, which surprisingly worked in his favor, giving him another second to continue his search while Nik wiped the muck from his face.

He just needed to feel...*there!* It happened so fast he almost missed it. But he felt the cool, familiar metal slide against his foot and spun to grab it with his hand.

He surged forward, arm outstretched, and just as his fingers connected with the coin, Nik slammed into him again. His face smashed into the mud once more and he pressed with all his might, trying to break the surface so he could breathe. But Nik was impossibly heavy. Maybe it was his weight, or maybe Eli was exhausted after hours of training, but it felt like he was no match.

Eli panicked as his lungs burned. His foot slipped, and he felt himself fall further into the depths. But that was enough for Nik's weight to lift, and Eli took the opportunity to twist and turn out of his clutches and pop his head up. He coughed and inhaled. The crisp air had never tasted so sweet.

Without bothering to clear his eyes, he started to trudge back to the border of the pool. It didn't matter what direction; he needed *out*.

"Giving up so soon?" Nik called.

Eli responded with one arm raised high in the air, a golden coin beneath a layer of mud held tight between his fingers.

He could've sworn he heard an impressed huff behind him.

Once out of the pit, they both did their best to clean themselves, especially Eli's eyes and nose, before they sat down for a break. Sam searched through Eli's bag for water and a snack so Eli didn't get mud all over his belongings.

"Well?" Sam asked.

Eli tossed a handful of nuts into his mouth, then washed away the saltiness with a swig of water. "Well, what?"

"I was right, wasn't I?"

"Don't get all cocky with us," Nik said. "It's not a good look."

Eli snorted. "He would know."

The words had no sooner left Eli's mouth than Sam burst into laughter. Nik stared, appalled, at the man who was supposed to be his friend. Once he regained his composure, Sam shrugged. "Sorry."

"You don't seem to be."

Sam's eyes met Eli's, and they both tried very hard to stifle another round of laughter.

"Don't be grumpy, Nik. *It's not a good look.*" Sam mimicked Nik's intonation, and Eli almost rolled over in amusement.

He tossed the bag of nuts back into his backpack and stood, clapping his hands together to remove the debris left by his snack. It was best to get back to training. Any more teasing Nik and his head might explode. "Ready to go again?"

Nik sighed, but stood and brushed his hands off as well. "Yes, let's get—"

His words tapered off, and he hardened to a statue.

"Something wrong?" Eli ran a hand over his face, feeling as if something were marking it. Something other than the dried mud which fell off in flakes. Did he have something in his teeth? A bug in his hair? "What are you looking at?"

"What the fuck is that?" Nik demanded, rage simmering in his eyes. He pointed at Eli's torso.

Eli searched himself, expecting to find some horrid, bloody injury or maybe one of the mud snakes had bitten him. But he saw none of those things. "What are you talking about?"

"That," Nik said again, angrier this time. He stepped closer and jabbed a finger at Eli's chest, right where a small tattoo covered his skin.

The moon to Ali's sun.

Eli smirked, tapping the dark ink on his chest. "This? Oh, that's just the tattoo I got with my best friend. Do you recognize it? They're not identical, but it is very similar to the one on her chest."

At the mention of Ali's chest, Nik launched forward and sent Eli tumbling to the ground. He was on him within seconds, pulling his arm back to throw the first punch.

Eli blocked it as well as he could, and Nik slammed his fist into Eli's arms over and over again, trying to get past his defenses. His punches were sloppy, full of fury, not the skilled blows Eli had seen him make plenty of times before.

Nik was like a wild dog. Eli had never seen him so riled up. He couldn't stifle the inappropriate laugh that bubbled out of him. There was just something so comical about seeing him this way.

"You think it's funny?" Nik said through gritted teeth, his cheeks and forehead a fiery red.

Eli chose not to answer. Instead, he smiled so wide he thought Nik might knock out every single one of his teeth.

Nik took one rabid look at Eli's smug grin before bending down and *biting* Eli's flesh.

Eli howled and tried to throw Nik off, but he only dug his teeth in harder, doing his best to pry the tattoo from Eli's body.

"Have you lost your fucking mind?"

Somewhere in the distance, Sam was yelling, but his pleas to end this nonsense were drowned out by Eli's pained yelps and Nik's ravenous grunts.

When he finally released Eli, blood trickled from his lips and tarnished his chin. He spat, and a mixture of reddish saliva landed next to Eli's head. Glancing down, Eli found a ring of angry teeth marks circling the tattoo on his chest. Likely deep enough to scar. He snarled at his attacker.

Now it was Nik's turn to look smug. When he smiled, red stained his teeth and the fire in his eyes turned to ash. "Now, wherever you may find Ali, you'll find me as well."

Eli shoved him, and Nik tumbled to the side. "You're insane. She didn't even know you when we got those tattoos. Why does it matter now?"

His fingers grazed the tender skin where Nik had sunk his teeth in, and he hissed at the stinging pain. He would never understand Nik. His jealousy was completely unwarranted. Ali was in love with him—something Eli would also never understand—and Eli had moved on too.

"She chose you," he said, gently wiping away the blood smeared across his chest.

Nik spoke quietly, anger still lacing his words. "She still *needs* you."

Eli could practically feel the pain it took for him to admit it. It was enough to almost make Eli feel sorry for him, but the burning pain in his chest ripped away that potential.

The silence that settled around them was unnerving. Even Sam seemed unsure of what to do, his gaze flicking back and forth between them, waiting for someone to make the first move.

"She loves you," Eli said finally. "For reasons that I'll never understand, but she does. Ali is my best friend, and you're right—we will always need each other. But not the same way she needs you. When are you going to get over it?"

The flare in Nik's eyes said it wouldn't be anytime soon.

Sighing, Eli pulled himself off the ground and stretched out a hand to Nik. A peace offering, even if he couldn't stand to offer Nik an apology for antagonizing him. He doubted Nik expected one and knew he'd never get one in return, either.

Nik's eyes narrowed to slits as he stared at Eli's hand, but after a moment's hesitation, he took it and Eli pulled him up.

They were still trapped in awkward tension when the sound of someone clearing their throat rang out.

"Hope I'm not interrupting anything, boys." Trevor sauntered toward them with a haughty grin and his shoulders slung back in an attempt to make him seem brawnier than he truly was. "Let me guess—Eli needed some extra time in the pit to ensure he wouldn't make a fool of himself."

Nobody joined in his chuckling.

Ignoring that, Trevor carried on, clapping Eli on the back. "First round shouldn't be too bad...even for a scrawny kid like yourself. Personally, I can't wait to kick your ass in the second round."

Eli shoved Trevor's hand away. Sam moved to step between them, but Nik pressed an arm to his chest, holding him back. Trevor merely looked at them like they were beneath it all. He was only here to torment Eli.

Eli looked him up and down. "Careful, Trevor. One of these days, you're going to get what you deserve. I only hope to be the one who gives it to you."

Chapter Seven

ELI

ELI'S HEART HAMMERED. IT felt as if waves were crashing against the walls of his organs, and they may collapse at any moment.

He stumbled a few steps to the right and grabbed a tree to prop himself up. Bending in half, he coughed and prayed he wouldn't lose his breakfast.

It was his last day to train before the first round was held tomorrow morning, and he wanted to make the most of it. In order to do that, he needed to keep his only meal down and maintain his energy.

Breathing in through his nose and slowly out through his mouth, he managed to calm his stomach enough to stand straight again.

Footsteps sounded, and Nik appeared at his shoulder. "You all right?"

"Yeah, I'm fine." Eli shook out his arms and cracked his neck, determined to finish his run.

"You look a little pale."

"It's very sweet of you to be concerned about me, but I'm okay."

Nik rolled his eyes before stepping back on the trail. He started off at a jog and called back to Eli, "If you're feeling okay, better get your ass back in gear. Don't want another man to steal your victory, do you?"

Eli groaned. Why had he ever agreed to let Nik train with him? He watched as Nik's figure shrank in the distance and then disappeared completely behind a hill. If he didn't get moving, Nik would beat him back to the pit and then he'd have to listen to his boasting for the rest of the day.

Absolutely not.

Eli forced his heavy feet to move forward and, after a few clumsy steps, picked up his pace to catch up with Nik.

By the time they reached the pit, several other suitors had gathered. In the past week, more and more had joined to practice before the first round, which was both helpful and a nuisance. It made it more difficult for Eli to get his practice in, but on the other hand, he could see what he was up against.

Only a few men stuck out to him as decent competition—Trevor and two others who had athletic builds. One sported shaggy blond hair and another had a buzz cut and even more tattoos than Eli. He wondered where the man had gotten them and if he could have the ones on his back retouched to hide the scars.

A few other men seemed average, not in excellent shape but could probably hold their own. They shouldn't be too difficult to take down if Eli found himself in a one-on-one fight for a medallion with any of them.

The other four contenders probably wouldn't make it past the first round. They should've been practicing for the past few weeks beside Eli, but thankfully they hadn't. It would improve Eli's odds.

"I think you're ready," Nik said, interrupting his thoughts. "You should take today to rest. Last thing you want is to be too tired or sore to give it your all tomorrow."

Eli nodded. He had a few things to take care of with Luka back in the lab anyway. He had been understanding of all the time Eli needed to prepare for the Rite, but Eli still felt guilty for missing so much work.

They gathered their things and headed for the trail that led through town and back to the mountain. Passing the shop that sold Eli's favorite afternoon beverage and the tailor where he'd replaced his wardrobe, a sense of peace washed over him.

The main street was alive and bustling with residents weaving in and out of the small buildings with baskets in their hands. Some of the shops had hung colorful banners at the start of the summer and they waved in the gentle breeze.

The town center didn't look nearly as intimidating as it had the first day he'd walked this dirt path. He didn't feel the same sense of dread and apprehension that he had that day as he waited to wake up and find it was only a dream.

Berland wasn't perfect, but it was *his*. In a world that had been torn apart and left him for dead, he'd managed to find his place. And in a few months, Grace would be his too.

He just had to make it through the Rite first.

A petite blonde woman caught his eye, and he watched Ali weave through the crowded main street. Her lips widened into a smile when she spotted them.

Nik greeted her with a quick kiss and a tight squeeze around the shoulders. Eli waited his turn before giving her a friendly hug.

"I was just coming to find you," she said excitedly, beaming at Nik—a look that would've killed Eli just a few months ago, but now he could stand to be in the shadow of their affection without feeling the darkness of abandonment.

"What's up?" Nik asked, wrapping a loving arm around her waist.

Ali quickly glanced at Eli before returning her attention to Nik. She clearly didn't want to say with him present.

He could take a hint. Although he was curious what Ali could possibly have to say that he couldn't hear, he didn't want to impose.

"Good to see you, Ali. I'll leave you two to it."

As he walked away, he looked over his shoulder and caught a glimpse of Ali's ecstatic smile—one he hadn't seen in so long. He'd forgotten it could be so enchanting. She said a few words to Nik and then he too broke out in a beaming grin, picking her up and holding her tight.

Eli turned and looked forward again, watching his step as he made his way through the busy crowd. Bright and cheery faces greeted him as if he were an old friend, wishing him luck for tomorrow's event. This was something he could get used to.

Belonging.

⁂

Eli's time in the lab was cut short when Luka came back from his lunch break and demanded that Eli take the rest of the day off.

"You need to rest and get your mind right," he said, hand on Eli's back as he shoved him out the door.

Eli didn't even have a chance to tell him he needed to pick up his notes for a project that was due in a week. Luka didn't let him get a single word in before he found himself in a dimly lit hallway leading back to the mountain's entry chamber.

There were still many hours left in the day, and he had no idea how he should fill them. The longer he walked, the more doubt crept into his mind.

What if he didn't get one of the coveted medallions?

What if his fight for Grace ended tomorrow?

What if he had to watch her marry someone else?

An image slipped into his mind of his hands wrapped around Trevor's neck before shoving him off a rocky cliff. He'd be exiled from Berland, maybe even sentenced to death himself, but it might be worth it.

Losing was not an option.

Eli made a left turn, and movement at the end of the hall drew his attention. A familiar face that he hadn't seen in over a month—hadn't heard his voice since he'd been trapped in a closet with Grace—looked up at him and almost turned around on the spot.

Eli called to him, "Noah!"

Noah forced a grin before waving to Eli. "Hello, Eli. How have you been?"

Eli jogged toward him. "I've been doing great. Can't say the same for you, though."

Noah tilted his head to the side, then glanced around, looking for potential eavesdroppers. "Not sure what you mean by that."

"I'm sure you've heard about Gabriel. He's been accused of treason for the fire that almost killed Ellen."

"Right." Noah shook his head. "Can't believe he'd do such a thing."

"I know what you mean. In fact, I don't believe he did such a thing."

Noah's eyes narrowed to slits. "What are you getting at?"

Eli took a deep breath. He wasn't sure how much he wanted to divulge. He certainly wouldn't admit that he'd been in Noah's office snooping around when he'd overheard Trevor threatening Noah. He needed to proceed carefully.

"If someone knew certain details...something that could clear Gabriel's name of this crime...the right thing to do would be to come forward and confess."

He studied Noah's eyes, hoping to see softening in them. A sign that Noah might be open to telling Ellen the truth and laying the blame where it truly belonged—with Trevor and the other rebels. But Noah's eyes turned black as night, and he looked Eli over like a predator about to attack its prey.

"Yes, if one did have any information, they should let it be known. If only someone had evidence to the contrary, Gabriel could be redeemed. Such a shame."

Eli's shoulders sagged. "A shame indeed."

Chapter Eight

GRACE

Steam rolled in clouds from the bathroom to Eli's bedroom, where Grace waited patiently, reading one of his many journals. It was fascinating to read his notes on his latest research projects—things she'd hardly been interested in before, but now that Eli was so heavily involved, she had a desire to read all of his thoughts. She was more interested in understanding how his brain worked than the research itself.

The sound of running water came to a halt and Grace laid Eli's journal on the small table beside the bed. She flipped to her stomach and pulled the clip out of her hair, letting it fall in waves, then propped her head on her palm and waited for Eli to enter the bedroom.

With a soft white towel wrapped around his waist, Eli appeared from behind the bathroom door, halting when he caught sight of Grace posing seductively on his bed.

She smiled, and her eyes roamed his body, still glistening with water.

"I figured you'd be staying home tonight," he said as he fell on the bed beside her.

She rolled to her side and slipped her hand into his. Warmth flowed from her fingertips through the rest of her body. "I will be. I just wanted to visit you first and see how you were holding up."

"Checking in on me, hmm?" His charming smile was irresistible as he pulled his bottom lip between his teeth.

She watched as a single drop of water moved down his stomach, inching closer to the sparse hairs peeking from below his towel. Suddenly, she felt parched.

"Are you surprised?" she asked, tearing her eyes away from his abdomen.

"I suppose not."

"Good. You shouldn't be. You should know by now that I care about you."

His grip tightened, and he brought their combined hands to his lips, kissing the back of her hand. "I do."

Grace pushed up into a seated position, her legs hanging off the end of Eli's bed.

"You sure you don't want to stay?" he asked, tugging her hand to prevent her from leaving.

"I *want* to stay, but you need your rest, and my mother is expecting me." She leaned down to kiss his cheek. "I'll see you in the morning, Eli."

Before she could pull her hand free, Eli yanked her back toward the bed. She fell on top of him, and their mouths connected. His lips were equally as soft and sweet as he was. Lips that she would get to kiss for the rest of her life, assuming he was successful in completing all three rounds of the Rite.

She smiled as she pulled back, running her hand through his short brown hair and getting lost in his hickory eyes. She had the utmost confidence in his ability to win, but every time she pictured their future together, a fragment of doubt snuck in. It was no use dwelling on it. She preferred to pretend it didn't exist. Pushing it aside, she planted another quick kiss on her future husband's lips. "Goodnight, Eli."

⁕⁘⁙ ⁙⁘⁕

"You're late." Her mother's voice drifted into the entryway before the door even had a chance to close behind her. Grace stepped farther into the mountain home she'd grown up in, peering into the study connected to the grand entrance.

Her mother sat swirling a glass of wine, wearing a burgundy robe and a judgmental frown.

Grace leaned against the doorframe and crossed her arms. "I said I'd be home. I never said when."

She almost laughed at her mother's exaggerated sigh. It wasn't that long ago when her mother's disapproval would've destroyed her. But the older she got and the closer to her future reign, the more she prioritized her own happiness over her mother's. It was both freeing and terrifying. For all the tension between them, she still loved her mother. She wanted her mother to be proud of her—of the person she *was,* not who her mother hoped she would be.

Maybe one day...

"Are you ready for tomorrow?" her mother asked, tactfully changing the subject.

Grace moved into the room and sat on the couch next to her mother, watching as she grabbed the bottle of angelfruit wine and poured it into a clean glass. She handed it to Grace and tilted her glass in a silent salute.

Something about the informality set Grace at ease. "I am."

"Not nervous at all?"

She slid her shoes off and propped her feet on the coffee table, knowing it would test her mother's patience. But her mother bit her tongue and merely waited for Grace's response. "Should I be?"

"I wasn't," her mother confessed, and Grace's brow rose. Her mother hadn't shared much about her own experience with the Rite. "Unlike you, I went into it with no expectations. No *hopes* or *dreams* or some fantastical idea of love. I knew what it was—a political arrangement. I lucked out with your father."

"Wouldn't that be all the more reason to worry? What if it had been someone awful?"

Her mother shrugged and sipped the last of the wine from her glass. "I had nothing to lose."

Placing her empty glass on the table, her mother rose, stumbling a step that had Grace questioning how much she'd had to drink. As she passed, she placed a hand on Grace's shoulder. "There will come a day when you realize that I only want the best for you."

⚘ ⚘

Grace woke to bickering voices outside her bedroom door—one lower pitched and a bit cautious, the other frantic.

"She should be up by now," Heather said.

"Knock again," Amaya answered. There came the sound of shuffling before Amaya continued, "I'm just going in."

"But what if she's—"

"You can come in," Grace shouted at her two best friends. She sat up and stretched her arms high above her head, the bones in her back cracking in a satisfying chorus.

The door flew open and Amaya came crashing through, jumping on Grace's bed with too much energy. Heather followed, though she thankfully kept her distance, attempting to give Grace a chance to wake up.

Behind her, a servant entered bearing a tray of assorted fruit, breads, and juice. She laid it at the end of Grace's bed and left without a word.

"What are you going to wear today?" Amaya asked. She was already dressed in a pale green sleeveless dress that cinched at her waist and flowed past her knees. Heather also wore a soft summer dress that slowly morphed from light pink off-the-shoulder sleeves to a bright fuchsia skirt that almost touched the floor.

While the Rite wasn't officially a formal event, many of the townspeople chose to dress up in the best summer style—bright colors and cool fabric to make it through the day without passing out.

Heather grabbed a glass of juice from the tray and headed toward Grace's closet. "You've only got a hundred dresses to choose from."

"Grab the white one hanging on the end."

When Heather emerged, she was holding a white chiffon dress that Grace had chosen days ago. It had one exposed shoulder and hugged her figure in a way that made her feel both sexy and sweet. Plus, the bright fabric would look stunning against her sun-kissed skin and brown curls.

Throwing back the blanket, she dragged her body out of bed and plucked the dress from Heather's arms, locking herself in the bathroom to change.

Once she finished dressing, she searched for her favorite pair of sandals—the tan woven ones with a small wedge heel. Her friends watched in silence as she slid them on.

"Don't you want something to eat?" Amaya asked, gesturing to the tray of fruit.

"Not all that hungry this morning."

Heather and Amaya exchanged looks of concern, but Grace spoke up before they could.

"You don't need to worry about me. Everything will be fine. Eli has spent weeks training for this. He will make it to the next round."

Heather's gaze softened. "What if he doesn't? Have you considered what will happen?"

Amaya looked like she might slap Heather. Her eyes burned with indignation on Grace's behalf. "Of course she's thought about it. Do you think she's a moron?"

"I'm right here," Grace said softly. Prior to Eli's arrival and his declaration of his intent to enter the Rite, she'd given a lot of consideration to who she may have to marry...and how miserable she'd be for the rest of her life. But now that she had Eli, there was only one outcome that felt real. She felt it in her soul that they would have their fairytale ending.

So she didn't need Heather's doubts or Amaya's concerns. She had enough faith for all of them.

Grace looked back and forth between her two friends and spoke it into existence. "Eli is going to win."

***

The path leading to the temporary arena was full of excitement. Children laughed and squealed, their parents chattering and ushering them forward, and vendors lined the path to sell food, drinks, and flower crowns. In addition to the joy and celebration the Rite brought, artisans and craftsmen had much to gain financially on days like this.

The summer sun had decided for once to give the people of Berland a reprieve, hiding behind scattered clouds. A light breeze shifted Grace's hair and let it dance across her neck. She almost regretted not bringing a shawl, but the sun would likely make an appearance soon and she'd be sweating per usual.

As she walked, familiar faces greeted her from every direction, the vast majority of them kind. Though she knew some of them must be associated with the rebellion and were likely rooting for Trevor to win, eager to see her quick demise, she held her chin high and refused to let them see her falter.

The field where the mud pit was centered had been transformed practically overnight. Temporary stands had been erected on the left and right side of the pit, decorated with the same purple and yellow flowers that adorned every little girl's head and some of the boys too.

In the center of the stands, a small stage with a canopy tent big enough to hold a dozen was waiting for her and her entourage. Heather and Amaya would join her as well as her newest guard, Nik. She felt his presence behind her, close enough to watch but far enough to be discreet. She'd also invited Ali and Sam, to her mother's dismay.

Her parents and Theo were already waiting. Despite their chat the prior evening, her mother looked pleased to see her and her brother waved excitedly.

She took her place on stage, on the seat in the center reserved for her, while the others sat in a back row. They still had a few minutes until the first round would begin, so she waited patiently while the crowd settled into their seats. She scanned the sea of people for Eli. With all the commotion, she had a hard time focusing, and every face blurred together as she sought him out.

She hadn't even realized her leg was shaking until Theo placed a hand on it. He smiled when she turned his direction. "It's going to be okay."

She knew that. Of course it would be. But for some reason, she found it difficult to form the words.

Then Theo pointed over her shoulder, and she followed his gaze. Near the northwest corner of the pit, Eli and the other suitors had gathered along with three members of the council who would oversee the competition—Diane, Fox, and Eamon.

She hated that he had weaseled his way into this aspect of her life. He should've been disqualified for the simple fact that his son was a suitor, but he'd convinced the rest of the council that he could be impartial.

But there he was, giving a pep talk to Trevor before things got started.

The other suitors were a mixture of old and young, tall and short, thin and brawny. Eli was one of the tallest and also one of the leanest. She wasn't sure if that would work in his favor today or not. His height would be an advantage in the pit, but would he be able to tussle with the bulkier men?

As she watched them stretch and prepare for the task at hand, rain began to fall and distorted her vision. A few moans of displeasure came from the crowd, but no one dared give up their seat. This was a once in a generation event. Another one wouldn't come along until Grace's firstborn daughter was old enough to wed. She shivered at the thought. The idea of forcing her own child to go through this made bile rise in her throat.

Grace turned in her seat and found Amaya in the row behind her. Catching her attention, she gestured toward Amaya's bag. Amaya chuckled but dug into her small purse until she found a silver flask. She passed it to Grace, who took several swigs of the fiery whiskey to calm her nerves, coughing a little as it burned her throat.

Theo muttered out of the corner of his mouth, "Careful. If Mother sees you drinking at an official event, you'll be grounded."

Grace smirked. "Let her try."

Chapter Nine

ELI

Rain began to fall more steadily, rattling Eli's nerves. Aside from the bad omen rain tended to signify, Eli hadn't practiced in these conditions. All of his training had been in perfect conditions. Already, rain dripped past his eyelashes and his fingers turned cold. The men around him looked equally disgruntled, except for Trevor and the man next to him. They both looked smug and eager to knock other suitors out of the running.

The man who had introduced himself as Fox explained how the first round would work. "In a few minutes, Lady Ellen will say a few words and then we will begin. You'll find markers spaced evenly around the mud pit, which is where you will stand until we tell you to go. One suitor per marker.

"There are only eight medallions, so half of you will be eliminated today. The medallions have already been tossed into the pit, and no one knows where they landed or which starting markers will be most advantageous. When I say 'go,' you must find a medallion and exit the pit with the medallion in your possession. If you drop it, it's fair game. If someone rips it from your hands before you exit, it's fair game. If you're bad at following directions and exit without the medallion still in your possession, it does not count. Have I made myself clear?"

Murmured acknowledgments rippled through the gathering of suitors.

"There are very few rules aside from exiting the pit with a medallion in your hands. It's expected that things may get physical. This will not be an easy task. There will be no pauses for injuries, foul play, or any other complaints you may have. The only rule we have is to not kill each other. I expect most of you should be able to abide by that."

Eli could've sworn he saw Trevor and the man beside him share a knowing look and then a grin.

Whatever. He didn't have time to interpret their weird behavior. Trevor wasn't stupid enough to try anything in front of an entire audience of people.

"Any questions?" Fox asked.

When no one spoke, he dismissed them to find their marks. Eli avoided the corner he knew to be the deepest. He chose the first marker available after that, on the opposite side of the pit from Trevor. As he waited for Ellen to make her speech, Trevor studied him through squinted eyes and pressed lips.

With any luck, Trevor would be out the first round and Eli wouldn't have to put up with him any longer. He wouldn't be intimidated by a barbarian pretending to be a noble. It didn't matter how long his family had been in Berland or how proud he was. Trevor was just a thief hunting for something that wasn't his.

The crowd went silent and Eli looked toward the stage where Ellen was standing. He was easily distracted by Grace sitting beside Theo, looking like an absolute angel sent straight from heaven. He smiled, and she tilted her head in acknowledgment. Her entire face seemed to brighten, and it warmed his cold, wet skin.

He shook out his drenched hair.

He could do this.

Ellen's greeting was short. Eli hardly heard a word of it while he stared at Grace. He couldn't wait to get the first round over with, so he could be one step closer to calling Grace his.

The crowd cheered and clapped, and Eli realized that Ellen was done speaking. She returned to her seat and Eli finally tore his eyes away from Grace, searching for Fox instead.

He held a hand up, paused, and then brought it down, shouting, "Go!"

Eli jumped into the pit, wasting no time digging in the mud and searching the bedrock for that solid circle of glory. Given how long the medallions had been in the pit, they had to be near the bottom. He felt his way along the surface, moving toward the deeper end in case the medallion had drifted farther down.

He did his best to tune out the surrounding competition, but when he heard roars of delight and chaos, his attention turned to his left. One of the men had found a medallion and two men were already at his back, clamoring to rip it from his hands. Another was headed in his direction.

Eli diverted his gaze back to the pit. It was no use even trying to retrieve that medallion. He was too far across the pit and his time would be better spent continuing his search.

Out of the corner of his eye, he caught movement. A suitor with a bald head and a pierced brow was searching the bottom just like Eli, but he kept a close watch. It was clear he was hoping Eli would find one first and the man could simply steal it from his possession.

Absolutely not.

Eli switched directions and moved away from the potential pillager.

Another round of applause rang out, but Eli ignored it. He couldn't afford to get caught up in the commotion. Not when his future with Grace was on the line.

Why was it taking so long? Every time he'd practiced on his own, he'd been able to find the medallion within minutes. Of course, the time it mattered most would be the time he struggled.

A large form moved into his vision from the right side, and he drifted to the left, hoping to avoid a confrontation. But when he looked up, he noticed the man was headed right toward him, beady eyes locked on Eli. Apparently, now that the first two medallions had been found, suitors were getting more aggressive.

The man shoved Eli aside, and Eli struggled to stay upright. The last thing he needed was to submerge in mud and lose his vision. His feet slid on the smooth surface beneath him, and he regained his balance just in time for the man to deal another blow.

"What the fuck?" he said through gritted teeth. He held up his hands, which were covered in mud. "I don't even have a medallion, you dipshit."

The man continued to charge at him, not seeming to care that Eli's hands were empty. It seemed as if he were only concerned with making sure they stayed that way.

There was no use fighting him, so Eli dodged away and headed toward the opposite side of the pit, groaning internally when he saw Trevor searching the muddy depths. He needed to find his medallion quickly and get the hell out of here.

Just as he began to search his new location, more cheers erupted and two men left the pit, medallions in each of their hands.

Four down, four to go.

Fuck.

He kept his head on a swivel in case the aggressive suitor had any intention of sneaking up behind him. Thankfully, the man seemed to have moved on to harass another, smaller competitor.

Eli shook his head and scraped the bottom of the pit with his fingers. He felt nothing but slimy, thick goo. The erupting crowd let him know that the fifth medallion had just been found.

His heart raced. It was only a matter of time before they were all found, and he *needed* to be one of the men who made it out of the pit with a muddy medallion in his hand. As his breathing became more frantic, so did his search. He felt his chance slipping away, his one shot at his happy ending with Grace—

There!

His fingers wrapped around a coin that was slightly smaller than the palm of his hand. He could tell before he even brought it out of the mud that it was the object he sought. He ran his thumb over the jagged edges and the star design imprinted on the face.

Without thinking, he darted toward the edge of the pit with a manic smile on his face. He'd done it. Just a few more feet and he could...

A body rammed into his side, jostling the medallion free.

"Won't be that easy, pretty boy."

Eli snarled at Trevor. If he punched him now, there would be no repercussions. He was well within his rights to defend himself and his claim on the medallion.

As if Trevor could read his mind, he threw the first punch, missing Eli's nose by a fraction of an inch. Blinding pain shot across Eli's face and his vision momentarily went black. He retaliated with a punch to Trevor's throat, sending him back a few steps.

Trevor wheezed as he gripped his throat with one hand. As much as Eli wanted to bask in the well-placed hit, he needed to grab the medallion and get out. It didn't take long to find the dropped prize, but as he stood up, another set of hands pulled him to the side and then wrapped an arm around his throat.

He choked, dropping the medallion once again so he could try to pry the thick arm from his airway. As he struggled to breathe, Trevor smirked and nodded in appreciation toward the stranger at Eli's back. He didn't have to look to know it was Trevor's friend, the one he had been chatting with before the match started.

Of course Trevor had people on the inside helping him. How had Eli been so foolish to not consider it? Was the other aggressive suitor also working with Trevor, or was that a mere coincidence? He suddenly felt as if he couldn't trust any of the other suitors.

Eli watched in horror as Trevor bent down to grab *Eli's* medallion. He waved it in front of Eli's face just to add salt to the wound before heading toward the rim of the pit.

Words failed to describe the devastation Eli felt as he watched Trevor climb out with a medallion in his hand.

Six medallions. That only left two still in play.

The brawny arm relinquished its hold on Eli, and after sucking in a sharp breath, Eli spun and landed a punch to the man's right eye. The man groaned and fell back a few steps, but not before Eli got in one more punch to his gut. The man coughed and for a moment, Eli thought he may throw up.

Dodging the path of projection, Eli slipped and stumbled, desperation sinking in. He put more distance between himself and Trevor's friend to buy some extra time to search. With a quick glance over his shoulder, he found the man still wheezing and looking around with one eye closed.

Eli felt a surge of satisfaction knowing he was the reason for the rapid swelling and purple tinge that marked his skin. Hopefully it would be enough to keep the man out of Eli's way so he could finish the round.

Sparing a glance at the rest of the pit, Eli found the remaining suitors scattered about, their heads down as they searched frantically. A couple looked as if they'd given up already, shoulders slumped and faces downcast. One man was splashing mud as he went, and Eli silently reproached him. He'd never find anything that way.

Choosing a spot he'd yet to visit, Eli waded into the deeper portion of the pit. He'd been avoiding it, knowing it would be more difficult to search, and he'd have to use his toes rather than his fingers to seek the medallion. He wouldn't be able to grab it without submerging in the mud and losing his vision for the remainder of the round.

He sighed and pushed forward until the mud rose above his belly button. Using the same method as he had before with his hands, he dragged his feet back and forth and hoped to strike a solid object that clashed against the slimy bed of the pit, praying to god he didn't come across a mud snake. As far as he knew, the ones in the region were not poisonous, but he preferred not to test that theory.

After what felt like hours, he abandoned the small square and moved to the left. He'd search the entire pit if he had to. Moving inch by inch, foot by foot. He'd do whatever it took to claim one of those medallions as his own.

As he moved another inch to the left, his foot grazed something that felt like a cool, hard metal coin. His heart soared, but he quickly masked his face in case any of the remaining suitors saw the glee in his eyes. He looked around, but none of them were paying him any attention. They all had their heads down as they continued their own searches.

Eli took a moment to consider. If he pulled the medallion out now, there was a good chance the other suitors would notice and rush him before he had the chance to make it out of the pit.

Using his foot, he slowly pushed the medallion toward the edge, pretending as if he were still searching. If he could just reach the perimeter, he'd be able to snatch his prize and climb out of the pit before anyone realized what had happened.

His ears rang with the roar of the crowd, and he realized the seventh medallion had been found. Judging by the splashing noises behind him, several of the suitors were now engaged in a fight to claim it.

The edge of the pit was just beyond arm's reach. He couldn't be distracted by the commotion behind him. Though it was only a few more feet, every nudge of the medallion felt like he was kicking a rock up a mountain. It was painfully slow, and his head throbbed from the adrenaline.

Just a few more inches...

The crowd erupted in cheers. Someone had been victorious in the struggle for the seventh medallion. It didn't matter, though.

He hid his smile as he reached into the mud and picked up the medallion beneath his foot. Then he placed both hands on the solid ground and pulled himself from the pit, raising his hand high above his head.

For a moment, he couldn't hear anything but a high-pitched buzzing. Couldn't see anything but a blur of muted colors as he turned toward the platform where he'd last seen Grace. It felt as though time stood still until the moment their eyes met.

He watched through the rain as her eyes moved from his face to the hand extended above his head and the medallion held high. Then she smiled and clasped a hand over her mouth, grabbing her brother's arm and pointing toward Eli. Theo saw the medallion in Eli's hand and wrapped Grace in a hug, cheering with the rest of the stands as their roars broke through the ringing in Eli's ears.

He felt a hand on his back, gently guiding him toward the platform where the other victorious suitors were waiting. Taking his place in line, Eli tried to calm the heart beating wildly in his chest. The moment felt surreal, like a dream, and he was only a spectator. He clutched the cool metal in his hand, reminding himself that this was real. He had successfully completed the first round.

One of the council members made a few comments and congratulated the eight remaining suitors, then offered condolences to those who were not fortunate enough to continue.

Eli hardly heard a word. His eyes were glued to Grace, a beacon of light through the dreary, rainy day. She beamed at him and mouthed a set of words that made his skin tingle. *I love you.*

He winked and responded in kind. *I love you, too.*

Chapter Ten

ELI

THE CROWD DISPERSED QUICKLY, leaving Eli with the other suitors, the three council members who oversaw the competition, Grace, and her mother Ellen. He thought he caught a look of disdain from the latter, but she quickly masked it. Had Grace managed to soften Ellen at all, or had she simply chosen to hide her contempt for him while in the presence of others?

Grace took a step forward and made a point to look each man in the eye, something Eli loathed but understood it was her duty. By now, it was certainly clear that Grace favored Eli, but she did her best to abide by Berland customs, appeasing the civilians that expected her to remain unbiased and placating the men who hoped to one day call her their wife.

Eli let out an irritated sigh. No one besides him would ever call her wife.

Clearing her throat, Grace spoke to the suitors. "Thank you once again for your participation in the Rite. I cannot express my gratitude enough for your commitment to Berland and our mutual prosperity. I am truly flattered and thrilled to congratulate each of you for making it past the first round. You are one step closer to standing by my side."

She offered them a smile, though Eli could see the strain behind it, the sour taste the words left in her mouth. Only one person would be standing by her side when all was said and done, and Eli was determined to be that man.

"The next round will be one month from today," Grace continued. "Pairs will be selected randomly for hand-to-hand combat. You'll have three chances to best your opponent, and the person with the most wins from each matchup will continue to the final round of the Rite. Simple enough. Are there any questions?"

When no one spoke, Grace dismissed them. Eli stalled for a minute, waiting for the other suitors to leave so he could have a moment alone with Grace. But some of the suitors had a similar agenda, feigning deep conversation with the person next to them while keeping one eye on Grace.

"Didn't expect you to be here," a grisly voice spoke from Eli's left.

Without turning to give Trevor his attention, Eli responded, "I'm sure you didn't."

No, surely Trevor thought his cohort would prevent Eli from gaining a medallion and moving to the next round. Unfortunately for him, he had underestimated Eli.

"That's all right. Better this way, in fact. Maybe I'll get to take you out myself in the next round." Trevor gave Eli's back a heavy pat.

Eli refused to give him the attention he so desperately sought, instead keeping his eyes on Grace.

As if he could read Eli's thoughts, Trevor chuckled and patted him one last time before withdrawing his hand. "That's right, kid. Save it for the next round."

Eli ground his teeth so hard his jaw ached. But then he saw Grace approaching, and his frustration fizzled into nothing.

"Congratulations, Eli." Grace kept a cordial but professional stance, placing her hand on his forearm for only a brief moment. After a quick glance to ensure they weren't being watched, she leaned in closer and whispered, "I have to make my rounds with the other suitors. Meet me back at my place?"

Eli nodded, keeping his voice low. "Of course. I will see you soon."

Before leaving the pit area, Eli was offered a bucket of water from one of the council members. The red-haired man named Fox told him to clean up before heading into the mountain. "Don't want to make a mess," he said.

Eli happily took the bucket of clean water. Despite the consistent rain, he was covered in mud and would need a good scrub once he returned home, but for now, the bucket of water would suffice to remove the muck covering his skin and clothes.

After retrieving his bag of belongings, he pulled on a clean shirt and pants, loathing the way they felt over his wet skin and undershorts. But the discomfort would be only momentary. He'd shower and change once he made it back to the mountain. Hopefully Grace wouldn't be far behind.

Rain continued to fall, and the puddles on the paths were impossible to avoid. The celebrations didn't stop, though. Eli passed hordes of cheerful Berlanders drinking and chattering with smiles on their faces. Musicians stood outside several shops, playing stringed instruments, pounding on drums, and singing while couples and children danced in the rain. It didn't matter that their feet and clothes were drenched and the wind whipped droplets in their face.

It truly was a celebration unlike any Eli had ever seen. Part of him wanted to stay behind and enjoy the festivities, but more than that, he wanted to spend the evening alone with Grace.

He continued walking the familiar path back to the mountain, weaving through the crowds and resisting the alluring smell of his favorite bakery. He was just about to make the last turn toward home when he caught sight of some familiar faces.

Ali, Nik, Sam, and Theo were all huddled under a small overhang, drinking pale amber liquid from large glass mugs. Ali was leaning against Nik's chest, but when she noticed Eli, she jogged over to greet him in the rain.

"Congratulations, Eli. I knew you could do it," she said, wrapping her mug-free arm around his neck.

"Thank you," he said as she led him back to the tavern's outdoor patio.

"You had us concerned for a minute there," Theo said, and Sam nodded his agreement.

"I wasn't concerned. I knew you had it in you," Ali said as she returned to her place wrapped in Nik's warm embrace.

"That makes one of us," Nik teased, but then he gave Eli a quick nod. "Congrats, man."

"Can we get you a drink?" Sam asked.

"That's okay. I don't plan to stay long."

"Oh, come on," Theo insisted. "Just one drink. What else could you possibly have to do?"

Silent looks were exchanged between the group of friends, indicating that they all knew where Eli would rather be and who he'd rather be with. It only took a second before Theo caught on.

"Ugh. My sister will still be there later. Besides, she has other folks to butter up before she'll be able to return home. You should be celebrating!

Not playing the part of a sad lovesick failure whose only redeeming quality is the woman who chose to love him."

"Harsh," Ali murmured. But Theo was grinning, and Eli knew every word was meant in jest. Theo would never truly utter a terrible word regarding his sister, nor the ones she cared about.

"Fine. I'll stay for *one* drink."

His friends cheered and clapped while Theo went inside the humble log cabin to fetch him an ale. As the door opened, Eli eyed the people packed shoulder to shoulder and understood why they'd chosen to stay outside instead.

What Eli intended to be one drink turned into two...then three...then four. Eli lost count around the time his head began to spin. The rain had softened into a light drizzle, and between the alcohol and the energetic atmosphere, Eli's cheeks flushed with heat.

He had almost forgotten that he was supposed to be meeting Grace until he felt a pinch on his left butt cheek.

He jumped and spun, expecting a drunken woman, but found Grace smiling up at him, her hair still damp from the rain and her clothes sticking to her skin.

Before she could say a word, he pulled her into a tight hug, squeezing her waist, and she wrapped her arms around his neck in return. There were too many eyes on them to enjoy a quick kiss, though Eli's dulled inhibitions were screaming at him to do it anyway.

"I was worried you'd get bored waiting for me, but I see you found a way to keep yourself entertained."

In a matter of seconds, a glass of ale was forced into Grace's hands. Eli wasn't even sure where it came from. The crowd had grown steadily over the past few hours, and now the area outside the door was just as packed as inside the building. People took turns heading inside and returning with as many mugs as they could carry.

"Don't worry, sis. We took good care of him," Theo told Grace.

She laughed as Eli swayed on his feet. "I can see that." She drained her own mug at an impressive pace before handing it to Theo. Then she took Eli's and passed it off to Sam. "Come on, Eli. Let's go home."

Instead of heading to Eli's apartment, where they usually spent their nights together, Grace led him back to her family's home. She still stayed there occasionally, but he had never stayed the night in their elegant underground mansion.

"Why aren't we staying at my place?" he asked, coming to a near stop in front of the threshold. She grabbed his hand, and he studied the way her delicate fingers intertwined with his rough ones.

"Because," she said, leading him up the staircase to where he knew her bedroom awaited. She skipped right over her bedroom door though and continued down the hall.

Eli glanced over his shoulder, wondering why they weren't going inside, falling onto the bed, and fooling around until one of them passed out. Probably him, given his condition.

"I thought you should see the spa."

When Eli turned to face forward again, he nearly tripped over his own feet as he entered the grandest bathroom he'd ever seen. Could it even be called a bathroom? The word seemed too insignificant for such a room. The *spa* was cut directly into the black mountain stone with metallic specks that shimmered in the warm glow of the hanging lanterns.

The walls to his left and right were decorated identically, featuring long stone benches placed below shelves stacked with towels, cloths, and an assortment of soap bottles. Two mirrors trimmed in ornate gold and iron woven together like vines hung beside the shelves.

There was even a chandelier with sparkling jewels hanging in the center of the room. But that wasn't the most mesmerizing feature of the room. Underneath the chandelier, a tub large enough for four was carved into the stone. The faucets matched the mirrors, with gold leaves circling the iron plumbing. And inside the tub, Eli spied a ledge that sat halfway down the wall.

"Impressive, right?"

Eli closed his mouth, which he realized had been hanging open. "You've been holding out on me."

Grace grinned wide, her eyes crinkling. "Now you know why I wanted to come here tonight instead of your place." She peered at his mud speckled skin. "I had a hunch you would need a nice, long bath."

Eli's shoulders shook as he peered down at the dried mud stuck underneath his fingernails. The bucket of water hadn't been nearly enough to clean himself thoroughly. "I suppose you're right."

Grace moved closer to the tub and gently turned the faucets. Water poured into the basin and steam rose. She ran her hand through the shallow depths, testing the temperature. Satisfied, she faced him again and stepped forward.

"Could you help me with this?" she asked, turning and pulling her hair to the side so Eli could see the zipper running the length of her spine.

He gently tugged, and the fabric of her dress fell open, revealing her perfectly smooth skin. He traced her spine with the back of two fingers, and she inhaled sharply. With one hand, she pulled down the single shoulder strap and let the dress fall to the floor, giving Eli the best view of her deliciously curved ass. He gave it a quick squeeze before his hands roamed around her waist and he pulled her body against him.

She giggled when Eli's lips brushed her neck. "You know you have to take your clothes off too before getting in?"

"Hmm." His lips vibrated against her skin as he rubbed his hands down her thighs and up her side. He was only half aware of what she was saying as she spun around.

"Let me."

She grabbed the hem of his shirt and lifted it over his head, unable to stop Eli from leaning forward and slamming his lips against hers. He felt her smile form beneath his kiss. She pulled away long enough to fall to her knees and fumble with the buttons on his pants. Their hurried breaths matched in tempo, her heart beating to the same rhythm as his.

She tugged his pants to the floor. He stepped out of them and saved her the hassle of removing his undershorts, ripping them off himself. He grabbed her hands and pulled her into a standing position before squeezing the backs of her thighs and hoisting her to his waist. She sucked in a sharp breath as their bodies collided, and he held in a moan as she showered him in kisses.

His neck. His jawline. His cheek. His temple.

Her hunger threatened to devour him whole.

Carefully, Eli carried her to the tub and climbed over the ledge. He sighed as the warm water swirled around his ankles and then engulfed his lower limbs. Grace continued to mark his skin with the soft impression of her lips, grinding her pussy against him until his legs wobbled.

He sat on the ledge and placed his hands on each side of her cheek, pulling back to get a good look at her face. When she bit her lip, his cock twitched beneath the water's surface.

"You're so beautiful," he said, mind spinning from the ale and the thick steam dancing above their heads.

Grace huffed a laugh and threaded her hands behind his neck, taking her time to study him. They stayed motionless, taking each other in as the water continued to pour into the tub. It was almost full now. They should break apart and turn the faucet off, but the sparkle in her eyes kept Eli glued to his seat. The tension between them was unbearably thick, but also delicate. Like a simple sudden movement or sound would easily shatter it into a million pieces.

Eli swallowed hard and leaned forward, his forehead resting against hers. He wasn't sure how long they stayed that way, frozen in time.

When the water reached his shoulders, Grace finally shifted in his lap and pulled away, crossing the tub to shut off the water. The silence only added to the tension. Eli cursed the space between them and began to move toward her, but she held out a hand.

"Wait."

He sighed but returned to his seat, stretching his arms along the edge of the tub on either side of him.

Grace made her way back to him and cupped the water in her hands, pouring it over his shoulders and arms. She gently scrubbed his skin and massaged his sore muscles.

He'd momentarily forgotten about the toll today and every day of training before had taken on his body, but as she ran her hands along his arms, down his chest, and over his thighs, he moaned. Then she wrapped a hand around his shaft and used her other to cup his balls, and he practically levitated out of his seat. Arching into her touch, he slid his cock through her fingers while she squeezed him with varying pressure. He leaned forward, seeking the sweet, sensitive spot between her legs, but she resisted his touch.

"Let me spoil you. You worked so hard today. I want to offer my gratitude."

Eli's body tensed as pleasure built in his abdomen. As much as he loved being taken care of by Grace, his favorite form of gratitude was the sight of her coming undone. He wrapped a hand around her wrist and pulled her flush against him, relishing the gentle caress of her breath against his face.

"Nothing would make me happier than to please you," he said, trailing his finger down between her breasts, over her stomach, and down to her clit. She gasped when he twisted his hand to stroke her folds, teasing her entrance. Wetness pooled between her thighs, a different slickness than the water in the tub.

He eased a finger inside, and she instantly clamped around him. Throwing her head back, she rocked her hips against his hand. When he added a second finger, she whimpered and squeezed tighter.

"Fuck, you are stunning," he choked out. His cock ached to be inside her, but he couldn't pull his fingers out just yet. Not while she looked to be seconds away from rapturous bliss.

He hooked his fingers inside her and moved them in a come-hither pattern. Grace's jaw went slack and a series of breathy moans escaped her lips. He felt the pulse of her cunt around his fingers and continued to move inside her until her orgasm faded.

She smiled and ran her fingers through his hair. "This night was supposed to be for you."

"This was for me," he said, leaning forward to pull her nipple into his mouth.

She squealed with delight as he wrapped his arms around her waist. He palmed her ass and held her close to him, driving her core against his swollen cock. The tip of his cock slid over her entrance, and he moaned against her chest.

Before he could say a word, he felt her hand grip his shaft, and she sighed as she slid down his length. The water sloshed against the side of the tub as he drove into her. Grace held onto his shoulders while he gripped her waist, mesmerized by the expression she made with each thrust.

It wasn't long before he felt the walls of her pussy clenching around him and smiled, knowing he had just delivered her second orgasm of the evening. Her pleasured cries sent a jolt of euphoria down his spine, and he spilled into her warm cunt.

Slowly, their labored breathing returned to normal, and Eli held Grace in his arms as they both came down from their high. She traced circles on his back while he dipped his hands in the water and let it flow over hers.

"Eli?" she finally said with a hint of apprehension.

"Yes?"

"I wish you didn't have to go through the Rite. That *I* didn't have to go through it. If I had my way, you wouldn't need to compete for my love. You already have it."

He kissed the place where her temple met her hairline. If it were possible to ease her troubles, he would do it in a heartbeat. Unfortunately, he couldn't see a way out of this.

"I choose you," she said quietly, resting her head against the crook of his shoulder. "I choose you."

Chapter Eleven

ELI

ELI'S EYES POPPED OPEN to pitch black. At first, he couldn't recall where he was, but as he inhaled sharply, he caught the scent of Grace's hair and felt the weight of her chest against his back. Then he remembered falling asleep next to her after they'd washed off.

He smiled and let his eyes fall closed again. He adjusted his arm, as it had fallen asleep at some point during the night. The sound of Grace's breathing lulled him into a state of tranquility.

Just as he was about to fall back asleep, a noise sounded from beyond Grace's bedroom. It sounded like someone fumbling around on the first floor. His heart raced at the thought of some unknown intruder wandering around Grace's home, but it was probably just one of her parents or Theo.

As gently as he could, Eli unraveled his body from Grace and slipped out from under the pillowy blanket still draped over Grace's silhouette. He felt his way to the door and quietly pried it open. A warm glow illuminated the hall, and he shut Grace's door and followed it toward the study located off the foyer.

When he reached the last few steps of the staircase, he heard coughing and the sound of a spoon swirling against a cup. He rounded the corner and found Grace's mother, Ellen, sitting in a navy cushioned chair with a teacup in her hands. Her eyes were closed, but he knew she was awake by the way she stirred the drink.

He cleared his throat.

She opened her eyes, but she didn't look surprised to see him. "Eli."

"Ellen."

"Please," she said, waving her arm at the couch across from her. "Have a seat."

He lowered himself to the sofa and studied her expression. Her eyes lacked the usual malice she held for him.

Silence stretched between them, and Eli ran his hands nervously over the fabric of his shorts. Ellen had made it clear time and time again that he wasn't her favorite person. She didn't think he was good enough for Grace. That by entering the Rite, he'd put a target on Grace's back and had further complicated things with the rebellion lurking in the shadows.

It had also been a source of contention for Grace and her mother. Eli and Grace had had many conversations on the topic, and Grace filled him in each time on the lengths she had to go to in order to defend him. He was grateful that she would stick up for him but hated that it was widening the divide between her and her mother. As if it hadn't been wide enough before his arrival.

Eli fidgeted, searching for the right words to break the uneasy silence, but it was as though every thought had scattered from his brain.

Ellen took a sip from her teacup and then reached forward to set it down on the coffee table between them. "It's been a while since my daughter has slept in her own bed."

Eli's throat constricted. Not the sentence he was hoping for. Rather than ease the tension, it only seemed to intensify it. "I...I'm..."

He considered apologizing, but he wasn't sorry. Not at all. And lying to Ellen didn't seem like a wise decision.

She waved her hand and saved him from responding. "I know it's no use telling my daughter what to do. She doesn't listen to me anyway. She's determined to do things her own way, and one day she'll understand that those actions have consequences."

Consequences. The way she said the word had Eli feeling like he was one of those *consequences.* A stain on their family's reputation. And he hadn't even won the Rite yet.

He leaned forward, placing his elbows on his knees and interlacing his fingers. "I think Grace is perfectly capable of making the best decisions for herself and for the people of Berland."

He chose to leave his other thought unspoken—that it was a shame that Ellen didn't see how smart, strong, and resilient Grace was. Very rarely did he have a cordial conversation with Ellen, and he didn't want to ruin it by insulting her.

"I know more than anyone what my daughter is capable of," she hissed. "I'm the one who raised the woman you're so fond of. I taught her to stand her ground...even if I may not agree with her all the time."

Despite his attempt to be on his best behavior, he had still managed to upset her. Perhaps they were never meant to be friends. A shame, since he planned to spend the rest of his life with Grace.

"I'm sorry, Ellen. I didn't mean to offend you."

She sighed and leaned forward, rolling her shoulders and cracking her neck as she stood from her chair. "I know you didn't."

She sighed again, this time heavier, like she had the weight of the world on her shoulders. And in some ways, he supposed she did. Berland was as close to paradise as he'd seen...and he'd seen more than most people. The responsibility of keeping an oasis like this running smoothly had to be a difficult burden to bear.

"I do hope Grace is right about you. If she were any other girl, born into any other role, I'd be delighted to call you family."

Eli's brows rose. He'd never expected such words to come from Ellen's mouth.

"But she isn't any other girl. She's the future Lady of Berland."

"I know."

"And any sign of weakness, any flaw that people perceive, will be scrutinized."

"I know."

"They'll put impossible expectations on her and blame her for all their problems."

"I *know*," he said. "You don't think I take this seriously, but believe me, Ellen, I do. I really do. I know what Grace is up against and I want to be the one by her side, supporting her each step of the way. I *can* do that."

Ellen slowly nodded, and Eli felt as though he'd finally made some progress with her. Maybe they could be a happy family when all was said and done.

"I still don't like that you went against my wishes," she said with a small uptick of her lips.

He smiled back. "I know."

"But you're not sorry for that?"

He shook his head. "Not at all."

She nodded again and started toward the study door, passing Eli on the way and resting a hand on his shoulder. It'd been so long since he'd felt a motherly touch, and he inhaled sharply when she removed her hand.

"Ellen," he said, turning to watch as she left the room. He wasn't sure what he was going to say. Thank you, maybe? That he was glad, at least, that her displeasure with him had nothing to do with his own faults and everything to do with Grace's position?

But he forgot all of that as Ellen stumbled a few steps and grabbed the door frame. She slid down the wall until she hit her knees, and her head slumped forward.

"Ellen!"

Eli jumped from his seat and rushed toward her, catching her before her torso hit the floor. Her head lolled to the side, and he attempted to cradle her in his arms.

"Ellen," he said again, gently tapping her cheek. "Can you hear me? Are you okay? Ellen, wake up."

Shit. He wasn't medically trained. He had no idea what to do in this situation. Should he yell for Grace? He hadn't seen her father Ben or Theo but had to assume they were sleeping peacefully nearby. Should he grab some water? But that would mean leaving her alone and maybe that would somehow make things worse.

He was fully prepared to shout again until someone woke and came to help when Ellen's eyes fluttered open. She peered up at him in confusion before glancing around the room and remembering where she was.

"Are you okay?" he asked. "Do you need water or something? Can you sit up?"

Ellen put up a hand. "I'm fine. Just a dizzy spell. It happens sometimes."

"Should I go get Ben? Tell me what you need."

"No, no," she said quickly. "No need to wake him. There's a bag hanging on the coat rack in the foyer. Can you bring it to me?"

Eli nodded and helped Ellen into a seated position. She leaned against the wall, looking pale and dazed.

There were only two bags hanging from the coat rack near the front door. Eli checked the first one, which was mostly empty except for a small coin purse and a set of earrings. He checked the second bag and, inside the largest pouch, he found three vials of a clear liquid substance. He could only guess what they contained, but this was likely what Ellen was looking for.

He removed the bag from its hook and brought it back to Ellen.

"What is that?" he asked, watching as Ellen pulled out one of the vials and uncorked it. She tipped it back and drank the contents with a grimace. Whatever it was, it must taste terrible.

"Don't worry about it," she said, replacing the cork and dropping the empty vial back into her bag. Some of the color returned to her face, and she seemed to regain some of her strength.

Eli didn't know much about health matters, but he knew enough to know something wasn't right. Did Grace know? She hadn't mentioned anything to him. Maybe it wasn't anything serious...

"Don't get any ideas," Ellen said sharply.

Eli frowned. "What?"

Moving to her feet, Ellen nodded toward him. "I can see you are overthinking this, Eli. I'm fine. So stop worrying."

Eli narrowed his eyes. The more she tried to convince him she was fine, the less he believed her.

"I mean it, Eli. This is not your business."

"Is it Grace's business?"

What little color had returned to Ellen's face suddenly drained once more. For half a second, Eli regretted his words.

Please don't faint again.

But then Ellen straightened her nightgown and peered down her nose at him. "Grace doesn't know anything. Because there is nothing to know."

"Sure," he said, shaking his head in disappointment. He didn't believe her for one second.

She sighed, and her icy demeanor began to melt. Her voice shook as she said, "Please, Eli. Do not tell Grace about this."

Eli was right not to believe her. There was obviously something wrong, but to what severity? From the glassy look in her eyes, he guessed it must be bad.

As terribly as Ellen had treated him, it was hard to say no when she looked so sad and pleading.

"I won't say anything...because you'll tell Grace yourself."

Ellen looked too exhausted to fight him. "Deal."

Chapter Twelve

ALI

"How have you been feeling?" The woman in a crisp white top and dark slacks turned to Ali with a notepad in her hand.

"Good," Ali replied. And for the first time in a long while, it was true. Things were going great with Nik. She'd mended her friendship with Eli, and they were both moving forward with their respective relationships. She had a job and a home.

And she was pregnant.

She smiled at the thought, placing a hand on her stomach. She wasn't showing yet, but she felt the magic of life growing inside her.

When she'd realized she was late, Nik had insisted that she see a medic before she got too excited. But a test had confirmed it, and she'd never forget the smile on his face when she told him with certainty that they would be adding a tiny member to their family.

"That's good news. If that changes, if you feel any discomfort, nausea, exhaustion, you can always come see me. I can't guarantee that I can alleviate the symptoms—it's pretty normal to feel those things—but I am here to support you and make sure everything goes as smoothly as possible."

The woman held up a bottle that rattled when she gently shook it. "These are some vitamins to make sure you're getting your nutrients throughout your pregnancy. You should take one a day. Do you have any questions for me or any other concerns?"

Ali shrugged. Her head spun with excitement and dreams for the future. It was hard to think straight these days. She was certain she would have questions, but right now she just wanted to find Nik and kiss him till she was breathless. And eat. Her appetite had increased exponentially in the past few days.

When the medic finished her exam, Ali was dismissed, and she left the sterile chamber with baby blankets and biscuits on her mind. She was supposed to meet Grace in the meadow where Nik and Eli were training for the second round, but she could be a few minutes late.

She stopped at a sweets shop first, drawn by the tantalizing scent of vanilla and cinnamon. The daily special featured cookies that were larger than her palm. She had a hard time deciding between the salted caramel or the shortbread with lemon icing, so she bought one of each.

Breaking off a piece of the lemon cookie, she popped it into her mouth and stepped into the town's largest clothing store. All of it was secondhand, but they had the biggest variety, and the stock was constantly changing as the townsfolk got rid of old items and traded for something different.

Ali broke off another piece of her cookie and stood on her tiptoes, searching for the section of the store that held the baby items. When she spotted a sea of pastels, she knew she'd found what she was looking for.

The store wasn't very busy this morning. In fact, there was only one other woman browsing the baby section. Ali smiled and began to sift through the racks of onesies, T-shirts, and sweatpants. She almost melted into a puddle at the sight of socks that fit in the palm of her hand. Each item she held up brought tears to her eyes as she thought about what her own child might look like in them.

There were so many items to sort through, but in the end, she picked out a gray onesie with a purple sleeping owl on it. There'd be time to shop more in the coming months, but she couldn't stop herself from purchasing one item. That tiny onesie made it feel *real*.

Morning dew glistened on the grass lining the pathway to the training field. Ali finished eating the first cookie and brushed her hands off. She'd meant to save some for Nik to try, but her cravings had gotten the best of her.

The onesie was safely tucked inside her bag. She wasn't sure if she was quite ready to share the news with the rest of their friends. In fact, she was a little nervous to tell Eli at all. The tension between him and Nik may have been easing, but their situation was delicate. Something like this might set Eli off again, and that was the last thing she wanted to deal with.

Still, it would be better to tell him first and preferably not in a group. Like the one gathered around a fallen tree trunk.

Ali approached her group of friends. Sam, Grace, Amaya, and Heather sat casually on the tree trunk, laughing at whatever story Theo was telling. Eli chuckled and spat out his water, which he drank from a canteen. Nik crossed his arms but did a terrible job hiding his amusement.

"What did I miss?" Ali asked.

"Just Theo trying his hardest to embarrass me. Little does he know, that's not possible," Grace said.

Theo laughed and ruffled his sister's hair. "It's true. No matter what story I tell from our childhood, she shows no shame. You just missed the story of Grace's first ball."

Amaya looked beside herself, struggling to breathe.

Heather clapped her on the back. "If you tell the story again, I think you might kill Amaya."

"Condensed version it is, then," Theo said. "She was, what...eight or nine years old?"

He looked at Grace for confirmation, and she nodded.

"I don't know if you know this, Ali, but as a public figure, it's expected that Grace politely accepts any invitation to dance unless she's preoccupied with another partner already.

"So there was this kid, Brady. He had a reputation for picking his nose in class."

The girls began to laugh again, and Theo shot them a quelling look.

"Well, he decides that he wants to dance with Grace. So we're both standing with our parents, on our best behavior..." He smirked and placed a hand on his chest, and Ali had the impression that they had been far from angels as children. "Brady comes and asks Grace if he could have the next dance. And you know what she says, Ali?"

Ali shook her head, grinning as she waited for the part of the story that had everyone in shambles.

"She says 'I'm not dancing with Boogie Brady!'"

Amaya began to wheeze again, but Sam urged him to continue. "It gets better."

"Our mother looked like she'd had a heart attack and told Grace that she *had* to accept since she wasn't currently dancing with anyone and that she would be kind and apologize to Brady.

"But that's not our Gracie, here. No, Grace instead says that she does have a dance partner already—herself. She moves out to the middle of the dance floor and begins to twirl in circles as if she's dancing with an imaginary friend.

"I don't know that I've ever seen our mother so furious in public. Every time someone tried to dance with Grace after that, she simply told them she had a better offer."

"I wonder if poor Boogie Brady ever thinks about his lost opportunity with Grace," Heather said.

"Poor shmuck. He was absolutely humiliated that day." Theo grinned, and it was clear he didn't feel sorry for him at all.

Grace rolled her eyes. "You make it seem like I'm heartless. I did end up apologizing to him years later. And for your information, he's happily married now with two kids and another on the way. So no permanent damage was done."

"Fair enough," Theo conceded. "It's probably for the best anyway. You would've eaten him alive."

"Speaking of...should we get back to work?" Eli asked, gesturing to the field.

Theo and Eli headed to the center of the clearing. After a quick greeting and a kiss on the cheek from Ali, Nik joined them. They briefly chatted, though she couldn't make out their words. It appeared as though Nik was giving instructions while Eli listened attentively and Theo nodded.

Ali took a seat on the tree trunk between Sam and Grace. "You didn't want to join them?" she asked Sam.

"It's not really my thing."

Grace leaned around Ali. "It's not our thing either, Sam. No, our thing is this," she said, gesturing toward the men.

"What is *this*?"

Amaya laughed. "Just watch."

Ali looked straight ahead as Eli and Theo squared up. Upon Nik's command, the two began to wrestle, shoving and pulling, dodging punches and blocking kicks. In less than a minute, they both hit the ground with a thud and a cloud of dirt.

They each struggled to claim their place on top, rolling around in the dirt while their sweaty backs glistened in the sunlight. Their muscles flexed and the sound of their grunts filled the air. Amaya whistled, and Grace cupped a hand over her mouth as she giggled.

"It's a bit erotic, isn't it?" Heather asked. "Whose idea was it for grown men to roll around half-naked?"

"Better yet, why didn't they choose to do it fully nude?" Amaya added.

Ali's shoulders shook from laughter, understanding now why the ladies wanted to hang out here for the day. Even Nik looked hot as hell standing with his shirt off and abs on display. When was it his turn to wrestle?

"Ms. Harper sure knew what she was doing when she devised the Rite," Grace said.

Amaya raised the beverage in her hand. "Cheers to Ms. Harper."

A round of cheers echoed her appreciation.

Theo was momentarily distracted by the hollers and clapping, leaving Eli the perfect opportunity to land him on his back with a forearm to his neck. Theo tapped the ground, and Eli released his hold. Too bad it wouldn't be that easy during the actual event. Ali doubted the contestants would be so easily distracted.

Rising to his feet, Theo waved at the girls and donned his most charming grin. Amaya and Heather both giggled as he wiped the sweat from his face and unnecessarily adjusted the waistband of his pants.

"Seriously though," Amaya said. "Who do I have to speak to about seeing Theo fight in the nude? I bet he could put on *quite* the show with his—"

"Ugh, Amaya," Grace said with a grimace. "That is disgusting. He is my brother."

"Whatever. He's hot. I know it, you know it, Sam knows it."

Sam smiled, nodding like even he could not deny how attractive Theo was. Something sparkled in his eye, and Ali's curiosity hit a new height.

Theo had a reputation of being a flirt, but she'd never seen him look at anyone the way he looked at Sam. Were they already more than friends but keeping it private? Sam was such a shy person; she didn't want to pry. There would be a lot of disappointed people—including Amaya and Heather—if Theo ever decided to settle down.

Ali placed her hand on top of Sam's and patted it, silently letting him know that she was there for him if he ever wanted to talk. He gave her a quick smile, and she knew he understood.

Her attention returned to the men and their training. Nik was demonstrating a move to Eli with Theo's assistance.

"Does Theo have much experience in hand-to-hand combat?" Ali asked Grace.

"Not really. He had a few lessons growing up and he still practices now and then just in case they run into trouble on the road, but he's not nearly as skilled as Nik or even Eli."

"What about the other suitors?"

Grace shrugged. "Some of them are well trained, like Trevor, and some are just as amateur as Theo. The pairs are drawn randomly, so I truly hope Eli finds himself across from someone half his size."

"You doubt him?" Ali asked, a bit surprised. Eli had been through more challenges than most in his lifetime, and he'd always risen to the occasion.

"Absolutely not! I just don't want another close call like he had in the first round. I don't think my nerves can handle it. I want a quick matchup and an easy win."

Ali had to agree. Waiting for Eli to climb out of the mud pit with a medallion in his hand had been excruciating. It had probably been much worse for Grace to watch, wondering whether her dream of marrying Eli would come to an end.

The men tussled again and Eli easily outmaneuvered Theo this time. After a few more easy wins, Nik stepped in. The ladies taunted Theo from the sidelines after he was removed from the practice.

"You'll get it them next time," Heather shouted.

Amaya added, "You did your best, sweetie."

The rest of their crew laughed as Theo headed toward them. He settled next to Sam. "I let him win," he said with a wink. "I was bored."

Nik dominated the subsequent contests, but he took time between each one to walk Eli through how he could improve. Toward the end of their practice, the fight seemed much more balanced. Eli even managed to beat Nik a time or two. Each time he did, Grace cheered the loudest and even Ali danced on the inside.

She could watch Nik wrestle all day and beam with delight at every win, but Eli had a lot riding on this. She wanted to see him succeed.

After another hour, they called it quits. Eli needed to head to work while Grace and Ali had a council meeting to attend. They packed up their belongings and headed back toward the mountain, Heather and Amaya breaking off when they reached Heather's family business.

Grace accompanied Ali and Nik back to their home. Nik needed a quick shower and since he was meant to be protecting Grace, she had to tag along.

Before he washed up, Nik quickly kissed Ali's cheek, and she felt his hand graze her stomach, resting there longer than normal. Her skin tingled and her belly fluttered with overwhelming joy. She had been a little worried that he wouldn't be too thrilled about having a baby. That it was too soon. But every time he touched her or she caught his eyes lingering on her stomach, she knew he was just as deliriously happy as she was.

Ali pulled a few things from their cupboards and set a pot on the stove. She dropped the ingredients in and watched as the broth began to bubble. Behind her, she heard Grace pull out a chair at the small dining table.

Reaching for a couple glasses, she turned around and asked Grace, "Can I get you something to drink?"

Grace was studying her. Appraising her. She had a thin smile, and her eyes were narrowed in suspicion.

"What?" Ali asked. She looked down, uncertain what she was looking for. Guilt sprang to the surface as if she'd been caught committing a crime. "What is it?"

"Ali," Grace said slowly. "Are you pregnant?"

"I... I didn't... How?" Ali stuttered. No one else knew except Nik and her medic. Maybe her medic had broken her trust?

Grace chuckled. "If you wanted to keep it a secret, you probably shouldn't hold your stomach like that. And tell Nik not to let his hands linger there either. You both look like you're about to burst from the seams with love. It's cute."

"Oh." Ali didn't know what else to say. She hadn't even realized her hand was resting on her stomach. In fact, it still was. She quickly dropped it to her side.

"So, you are then? Pregnant?"

Smiling, Ali tucked her hair behind her ear. "I am."

Chapter Thirteen

NIK

THE SOUND OF SIZZLING bacon filled the air. Nik flipped each piece on the hot surface and then stirred a small pan of eggs. While breakfast cooked, he squeezed a couple of angelfruits over two glasses, filling them with sweet pink juice.

In the bedroom attached to the open kitchen, Ali was still nestled in the thick blankets. Despite the summer heat, the homes under the mountain stayed comfortably cool. Nik watched her breathe, her chest rising and falling with each peaceful inhale and exhale.

She'd been extra tired lately, and he wanted to do something nice for her. Breakfast in bed seemed like the best idea to allow her to sleep in and show her how much he cared.

As he removed the pans from the stovetop, he heard rustling from their bedroom.

"Nik?" Ali's voice carried through the quaint apartment.

"Don't get up," he called, rushing to dish the food onto plates. "I'll be right in."

After placing the plates and glasses of juice onto a small server, he carried it into the bedroom and sat it at the end of the bed. "Surprise," he said, rounding the end of the mattress to crawl back into bed with her.

"You did this for me?" she asked with tears in her eyes.

Nik felt a little uneasy. "Yes..."

She wiped her cheek with the back of her hand. "That's so sweet. Thank you."

Then she swung her legs over the side of the bed and stood, sliding a pair of shorts over her bare legs.

Nik stared in confusion. "Where are you going?" The tray of food sat untouched in the middle of the bed. Ali walked into the bathroom and shut the door without another word. Each second that passed caused Nik to worry. Was it morning sickness? He'd heard that was a thing pregnant people went through. Maybe he should check on her.

He was just about to get up when the door opened again and Ali strolled out, no sign of tears on her face.

"Are you all right?" he asked.

"Yes, I'm fine."

She crawled back onto the bed and leaned against the headboard. When she realized he was still staring, waiting for some sign that she was truly okay, she sighed. "I just have to pee all the time right now."

Nik chuckled. Thank god that's all it was.

Ali playfully smacked his arm. "It's not funny. It's actually very annoying." He laughed even harder, and Ali joined him. "You won some points with this breakfast, but I think you just lost them."

Nik reigned in his laughter and passed her a plate. "Would I win them back if I tell you there's also a cinnamon bun with your name on it in the kitchen?"

She paused, raising a forkful of scrambled eggs to her mouth, and her lips curved into a wide smile. "Yes, that would win you a lot of points."

Once Ali had finished her eggs, bacon, and a slice of toast, Nik fetched the cinnamon roll as promised. He hadn't been certain that she would be hungry enough to eat it all, but he should've known she would always have room for sweets.

Before he left for the day, he kissed her lips—quickly at first, but then he went back for seconds, relishing the way her lips formed to his. The softness and the taste of sweet cinnamon that still lingered there. "I'll see you later."

Since he'd settled into his job as Grace's newest guard, he'd gotten into a routine. Each morning, he met her outside of the cafeteria and followed her around as she took care of her various responsibilities. Sometimes it meant standing outside of meeting rooms, while other times it meant tagging along to watch Eli train. Those times always ended up with him taking an active role in helping Eli rather than watching from the sidelines. He had a hunch that Grace and Ali had planned it that way.

Today they'd be assembling food packages for some of the less fortunate members of Berland. It was a surprise that anyone would struggle here since he and his friends had been taken care of so well. But Grace explained that not everyone adapted to life in Berland so easily. Regardless of whether they were newcomers or had been here for decades, some struggled to find the right job to fit their skills. Some had large families and needed more to provide for their children, while others had just fallen on hard times and needed help getting back on the right track. In the same way that the newcomers had been provided for, the community came together to help those in need.

When he met Grace outside the cafeteria, she bounced on her feet and greeted him excitedly. Was she ever calm? She always seemed to have enough energy for an entire army.

Nik did his best to put on a smile, but it paled in comparison to her excitement. "Lead the way," he said, gesturing for her to move into the cafeteria.

Grace chattered the entire time they walked to the attendant at the register. Nik hardly heard a word she said, but nodded and furrowed his brows to make it seem like he was fully engaged in the one-sided conversation.

Grace exchanged a few words with the worker stationed next to the buffet, who pointed to a semi-hidden door behind several stacks of wooden crates. Nik followed Grace through the door to a small storage area. The walls were lined with fruits and vegetables and an assortment of non-perishable items. In the center of the room, a large rectangle table stretched from one wall and stopped only an arm's length away, leaving very little room to maneuver around.

One elderly man waited for them. He held a small clipboard and read it with the utmost concentration, biting on the end of a pencil. He scribbled something and then looked up, perusing the shelves on the wall. He jumped when he caught sight of Nik and Grace waiting patiently by the door. Clutching at his chest, he nodded politely toward Grace. "I'm sorry, Miss Grace. I didn't see you there."

She smiled and squeezed her way around the table. "Preston, it's so good to see you. How have you been?"

"As good as an eighty-year-old man could be, I suppose."

She laughed and gave him a quick one-armed hug. It was all she could reach in the crowded space. "Preston, this is Nik. He's a new guard assigned to me, and he'll be helping out today."

"Nice to meet you," Preston said, stretching an arm toward Nik. Nik had to reach around Grace to shake his hand.

"You as well."

Preston pulled a sheet of paper from his clipboard and offered it to Grace. He pointed toward the top and Nik leaned to see what Grace was seeing. It appeared to be some type of fulfillment sheet with a log of items required.

"I've filled these boxes already." His finger traced the first few lines. "We still have these to go."

More than half the page had yet to be crossed off.

Grace read through each line, nodding occasionally. "Right. I'll start with these. Nik, you can take the next three. The items are clearly marked on the shelves, but if you need help finding anything, you can ask Preston or me."

Nik nodded and claimed a crate, searching for items along the walls and filling it until each item had been crossed off. By the time he was done with the first crate, its contents looked very similar to the items he and Ali had been given when they first arrived in Berland. Nik hoped the recipient would find as much comfort in it as he had.

Nik worked quietly while Grace and Preston sang unfamiliar tunes off-key. Their energy was so contagious that by the end of the first hour, he found himself tapping his toe to the beat.

Between filling crates, he was tasked with taking the fulfilled orders outside of the small storage room and stacking them neatly against the wall behind the buffet line. Then he'd grab a few of the empty crates to replace the ones he'd just moved.

Shortly after their lunch break, another worker knocked on the door frame. He was a young man, barely out of his teens, with short blond hair and a patchy beard. "Sorry for the interruption. Miss Grace, your mother sent me to tell you she just received word of a small group of newcomers arriving in a few days. She says that we'll need four rooms prepared."

Grace frowned. "Okay. Why is she telling me?"

The man straightened and his cheeks flushed. "She said that you would take care of it."

Not requested. Not asked. Just demanded.

In the few days that Nik had spent working as Grace's guard, he'd noticed the immense pressure her mother put on her. He almost felt sorry for her, though she rarely seemed fazed by it. She kept the pep in her step and her cheery demeanor almost to spite her mother. He would've found it admirable if her sunny disposition wasn't too bright for him to handle.

"I'm a little busy here," Grace said, but the man wasn't deterred.

He cleared his throat, and Nik could tell he did not enjoy being the messenger between two ferocious women. "I'm sorry, but Lady Ellen insisted."

Grace sighed. "Fine. Let her know we'll be there soon."

The man let out a big sigh of relief. He nodded and left the room. Grace apologized to Preston, but he waved her off. According to him, any help was better than nothing.

Before they left to prepare the rooms, Nik carried two more crates full of food and toiletries to the stack of completed packages. His chest swelled at the sight of more than a dozen crates ready to be delivered to those in need. It was worth spending hours listening to Grace and Preston's awful singing.

⁂

"What do you think?" Grace asked with a bright grin.

"It's...empty," Nik said, glancing around at the dusty floor and four blank walls. The only thing to break up the monotony were two white painted doors that separated the main living space from the bedrooms.

"Yes, but when we're done, it's going to be a cozy little home for the next family to walk Berland's streets. I'm going to make a list of the furniture we'll need—the shop will have everything brought down—and then we can start cleaning."

"Sounds great," he said.

While she wrote, Nik wandered around the empty apartment. It seemed bigger than Ali's and his. He reached for the door handle, expecting a bathroom, but instead found a second empty room. Unlike his studio apartment with Ali, this home had more than one bedroom. He went to check the second door and, sure enough, another separate bedroom lay beyond the living room. Each bedroom had a bathroom attached as well.

For a moment, he pictured himself and Ali living in this apartment, taking turns getting up in the middle of the night to check on their baby in the adjacent room. It was small, but there was enough space to add a chest full of toys and still be able to play in the center of the room. He could see it so clearly—him teaching his kid to walk across the smooth floor with a smile on his or her face while Ali cheered them on.

"That should do it," Grace said, reviewing the list of items she'd made. The image of his future faded as she left the room to send the message along.

When she returned, she carried a handful of cleaning supplies. She offered a broom to Nik. "Do you have a preference on which room you'd like to clean?"

He chose the main room and began sweeping the floor, but something nagged at him. "Grace?"

She popped her head out of the closest bedroom. "Yes?"

"How does Berland distribute apartments?"

"Well, there's a registry and we keep track of which units are available for whenever more newcomers arrive."

"But what about those who already have homes? Like children growing up and leaving their parents. Or—"

"Or a couple in need of a nursery?" she asked, one corner of her lips curving upward.

Nik's brows rose and his neck turned so fast he heard a crack. "Ali told you?"

"No. I guessed it, but she confirmed it."

Nik was surprised. He had assumed Eli would be the first person Ali told. "And Eli?"

"He doesn't know. And I won't tell him either. As far as the apartment goes, I've already looked into it for you. There's an older woman who just lost her husband and will be downsizing in the next few weeks. I've made sure that once she's moved out, it'll pass to you and Ali."

Nik suddenly felt horrible for every occasion he'd ever considered Grace annoying. She was more thoughtful and generous than he deserved. He made a vow to be more kind—to be a better friend and live up to the man that Ali believed him to be. "Thank you, Grace."

She beamed, and for once he smiled back.

Chapter Fourteen

GRACE

GRACE TWISTED IN HER seat, leaning against the arm of the couch and propping her feet on the middle cushion. She bent her legs and leaned her notes against her lap, trying to make sense of the gibberish she'd written during yesterday's meeting.

She was supposed to be going over a proposal submitted by Walter. His family had been the single source of livestock for generations and he was coming to the council now to request more land and resources for expansion. The plea was rich, given his contempt for anyone else in need of additional resources. He was quick to judge her mother for "excessive expenditures," insisting she didn't have the financial prowess that a man might hold. Grace couldn't be certain that he was a member of the rebellion, but his behavior proved he was no ally to her or her family. And the fact that he was now asking for more land and funding made Grace's blood boil.

It wasn't even a bad proposal. The town needed the extra livestock, and there was plenty of land in the valley to spare. But the hypocrisy made Grace grind her teeth. As much as she'd love to tell him to shove it, she knew the council would vote unanimously in his favor.

She turned the page to find a long list of data and projections that her sleepy mind couldn't comprehend. She rubbed her temple with one hand and tapped the sheet with her other index finger.

"Everything all right over there?" Her mother's voice was low and soothing. It reminded her of when she was young and her mother would read bedtime stories to her and Theo. She smiled, recalling one of the few tender moments her mother had ever exhibited. By the time she was a teenager, those moments had been long gone.

Grace straightened her legs and stretched her arms over her head. "Everything is just fine, Mother. I think I'll head to bed, though. I don't know how many more times I can read the word 'profit' without dozing off."

Her mother simply nodded, and Grace took it as permission to leave the quiet study. Before she did, she laid the proposal on the end table next to her mother. "Just in case you want to read this one, too."

She wasn't a fool. She knew that every task her mother assigned to her inevitably would be reviewed and scrutinized. In the first few months that Grace shadowed her, she had noticed notes written in the margin, markings throughout the texts she'd been reading. None of these items had appeared until after Grace had done her initial review, and when Grace mentioned it, her mother had feigned ignorance. It didn't take a genius to realize her mother was redoing all of Grace's work. She didn't know what it would take for her mother to trust her or believe in her.

Now there was no point in pretending. Grace didn't have the energy for it.

"How is everything else going? How are things with Eli?" her mother asked, and Grace froze in her tracks. In all her years, she couldn't recall a time when her mother had voluntarily inserted herself into Grace's social life.

"They're...good," she said cautiously.

Her mother sat her own notes down and crossed her legs at the ankle, rocking back in her chair. Her undivided attention made Grace's pulse race. "Is that all you have to say about him? For all the chaos you've caused, I would've expected a much bigger show of affection."

"You'll have to forgive me if I choose to protect my relationship with Eli. You haven't been very supportive in the past." She added under her breath, "Nor the present."

Her mother fidgeted, a movement that looked completely unnatural for such a stoic woman. "Yes, well, perhaps I've been a bit extreme."

Grace's knees wobbled. She couldn't recall a single occasion in which her mother had admitted to being wrong. Unsettled, she felt her way around a chair and took a seat. "Why the change of heart?"

Her mother shook her head, lost in thought. "I just realized this is a fight I won't win. What's done is done and there's no point in continuing to argue over it. I'd rather focus on what's ahead of you. I still believe your affection for Eli will cost you. The people of Berland won't like—"

"The wealthy, arrogant, entitled people of Berland," Grace corrected. "The ones who already think the worst of you and me and every woman before us. They'll have to get over it. I won't give in to someone like Trevor just to placate them."

Her mother sighed and pinched the bridge of her nose. "I'm not trying to start this again with you, Grace. I just...I just..."

Grace waited patiently for her mother to find the right words, but they seemed to evade her. "Mother?"

After a deep inhale, her mother asked, "Are you happy?"

"Of course I am."

"Good. That's...good."

Grace studied her mother, who appeared completely lost in thought. "Mother, is everything okay?"

"Everything is absolutely as it should be." Her mother rose from her seat and Grace followed suit. Then her mother broke character even more by wrapping her arms around Grace's shoulders and hugging her. The gesture was so unfamiliar that Grace was momentarily immobilized before she hugged her mother's slender figure.

"Goodnight, Grace. Don't stay up too late. We have a council meeting in the morning."

Grace watched as her mother left the study and listened to the stairs creak with each step toward the bedroom. She shook her head, trying to dismiss the strange feeling that had settled over her.

Something was wrong.

***

Early the next morning, Grace snuck out while her parents were still fast asleep. Nik was already waiting in the hall for her, leaning against the wall with his eyes half closed.

"You won't be able to keep watch like that," she joked.

Nik perked up and pushed his shoulders back. "Sorry."

"I was just kidding. It's highly unlikely that anyone is even awake to attack me right now. I'm sure the entire mountain is still asleep."

"You're probably right. Still, it's what you're paying me for."

Grace shrugged. There hadn't been any violence in recent weeks. She was beginning to doubt she even needed a full-time guard, but she'd already given him the position, so he may as well keep her company.

Nik was an interesting person. From the way Eli spoke of him, she thought he would be more antagonizing. He was surly, but really, he just seemed lost to her. Like he hadn't quite figured out his place in the world.

It was the exact opposite of her troubles, since she was only meant for one position. Maybe having her life planned out for her wasn't so bad.

The cafeteria was quiet during these early hours. There were only a few others spread out among the freshly cleaned tables, still perfectly organized in neat lines before the morning rush when people would push tables together and borrow chairs for larger groups. It was peaceful.

Sitting at a table near the buffet line were most of Grace's friends. Theo was out of town and wouldn't be back for a few days, and Heather had worked late the night before and had no doubt slept in this morning, but the rest of the familiar faces turned to look their way. Eli smiled at her while Ali and Sam waved. Amaya had her back toward them, but when she noticed the waving, she turned and nodded in greeting.

Grace sat beside Eli, who planted a kiss on her cheek. She rarely slept in her own bed lately and the few times she did, she missed him far more than she expected. She had slept terribly last night, and just his embrace had her melting into his side and wanting to doze off again.

"Can I get you anything?" Eli asked.

Stealing a piece of bacon from his plate, Grace grinned and took a bite. "Nope. I have what I need."

He squinted at her, but she could tell by the enormous heap of food on his plate that he had already planned to share his food with her. She liked that he was attentive enough to know she preferred to steal things off his plate over making her own.

They took turns sharing details about their lives—Amaya's latest date, Sam's hilarious experience taking care of a baby goat that nipped his fingers, and a breakthrough Eli had at work with a communication device that could supposedly transmit from opposite sides of town. Quite the feat if they could get it to work properly.

The cafeteria filled with people too quickly. Before Grace knew it, it was time to head toward the council chambers. Without thinking, she leaned into Eli and kissed him on the cheek, then another quick peck on the lips.

He licked his lips, eyes widening as he enjoyed the taste of her. But when she pulled back, she noticed two of her suitors staring with disgruntled looks. Though their trays were full of food, they looked like they may be too nauseated to eat.

She forced a pleasant smile and timidly waved. "Jae, Zack. Good morning. How are you?"

Jae, the shorter one with black hair and pale skin, looked between her and Eli, not bothering to hide his irritation and...jealousy? Grace knew it was a risk spending time with Eli so openly, but after he'd made it through the first round, she'd become careless. She mentally smacked herself for being so reckless, angering her suitors and, with the way the two men eyed Eli, putting a target on his back.

"I'd be much better, Miss Grace, if I could have some alone time with you as well. You are still an available woman, are you not?"

Eli's fork clattered to the table, and he swiveled in his seat, but Grace cleared her throat and shot him a look that said *I've got this. Don't do anything stupid.*

"I am. And as such, I'm allowed to spend my time however and with whoever I desire."

"I see," he responded. "I hope that if I or my friend *Zeke* here wins the Rite, that your desires will be rerouted."

Grace bit her lip, understanding now why Zack...or Zeke, hadn't said a word. His jaw rippled, aggravation written clearly on his face as he watched her realize her mistake. Tiny creases around his eyes disrupted his otherwise flawless golden-brown complexion.

While she wasn't sorry for spending time with Eli, she did feel guilty for not even knowing her other suitors' names. She turned to Zeke and said softly, "I'm sorry. It was an honest mistake. Please forgive me."

His expression softened a little, but his eyes still burned a hole in Eli's back. "Of course. You can make it up to me by saving me a dance at next week's ball."

Her heart pounded against her chest. The next big celebration was a little over a week away, the eve before the second round. Time was moving faster than she was prepared for. While she'd rather spend the evening with her friends and Eli, she knew the proper thing to do would be to mingle with the other suitors. It might even get her mother off her back for a few days.

"I will."

Beside her, she felt Eli flinch and inhale sharply. Once Zeke and Jae moved along, she spoke before he had a chance to. "Please don't be upset with me. If I'd turned him down, it would've been—"

"It's okay, Grace. I understand." His mouth said one thing, but his deep brown eyes said something else.

She leaned in close and whispered so only he could hear, "I'll make it up to you."

As much as she wanted to kiss him goodbye, there were many sets of eyes on them now. The shared dining space was full of people, some even hovering and hoping they would move from their table soon since most of the seats were now occupied.

Ali stood first and Grace took that as her sign that it was time to go.

⁕ ⁕ ⁕

Grace and Ali were two of the first council members to arrive in the chambers. Nik escorted Grace but spent most of the time speaking in hushed tones with Ali. She was envious that they could be open with their relationship and no one came up to them with an attitude, demanding that Ali give them her attention or that Nik give them his time.

121

One day very soon, she reminded herself.

The rest of the council members slowly filed in until every chair in the circle was filled. Her mother took her position at the head of the room, and everyone grew quiet as she sat down.

It was a typical meeting—long, tiring, and at some points boring. Grace loved helping her community and leading them, ensuring they were happy, healthy and prosperous, but even she had to admit sitting in a room for hours could be tedious and mind-numbing.

Finally, it was Walter's turn to speak. As expected, he dove into his proposal to expand his farming practice. He gave an impressive presentation and then opened up the floor for questions.

Grace fidgeted but ultimately raised her hand. She could tell the sight of her arm held high irritated Walter, but he gestured for her to speak.

"Walter, in your proposal, you mentioned that you'll need another twenty to thirty employees to help you raise and care for the new animals and maintain the land and by products. Potentially even more if all goes well."

He nodded. "That's right."

"Are you aware that we currently only have six people on our unemployed listing? And"—she ruffled through her notes—"eight turning of age in the next twelve months?"

"I'm aware of the numbers, yes."

"And how do you hope to fill the necessary positions for your operations to run smoothly?"

Walter huffed, and she knew she'd hit a nerve. "We can cross that bridge when we come to it. But if it comes down to it, we can have volunteers or perhaps people would like a second income."

Grace bit her cheek and tried her best to keep her calm composure. "So your plan is to *hope* that people will work for free while you profit?"

Beside her, Ali cleared her throat. "If I may? You mentioned that there is another caravan of people coming soon. Surely there will be enough to fill the open positions?"

It was an innocent question from someone who hadn't been privy to these conversations like Grace had. Someone who didn't realize just how misogynistic and arrogant these men could be. Those who insisted they had all the answers and couldn't fathom that a woman, especially a newcomer, might have better ideas than them.

As predicted, Walter's face reddened. He sputtered but couldn't find the words to admit that his proposal *required* growth and acceptance of newcomers. The problem with men like Walter was they believed they were entitled to wealth, success, and influence. But in order for him to succeed, others must as well.

Eamon saved him the embarrassment of trying to answer the question. "It's an option, but I think we'd like to explore other options before simply opening up our gates to any stranger that stumbles by."

Heat rose in Grace's chest. "They're not just some *strangers*. The group currently on the way had their homes destroyed by severe flooding. They have nothing but the clothes on their backs. We have been blessed here in Berland; the least we can do is offer them shelter and food."

"Or we could encourage them to help themselves by rebuilding and staying strong."

It took everything in Grace not to roll her eyes. "Wise words from a man who's never had to display strength in trying times."

"Grace," her mother hissed.

She knew she'd overstepped, but the look of indignation on Eamon's and Walter's faces was worth every second of scolding she'd endure from her mother later.

"Apologies," Grace said with as much bitterness as she could muster.

Eamon sneered at her in return but nodded. "No need to apologize, Miss Grace. We all just want what's best for Berland, even if our ideas differ."

Everyone in the room could see through his false niceties, but it was enough to move the meeting forward. Grace tried her best to focus for the next few hours, but it was difficult with Eamon and Walter whispering to each other across the circular room. Every so often they'd break apart to look over at her and she glared back. If they thought she would back down just because she was a woman or younger than them, they were severely misinformed.

⚘ ⚘

"And then they just sat there staring at me for the rest of the meeting like I was on the verge of exploding." Grace sliced through a loaf of bread with far more force than necessary.

Eli came up behind her and wrapped his arms around her waist, pressing his lips to the exposed nape of her neck. "They're threatened by smart, beautiful, and charming women such as yourself."

She jerked her wrist, and the jagged edge of the knife tore into the loaf, shredding it and leaving crumbs everywhere.

"You know, maybe I should slice the bread," Eli suggested. "Would you like to stir the soup instead?"

"No," she said, stabbing the loaf with too much force and slicing the tip of her finger. A small red sliver formed. "Shit."

Eli sighed, then grabbed a rag and ran it under the faucet. He wrapped her finger and applied pressure to stop the bleeding. "Are you all right?"

She knew he was asking about more than the finger. "Yes," she replied angrily. Frustrated tears welled in her eyes. "No."

Eli simply wrapped his arms around her, holding her close. The sound of his heart beating helped calm her burning rage.

"What can I do to help?" he asked after a few moments.

"Just...be here. Be with me."

He kissed her temple. "Always."

Chapter Fifteen

NIK

Sweat dripped down Nik's back and his bangs stuck to his forehead as he ran down the dirt path nestled in the woods. He and Eli had chosen to run a different path than usual. It had seemed like a good idea—new scenery to make the run more enjoyable—but Nik hadn't realized this path followed the mountain up and down and up, up, up again. At least the tree canopy kept the sun off their backs.

The other unexpected consequence of choosing a new running path was this one was at least twice as long as their old route. They'd been running for an hour already with no end in sight.

"Watch your step," Eli shouted.

Nik looked down just in time to jump over an overgrown root.

Eli slowed to a walk ahead of Nik, and Nik matched his pace. They both breathed heavily but continued to travel at a brisk walk along the running trail.

"How's Ali?" Eli asked.

Nik knew he was only making small talk, but he cringed regardless. Ali still hadn't told him she was pregnant, and it was beginning to feel like a big secret, a heavy one that plagued Nik every day that he trained with Eli. "She's good. She really loves her job on the council, even though some of those guys can be assholes."

Eli snorted. "Tell me about it. Grace came home the other day in a full rage over something Eamon said. I thought I'd have to restrain her so she wouldn't sneak out in the middle of the night and murder him in his sleep."

"I can't picture Grace being violent."

"You'd be surprised. She's an expert at keeping her composure in public, but underneath it all, she's still a human with fears and anger and disappointment."

"She seems so bubbly all the time." He didn't add that he found it annoying.

"She's a lot of that, too."

When Nik glanced at Eli, he found him smiling, eyes distant like he was off in a daydream with Grace by his side. He'd happily suffer through Grace's overwhelming positivity if it meant Eli was smiling like that over her and not Ali.

Just when Nik was about to suggest turning around and heading back, the path curved and sloped downward to a familiar landmark. His shoulders relaxed; they were almost back in town.

When they made it to their training site a short distance from the main strip, both Eli and Nik dug into their backpacks and chugged an entire bottle of water each. Thankfully, he'd brought more than one, so he could still quench his thirst throughout the day.

Nik had to admit Eli had progressed immensely in a short amount of time. He moved with more confidence and aggression than when they'd initially started their hand-to-hand combat training. Although he still didn't have the size advantage that Nik did, he made up for it in nimbleness and resolve. Sometimes Nik would land a blow that he thought for certain would have Eli crumbling and caving, but he took each hit in stride and kept going with the ferocity of a man driven mad.

Nik shook his head as Eli rebounded from another impact that should've had him on his knees. The promise of Grace's love was enough to dull the pain and exhaustion, he supposed.

Halfway through the day, Eli and Nik paused to grab lunch. There was a soggy nut butter sandwich in Nik's backpack, which he tossed aside when Eli mentioned grabbing something in town instead.

They neared the center of town, where a man in an apron stood outside his shop. His face was red from the heat of a sizzling pan positioned over a blazing fire. Nik's stomach growled as he inhaled the scent of meat, veggies, and spices. As he got closer, he saw the char marks on the chicken, peppers, and tomatoes. The man added a brown sauce and continued to stir as people lined up to be served.

When it was Nik's turn, he handed the man a few coins and received a steaming hot sandwich with a freshly baked bun in exchange. Much better than the lunch he'd packed for himself. He'd need it, considering they still had a few hours of training left.

They ate as they walked, the silence only broken by the occasional moan of satisfaction. Nik didn't think he'd ever eaten something so savory and delicious.

They were almost back at the training site when they heard a chorus of mocking chants. Nik shot a glance at Eli before breaking into a jog. The commotion was coming from the clearing where they'd left their belongings.

Once the trees opened up, Nik found three young boys dancing in circles at the bottom of a tall pine. Heads tilted back; they yelled toward the sky.

"Lucy is a loser. Lucy is a loser."

"Lucy, come down here."

"Or else we'll come up there!"

Searching the branches above their heads, Nik found a young girl, her hair tangled in a mess of brown curls. She was wedged between two sturdy branches at least ten feet above the ground. Her eyes shone with tears, but they were narrowed with anger and determination.

"I'm gonna tell Mom!" she threatened.

One of the boys laughed. "No, she won't. I'll make sure she doesn't tattle. I'll pop all the heads off her dolls...at least the ones I haven't already." He laughed again, and the other two boys joined in.

"Come down, Lucy! We won't hurt you."

Doubtful, Nik thought.

"What's going on here?" he asked.

The group broke apart, and the boys exchanged startled looks that settled on the boy to the right—the leader, Nik presumed.

The boy straightened and masked his features with a look of innocence. His eyes softened and lips curved into a polite smile. "Nothing, sir. We were just playing hide and seek with my sister and she got stuck up there. Do you think you could get her down?"

Nik looked up into the tree, where the little girl frowned and sniffled. "Is that what happened?"

From the corner of his eye, he caught her brother making a motion with his hands that looked suspiciously as though he were pulling the head off a doll.

The little girl pressed her lips into a thin line. "Yes."

Beside him, Eli was glaring at the young boys. An image flashed before Nik's eyes of a young Ali getting picked on and Eli coming to her rescue. An image of a young daughter with his eyes and her hair climbing up a tree to get away from her bullies.

He pushed his shoulders back and turned to the boys. "I know you're lying, but lucky for you, I'm going to let you go. Leave your sister alone and go play somewhere else, and I won't tell your parents what you've been doing out here."

The head of the boy gang side-eyed his friends, daring them to step out of line. The faux friendliness disappeared from his face, and he squinted at Nik and Eli. Crossing his arms, he said, "Who are you anyway? My mom won't believe you."   .

What a little shit.

Eli spoke before Nik could threaten the tiny terror of a human. "My name is Eli, and I happen to be good friends with Grace. Perhaps you know her? Maybe your mother won't believe the two of us,"—Eli pointed between himself and Nik—"but I think she'd believe the next Lady of Berland. And if we get her involved...well, I don't know what kind of trouble you'll get in then."

The other two boys looked frightened now. Nik had to hand it to Eli; threatening them with authority was more effective than their mother.

The boy on the end gritted his teeth and looked back up into the tree. "I'll see you at home, Lucy." The last word was etched with a menacing threat, but at least they'd gotten rid of them for the time being.

The boys ran from the clearing, laughing and shoving one another as they went. Once they were completely out of sight, Nik stepped closer to the tree.

"Hi, Lucy. My name is Nik. It's all right to come down now."

She eyed him warily but carefully began climbing down the tree. When she was within his reach, he grasped her under her arms and helped her the rest of the way, planting her solidly on her feet.

"Thank you," she murmured. She eyed the winding path where the boys had fled, wiping the tears from her cheeks. If Nik had to guess, they were probably waiting for her just beyond the tree line, hoping to catch her on the way out.

"You don't have to go. You can stay if you'd like," he said. "I was just teaching my friend here how to fight. Would you like to learn, too?"

"Girls aren't supposed to fight," she said softly.

Nik scoffed. "Says who?"

She didn't have to answer. He was certain she meant her brother and his friends.

"Maybe you just want to watch, then?"

Lucy nodded and sat with her back against the tree while Eli warmed up. They began going through the motions, practicing simple offensive attacks and beginner defensive moves—things that Eli had long since mastered, but he played along, understanding what Nik was doing.

Lucy watched with rapt attention, her eyes lighting up as Eli dodged Nik's advances and Nik blocked Eli's punches. When they took their next break, Nik approached the girl again.

Between sips of his water, he asked, "Are you sure you don't want to give it a go? I can at least teach you how to protect yourself."

She bit her bottom lip. "What if I'm not good at it?"

"We're all shit until we've practiced."

Lucy gasped and her eyes went wide. "You said a bad word."

Fuck. Hopefully she didn't go back home and repeat that word to her parents.

"Let's pretend I didn't." He smiled, and Lucy returned an even brighter one. Then he held out his hand, and she placed her tiny hand in his, allowing him to pull her up.

After an hour of practicing with Lucy, Nik had taught her a few different punches and kicks. Eli kneeled on the ground at Lucy's level, his fists blocking his face. Somehow, Nik had convinced Eli to be Lucy's personal punching bag, and he watched with amusement as Lucy hit Eli in the stomach. Her small frame and tiny muscles lacked the weight to do much damage, but it was still entertaining watching her release her aggression on Eli's torso.

A well-placed punch to Eli's ear had both Nik and Eli hunched over—Eli cupping his ear and assuring Lucy that he was okay, and Nik doubled over in laughter.

"What's going on here?"

Grace and Ali emerged into the clearing.

While Nik approached Ali, Grace kneeled beside Eli and checked his reddening ear.

"We're teaching our new friend Lucy how to make sure her brother and his friends don't fuck with her."

Lucy gasped and pointed at Nik. "You said another bad word."

Nik motioned zipping his lips closed and Lucy grinned, her smile stretching from ear to ear.

He felt Ali's arm slink around his stomach, and she beamed up at him. "You made a new friend?"

"I did," he said before planting a kiss on her lips.

"She seems to really like you."

"What's not to like?" he joked, but the compliment meant more than he let on. Nik wasn't *likeable.* He'd spent so many years alone that he'd forgotten how to be likeable. It was still a mystery to him how he'd wound up with Ali by his side.

The idea of raising a child caused him to sweat more than any amount of physical exertion. What would he do if his own kid didn't like him? Would the same tension that marked his own relationship with his father define his relationship with his child? He tried to swallow, but his throat was suddenly dry.

As if Ali could read his thoughts, she leaned in close. "Don't doubt yourself for one second. You're going to be an amazing dad."

Chapter Sixteen

ALI

ALI STARED IN THE mirror, braiding her hair to the side. Her eyes lingered on her stomach, where the smallest bump was beginning to form on her slender figure, though it was mostly hidden by her long, flowing emerald-green dress with thin straps and a plunging neckline.

On the counter, a variety of necklaces and bracelets were on display, all of them borrowed from Grace. She held up a necklace with green gemstones that matched the dress but shook her head and set it back down. There was only one necklace she ever wore, and it was the one Nik had given her with the amethyst rose on a gold chain. She paired it with a dainty bracelet with stones that shimmered green or violet depending on the light.

Moving from the bathroom to the bedroom, she found Nik lounging on the bed, one arm tucked behind his head. She might've thought he was asleep, except his gaze was fixed on her.

"Can you zip me up?" she asked, turning around and holding her braid to the side.

The bed creaked, and she felt his presence behind her, grabbing the zipper near her lower back and gently pulling up. When he was done, he placed his hands on her hips and spun her around. "You look absolutely stunning."

Heat rose, spreading from her cheeks down to her chest. It didn't matter how many times he complimented her. She'd always turn into a flushed mess at his praise.

"You're quite handsome as well," she said, lacing her fingers behind his neck. He wore black slacks and a white button-up shirt, but he'd left the top two buttons open, showing off a small amount of his tan chest. Part of her wanted to open the rest of the buttons and pepper kisses down his stomach and then a little farther, but they had company arriving any minute now.

Nik caught her staring at his groin and smirked. Sliding his hands around to her ass, he licked his lips and squeezed. "What are you thinking about?"

Ali huffed a laugh. "Nothing in particular."

"Mm," he hummed. "Do you want to know what I think?"

She nodded, admiring the way his eyes darkened as they roamed her body.

"I think you were visioning my cock inside your mouth." He pulled her close and pressed a kiss to her chest, his lips grazing the bare skin where her dress dipped low. "Or perhaps inside your pussy..."

Somehow, his hand had moved from her ass to under her skirt without her noticing. He slipped it between her thighs, and she bit back a moan. Her eyes fluttered closed as Nik continued to stroke her slick center, building her into a frenzy.

She felt like a river of water seconds away from toppling over a dam. Her legs felt like they were about to give out at any moment, and he hadn't even pressed inside her yet. When she opened her eyes again,

Nik was staring at her with such intensity that she couldn't look away. Neither of them blinked, completely entranced by the other.

With one sharp inhale, Nik slid his fingers inside her.

Ali pitched forward, and he was there to catch her as her pussy clenched around his fingers. She wasn't sure how long it was before he removed his hand from between her thighs. Her racing heart had settled, and his lust-filled eyes had turned from dark iron gray to a dazzling metallic blue.

He released a heavy sigh as she picked herself up, standing straight once again. She brushed out the rumples in her skirt and made sure her breasts were still tucked into the top of her dress. Running a hand over her braid, she let out a breath of relief that her plait had suffered minimal damage.

Nik headed toward the bathroom to wash his hands, and Ali once again found herself eyeing his straining pants. She'd been thoroughly satisfied, but what about him? She still wanted to wrap her hands around his cock and taste the result of his unraveling. She reached out and grabbed his forearm.

He tilted his head. "Yes?"

Before shame or embarrassment could block her speech, she asked, "What about you?" Her eyes briefly flicked to the button on his pants.

Nik gave her a crooked smile. "I'll be fine, Ali. If you get your hands on me, we likely won't leave this room at all. Save it for after the dance, sweetheart."

She might've argued, but a knock at the door reminded her they were expecting company. She greeted Sam and Eli, who walked in holding bags full of sealed containers. They placed them on the table and began to peel back the lids, revealing an assortment of steaming side dishes. Mashed potatoes, a vegetable medley, a loaf of bread that smelled like nuts and angelfruit. The scent alone made her stomach growl.

She took turns hugging Eli and Sam once their hands were free.

"Hey, Ali," Eli said, ruffling the hair on the top of her head. She dipped down to avoid his hand and made sure her braid hadn't been messed up.

Eli looked dapper with a fresh haircut and a crisp black shirt and gray trousers. Though she could tell he had forgotten to shave the stubble on his chin. It suited him, though. Without it, he looked like a teenager. This way, he looked more distinguished and mature.

"Good to see you again," Sam said, more formally than Eli. Sam's dark hair was slicked back, and his deep red shirt complimented his tan skin. He had dressed to impress at tonight's ball too, and Ali had a hunch who had inspired such an effort.

Nik returned from the bathroom and greeted the guys. He even clapped Eli on the back. It was a sight Ali had never expected to see, but it made her heart swell with affection for the love of her life and the best friend she'd ever had.

While Nik pulled the main course from the oven, Ali set the table with plates, glasses, and silverware.

"Damn, I didn't realize you were such a chef," Sam joked.

Nik shrugged off the unexpected compliment. "It's just chicken."

Chicken that he had painstakingly marinated and seasoned to perfection. The skin was the most delicious shade of brown, and if the sides hadn't made Ali salivate already, the savory aroma of the roasted fowl would have.

Eli sucked in a sharp breath and snapped his fingers. "I completely forgot to bring a bottle of wine. I'm sure you guys have one, right?" He moved toward the cabinet that they usually kept theirs in, but Nik stopped him.

"Actually, we're all out. I can go to the supply chamber and grab a couple bottles."

"Don't be silly," Ali said. "We can do without."

Nik shook his head. "It'll only take fifteen minutes. Angelfruit okay? Or do you want something else?"

"That's fine with me," Eli said.

"I'll come with you. I'd like to see what other options they have," Sam added.

Once Nik and Sam had left, Eli pulled out a chair and gestured for Ali to sit.

With a grin, she lowered to the cushioned seat. "What a gentleman."

"You know me so well," he said, finding his own seat across from her. He began to place the lids back on the dishes to keep them warm while they waited for Nik and Sam to return.

She really did know him so well. Probably better than anyone else. Even though they hadn't had a moment alone together in weeks, she felt as close to him as ever.

Well, maybe that wasn't entirely true. There was currently a chasm between them, one that grew wider with every day that Ali didn't share her big news. But every time she tried, her hands got sweaty and her heart began to race.

Initially, she couldn't determine what she was so scared of. But then she realized she'd be devastated if Eli wasn't happy for her. She pictured a bright future where her child was surrounded by a loving family, including an "Uncle Eli."

But what if he didn't want to be part of that future?

She thrummed her fingers nervously on the edge of the hardwood table. Finally, she said, "You and Nik seem to get along well these days."

Eli grinned. "I suppose so. He's...tolerable."

"You can't fool me. You forget that I've seen the two of you training together on many occasions. You almost look like friends."

A pleasant change that could all be undone if Ali's news didn't land well with Eli.

Leaning forward in his seat, Eli rested his elbows on the table and ran a hand over his scruffy chin. "I don't hate him."

Ali's smile stretched across her face.

"It's good to see you smiling again. How are things going...with you?" he asked.

Although he hadn't been there to witness her darkest days spent searching for him, she'd filled him in on nearly every bitter moment. The hollow feeling that had consumed her. The restless nights spent replaying every loss of life around her. Some days she still woke up with an overwhelming weight on her chest, but she was getting better at coping and learning to lean on Nik when she was unable to face the day on her own.

"Good," she answered honestly. "It's weird, isn't it? Did you ever think this is where life would lead us? I still miss Andus and my mom and your dad, but I can see us growing old here together. Getting married, having children..."

Eli's brows rose. "It is unbelievable, huh? Assuming I win the Rite, Grace and I will be married by the end of the year." His eyes went wide at his own words, and Ali almost giggled.

"Are you ready for that?"

He only took a few seconds before he responded with certainty. "Yes, I am. As crazy as it sounds, I feel like I'm the best version of myself with Grace."

"That's not crazy at all." Ali recalled the moment she had first met Nik and the things he'd made her feel. It had been so hard to explain those feelings to Eli back then, but by the look on his face, he understood them now.

"Kids, though..." He laughed. "Can you imagine us with kids? We can hardly take care of ourselves. That'll have to wait a few years, don't you think?"

Ali struggled to swallow—some invisible object the size of her fist had gotten lodged in her throat. She stood up and grabbed a pitcher of water from the counter, pouring some into her glass. "Water?" she asked Eli. When he nodded, she filled his glass as well.

She took a few sips and set the glass down with shaky hands. "Eli, I have something to tell you."

Eli leaned forward and slid the lid off one of the dishes. "I'm starving. Do you think they'll notice if we dig in without them?" Unsatisfied with the first bowl, he peeked under the lid of another and inhaled a deep breath, moaning at the delectable scent emanating from underneath.

"Eli..."

"Do you have a serving spoon?" he asked, still distracted by his rumbling stomach.

Why was this so hard?

"I wanted to tell you—"

The door swung open, and Nik and Sam came in, laughing about something she hadn't heard.

"Thank god. I was about to start eating without you," Eli said, taking a bottle of wine from Sam's hands. He read the label and nodded approvingly. "Peach, huh? I don't think I've had this one."

Nik sat another bottle on the table and Ali recognized it as their favorite angelfruit wine. Then he pulled a third bottle from a bag. "We also got this angelfruit lemonade. It sounded too good to pass up."

Ali smiled, knowing he'd gotten it for her benefit. Now she didn't have to make an excuse for not drinking wine when there was a non-alcoholic beverage to choose from.

The guys found their seats around the table and took turns dishing food onto their plates. Her stomach turned and her appetite all but disappeared.

While she poured herself a glass of lemonade, she tried not to focus on the fact that she'd missed another opportunity to tell Eli her good news. Or the fact that he might not consider it to be good news at all.

Chapter Seventeen

GRACE

GRACE GENTLY BRUSHED THE tangles from her long brown hair, star-ing into her mirror but paying no attention to her reflection. Her mind was elsewhere. Mostly wishing she could simply skip the ball and spend an evening alone with Eli. She wanted rest and peace and comfort. Eli provided all those things and more.

The dance, however, was going to test her patience and force her to socialize with people she did not care to entertain. Not that she didn't appreciate the civilians of Berland. In fact, she put their needs before her own most of the time, though she rarely felt the sentiment returned. These formal events only highlighted the way they perceived her as in-human. Either a pawn in their games—a brainless girl who needed a man to steer her—or a trophy on a pedestal, too perfect and pristine to have needs of her own.

The burden of their expectations weighed heavily on her, but none as much as her mother's. Though she had taken a step back and had given

Grace more free rein, Grace still felt the pressure to prove she was capable of everything her mother could do and more.

She sighed and opened a tin of rose-tinted powder, gently applying it to her cheeks to give her face a more flirtatious appeal. Then she stepped into her long white gown and pulled the straps over her shoulders. The luxurious fabric stretched over her curves and didn't even require a zipper. Of all the gowns she owned, this was the comfiest. It was also the most bride-like, with a flattering sweetheart neckline, an open back, and a long flowing skirt.

From her bedroom door, she heard a gasp and swiveled to find her mother with a hand to her mouth.

"What?" she asked, looking down and searching for a tear or a stain that would explain the look her mother was giving her. "What's wrong with this one?"

Her mother dropped her hand and squinted. "Nothing is *wrong*, Grace. You look absolutely beautiful. I don't know why you always think the worst of me."

Probably because her mother always thought the worst of Grace.

"Thank you," she said politely.

"Are you almost ready? We should leave if we don't want to be late."

"Just about. Why don't you and Dad go ahead? I can meet you there."

In reality, she didn't have anything else to do. She just wanted to be left alone. If she'd been given the choice, she would've attended the ball with Eli, but her mother had insisted that she make time for other suitors and go without a date. Because of that, she didn't feel like feigning excitement in her mother's presence. She wanted some time to herself to get in the proper mindset.

Her mother nodded. "Your father and I will head out then. But there's someone here to escort you."

Grace straightened. Had her mother reconsidered?

Her bedroom door opened a few inches farther and Theo slipped in. His lips curved into a bright smile upon seeing his sister, and Grace couldn't contain her own.

"Theo!" She bolted forward and wrapped her arms around him for a hug.

"Hey, sis."

"I thought you were going to be out of town this evening." Theo was often on excursions to nearby towns for trading and to ensure peace with their allies. While he did his best to stick around for all the festivities the Rite brought to town, it was inevitable that he'd have to miss some things. "You came back early?"

"I did. Our negotiations went smoother than expected. No reason to stay away from home another night." He released his hold on her and spun her in a circle, then frowned. "You're going to keep me busy tonight, aren't you?"

"What do you mean?"

"If I see one man's hand placed somewhere it doesn't belong, I'm going to have to break all his fingers."

Grace chuckled. Her brother was one of the least violent people she knew. His bark was far worse than his bite. More like a nibble, really. "I can handle myself."

"Damn right, you can."

Behind Theo, their mother cleared her throat, and Grace flinched. She'd completely forgotten she was still there. "I'll be going now. Don't take too much longer. You're the main event of the evening, after all."

As their mother turned to leave the room, Theo and Grace exchanged a look that said, *Can you believe her?*

When the two of them were left alone, Grace relaxed. She sat down at her vanity and ran her comb through her hair a few more times. Theo sat on the edge of her bed, and she peered at him through the mirror. "Is that what you're wearing?"

Theo looked down at his dark jeans and gray henley shirt and shrugged.

"No," she said, spinning in her chair. "You can't wear that."

"Why not?"

"Well, besides the fact that Mom would drag you by your ear out of the hall, you're not going to impress anyone with that lazy look."

Theo laughed. "I'm not trying to impress anyone."

"Aren't you?"

His eyes turned to slivers, but his mouth curled mischievously. "Do you have something to say to me, Grace?"

She forced her gaze back to the mirror and tucked a stray hair behind her ear. "Did you know Sam's favorite color is blue?"

Through the mirror, she watched Theo's playful grin widen. Pride radiated from his big brown eyes as he said, "I did."

⁂

The halls were empty except for a few stragglers running late for the ball. Grace held onto Theo's arm as he guided her toward the ballroom. Smiling, she took in his dark gray slacks and the royal blue shirt he'd changed into. He paired it with a confident smirk that would win every available heart in Berland, at least those that weren't competing for Grace.

As they approached the double doors leading into the ballroom, Grace squeezed his arm. "Stay close by? I might need you to break some fingers for me."

He chuckled. "Of course."

Despite her mother's warnings, she'd appeared late enough that she'd missed the welcome speech. Couples were already on the dance floor,

145

and trays of burgundy beverages floated through the crowd. It took less than five minutes before suitors surrounded her like vultures, eagerly extending their hands for the first dance.

Grace took a deep breath and did her best to greet each of them sincerely, but her eyes were drawn to the left corner of the room, where Eli was surrounded by his friends. By the time she found him, his eyes were already locked on her. He gave her an encouraging smile and raised his glass before taking a small sip.

He hadn't been thrilled about the idea of Grace attending the ball on her own, but he understood the necessity of it. She'd love nothing more than to have Eli by her side and holding her hand all evening, but unfortunately, that wouldn't gain her any favor with the other suitors. She still had a duty to uphold and a Rite to respect. The last thing she needed was another reason for the rebels to degrade her.

Eli's reassurance gave her the confidence to accept the first dance from another man. Zeke, the man she'd run into in the dining hall a few days prior, led her to the center of the ballroom and placed his hands on her waist. She flinched but did her best to relax and placed her hand on his shoulders. They began to sway to the music, and Grace took deep and controlled breaths.

"You look amazing, in case no one has told you," Zeke said with a friendly smile.

She peered up into his eyes, dark green like pine trees. His jet-black shoulder-length hair was pulled into a half bun and his beard was neatly trimmed. There was a kindness in his eyes that contrasted his chiseled jaw. Her shoulders relaxed a little. "You do, too."

"Are you ready for tomorrow?" he asked.

"Shouldn't I be asking you that question?"

The second round of the Rite would take place the following afternoon. Eight men would be narrowed down to four and Grace would be one step closer to an engagement. She'd been watching Eli's practices and felt pretty confident in his ability to advance. But any time she thought too hard about the way it would play out, her mind played tricks and showed her an image of him with his back on the ground, tapping out. So she tried not to think about it too much.

"I'm more than ready," he said. Confident, not cocky. It was hard to find fault with Zeke, which made her feel even worse for forgetting his name earlier.

"Listen, I really am sorry for the other day."

"Don't worry about it."

"No, it was so incredibly rude of me—"

He suddenly stopped spinning in circles, and Grace came to a halt, too. "If you'd like to make it up to me, please...please say that you won't get in too deep with that guy." He nodded his chin over her shoulder. She didn't have to look to know he was talking about Eli.

"I..." She didn't know how to respond to his request. She couldn't promise him that. She was already in too deep with Eli. "I'm sorry," she finished lamely.

Zeke removed his smooth hands from her waist, but he didn't berate her. He didn't scold her like her mother would have. Instead, he looked defeated. "I wish the best for you, Grace."

He took a few steps backward before turning and leaving Grace standing in the center of the floor, feeling like the smallest person in the room.

Tears welled in her eyes, and she wasn't sure why. It wasn't like she had feelings for Zeke, but knowing she'd let him down, just like her mother had said she would, was enough to make her feel like a heinous human being. Careless and reckless with the feelings of those around her.

Unfreezing her feet from the floor, she walked toward the exit. She needed a few moments to compose herself before the next dance, but before she could take five steps, Trevor was standing in front of her, blocking her path.

"My turn for a dance," he said, extending his hand.

"Give me a minute." She stepped to the right, but he caught her with a hand around her waist.

"It wasn't a question."

Chills ran down her spine, but with so many eyes on her, she felt trapped. If she shoved him like she so badly wanted to do, a scene would follow. One in which *she* would look like the bad guy. The ungrateful one. The incompetent one. There was nothing she could do. Any retaliation could only be played out in her mind while she gritted her teeth.

He pulled her body towards him, and she felt the hard planes of his chest and hips collide with hers. Though she attempted to pull back and create space between them, his hold on her was too strong and he kept her glued to his body. The friction between them as he moved to the music made her nauseous.

Then his breath was hot and heavy in her ear. "Sometimes I think about you and me. Remember when we used to be friends? I often wonder what could've been if only things had gone a little differently." His voice was soft and soothing, but it had the opposite effect on her nerves. Her skin crawled. There was no sincerity in his words.

While Zeke had made her feel selfish and entitled, Trevor made her feel used and objectified.

"You mean if you hadn't treated me like a steppingstone to power and prestige? We'll never know, Trevor. You're still doing the same thing today."

He chuckled, and she felt the rumble of his chest against hers. She hated every second of this dance...this game she was forced to endure. "I have no idea what you're talking about, Grace." His words were like molasses, smothering her and making it impossible to breathe. "I'm simply a man who's head over heels for you."

He hit her with a crooked grin, and she could no longer contain her disgust. She pushed against his chest with more force, and this time he didn't stop her. Taking a few steps back, his grin slowly began to fade. His eyes locked on something—someone—behind her.

She knew without looking who had come to her rescue. Her anger and tension eased as she turned to find Eli standing tall, only a foot behind her.

His eyes flicked to her for a brief moment, long enough for her to nod and give him a small smile. Once he was satisfied that she was okay, his hard glare returned to Trevor.

"Your turn is up." His voice was low and threatening. It made the tiny hairs on Grace's neck stand on end...and her thighs clench. The confidence he exuded made her feel safe and secure. She took a few steps to stand by his side, gripping his forearm.

Trevor raised his hands in surrender, but the cocky grin on his face said he wasn't finished tormenting them. Maybe he never would be. It was hard to imagine him giving up, even if he lost the Rite. The words her mother had spoken once before echoed in her ear. That Eli shouldn't have entered the Rite. The rebels wouldn't stand for it; he wasn't one of them. Grace had thought she was overreacting, but maybe her mother had been right. What road to destruction had she led them down?

What other choice did she have, though? Eli wasn't just an option. He was her one and only.

"Are you okay?" he asked softly, wrapping his arms around her.

She sank into the warmth of his embrace and let out a heavy sigh. Then she pressed her cheek against his chest and listened to the rhythm of his heart, steady and strong. "I am now."

There was a brief pause in the music before the next song began to play.

"I've been going out of my mind watching you dance with other men," Eli confessed. He planted a soft kiss on her temple before letting his chin rest on the top of her head.

"I've only danced with two," she said, smiling against his chest.

"And that was two too many."

Leaning away, she tilted her head back so she could see his face. "My mother won't be happy if I don't dance with the rest of the suitors."

His jaw tensed and his throat bobbed as he swallowed. "I'll survive your mother's wrath, because your next dance is mine. And the one after that. And the one after that. For the rest of our lives, every single song, every touch, every smile and laugh, every kiss is mine."

Chapter Eighteen

ELI

ELI THREW A ROCK across the river, watching it skip like he used to do back on the lake in Andus. The rock made it halfway across the stream, then lost momentum and sank to the bottom.

Beside him, Ali took her turn. "Beat you," she said with a little shimmy of her shoulders.

"That was luck," he teased. He searched the ground for the perfect pebble for his next toss while Ali fidgeted in her seat on the tree stump.

Somehow, she was more nervous than he was. The second round of the Rite would take place that afternoon, which meant he and the other suitors had all morning to kill. Time seemed to move even slower than normal as he anticipated the competition to take place later that day.

He had tried to go to work, but Luka had immediately sent him home and told him he wasn't needed in the lab and to come back tomorrow after he'd completed the second round. He had contemplated going for a run, but figured it would be better to save his energy. Grace was busy with her own responsibilities while Nik played bodyguard for the day, so it gave him some alone time with his old friend.

Ali fidgeted again, folding her legs and tucking them underneath her.

"Why are you so anxious?" he asked.

Her cheeks turned pink. "I'm not."

Eli looked pointedly at her knee bobbing up and down and her fingers thrumming against the tree stump.

She quickly uncrossed her legs and set her feet flat on the ground with her hands folded neatly in her lap.

"Now you look even more uneasy."

Ali swatted at his arm. "I'm just...I guess I'm just hoping today goes well. That's all."

"It'll be fine," he said, patting her knee before tossing his stone across the water. He'd seen enough of the competition to know his odds were pretty good. More than good, but he didn't want to get too comfortable after what had happened in the first round. He was determined to stay focused and keep a level head. Nothing would force him to falter. "You're not doubting me, are you?"

Her brown eyes went wide. "No, not at all. It's not that. It's...it's...never mind."

"Don't do that. What's on your mind?"

Biting her bottom lip, she turned away from him.

Now *he* was the one concerned. Ali dealt with anxiety, but the way she avoided his gaze told him this was something more. His heart pounded in his chest, and he inched closer to her, trying to get her to turn back his way. "Ali?"

She sighed heavily and stared up at the sky. "I've been—"

A group of men erupted in laughter behind them, walking along the path that led to the site of the second round. Eli watched them disappear before turning back to Ali. "You were saying?"

She shook her head. "Nothing. It's not important. You need to get going or you'll be late." Her forced smile did little to ease his nerves, but she was right. More people were making their way along the path, including one man he recognized as a suitor.

He took Ali's hands in his. "Promise me everything's okay?"

She tilted her head, clearly taken aback by his request. "Of course it is."

Unable to sense a lie, Eli stood and pulled her up with him. Whatever was troubling her, she'd tell him in her own time. He'd have to trust in that. Besides, he had plenty on his mind to keep him occupied.

Together, they made their way along the trail leading to the temporary arena. Much like the first round, makeshift stands had been erected, surrounding a wide-open space where the hand-to-hand combat would take place. In the center was a long rope laid in a circle, a boundary for the fights.

"Good luck. I doubt you need it," Ali said, briefly squeezing his arm and leaving his side to find a seat.

Eli found the group of other suitors huddled around the council members who'd be overseeing today's round. The woman, Diane, gave him a brief nod and said, "Looks like we're just waiting on Zeke. Why don't you all stretch and do what you need to do while we wait for him. I'd rather not repeat the instructions a second time."

The arena grew louder as more people filed in. While Eli stretched, he kept an eye out for Grace. During the ball the night before, her light had been diminished, and he needed to know she was okay. To no one's surprise, her mother had been furious after Grace danced with only two suitors and then spent the rest of the evening with Eli. Grace had gone home to her own bed to prevent her mother from having a meltdown, which had left Eli tossing and turning. He wondered if Grace had spent all night doing the same.

A few minutes before the round was to begin, Grace walked in with her entourage and took her place on a small, shaded stage with the best view of the ring. Eli waved, catching Grace's attention. Her face brightened, and she offered a delicate wave of her own before touching her forefinger to her lips. The movement reminded Eli of how soft and sweet those lips were, how he'd like to kiss them again right now.

Diane called the suitors over, and Eli abandoned his sultry thoughts.

"We can't wait any longer, so we'll go ahead and get started with the rules." Diane explained the basics of the round—no weapons other than your hands, step out of boundaries or tap out and lose the round, best two out of three wins, etcetera—and Eli looked around at the other suitors. Zeke was still missing. The others didn't seem concerned, so Eli tried to brush off the uneasy feeling in the back of his mind.

"Each of you will pull out a rock from this bag," Diane continued. "There's two of each color, which will indicate your match-up."

Fox held out a bag, and each of the suitors pulled out a stone. Eli reached in and grabbed the first one his fingers touched—a jagged-edged stone painted bright green.

Eli sought out his partner first. He thought the man's name started with a 'D.' Dom or Damien or something along those lines. He had a slender build, similar to Eli's, but 'D' was about six inches shorter. Eli hesitated to breathe a sigh of relief, but he felt good about the matchup.

Around the circle, he noted a pair of strangers had pulled the gold stones. Jae and another bulky man with a frown pulled the blue stones and Trevor had pulled a red stone. Which left another red stone waiting in the bag for Zeke whenever he showed up.

Trevor caught Eli's glare and winked at him, tossing the stone up in the air and catching it in one hand. Eli clenched his teeth but kept his mouth shut. He wouldn't give Trevor the satisfaction of getting under his skin. Not anymore. His newest method of handling Trevor's bullshit was to ignore him. Treat him like the insignificant rodent he was.

The duo that Eli hadn't met went first. Once the committee welcomed the crowd and ushered the first two suitors out into the center, the round began. Since Eli didn't know either of these men, he paid little attention. Instead, he focused on his own strategy, which moves would be best suited for his competition and how he could use the boundary to his advantage.

He kept glancing at his match, sizing him up and doing his best to determine if he had any weak spots. He thought he could recall 'D' practicing once or twice while Eli was present. While he was quick and agile, Eli recalled his balance to be lacking. If Eli couldn't pin him, forcing him out of bounds might be the better option.

Cheers erupted. The first match was already over. In a two to zilch fight, the victor had easily overcome the smaller of the suitors and claimed his place in the third and final round. Eli's stomach turned as time crawled forward, closer to his match and the final round of the Rite.

The only thing keeping him sane was the promise of Grace waiting at the end of it all. For her, he would do everything imaginable to win.

Jae and his match were the second duo to take their place in the ring. Eli paid closer attention to their fight, mostly to take his mind off his developing nerves.

Jae was smaller than his competition, but he was clearly very skilled. He dealt a perilous punch to the man's jaw and threw a kick that had the man stumbling backwards and out of bounds.

The man reentered the ring with blood running down his nose and charged at Jae. Eli flinched and hissed as Jae hit the ground with a crack. He wasn't sure which bone he'd broken, but *something* had snapped. Jae tapped the ground and then it was one to one. The winner of the next fight would move on to the third round.

Jae had a chance to inspect his injuries but ultimately shook off the medics, determined to get it over with. Either his injuries weren't as bad as it sounded or adrenaline was keeping him in the fight. He shook out his arms and rolled his neck before stepping back into the circle.

The larger suitor ran toward him again, but this time Jae stepped out of the way, tripping the man as he stumbled past. He regained his footing, but not before Jae landed a right hook and a jab to his nose. The man groaned but countered with a few sloppy punches of his own. Jae didn't allow a single one to strike.

Taking a few steps back, Jae taunted the man with a few words that Eli couldn't hear. Whatever he said left the man fuming. His ears turned red, and he ran toward Jae again, wrapping his arms around his torso and tossing them both to the ground. They tussled around and, to Eli's surprise, Jae held his own. Every time it seemed as though he was about to tap out, he managed to slip and squirm till he was on top again.

This happened a few more times until Jae finally escaped the man's hold. Jae taunted the man again, and he staggered forward like a wild, angry animal. Jae gripped him by the shoulders and swung around, using all his energy to push the man backwards. They struggled, seemingly at a standstill, then the crowd erupted in cheers again.

They'd been so close to the edge; the man hadn't even realized he was about to step over the rope until it was too late. He was still holding onto Jae when he realized his mistake. He shoved him away and swung.

Jae was too enamored by the cheering crowd to notice the man's lack of sportsmanship. He took the blow to his jaw, and a wave of concern swept through the crowd before it turned to angry jeering.

The man was ushered out of the arena before he could strike Jae again, and Eli turned to find Grace. Her lips were turned down in a frown, her brows pinched together in distress. Beside her, Ellen spoke animatedly to someone at the edge of the stage. Even from a distance, he could see her brows furrow and her eyes squint. Taking care of business, he assumed. The man wouldn't get away without repercussions.

As if she felt his gaze, Grace turned to Eli and forced a smile for him.

He subtly shook his head, sending a silent message. *You don't need to pretend for me.*

She never had to hide her fears or her doubts with him. She didn't have to be the epitome of perfection that her mother and everyone else in this town expected her to be. It was okay to have flaws and insecurities. It was okay to be sad or frustrated. It was okay to be *human*.

Her forced smile straightened into something resembling acceptance. Then her mother returned to take a seat beside her and motioned for the competition to continue.

Eli's turn was next. Diane called him forward along with his match, Dom. Ah—that was the man's name.

Loosening his limbs one last time, Eli entered the ring and Dom followed shortly behind him. They squared up.

Someone shouted, "Go!"

Dom was calculated with his movements, circling Eli, advancing when he could and retreating when he had to. Eli silently cursed the fact that he wasn't reckless like the last suitor. Just his luck that he'd be paired up with one of the few competent fighters.

Dom wasn't arrogant like Trevor, either. His face was hardened to stone, no mockery or taunting. His eyes were narrowed as he focused all his attention on Eli. It would be hard to exploit any weaknesses.

They continued in a delicate dance around the ring, neither making the first move. The crowd began to chant as their patience grew thin.

"Tackle him!"

"Get on with it!"

For these people, the Rite was a show. A form of entertainment. They didn't understand how much was on the line for Eli. He refused to be careless with his chance to earn his place beside Grace.

But their calls had some effect on Dom. His eyes moved from Eli to the crowd and back again. Then he did it again. The third time, Eli was ready. He struck hard and fast, dealing a blow to his opponent's jaw. Dom groaned, but his attention snapped back to Eli before he could land a second punch.

Dom spat blood into the dirt. Then he wiped his mouth with the back of his hand, leaving his right side exposed. Eli didn't have time to second guess himself. He took the opening and plowed into Dom, tackling him to the ground.

The sudden assault took Dom by surprise, and Eli knew he had to make each second count. He dug his forearm into Dom's throat, restricting his airway until his cheeks turned red. With his other hand, he pinned Dom's left arm to the ground and kneeled on his right arm. Though he twisted with all his might, Dom wasn't able to slide out from Eli's hold. He thrashed and bucked his hips, almost unseating Eli, but he was prepared for it. With each wild movement, Eli adjusted and ensured that he remained on top.

Dom didn't give up, though. Sweat formed on Eli's brow, and he began to wonder if Dom would ever tap out. *Let him struggle,* he thought. The more he wore himself out in the first fight, the less energy he'd have for the next one. Eli was still in a position of power and exerting much less energy than Dom.

Eventually, Dom's face turned from red to purple. What would happen if he passed out? Would he really allow that to happen before tapping out? Perhaps Eli had underestimated him.

Dom's eyes went wide, bulging out of his head. He gave Eli a manic look and Eli almost felt sorry for him, wondering if he should pull back before he lost consciousness. Instead, he dug his forearm into Dom's throat even harder, and finally, Dom patted the ground beside them.

Eli heard someone yell for them to cease and immediately fell back. Dom choked and sputtered, massaging his neck and glaring daggers at Eli. Ordinarily Eli hated violence, but he wouldn't apologize for doing whatever it took to win.

Rising to his feet, he took a few deep breaths and used his shirt to wipe the sweat from his face. His arms ached, but it was a dull throb, nothing he couldn't handle. He quickly shook them out and readied himself for the second fight.

If he could win this one, it would be over.

Dom moved slowly as he rose from the ground. He turned to face Eli, dragging his legs and breathing heavily. Eli's confidence soared, thrilled that the first match had taken so much out of him. He could feel it—the win was almost his.

When a male voice shouted for them to begin, Dom immediately surged forward, tossing Eli to the ground. He rolled backwards and sprang to his feet, but Dom was already there, ready to deal his next blow.

He slammed a fist into Eli's temple, leaving a ringing in Eli's left ear. He stumbled a step but quickly righted himself and blocked a second punch. Dom's attacks were coming so quickly now, it was nearly impossible to reverse the tide. Eli sloppily kicked in front of him, right into Dom's stomach. It was only enough to send him back a few steps, but it gave Eli a moment to breathe and collect himself.

When Dom pressed forward again, Eli threw out his arms and caught him by the shoulders. They rocked back and forth as they each tried to toss the other to the ground. Although they were evenly matched, Eli could feel his feet slipping in the dirt. Dom was making progress and pushing Eli toward the rope marking the edge of the ring.

Eli gritted his teeth and dug his feet into the loose soil. But soon he was sliding again, and he felt his chance with Grace slipping away with each inch he lost. He glanced over his shoulder to see how much space he had left.

A little more than a foot...

He didn't know how much longer he could hold Dom off. Sweat ran down his face and neck. His muscles were taut and nearing their breaking point. He couldn't even feel his toes anymore from the effort it took to resist sliding backwards.

Dom was struggling just as much. His face was bright red and his eyes had that manic look again. The vein in his forehead bulged with the effort of pushing Eli back. He licked the sweat dripping above his lip and released a heavy breath.

Eli chanced a glance behind him again. His heel was almost touching the rope. If he didn't do something, he was going to lose. The last thing he wanted was to fight Dom for a third time, but every second brought him closer to that reality.

Over Dom's shoulder, Eli's eyes caught on something...someone. Grace was standing on the platform. She watched with both hands clasped over her mouth. Nik stood beside her. His arms were crossed, and he was looking at Eli with disappointment. He tilted his head a little and Eli could practically hear Nik's voice in his ear.

You're better than this.

Fucking Nik. Even from fifty feet away, he was a pest buzzing around Eli's brain. He'd love to throw a punch or two his way. Side-step and watch him face plant in the mud like Eli had in one of their earlier practices—

Hold on.

That was it. Dom was using all of his weight to push Eli back. If he just...

Eli couldn't have timed it better. Just as his foot was about to slide out of bounds, Eli spun to the side, releasing Dom as he moved. Dom's momentum sent him flying forward, and he came to a halt several feet beyond the border, a look of complete bewilderment on his face.

The crowd erupted in applause.

Eli looked up at a sea of cheerful faces, but there was only one he cared about. Behind him, Grace bounced on her heels with the brightest smile in the arena. She was glowing with pride, and Eli wanted nothing more than to cross the ring and wrap her in his arms.

He'd completed the second round. Only one more to go.

Footsteps sounded behind him, and Eli turned to find Dom with a hand outstretched. "Well done," he said in a low rumble.

"Thank you," said Eli. "You fought well."

Dom disappeared into the crowd, officially eliminated from the competition, and Eli found a spot on the edge of the arena to watch the fourth and final match.

Except Zeke was still nowhere to be found.

The crowd simmered, and Eli watched as Ellen crossed to the side of the platform again, chatting with Eamon. He couldn't make out the words, but Eamon seemed excited. Which meant that Eli wasn't.

After exchanging a few sentences, Ellen addressed the crowd. "Thank you, everyone, for coming out today. And congratulations to the suitors who won their respective matches and will be competing in the final round." She gestured toward Eli, Jae and the other victor, and the crowd applauded. Once they quieted down, she continued, "Unfortunately, one of the suitors has dropped out, which means our fourth matchup goes to Trevor by default."

The news was met with mixed results. Some onlookers cheered as Trevor raised a hand in unearned triumph, while others looked disappointed by the event's premature ending.

And Eli...

Heat rose up his neck. He watched his least favorite person strut to stand beside the rest of the victors, an arrogant smile plastered on his face. It had always been a gamble that Trevor would meet his end during the second round, but to have that chance stripped away? It was unfair and difficult not to feel slighted by fate. Why should he have an easy path to victory while the others gave their blood and sweat in the ring?

Trevor grinned and murmured as he passed, "Might as well get used to seeing my face, Eli. You're going to see it a lot more often when I'm standing next to Grace."

Eli scowled. "Over my dead body."

Chapter Nineteen

GRACE

THE LONGER HER MOTHER paraded her around, the more Grace itched to get away. Her mother was most interested in having conversations with Berland's wealthiest and most prestige families, Grace only wanted to celebrate the end of the second round with Eli.

Sensing her eagerness to flee, Grace's mother leaned toward her and whispered, "One day it'll be your responsibility to maintain these relationships. You could act a little more invested in the community you are meant to lead."

Grace inhaled deeply and counted to three before responding. "These upper-class families aren't the only civilians worth entertaining. Just because I don't want to suck up to the snobs doesn't mean I'm not doing my job. I'm taking part in weekly community service and making rounds to ensure that families have what they need. I welcome the newcomers and help them get settled. I meet with local businesses to hear their concerns. I do so much, but you only see my faults."

Grace faced forward, but she could feel her mother's eyes burning a hole in the side of her head. She was sick of holding back. Sick of letting her mother tear her down and belittle her.

Her mother opened her mouth to speak, but Grace couldn't take it anymore. She stepped forward, moving through the crowd back toward the mountain.

"Where are you going?" her mother shouted from behind her.

Tuning her out, Grace kept pushing forward and didn't look back.

***

Grace made a quick stop at home to pick up a few things—clothing to change into along with some accessories, her toiletries for the evening, and something lacy and revealing to sleep in. She had no intention of coming back home tonight. Partly because she wanted to spend her time with Eli, but also so she wouldn't have to see her mother again. She couldn't recall a time she'd ever defied her mother so boldly, and she wasn't looking forward to the fallout.

Locking up behind her, she skipped down the hall to Eli's apartment. Her knuckles had barely rapped on the door when it flung open and Eli pulled her inside, kissing her swiftly. Grace dropped her bag and slid her hands around his back. Finding the hem of his shirt, she lifted until she could trace his skin with her fingertips.

His lips opened with a gasp at her cool touch, and she slid her tongue in, reveling in the way his body curved into hers. He moaned, sending a surge of electricity down her spine. She angled her hips toward him, and he slid a leg between her thighs, applying just enough pressure to make her tremble.

She hadn't realized they were slowly backing up until her back hit the door. Eli trapped her, placing both his palms on the wood surface next to her head. She moved her hands through his soft brown hair and gently broke their kiss.

"As much as I'm enjoying this, I have plans for us tonight," she said with a sparkling smile.

Eli's cheeks were flushed, and he studied her like the last thing he wanted to do was to stop kissing her. To stop touching her and eliciting those desperate moans from her mouth. She could feel his hard length pressing into her stomach and knew how badly he yearned to toss her on the bed and settle between her thighs.

But her plans were better than that.

She pushed off the wall and leaned down to grab her bag. Reaching in, she pulled out her outfit for the evening and two familiar black lace masks. Eli's eyes glossed over at the skimpy black dress in her right hand. There wasn't much fabric, and the longer he studied it, the darker his eyes went. Then he looked at her left hand and saw the masks.

His smile was devilish. "Grace..."

"Surprise," she said, tossing him his mask. "I thought you might enjoy a trip to Azalea's this evening."

Eli caught the mask with ease and licked his lips. Unable to hide his excitement, he adjusted the front of his jeans before inching toward Grace for another kiss.

As he pulled away, Grace ran her hands down his chest, toying with the buttons on his pants. Rather than stopping her to do it himself, Eli watched while she unzipped his jeans and tugged them down his hips. His large cock pressed against the fabric of his underwear, and it took everything in her to leave him unsatisfied. She ached to feel him inside her, but if they eased their desires right now, they wouldn't make it out of Eli's apartment.

"Hurry," she said. "Get changed so we can get out of here."

Eli groaned but obeyed. He knew that waiting would be worth it for both of them.

While Eli dressed in dark jeans and a button-down shirt, Grace slipped into her silky black dress and matching wedge shoes with lace that tied in a bow around her ankles. Although it was the middle of summer, she pulled on a light jacket that extended past her knees. She didn't want to give anyone a heart attack as they walked through town on their way to Azalea's.

They held hands as they left the mountain. By now, people had been drinking and celebrating for hours and most of them didn't give Eli and Grace more than a second's glance. They only ran into one council member, who frowned as they took in Grace and Eli's interlaced fingers. Grace just smiled and proceeded down the path.

Once they got closer to the scandalous hidden bar, they put on their masks. No one was around to see them slip into their disguise, so their true identities would remain a secret once they stepped inside the little gem that was Azalea's.

Eli opened the door and held out a hand. Under the mask, Grace spotted a small smile on his lips. "After you," he said.

She stepped in to find the hostess waiting. A young woman with red curly hair and gold jewelry decorating her ears and neck. In fact, one gold chain dropped low between the curve of her breast and disappeared into her black top.

"Just the two of you? Would you like a table or a private room?"

"A table, please."

The woman nodded and led them through the entry hall and into a room to the left side of the building. Many of the tables were already occupied with folks of all ages and genders, sipping out of glasses while their shadows danced in the candlelight. The focal point of the room featured a man hidden behind a mask like everyone else, but he held a guitar and sang in a deep voice that had the room hanging on his every word.

"Here's your seat. What can I get you?" the hostess asked quietly.

"I'll take a wine," Grace said, removing her jacket and hanging it on the back of her chair.

Eli nodded. "Same for me."

Grace waited for Eli to sit, then ignored her own seat and moved to his lap.

Eli wrapped a hand around her back and placed the other on her bare leg. He immediately slid it higher, his finger delicately grazing her sensitive skin.

She smiled as she thought about their first trip to Azalea's. He'd been so shocked and timid but also up for anything. She loved that about him. He never tried to tame her or expected her to settle down. Eli saw her for who she was and loved everything about her. He encouraged her to be wild and free.

Now he was pushing his hand up her inner thigh with no inhibitions. Not once did he glance around to see if anyone was watching. Grace, however, looked over his shoulder and surveyed the room. The idea of watching and being watched was one of her most frequent fantasies, and why she had so often come to Azalea's even before she'd met Eli.

Most people's attention was directed toward the man serenading them, and she could hardly blame them. His voice was mesmerizing and even with a mask, his eyes were beautiful enough to melt the coolest patron.

Eli nibbled her ear, and her eyes rolled back in her head. She shifted so her back was against his chest, wrapping an arm behind his neck as her head rolled to rest on his shoulder.

Beneath her, she felt him suck in a sharp breath as his fingers finally met the apex of her thighs. "No panties?" he asked, rubbing a gentle circle over her clit.

She sank further into him, her breathing turning shallow.

His lips grazed her ear. "I asked a question."

Biting her lip, she tried to focus beyond the mind-numbing sensation currently happening between her legs. What had he asked? She felt a finger slide inside her and pushed her ass against the ridge in his pants. Right. No panties.

"I didn't want lines."

Eli chuckled. "That's the only reason?"

His finger stroked her inner wall, and he patiently moved it in and out of her. She clenched around him, desperate for more.

"N-No."

"Why else would you leave the panties behind?" he asked in a low voice that rumbled in his chest.

Grace's eyes fluttered closed, and she rocked her hips, praying he'd give her more. Her body shook with anticipation.

"Grace." He spoke again, more commanding this time.

"Hmm?"

"Answer me." His words were pleading. Like he ached to be satisfied, too. As if the hard length pressed into her bottom wasn't sign enough.

"I wanted you to have easy access." She gasped when his finger slid out of her and began to circle her clit again. Squeezing her thighs together, she could feel just how wet she was from his touch. Her speech was needy and breathless. "I was hoping you would touch me."

"Like this?" he asked, pushing two fingers inside her.

"*Fuck.*"

"My god, Grace. You look so pretty when you're riding my fingers."

A wicked grin flashed across her face. "Even prettier when I'm riding your cock."

Eli moaned and used his free hand to grip her face. He forced her to face him, devouring her lips while he continued to play with her pussy.

When he broke the kiss, Grace leaned forward. He pulled his fingers from her, and she missed them immediately, but he worked quickly to unbutton his pants and pull them down. His underwear followed shortly after and once his cock sprang free, Grace returned to her position.

Wrapping an arm around her waist, Eli reached for his shaft and pressed it against her entrance. He teased her, covering himself in her arousal before gently pushing the tip in.

Her entire body pulsed with uncontrollable energy. With Eli's free hand, he held her firmly against his chest and pushed farther inside her, stretching and filling her until she couldn't take it anymore.

"Open your eyes, Grace," Eli said.

She hadn't even realized she had closed them, but she opened them at his request. Looking around, she noticed that multiple couples were now focused entirely on them. Watching as Eli's cock worked in and out of her. A woman to her right sat on her partner's lap, grinding on him while his hand traveled up her shirt. On her left, she caught a man with his hand hidden beneath the table. The woman next to him bit her lip while her chest heaved.

"You're right. You're a fucking piece of art while you ride me. Everyone thinks so."

Grace's legs fell open further, and she threaded her fingers in Eli's hair. Seeing the small crowd so enamored by their bodies moving together was a feeling unlike any other. She'd never felt freer of the obligations that always held her down. Unconfined by the expectations that kept her lifeless like a statue. A doll that the people around her got to dress up until she looked and acted the way they needed her to.

Here, Grace was no one. Just another faceless guest in the house of pleasure. And yet she felt more like herself than she ever did outside these walls.

She rocked her hips and Eli picked up his pace, thrusting into her with passion and enthusiasm. Her legs tightened, but she couldn't squeeze them closed while Eli's knees held them open.

At the center of the room, the musician had stopped singing, though he continued to strum his guitar. A beautiful melody filled the air, and it sounded how Grace imagined lust and ecstasy would. Quickening in all the right places and hitting notes that made the hair on her neck stand straight. It seemed as though he played a tune just for her. For them.

Eli rubbed her clit to the melody and drove into her with everything he had while the music swelled, reaching its peak and dancing back and forth between the highest notes. Everything hit her at once. The pressure inside her, the captivated gazes of the patrons, the soft, pleasured moans of Eli behind her...

Grace shivered as waves of agonizing bliss rippled through her body. Her pussy spasmed around Eli's cock and he groaned his approval. She struggled to catch her breath as the aftershocks of her orgasm coursed course through her. By the time they ceased, her body was limp and completely spent.

Eli pumped into her a few more times before he came undone and spilled inside her. She fell back against his body, breathing heavily while he peppered kisses over her neck. His fingers still massaged her clit, and she whimpered, grabbing his hand and forcing him to stop. It was too much for her to handle.

She faintly heard the musician begin to sing once more, but she found it hard to focus on anything at all.

"You okay, my love?"

Grace smiled. "Never better."

Chapter Twenty

ALI

"HAVE YOU SEEN MY blue sweater?" Ali asked. She kneeled to peer under the bed, then looked under a pillow before heading to the kitchen and opening random cabinets.

Nik raised his brows. "I definitely have not seen it in the cupboards. Did you check the laundry basket?"

The beige corded basket was overflowing with clean clothes that neither of them had put away. She flipped through a couple items before spotting the sweater she was hoping to find.

Sliding it over her head, she mumbled, "I don't know what's wrong with me." Her head had been all over the place in the past few weeks. She couldn't seem to focus on anything and kept forgetting where she'd placed things. It was frustrating, but Nik brushed it off, stating it must be "pregnancy brain."

Since she'd made it past her first trimester, the nausea had subsided for the most part, but now she had the added anxiety of trying to hide her growing belly. Thankfully, a wave of cool weather had rolled into Berland and she could throw on baggy sweaters while out in public.

"Why don't you just tell Eli?" Nik asked. She wasn't sure how he'd moved so quickly. One moment he was in the kitchen eating his breakfast and the next he was standing next to her beside the bed with his arms wrapped around her waist.

"I will. Tomorrow."

He groaned. "Ali..."

"I mean it. I said I'd meet him for lunch tomorrow, so I intend to tell him then."

"What are you scared of? You don't think he'll be upset, do you? It's not like he's hung up on you...right?"

"No, it's nothing like that."

"Then what it is it like?" His arms fell from her waist, and he took a seat on the edge of the bed. He didn't look angry, more confused. And honestly, Ali wasn't sure why she was having such a hard time telling Eli, either.

"Eli has been family to me for as long as I can remember. I don't know...something about having a baby and starting a family of our own...it feels like he's being pushed out. Does that make sense? I just don't want to upset him."

Nik nodded, though he appeared to be lost in thought. She couldn't blame him if he didn't fully understand. He'd been without family for so long; how could he possibly know what she was feeling?

"You look sad," she said. An ache grew in her chest as she took in his somber face.

"Not sad. I'm just so goddamn happy about this, Ali. But I feel like I can't celebrate—like *we* can't celebrate—until we've jumped this hurdle. And it shouldn't be a hurdle."

The ache was replaced with the heavy weight of guilt. "I'm sorry. You're right. I will tell him tomorrow and then we will celebrate however you want. Dinner by the river at that cozy bistro you like?"

His mouth curved into a smile. "I'd like that."

Wrapping her arms around his neck, Ali stood between his legs and leaned in for a kiss, which he happily accepted. She meant it. She would not chicken out this time. Nik deserved her bravery, and Eli deserved her honesty.

Not to mention she couldn't keep wearing these sweatshirts once the weather heated up again.

A few moments later, Grace knocked on their door. A group of newcomers was set to arrive today, and Ali had agreed to help get them settled. Since Nik was on guard duty, he was automatically included in their welcome committee, too.

The paths were crowded as people took to the town to enjoy the small reprieve from the scorching summer heat. Families and friends strolled from shop to shop, stopping for a cup of freshly squeezed juice or a sample of the latest batch of jam. These were Ali's favorite days in town—when the whole of Berland seemed to come alive and everyone seemed so happy while they basked in each other's company. It reminded her of Andus.

As they approached the center of town, two familiar faces caught Ali's attention. A pair of women, one with dark tan skin and two long braids running down her back, the other with a short wavy bob of hair. The latter held onto the hands of two children, who peered around nervously.

"Genna, Isabel!" Grace called, running toward them. They both smiled, and Isabel waved while Genna's hands were busy. "It's so good to see you."

Ali and Nik both greeted the pair of women who had once shown them the way to Berland.

"Great to see you again," Genna said, dropping the hands of the two children and patting Nik on the back. Then she turned to Ali and gave her a brief hug. "How has Berland been treating you?"

"Very well," Ali confessed. "Better than I could've hoped."

Nik echoed the same sentiment.

"Ali is the newest council member," Grace boasted, and Ali's cheeks heated. She wasn't the biggest fan of attention, but Grace continued to gush. "She's been helping me a lot."

"You're exaggerating."

"I'm not. Trust me. Even if it doesn't seem like you've been of much use, just having you there to back me up is more than enough. And you were the only one to volunteer to help today."

That much was true. Ali wasn't sure why no one else wanted to help greet the newcomers, but she had nothing better to do. And it felt like a small way to give back. It hadn't been that long ago when she, Nik and Sam had ventured to Berland, and she hadn't forgotten how anxious she'd felt that day. Uprooting your life and starting over was a terrifying task.

"How many are with you?" Grace asked, studying a small group of people standing nearby.

"Sixteen," Isabel said. "Three couples, a family of four, and two single adults. And four children without parents."

Ali's face fell. The two children who had been holding Genna's hands were now picking flowers off the path. They looked no older than four or five years old. Beyond them, she studied the rest of the group and tried to determine which were the other two orphans, but she couldn't discern them from the two who still had their parents.

"What happened?" Grace asked.

"Wildfire. Ripped through their village and destroyed their homes and crops. It happened during the middle of the night and caught them off guard. Most were able to get out of their burning houses, but some died in the flames."

"This is all that's left?" Nik asked.

"No. This is about half. After the fire struck, they picked up what they had and began to head south, looking for a new place to settle. But on their trek, several more died from the elements and starvation. They've had a pretty rough go of things. When we stumbled upon them, they were knocking on death's door."

Ali glanced at the group again, paying more attention to their faces. Some of them still looked as though they were seconds from the grave. Was that what she had looked like at one point, too?

"We'll take good care of them," Grace said.

"We knew you would." Genna smiled and waved them forward. "Let's go meet everyone."

While Grace introduced herself and answered questions from the newcomers, Ali kept the two youngest children entertained. The two little girls couldn't keep their hands off the wildflowers that grew along the side of the path, so Ali sat down with them and plucked a few herself, weaving them into a crown like she'd done so many times as a kid. When she finished the first, she offered it to the little blonde girl with big brown eyes. She was so similar to Ali at that age, and Ali silently wondered if her own child would look more like her or more like Nik.

The little girl eagerly placed it on her head and began to dance in circles.

"What's your name?" Ali asked.

"Julia," she said, emphasizing the 'u.'

"That's a pretty name. Mine is Ali."

She finished the second crown and held it up for the other little girl, a brunette with freckles all over her cheeks and shoulders. "And what's your name?"

The second girl was much shyer than the first. She didn't step forward to accept her crown or answer Ali's question. Instead, she crossed her arms over her chest like she was giving herself a hug, shrinking inside herself.

"Do you like to play princesses? I used to love it when I was your age. You know the woman over there?" Ali pointed to Grace. "She's basically a *real* princess!"

The tension in the girl's arms eased slightly, and she looked over her shoulder to see Grace smiling and talking with all the adults. "I can promise she won't mind sharing the title with you for a day, though."

Ali's encouragement seemed to do the trick, and the little girl reached for the crown made of daisies and purple bellflowers. The girl spoke in little more than a whisper. "Kaydence."

"Nice to meet you, Kaydence. I'm Ali."

Kaydence placed the crown on top of her head, and it tilted a little to the left. It didn't seem to bother her, though. She rushed toward Julia, and Ali watched as the two of them took turns chasing each other.

"Having fun?" Nik asked, coming to her side.

Ali nodded and wrapped an arm around Nik's waist, letting her head fall to his shoulder. "One day, those will be our kids playing outside, laughing and running wild."

"Kids as in multiple?" he asked, his lips curving into a grin.

Ali prodded his side. "Can't you picture it? The two of us growing old, chasing around half a dozen kids?"

He coughed. "Half a dozen?" His eyes were wide with something between terror and amusement.

Laughing, Ali responded, "Or however many you want."

Nik recovered quickly and squeezed her shoulder. "I want whatever you want."

Ali wasn't sure what she wanted—two kids or eight. All she knew was that she wanted a family with Nik and she'd accept however many fate had in store for them.

While they waited for Grace to finish speaking with the rest of the party, Julia and Kaydence kept them entertained. Surprisingly, the latter took no time at all to warm up to Nik. Kaydence brought him one yellow flower. Nik expressed his gratitude, and before they knew it, he had a whole pile of yellow flowers.

Each time she came back with another, Nik put on the biggest show of gratitude and her smile brightened before she set off to pick another. It was one of the most precious things Ali had ever seen. If she wasn't already pregnant, she would've taken him back home just to let him impregnate her again.

The sound of raised voices reached Ali's ears, and she turned around, expecting to find Grace and the newcomers headed their way. It had to be time to go inside the mountain by now. But instead, she found Grace face to face with one of the council members.

Scott, the newest council member aside from Ali, was hovering over Grace with one hand on his hip while the other pointed aggressively at the group of newcomers, who watched with apprehension. She couldn't make out the words, but whatever he was saying was enough to cause the newcomers to clutch their loved ones, and Grace to jab a finger into Scott's chest.

At the sight of the two of them, Nik hopped up, ready to defend Grace. Scott looked ready to throw Grace off the side of the mountain; his cheeks were bright red, and a vein pulsed in his forehead.

"Come here, girls," Ali called for Julia and Kaydence. Neither of them was paying attention to the scene, but Grace and Scott were drawing an audience from the civilians of Berland. Most watched with curiosity, but a few looked like they were ready to take a side. Ali didn't want to find out what would happen if this verbal altercation became a physical one.

She moved closer but kept the two girls safely behind her. "What is going on?"

"These people can't stay here," Scott said, not taking his eyes off of Grace.

"You're not in a position to tell me who can and cannot stay," Grace retorted. She spoke with such authority and self-assuredness that Ali was surprised Scott didn't crumble in her presence.

"The council didn't approve this. Where will you even put them?"

Grace looked like he had just slapped her across the face. "We have *never* needed the council's approval to bring in newcomers. And we have the space for them. There are multiple units prepped and ready, but if you're so concerned, we could always give them your home."

A sound resembling a growl came from Scott. He took a threatening step forward, but Nik positioned himself in front of Grace. He held his hands up and said calmly, "This is not the time nor the place for this conversation. Why don't we go inside and—"

"And who do you think you are?" Scott interrupted. "Your opinion matters even less to me than *hers* does."

Ali flinched, but Nik only stood taller, a few inches above Scott's head. He pulled back his shoulders and glared at Scott, cracking his knuckles as he readied to throw a punch.

Grace moved around him and spoke directly to Scott. "You're out of line, Scott. I know you think you're more important than everyone else, but you can't speak to people that way. And you definitely cannot speak to *me* that way."

Scott sneered but remained quiet. Perhaps he sensed the crowd around them and made an effort to keep his emotions in check.

"Nik is right," Grace continued. "We should take this conversation inside, preferably in a private council meeting. But you should know that any more outbursts like this will result in your expulsion from the council."

"You don't have the power to do that," Scott said.

"Try me."

Chapter Twenty-One

ALI

Ali hadn't expected the day to be so draining, but by the time all the newcomers were settled into their new homes, she was ready to crash. The hardest part was leaving behind Julia and Kaydence with a middle-aged woman they'd never met. The girls clung to Ali and Nik, but with a little encouragement, they were finally convinced to stay with the kind woman.

Grace explained that Ms. Carpenter took care of any children without parents until they could find a more permanent placement for them. It was heartbreaking to know that such a role was necessary, but Grace assured them she was a sweet and caring woman and the kids would be safe there.

Ali promised to meet them for breakfast the next morning and Kaydence shyly asked if Nik would come along.

"I think she has a little crush on you," Ali joked, and Nik shrugged her off. He sat next to her, casually massaging her shoulders in Grace's private office space. The room was small and nearly empty aside from a wooden desk and a few mismatched chairs. Given that this was the first time Grace had even mentioned the office, Ali figured she rarely used it, choosing instead to spend her days actively involved in the community.

"Thank you both for helping today," Grace said. "And stepping in to protect me."

"Of course," Ali said. "I had a great time today, even after Scott showed up. It was nice being on the other side of things and getting the opportunity to welcome people to Berland like we were."

"It's a shame that asshole ruined it," Nik commented.

Grace shook her head, and her brown hair rippled. "Things are far from ruined. I spoke with everyone afterwards to reassure them they are safe here."

"Are they? Safe here?" Nik asked, and Grace frowned. "This rebellion...they truly seem to hate you and, by extension, anyone who associates with you. What if something does happen and Trevor winds up by your side? Or, god forbid, Eamon finds a way to forcibly remove you and your family from power. How can you guarantee their safety?"

Grace thought hard about this before responding. "Nothing is *guaranteed* in this life. Any one of us could lose everything tomorrow. But that possibility can't stop us from pursuing our dreams, our goals, and our happiness. I won't stop pursuing a better community for my people, new and old. The rebels might be bold with their hatred, but they are not the majority, and we won't let them silence us. I can't guarantee my people's safety, but I can promise that I will always fight for them."

Nik considered her words before nodding, satisfied with her answer. Ali, on the other hand, tried not to think too hard about the frequency of attacks against Grace and her family.

"Should we get going?" Nik asked as he rose from his seat. "It's getting late and we haven't even eaten yet."

Grace yawned and stepped out from behind her desk while Ali followed Nik out of the office. Together they headed toward the entry chamber, which was quieter than usual. Given how late it was, most people were home fast asleep already.

The dining hall was still open, however, and a few stragglers were seated near the buffet line. Their heads were huddled together as one woman showed the others something in a notebook.

"Shoot," Ali said suddenly. "I left my bag back in the council chamber. It has all my stuff, including my notebook."

Nik shrugged. "You can grab it tomorrow."

Ali shook her head. "I need those notes to prepare for a meeting tomorrow. It can't wait. You go on and grab something for us to eat and I'll run back and get my bag. Meet you at home?"

Nik frowned like he'd rather she not venture out alone, especially after the day they'd had, but the halls were empty. She'd be fine.

She gave him a quick peck on the lips before turning back in the direction they'd come from. It wouldn't take long to reach the council chamber and return home.

The halls were dimly lit, but she met no one on her way to the chamber. She used her key to unlock the room and slipped in, leaving the door cracked so light from the hall filtered in. Her bag was right where she'd left it earlier in the day, and she snatched it from the table and slung the strap over her shoulder.

On her way out, her eyes caught on an envelope lying beneath the table. She bent down to pick it up, figuring someone must've dropped it and she could return it to its owner. Once she grasped it, she stood and checked the outside for any sign of who the envelope belonged to.

It was larger than a letter, but thin. She guessed it held important contracts or something along those lines. It was light brown and bent in places but otherwise had no clues to what it held.

She thought for a moment, turning the envelope in her hand. If it did hold important documents, they might be confidential. But how could she know who it belonged to if she didn't open it? She supposed she could just leave it where she found it and the owner may be back the next day to claim it...

After another moment of hesitation, she slid her finger under the folded edge and opened the envelope. But when she peered inside, she couldn't find anything. She reached in, thinking perhaps it was too dark to see and maybe there was something at the bottom. The only thing she felt was a powdery substance.

She was left with nothing more than disappointment when she pulled her hand back out. Her fingers were covered in a reddish-brown dust and she rubbed it between her fingers.

What the...

She brought her hand closer to her face and inhaled an earthy scent with a hint of something fruity. Her head spun at the same time her fingers began to tingle. She staggered a few steps backward, and the room began to turn sideways. Her body felt as though it were tumbling forward even though her feet remained on the ground.

Panicking, she stumbled for the door, but each step felt heavy and impossible. Something was wrong, and she tried to say as much, but no one was around to hear her. She shouldn't have come alone. She shouldn't have picked up the mysterious envelope. And she *definitely* shouldn't have checked its contents.

Whatever was on her fingers was toxic. She wiped her hand against her pant leg, though it was too late. Her vision was growing blurrier by the second, but in her terror, she couldn't think of what else to do. What could be so potent to have such an instantaneous impact? What if it was *lethal?*

Her throat constricted, but she wasn't sure if it was the poison or her fear. She reached for it, realizing too late that she'd inadvertently spread the powder to her neck.

Shit.

Her knees slammed to the floor, and she lost her balance. Her only option was to crawl toward the door and hope someone passed by in the hall. "Help," she cried, but it was little more than a whisper. "Help!"

Silence was the only response. She could hardly feel her toes, and she used her forearms and knees to push herself forward. Her stomach roiled, and she dry heaved.

She was going to die here alone. The thought of Nik finding her lifeless body brought angry tears to her eyes.

Her heart was full of regret, disappointment, and longing for all the things she had yet to experience in her life. Soul shattering hurt for the family she'd leave behind.

For her unborn child...

Her body was giving up, but her mind stayed determined. The harder she fought to stay awake, the more her eyelids resisted. With each passing moment, the darkness swirled closer, enveloping her in a suffocating blanket of permanent night.

Finally, her strength gave out. Her chin slammed into the hard floor and a muffled cry escaped her lips. Her heart beat faster and faster until it seemed to cease altogether, thudding irregularly inside her aching chest.

Ali's eyes fluttered closed, and she surrendered to a deep sleep.

Chapter Twenty-Two

NIK

After seeing Grace safely back to her home, Nik waited for Ali to return so they could eat together. He set the carry-out container filled with grilled chicken, vegetable mix, and roasted potatoes on the table and lay on the bed to relax a bit.

It wouldn't take long for Ali to return, but it had been a long day, and the bed was far more comfortable than the hard chairs at the table. He positioned one arm behind his head and stared at the ceiling. The small wall light fixture hummed, and he closed his eyes to block out the warm illumination. His body sank into the mattress and he slowly drifted to sleep.

When Nik woke, the room was significantly darker than before. It took his eyes a moment to adjust, and he blindly felt the bed beside him, but Ali's side was empty.

"Ali?" he whispered.

He sat up quickly and stumbled to turn on a lamp. His mind went into a tailspin; he needed to see with his own eyes that she wasn't where she was supposed to be. The light fell over the bedroom and even though he felt her absence, some part of him hoped he was wrong and that she'd be on her side of the bed, blocking her eyes from the brightness and wondering why he'd gotten up so suddenly.

But she wasn't there.

"Ali?" he called again. The door to the bathroom was cracked, and he pushed it open to look inside. No sign of her there, either. There were only so many places she could be, and with one glance into their dining area, he'd searched all of them.

Nik quickly found his shoes. Having fallen asleep by accident, he was still dressed in the clothes he'd worn that day. He wasn't sure how late it was, but she should've been home by now. So he set off for the last place he knew she'd been: the council chamber.

The halls were entirely empty, and Nik opted to run rather than walk. It wasn't like Ali to stay out so late, especially when she was just supposed to be grabbing her belongings. It set him on edge and forced him to move faster. He didn't have to think twice about directions. Since he'd taken over as Grace's guard, he'd visited the council chamber many times and knew the way by heart.

He was nearly there when he considered that the council chamber was usually locked and he didn't have Ali or Grace with him to use their key, but as he turned down the hall that led to the chamber, he noticed the door was already cracked open.

He sprinted toward it, and when he opened the door, his chest tightened and his stomach did a somersault. A dim light from the hall barely illuminated the figure of a lifeless Ali lying on the floor.

Nik dropped to his knees and pulled Ali to his lap, gently tapping her cheek. "Wake up, Ali. Wake up!"

What the fuck had happened here?

"Ali!" he screamed, but her head bobbed in his hold and her eyes remained closed. Terror gripped his heart as he carefully put two fingers to her neck and checked for a pulse. He felt the faint beat of her heart and let out a sigh of relief. She was alive, but for how much longer?

Wasting no time, he wrapped one around her shoulders and tucked the other under her knees and ran back down the hall toward the medical facilities.

As he ran, he looked down at her every so often, checking to see if she'd woken up, but she remained motionless except for the rocking of her body with each step he took.

Please don't die, he silently pleaded.

His eyes drifted to the bump on her belly, and he silently said another prayer to the gods that never listened.

Don't let either of them die.

When he made it to the medical chamber, he found a young woman with her eyes half closed, drawing little symbols on a notepad in boredom. At the sound of his heavy footsteps, the woman looked up and her eyes went wide.

"What happened?" she asked, stepping out from behind the front desk and crossing the room to knock on a door. Nik knew from prior visits that it led to a spare bedroom that the medics used when they weren't busy. A place for one of them to stay overnight so someone was always available. After a brief pause, she knocked again.

"I don't know," he told the woman. "I found her like this. She's not waking up." He did his best to remain calm, but his voice shook.

Right as she was about to knock again, the door opened and an older woman appeared, blinking at the light. She looked between Nik and the receptionist and suddenly was wide awake. "Bring her this way," she said, pulling her black hair into a ponytail.

She led them down a hall and into the first available room. Nik gave her Ali's name and answered her questions as best he could. Which was painful, since he had no clue how Ali had wound up this way. He couldn't offer anything to help the medic determine what was wrong with her or what needed to be done.

"She's pregnant," he told her. "And she has anxiety and possibly depression, too." They'd never explicitly talked about it, but Nik had a hunch from her behavior throughout those months that Eli had been missing. After everything she'd been through, it had made sense that she was having a hard time. But even now that the two friends had been reunited, there were still days Nik could sense that shadow lingering beneath the surface, threatening to make an appearance again. On those days, he held her and comforted her and waited for it to pass. "I'm sorry. I don't know much else about her medical history."

The door opened and a man with black hair that fell to his shoulders and warm brown skin walked through. Nik recognized him as one of the former suitors, the one who didn't show up to the second round. The man rolled up his sleeves, ready to assist the medic. She turned to face Nik. "Thank you. That's helpful. I'm Meg and this is Zeke. We'll be taking good care of Ali, but I need you to return to the waiting room with Linsey so we can do our job."

Nik's shoulders tensed. Ali was lying on a stiff bed, her small hand still frail and pale inside Nik's grasp. The idea of letting her go made him sick. "I can't stay?"

Meg shook her head. "I promise we will do everything we can. But we need to have zero distractions."

He swallowed the lump in his throat and his eyes flicked to Zeke, who gave him a quick nod. Nik knew little about the man, other than he had stepped aside when he realized Grace was in love with someone else, and that alone gave him a few points in Nik's eyes.

Nik took a few deep breaths and then gently rested Ali's hand on the bed. He stepped back, and each inch felt like a dagger in his heart.

Linsey placed a hand on his back and he reluctantly allowed her to lead him out to the reception area to wait.

※

Nik had no idea how much time passed. His eyes felt heavy, but he never once let them close. He kept them fixed on the door he knew led to Ali's room and strained his ears for any sign, whether it was good or bad.

Early in the morning, Linsey switched shifts with another worker and said she'd be back to check on him. It wasn't too long before she returned with fresh donuts and two familiar faces.

Nik leaped to his feet as Grace threw her arms around him. "What happened?" she asked.

He shuddered and hardly recognized his own voice. "I don't know."

Grace released him and looked him over with tear-filled eyes. Behind her, Eli looked pale and distressed. Nik wished he had good news to give them, but he hadn't heard anything from the medics.

Frustration consumed him, and he clasped his hands behind his head before running them down his face. "Something happened when she went to get her bag. I don't know what. I...I fell asleep and when I woke up, she still wasn't back, so I went searching for her and..." He struggled to finish his sentence.

And she was lying lifeless on the floor.

Grace rubbed his arm in comfort. "How long have you been waiting? Linsey ran into us in the hall and told us there was an emergency, but she didn't say much else."

The previous night's desk attendant had left again, leaving behind the donuts and cups that likely contained juice or tea.

"I'm not sure how long I've been here, but they've been in that room and I haven't gotten any updates."

Grace nodded and looked toward Eli. They stared as if having a silent conversation, but Nik was too tired to decipher its meaning.

"I'll be right back," Grace said, moving toward the patient rooms.

"It's the first room on the left," he told her. As future Lady of Berland, Grace held more sway than he did. If he couldn't see Ali, maybe Grace could at least get an update on her condition.

The lack of information was driving him mad. He pushed his hands through his hair again and huffed in aggravation.

"Why don't you sit down?" Eli said, offering a donut to Nik.

Nik shook his head. His throat was dry, and he didn't think he could eat anything right now. He'd likely just throw it back up.

But he did sit down, his elbows resting on his knees and his head tucked between his hands.

Eli's hand awkwardly patted his shoulder. "It'll be okay. Ali is a fighter."

"What if she isn't?" Nik's voice cracked, and he squeezed the bridge of his nose. Something burned behind his eyes and he needed it to go away.

"Don't let your head go there, man." Eli sighed. "I don't know if it helps at all, but the fact that they haven't come out and updated you is a good thing. It means she's still in there fighting. Trust that they've got her."

Words that Nik would've told anyone else in his position, but hearing them didn't make it any easier. He was being asked to put his faith in complete strangers. Leave his entire world in their hands.

"You sure you don't want something to eat?" Eli asked. He was trying so hard to comfort Nik, even if he was doing a horrible job at it. Nik couldn't fault him, though. That he was even trying at all was a testament to his character. Who would've thought the man who had once hated him for taking his girl would be the one sitting here now, consoling him while that same girl's fate hung by a thread?

"Thank you," Nik said, finally taking the donut from Eli, along with a glass of juice to wash it down.

He'd barely taken his first bite when raised voices sounded from Ali's room. Eli and Nik exchanged glances. It didn't sound like panic or something he should be alarmed about.

It sounded like Grace wasn't taking no for an answer.

For the first time in hours, a smile spread across Nik's face. "She's a force to be reckoned with," he told Eli.

Eli grinned. "I know."

The door swung open and Grace appeared, waving at them. "You can come in now."

For fuck's sake. If Nik had known all it would take was Grace's persuasion, he would've gone to find her hours ago. He tossed his barely touched donut back into the paper bag and left the glass of juice on an end table.

He crossed the waiting room in three long strides and met Grace in the hall, Eli following closely behind.

When he entered Ali's room, he wasn't sure if he wanted to break down and sob or exhale in relief. She was still asleep, but the color had returned to her cheeks. She looked as though she was merely dreaming peacefully with a soft smile on her face. He ached to hold her in his arms, but he still wasn't certain of her condition.

"She's stable for now," Meg said, sensing his questions. "We still want to monitor her, though."

A sound like a fake cough came from Grace, and Meg grimaced.

"I apologize for keeping you waiting so long. We wanted to wait until she woke up before bothering you. Shouldn't be too much longer now."

Bother him? Like the past few hours hadn't been some of the most agonizing moments of his life. Did she have any clue how close he had been to breaking down the door?

"Did you figure out what happened?" he demanded.

Meg walked around Ali's bed and held up one of her hands. The fingertips looked darker than the rest of her skin, like a rash. He hadn't noticed it in the darkness of the council chamber. "She was poisoned. That reddish tint is from helberries—a deadly fruit that grows in the depths of the mountain. It's actually a fungus and not a fruit at all, but it looks like a bundle of berries... Anyway, you didn't come for an etymology lesson. Where did you say you found her?"

"Um..." Nik hesitated. If this poisoning was intentional, should he share where Ali had been? Was that meant to be Grace or Ellen lying on the bed in front of him?

Grace noticed and stepped in for him. "That's not necessary, is it?"

Irritation crossed Meg's face. "I only want to make sure there isn't a bloom of it anywhere children could stumble into. We haven't had a helberry poisoning in years and I'd rather not have another one." She turned to face Nik again. "We have an antidote, but supplies are limited, as you can imagine. It's a good thing you got her here when you did. Any later and I'm not sure the antidote would've been much help."

Nik swallowed hard, a million thoughts racing through his mind. Kicking himself for falling asleep and not realizing she was missing sooner. He should've come with her in the first place to retrieve her things. His stomach turned at the possibility that Ali could've died, and he sat on the side of her bed, taking her hand in his. He ran his thumb over the back of her hand in small circles, wishing he could see her pretty brown eyes and know for certain that she would be okay.

"I can assure you that we will investigate the incident and make sure any helberry growths are taken care of," Grace said.

In the corner, Zeke cleared his throat. "There's something else."

Nik's chest tightened, and he wasn't sure why, but instinct had his eyes flitting to Ali's stomach. He shook his head and furrowed his brows, his relief that Ali was okay coming to an abrupt halt. "Please…"

He knew. Somehow, he just *knew*. A space had been carved out in his chest, and it felt painfully hollow. He knew, but he wished he didn't.

He waited for Zeke to speak, to deny what he felt in his heart. He begged the gods to reverse time and let him have another chance, a moment for him to change the unbearable course they'd taken and stop Ali from making the one choice that would change their future.

"Don't…"

Don't say it.

Zeke's eyes were full of apologies, but he opened his mouth to speak anyway. Nik's ears rang as the words hit him like bullets. "We couldn't save the baby."

Chapter Twenty-Three

ELI

Eli must've heard incorrectly. There was no other explanation. The *baby?*

But he watched as Nik hunched over and sobbed against Ali's torso and knew that Zeke hadn't misspoken.

Ali had been pregnant...and now she wasn't. How long had she known? It was evident that Nik already knew. Eli caught Grace softly crying out of the corner of his eye, and he turned to hug her. Something about her expression told him she wasn't surprised by the pregnancy either.

Was he the only one who hadn't known?

A piece of him ached over the knowledge that his best friend had kept something so special from him, but he couldn't linger on that hurt when too many of his thoughts were consumed by the fact that he'd almost lost Ali again...this time permanently.

He was sure she had her reasons for keeping this secret, and hopefully one day she'd share them with him. For now, he could only pray she would wake up.

He studied her. Ali continued to breathe quietly with her eyes closed. Her blonde hair was pulled back in a messy braid and her lips were slightly parted. A blanket was pulled up to her chest and underneath, Eli spotted the smallest bump on her stomach. She had been gaining weight, but he'd assumed that, like him, it had been the result of no longer wondering where their next meal would come from.

He should've been paying closer attention. He'd been so absorbed in his own life and hardships that he hadn't noticed his best friend was pregnant. And as soon as he'd discovered it, it was over. His mouth turned dry, and he tried to swallow his hurt and disappointment.

It was nothing compared to what Ali would face when she woke up. He could only imagine the devastation she would feel. The overwhelming loss that Nik visibly felt.

Eli reached forward to comfort Nik, gently patting him on the back. His pain was so significant, it expanded and filled the entire room with heartbreak and despair. It was impossible not to feel for him.

"I'm sorry," Eli said softly.

Grace echoed his sentiments and pulled at Eli's arm. "We should give him a moment," she whispered. Then she spoke louder for Nik to hear. "Let us know if you need anything."

Nik didn't look up, still nestled against Ali's chest. Eli wasn't certain if he'd heard Grace, but they left the room regardless, Zeke and Meg not far behind them.

They walked in silence until they reached the hallway outside of the medical chamber, and then Eli turned to Grace. "You knew... You knew that Ali was pregnant?"

Grace nodded and tried to read his expression as he did hers. She looked sympathetic but firm in her decision not to tell him, the weight of defensiveness bringing down her shoulders.

"Why didn't you say anything?"

"It wasn't my news to share." She reached for his hand, but he pulled back, his mind still whirling with tangled thoughts. Grace frowned. "Ali didn't even tell me—I guessed it. She planned to tell you."

"Then why didn't she?"

Her brows pulled together. "Just waiting for the right moment, I suppose."

Eli rubbed the back of his neck and looked both ways down the hall, unsure of what he was searching for. He felt lost in more ways than one.

Grace reached for his hand again and this time he accepted, letting the touch of her skin bring him back to earth. He was grateful for the stability she provided, even if she'd kept this knowledge from him. He pulled her into his arms and squeezed her tight, releasing some of the tension he'd been clinging to.

"I'm sorry, Eli," she said against his chest.

"You don't need to apologize. I understand why you didn't tell me."

"Not for that," she said. "Ali is the only family you have. That child would've been like a niece or nephew to you. I'm sorry for your loss."

Eli struggled to breathe. It was true. As her best friend, Eli would've had a significant role in the child's life.

The blows kept coming.

He pressed his cheek against Grace's head and lost himself in her embrace. They stood in the middle of the hall while people passed on their way to work or social engagements for the morning. Eli didn't know how long they remained immobile. All he knew was that he didn't want to lose Grace's touch.

Eventually, he sighed and pulled back. "Thank you. For being here for me."

He pushed her brown hair behind her ear, and Grace smiled. "I'll always be here for you, Eli."

The research lab was bustling with lively and energetic faces. People hustled around gathering materials and scratching down notes at the surrounding worktables.

Eli propped an elbow on his table and rested his chin on his palm. His pencil was reduced to a dull stub, but he continued to scribble mindlessly on his notepad.

In the chair across from him, Luka tinkered with a metal device, attempting to disassemble it but failing miserably.

Eli was supposed to be helping, but his mind was elsewhere. He would've taken the day off work if he hadn't already missed so much due to his training schedule for the Rite. Luka was extremely understanding, but Eli refused to take his patience for granted.

"Could you grab those pliers over there?" Luka asked, pulling Eli from his thoughts. He glanced at the counter behind him, noting several tools they commonly used in the lab. He picked up the ones that looked similar to shears but with serrated pincers at the end and handed them to Luka.

"Thanks," he said. "Are you all right?"

Eli sighed, meeting Luka's gaze for the first time all day. He should've known he couldn't be distant-minded all day without someone noticing, especially Luka, who never let anything slip by him. "I've got a lot on my plate right now. Makes it hard to focus, I guess."

Luka huffed a laugh. "I hear you. I remember being your age, running wild with friends and chasing my future wife. Living like sleep was optional and suffering the repercussions the next day." He sighed as though fondly recalling those days.

Eli wished that was all he had going on. He gave Luka a half-hearted smile.

"You must be even more occupied with the Rite. Well done on the second round, by the way. I see all that training is paying off."

"Yeah, it is. Thanks again for letting me take time off. Once this is over, I promise I'll make it up to you."

Luka brushed his comments aside. "Forget about it. What kind of man would I be if I stood between two soul mates?"

Eli's smile was genuine at the thought of his *soul mate*. While the morning had been rough and there was still much healing to come, Eli was grateful he had Grace on his side.

That moment of gratefulness was short-lived with the threat of the third round just weeks away.

He could already picture it: standing at the end of the Rite, watching another man hold Grace's hand and kiss her lips. Ali might try to console him, but she had her own heartbreak to work through. And she had Nik too. He'd be left alone—completely abandoned.

"Eli," Luka said, snapping his fingers.

Blinking, Eli cleared the nightmare from his mind. "Sorry," he said. "Did you need something else?"

Luka snorted. "I need you to go home. You're certainly not in the right headspace to be here."

Eli shook his head. "No, I can stay."

"I mean it, Eli. The lab can be a dangerous place if you aren't paying attention. We don't need any injuries today."

He wasn't wrong. A month after Eli had started working in the lab, a coworker had sliced through a finger with a blade because he'd been distracted. Instinctively, Eli flexed his hand and counted each of his fingers—all ten still attached.

"Okay, but I'll be here early tomorrow," he said, gathering his things and heading for the exit. "Thanks, Luka."

"Don't mention it."

Eli walked aimlessly from the lab. He wasn't hungry, and it had been raining all day, so he didn't feel like going for a run or visiting his horse, Obsidian. Grace would be in meetings until later in the afternoon. The only place he felt called to be was in the medical chamber, next to Ali. So it was no surprise when he looked up from his wandering feet and found himself in the reception area.

The woman at the desk greeted him with a warm smile, which he returned before heading to Ali's room. He gently opened the door, and his eyes were immediately drawn to Ali's face—still fast asleep. Nik hadn't moved positions either. He was still draped over her body with his cheek pressed against her chest. By the soft sound of his breathing, he was asleep as well.

Eli quietly pulled up a chair and sat on the opposite side of Ali's bed. Then he leaned forward and held her other hand, staring at it as if she might squeeze his at any moment.

When she didn't, he sighed. All he wanted to do right now was talk to his best friend. He couldn't help but think of their life before Andus was attacked. How simple everything had seemed back then. They had been foolish to think that life would always be that carefree.

Or at least he had been. Ali had always dreamed of a life beyond Andus's borders. She had craved adventure and experiences that she never would've found back home. Would she have chosen this if she'd known everything she'd lose in the process?

"You deserve better than this," he said softly.

Across the bed, Nik grumbled indistinctly. His shoulders shifted, but then he settled back into place, breathing heavily.

"Nik," Eli whispered.

Nik didn't stir.

"Hey, you asshole."

Still no movement.

Satisfied that Nik wasn't eavesdropping, Eli relaxed and returned his attention to Ali. "I'm sorry this happened to you, Ali. And I'm sorry you felt like you couldn't tell me. I don't know how we got here. I suppose it was silly to think that nothing would ever change. You've got Nik and I've got Grace. I just thought we'd always be close, you know? After Nik and Rysburg, I thought we'd made it through the worst of it. Maybe I should've made it clear that you can always come to me with anything. I know I reacted poorly when I found out about Nik, but I'm a different person now. I'm more mature and less stubborn. You can tell me things. I *want* you to tell me things."

Eli's shoulders slumped, and he leaned back in his chair, dropping Ali's hand. "I miss who we used to be, Ali. I miss my best friend."

"I'm still here," a hoarse voice said.

The words hit Eli in the heart. His head shot up to find Ali smiling faintly at him, though there was confusion in her eyes.

"Where is *here* exactly?"

"Thank god," Eli said, lunging forward to embrace her.

He bumped Nik's head on the way, and Nik grunted unintelligibly as he sat up. "What the fuck is wrong with—" His words faded before he inhaled a sharp breath. "Ali."

Nik nudged Eli out of his way and held Ali in his arms. From the way his shoulders shook, Eli assumed he was crying tears of joy.

Ali's face was visible over Nik's shoulder, and she still looked bewildered. "What happened?"

Nik pulled back enough to meet her gaze. "I'm hoping you can tell us."

She shook her head. "I don't... I..."

Understanding slowly sank in, and her demeanor shifted from confusion to fear to all out panic. Her breathing became erratic, and she pushed up into a sitting position on the bed.

"Hey, it's okay. It's okay," Nik repeated, rubbing her arms in a feeble attempt to soothe her.

"It's not," she said frantically. "I was... I was grabbing my bag and there was... I opened it and then... and then it was black and everything was black and..."

She was hyperventilating, and even Nik was struggling to ease her anxiety.

Eli moved toward the door, opening it quickly and shouting down the hall, "We need help in here!"

Meg, the medic from that morning, rushed through the door, pushing Eli's chair back and taking his previous spot. After some convincing, Nik sat back and allowed Meg to check Ali over. She continued to breathe heavily, so Meg procured a clear vial with a translucent pink substance. She convinced Ali to drink it, that it would calm her nerves, and Ali did as the medic asked.

After a few moments, her breathing seemed to steady, but her face was still full of terror. "How did I get here?"

Nik moved closer now that her panic had subsided. He rubbed circles on her back and explained how he'd found her in the council chamber, passed out and alone. Then Meg explained the steps they'd taken to treat her and that she'd been poisoned with helberries.

"Was anyone there with you?" Nik asked. "Did someone give them to you?"

Ali shook her head. "No, no one else was there. It was... It was an envelope. I saw it lying there, and I didn't know who it belonged to. It wasn't berries, though. It was a powder."

Meg crossed her arms and nodded. "When they're dried and ground up, they become even more potent. That explains why you reacted so quickly."

"Who would do that?" Ali asked, looking between the medic, Eli, and Nik. "Why would they leave it there for someone to find?"

Eli clenched his jaw. He had a guess as to who might be miserable enough to poison one of the council members. That poison hadn't been meant for Ali. There was a very high likelihood that it had been meant for Grace or her mother. He ground his teeth at the thought of Eamon, Trevor, and every other rebel who wanted to take Grace's family down.

"I'm sure there will be a full investigation," Meg said. "But there is one more thing we need to discuss."

Eli shifted uncomfortably. "I'll step outside."

No part of him wanted to be present when Ali heard the fate of her and Nik's child. Not when she hadn't even told him about her pregnancy. He felt like an intruder in this difficult moment.

Ali frowned as she watched him move toward the door. After he closed it, he leaned against the wall and clutched his aching chest.

Moments later, a devastated cry shattered his already broken heart.

Chapter Twenty-Four

ALI

Returning home after a few days in the medical chamber should've raised Ali's spirits, but stepping through the door left her feeling empty and incomplete. She had left a piece of her heart back in that sterile medic room. A piece that she would never get back.

She could hardly recall the events of the procedure following her miscarriage. Her mind had been so hazy, but perhaps it was best that she didn't keep those memories. She'd had enough hardship to fuel her nightmares for the rest of her life.

Meg told her the first few days might be rough. That she might experience some cramping, and it was normal. Although the physical impact of losing her baby would heal in time, she wondered if her soul ever would. It didn't seem possible to move forward. It felt like someone had stolen a piece of her.

Nik's hand rested on the small of her back as he guided her to the bed. Her lower body felt numb, but her legs pushed forward anyway. The mattress yielded to her weight as she sat on the edge.

"Do you need anything? I can make you something to eat or something to drink."

"I'm fine," she said softly. She was far from fine, but it wasn't anything food or water could fix.

Nik searched for clothes in their shared dresser so she could change into something more comfortable. When he turned to face her, his eyes were bloodshot. The sight of him made her eyes sting with tears once again.

They'd spent countless hours crying together in the medical chamber, taking turns comforting each other. Right now he was doing his best to keep it together for her sake, but she knew he was hurting just as much as she was.

He handed her a soft tank top and loose-fitting sweatpants, and she placed them beside her on the bed. "I think I'd like to take a quick shower first. Rinse off...everything."

The smell of the medical chamber still lingered on her, tainting her skin and haunting her when she closed her eyes. There was no amount of soap or scrubbing that would diminish the despair that clung to her, but that wouldn't stop her from trying.

It was strange how everything felt so unfamiliar. Like she was seeing it all with new eyes. This was her home, where she'd been living with Nik for months. That was her white tiled shower she'd used daily. On the sink lay her toothbrush and spare hair tie right where she'd left them.

And yet none of it felt the same. It was all *wrong*. There was no other way to describe it. This was someone else's life—a version of her that no longer existed.

Hot water rushed over her skin, and she rubbed her face. Her eyes were swollen, and she gently massaged them before squeezing soap onto her hands. She lathered it and scrubbed her scalp. She'd spent four days in the medical chamber, and her hair was oily and matted to the back of her head. After rinsing her hair, she repeated the steps, massaging her scalp a second time with the shampoo.

When she finished washing her limbs and torso, she stood under the water, letting it rain on her skin. She closed her eyes and tried to imagine she was somewhere else, some place happy, but every image she conjured, every wistful escape, was overrun by the prospect of what could've been.

A child danced through her imagination, but she couldn't make out the details—did the child have her brown eyes? Nik's dark brown hair? It was too fuzzy to tell. Her memory desperately tried to hold the image together, but it was an impossible feat when she'd never known their face.

Tears began to fall, and Ali dropped to her knees in the shower, sobbing into her palms. It felt as though someone had reached into her chest, pried her ribcage open, and yanked out her heart. She sucked in a sharp breath and pulled her knees to her chest, wrapping her arms around her legs. She dug her nails into her arms and relished the pain. The physical hurt was so much easier to bear than the emotional.

"Ali?" Nik's faint voice called from beyond the pattering shower. She could just make out his figure through the cloudy glass. He slid the door open and silently turned off the water.

She could see the pain etched in his face even if he didn't speak. Several lines ran vertically between his brows, and he seemed unable to look her in the eyes.

He disappeared for a moment and returned with a towel, wrapping it around her shoulders and pulling her up from the shower floor.

Love and compassion radiated through his body and engulfed her, which only made her tears fall more freely. With him, she felt safe enough to break down.

He ran his hand over her damp hair and held her body close. "Shh," he said, kissing the top of her head. "It's going to be okay. It's all going to be okay."

She didn't know how he could be so certain. How could he find hope when she no longer believed it existed? It was one thing she loved about him: his ability to move toward the light when all she wanted to do was dwell in the darkness. She wanted to let it swallow her, but Nik protected her from that endless abyss.

Slowly, her tears subsided, but she held onto Nik, not wanting to lose the comfort of his solid embrace. He swayed back and forth until both of their bodies relaxed.

"Come to bed with me?"

It was a plea, not a command. She was certain he'd do whatever she wanted at this moment. If she wanted to stand here all night, crying on his shoulder, then that was what he would do.

When she shifted on her feet, her legs wobbled and she recognized that rest was the better option. She was exhausted physically, mentally, and emotionally. If she didn't climb into bed, her body may very well collapse without her permission.

Nik followed as she headed toward the bed. She didn't even bother with the clothes he had laid out for her, dropping the towel on the floor before climbing into bed naked.

"I made dinner," Nik said. "Will you eat? I can bring it to you."

She wasn't hungry, but a small part of her knew she should eat something. She couldn't even recall the last meal she'd had. They'd served her a few things during her stay in the medical chamber, but she'd mostly picked at it. "Yes, thank you."

Ali sat up, pulling the blanket to her chest and tucking it under her armpits. She relaxed against the headboard and waited for Nik to bring a bowl of steaming hot pasta with a white sauce mixed with peas and carrots. It smelled and looked delicious, but her appetite was still nowhere to be found. She forced herself to take a few bites while Nik returned to the kitchen. When he came back a second time, he had his own bowl in hand along with a few slices of garlic buttered toast.

"Thanks," she said when he offered her one.

An unpleasant silence swept the room while they ate. Normally, Ali didn't mind sitting in the quiet with Nik, but tonight the air felt thick with the weight of tragedy.

"How are you doing?" she asked lamely, but it was the least she could do considering everything he'd done for her. She hardly had it in her to shower, let alone cook dinner.

He finished chewing a bite of bread and swallowed. "I'm—" She was pretty certain he was about to say 'fine' but thought better of it. "In shock? Disbelief? I'm angry that this happened to you...to us. And I'm sad, too. Since the day we found out you were expecting, I haven't stopped thinking about what our lives would look like. What our kid would look like. I was ready for it all, Ali. I wanted to teach them to throw a ball and swim in the lake. I wanted to teach them to read and how to fight. I wanted to see the person they grew up to be, their personality and which hobbies they chose. And I'm so damn heartbroken that they were stolen from us."

Ali's eyes glassed over, but she wiped her tears before they had a chance to fall. "I wanted that, too."

Nik leaned close and brushed her hair behind her ear, gently rubbing her cheek with his thumb. He closed the space between them and kissed her softly on the lips.

"I don't know if it's possible to survive this," Ali quietly confessed.

Nik winced in pain. "You will. *We* will."

The next morning, Ali woke to Nik's lips against her temple. Her eyes fluttered open to find him sitting on her side of the bed, one hand on her hip. He was fully dressed in dark blue jeans and a gray short-sleeved shirt, showing off his biceps and tan skin. His hair was still wet, like he'd just gotten out of the shower.

"Hey," he said quietly.

"Where are you going?" she mumbled, still half asleep.

"I need to take care of a few things, and I have to meet with Grace."

"You don't have to work, do you?" They had only come home yesterday. Surely Grace wouldn't expect him back to work so soon. Ali had been given another week off. Grace would've offered more, but Ali had insisted that returning to work would help bring back some normalcy to her life.

Nik shook his head. "No, she has someone filling in for me. I'm meeting him as well for an orientation."

"Oh," she said softly.

Nik frowned and looked away, and Ali knew he was reconsidering going out.

"It's okay," she told him. "I'll be fine on my own for a little bit. You'll be back soon?"

"It won't take long at all. And you won't be alone."

Ali tilted her head. Before she could question him, Eli stepped into view. The sight of him brought a smile to her face, and even Nik grinned.

With a quick hug and a peck on her cheek, Nik stood and headed toward the door. On the way out, he slapped Eli's shoulder, muttering, "Take care of her."

Eli nodded. When the door shut, he approached the bed.

"Wait," Ali said suddenly.

Eli halted and looked slightly confused.

"Turn around," she said.

"Okay…" He turned to face the opposite direction and put his hands in his pockets, rocking back and forth on his feet. "Is there a reason I'm doing this?"

Ali scrambled out from under the blanket and found the clothes Nik had laid out the night before. As quick as she could, she pulled the top over her head and slid the sweatpants on. "Okay, you can turn around now."

If Eli realized what she had done, he didn't comment. Instead, he sat on the edge of the bed and Ali sat next to him. He squinted his eyes at her like he was trying to discern how close she was to falling apart.

Very close.

"So," she said.

"So…" he repeated.

When it became clear that neither of them knew what to say, Eli leaned forward and pulled Ali into a hug. "I'm so sorry, Ali."

Her words lodged in her throat, and she choked back a sob. If she opened the floodgates now, there'd be no stopping it. "Thank you," she said in barely more than a whisper.

"What can I do to help?" He pulled back but held onto her shoulders, keeping her steady and upright.

"I don't think there's anything you can do," she admitted. "Nothing could ever make this right. Nothing will bring back my baby." A single tear escaped, but she quickly wiped it away.

Eli frowned. "It's okay to cry, Ali. I can't imagine what you're going through right now. Let it all out and don't be afraid to lean on your friends and family. You can lean on me. You know that, right?"

"I know," she said, brushing away another tear with her thumb. It was more than that, though. She was terrified if she let herself crumble that she wouldn't be able to put the pieces back together. If she tiptoed into the darkness, would she ever make it back to the light?

She could see it in Nik's eyes every time he looked at her. He was terrified of losing her, not just physically but mentally. And she couldn't even tell him not to worry because she knew at any given moment, she was one dark thought away from slipping into a depressive episode.

The love of her friends and family strengthened her, but she wasn't sure how much longer she could stave off the inevitable. She was just waiting for the moment when her emotions crashed into her, knocking her over and pulling her under the surface.

For now, she'd live in the reality where she was surrounded by love. She looked at Eli with his boyish grin and the bright, familiar light twinkling in his eyes.

"Thank you," she said. "For being here."

"Always," he replied.

Chapter Twenty-Five

NIK

Sleeping had never been so hard for Nik. He couldn't recall a single time where his mind and body had betrayed him so deeply. Every night for a week, he tossed and turned, pleading with his thoughts to cease, until exhaustion finally took over. But it never lasted.

His eyes flew open. He stared at the ceiling in the darkness, taking a moment to orient himself. His head throbbed and his eyes felt swollen and bloodshot. He couldn't have gotten more than two hours of sleep.

A muffled cry came from beside him, and he turned his head toward Ali. It was too dark to see, but he could sense her body next to him. Feel her warmth against his side. She sobbed again, and the mattress shifted slightly under her weight.

She didn't know he was awake.

It had been a week since they'd come home from the medical chamber and after that first day, she'd refused to let him see her cry. It was as though she had something to prove, determined to remain strong even though it was clearly killing them both.

But now, in the dead of the night, she let down her guard and cried into her pillow. The ever-present lump in Nik's throat grew larger.

The sound of her heartbreak absolutely gutted him.

He clenched his jaw and turned onto his side, moving his arm across the bed to find Ali's torso. She jolted when he grabbed her waist and pulled her closer to him. Her back melted into his chest and he nuzzled the nape of her neck.

She sniffled. "I'm sorry. I didn't mean to wake you."

"Don't apologize," he whispered against her skin. "I'm here."

Her body shuddered as she stifled another wave of tears. Nik tightened his grip, keeping her tucked safely against him. Slowly, her crying ceased and the rhythm of her breathing told Nik she'd fallen back asleep. He closed his eyes, hoping he could join her...until the next time she woke up sobbing.

Morning came far too early. The dim light of the lamp on the wall illuminated the bedroom in a warm glow and Nik peeled his eyes open. He was certain the bags under his eyes had doubled in size overnight. Ali slept peacefully under the weight of his arm, her head tucked just below his chin.

No part of him wanted to wake her, but today was supposed to be his first day back at work. As gently as he could, he slid his arm out and rolled toward the other side of the bed. He kept his movements slow and quiet and when he rose to his feet, Ali's breathing remained steady.

After a quick shower and a stale bagel, Nik kissed Ali goodbye on her forehead. She stirred, but her eyes stayed closed. Honestly, Nik was glad. As much as he wanted to properly say goodbye and tell her he loved her, it was better that she rested. At least one of them should.

He hurried to meet Grace at her home. More often than not, she stayed with Eli these days. He'd check both locations since they hadn't had a chance to catch up recently.

He'd no sooner reached the entry chamber when he spotted Grace walking through the door to the cafeteria. Problem solved.

Inside the cafeteria, people chattered in a low hum, most of them still half asleep but determined to grab a bite to eat before their workday started. Searching the small crowd, Nik found Grace had taken a seat next to Eli at a table on the far left.

As he approached, Grace looked up and waved him over.

"I didn't expect to see you here," she said as Nik took a seat next to Eli.

"Today was supposed to be my first day back, wasn't it?"

"Well, yes, but I figured you could use more time off. I've already asked Soren to meet me here this morning."

Soren, Nik's replacement while he'd been off work, was a young boy, barely eighteen, but eager to earn some spending money. He was a kind kid but tall and muscular, which intimidated those who didn't know him. At first glance, he looked like he could rip a person apart with his bare hands, but within five minutes of meeting him Nik could tell he was nothing but a teddy bear. He had a good heart, and Grace trusted him.

"Oh. I guess I'll just go back home then." Nik began to rise from his seat, wishing he had something else to do to keep his mind off of things. He was happy to keep Ali company and take care of her, but during the moments of silence, the loss hit him like lightning, sending bolts of pain and shock through his body. He'd been looking forward to the distraction that work would provide.

Grace must've picked up on his disappointment because she said, "Eli could use a training partner. Isn't that right?"

Beside him, Nik could've sworn he caught Eli rolling his eyes. "Yeah, sure. I've missed having someone talk shit and belittle me."

Grace's eyes narrowed, but Nik huffed a laugh. "You can count me in then."

"You should get something to eat. Wouldn't want you to get all weak on me," Eli said.

It was Nik's turn to roll his eyes, but Eli was right. So Nik filled a plate with eggs, sausage, and breakfast potatoes.

As he ate, he asked Grace, "Have you discovered anything about who poisoned Ali?" He didn't add, 'and murdered my child,' though he wanted to. It brought a mix of unbearable anger and sorrow that he wasn't ready to confront.

Grace sighed and shook her head. "Not yet. Unfortunately, we don't have much to go off other than the envelope and the fact that it had to be either a council member or someone who had access to a council member's key. No one else should've been able to enter the room. We can't even be certain who the poison was meant for since the envelope wasn't addressed to anyone. I'm pretty confident it was either for myself or my mother though."

"It had to be Eamon," Eli said.

Nik ground his teeth and nodded in agreement.

"That's a good probability," Grace said, her voice calm, "but we can't do anything without proof."

Nik scowled. "So whoever did this is going to get away with it?"

Grace's eyes were full of sympathy. "We're doing everything we can."

Nik knew that, and it still wasn't enough. He wanted to snap someone's neck in half. Wanted to gut them and watch them bleed. Make them feel the pain that he did. Leave them to die alone like they'd left Ali.

Grace apologized again, but Nik remained lost in thought for the remainder of breakfast. When Soren arrived and Grace left with him to meet the council, Eli said in a hushed tone, "We'll make them pay."

Nik turned to him, spotting a bitter determination that matched his own, and he gave Eli a small nod.

Yes, they would.

***

Nik couldn't recall the last time he'd pushed himself this hard during a run. He didn't bother glancing behind him but could tell by the silence that he'd left Eli in his dust. Each inhale pumped his legs harder, and each exhale solidified his unyielding drive.

Sweat dripped down his forehead, and he wiped it with the back of his hand. He saw the finish line nearing and increased his pace more than what should've been humanly possible. As he bolted between two tall evergreen trees that marked the end of his run, his body stumbled forward and he collapsed on the ground, panting and clutching his chest. His heart felt like it was trying to escape his ribcage.

After a few minutes, the sound of footsteps came from the woods and then Eli ran between the same two trees, slowing to a halt next to Nik. He bent over and put his hands on his knees, breathing heavily. He glanced at Nik and it was obvious he wanted to say something, but he seemed to think better of it.

Please do, Nik thought. *Please give me a reason to bust your lip.*

Fighting with someone was just what he needed right now.

Eli straightened and used his shirt to wipe the sweat from his face. Then he held a hand out to Nik...the opposite of what Nik had been hoping for. Nik sighed and gripped Eli's hand, allowing him to pull Nik to his feet.

"The third round is a race down the mountain and then back up again," Eli explained, still catching his breath. "Not much to train for this time, aside from stamina. I figured I'd just repeat the process over and over again until my legs collapse."

"Sounds perfect," Nik said, thrilled at the prospect of endless physical activity that would leave him no time or energy to remember what he'd lost. Maybe he'd even get some decent sleep afterwards.

Eli led him to the designated starting point of the third round. It was a little over a week away, but crews were present, setting up the makeshift stands for spectators.

"The starting point at the top and flag location at the bottom are set in stone, but the path between is up to each suitor. Meaning we can navigate and determine the best route during practice."

At the same moment Eli finished explaining, a man climbed up a steep part of the mountain and rose to his feet. The dark-haired, fair skinned man with a wiry beard took one step before his eyes met Nik's and he broke into a sinister grin.

Trevor.

Nik's feet were moving before his thoughts could catch up. This man was responsible for the loss of their child. Well, his father was, but Trevor was just as guilty by association. If Nik couldn't get his hands on Eamon, then Trevor would do.

The rebels had almost killed Ali too. It didn't matter who the poison was intended for—Ellen, Grace, another council member...Ali had paid the price. Fury coursed through his veins like nothing he'd felt before.

Trevor must've seen in it his eyes because he took a step back as Nik approached. His hands went up in surrender. "Whoa there, buddy. What's got you so bothered?"

Nik's fist connected with Trevor's jaw with a vicious crack. Trevor stumbled back a step. Before he could regain his footing, Nik hit him again. Then he grabbed him by the neck and pulled him forward, ramming his knee into Trevor's stomach.

Trevor shouted unintelligibly, but Nik tuned him out. He continued to unleash his anger, beating and striking any way he could. His muscles ached, but he tuned that out too, concentrating on the sound of his fists and legs connecting with Trevor's body instead.

It was a beautiful sound.

Trevor finally managed to break free from Nik's furious onslaught, but Nik darted forward and tackled him to the ground. He was vaguely aware of Eli on the sidelines, watching but not interrupting. He probably knew how useless it would be.

If Trevor fought back, Nik didn't notice. He felt nothing except the wrath of a madman. He would've happily beaten Trevor into a bloody pile of flesh, but two pairs of hands gripped his arms and pulled him to his feet.

Trevor leapt to his feet, but Eli stepped in front of him before he could retaliate, protecting Nik.

Nik growled and turned to spit, blood and saliva landing on the ground. He tried to yank his arms free, but more hands held him back. Finally pulling his eyes away from Trevor, he realized several members of the setup crew had seen his attack and intervened.

He breathed heavily but stopped resisting. If it had been one or two, he could've taken them, but he'd drawn a crowd of five extra bodies and couldn't take them on his own.

"You can let go now," he grumbled.

The two men on either side of him exchanged a look and hesitated, clearly afraid he'd lunge at Trevor again if they released him. Nik tried his best to relax his muscles and prove he wouldn't cause any more harm.

Meanwhile, Eli was arguing with Trevor, yelling at him to calm down while Trevor shouted useless threats. Nik's nostrils flared, which unfortunately made the two men tighten their grip on his arms. He rolled his eyes and muttered under his breath, "Damn it."

He was forced to watch as Eli tried to reason with Trevor, a hopeless task. "Think about what you're doing. Nik is Grace's guard."

"Grace isn't here," Trevor spat.

"You're right. She isn't. But if she finds out you harmed him, there will be consequences. Perhaps she'll see fit for you to be disqualified from the Rite."

Trevor's gaze whipped from Nik to Eli. "She can't do that."

"Is that a risk you're willing to take?" Eli asked.

Trevor snarled and pushed his shoulders back. He glared at Nik but stopped trying to get around Eli. "You just wait. When Grace is *my* wife, I'll have you whipped and thrown to the wolves."

Nik couldn't see Eli's face, but his posture said it all. He was holding back his own rage toward Trevor. Calling Grace his wife sent chills down both of their spines. Grace might've been annoyingly positive, but she was a good person and didn't deserve to be shackled to a man like Trevor. And despite everything they'd been through, somehow Nik found himself rooting for Eli's happiness.

Eli took a few steps back until he was in line with Nik and turned to the two men restraining him. "You can let go now."

They exchanged hesitant glances again but ultimately loosened their grips. Nik shook out his arms and rubbed the irritated skin where their hands had been, red from where he'd resisted.

"Let's go," Eli said, turning his back to Trevor and the two crew members. He had more faith in them than Nik. As Nik walked backwards, he kept his eyes locked on Trevor. And when Trevor winked at him, Nik nearly lost his temper again. Beside him, Eli kept a cool head and urged Nik forward. "He'll pay for it, Nik. Not now...but soon."

When Nik returned home, he expected Ali to be awake, maybe reading or working on one of her sewing projects. Anything to prove that she wasn't spiraling into the depths of despair.

Instead, he found her curled up under a blanket in bed, sleeping on her side with something twisted in her hands. As he stepped closer, he reached for the tiny green fabric she held, gently pulling it out to find a onesie with a pattern of little yellow stars.

He wasn't prepared for the impact, and his shoulders shook as he gasped for breath. Tears welled in his eyes, clouding his vision. He couldn't remember the last time he cried, but he also couldn't remember the last time he'd felt this level of pain. The inconsolable kind that couldn't be shoved aside.

He pinched the bridge of his nose and took deep breaths. Then a hand grazed his thigh and Ali's voice reached his ears. "Nik?"

"I'm okay," he said, half speaking to her and half convincing himself. "I'm okay."

"You're not. I'm not either. But we will be."

Nik dropped his hand and met Ali's gaze, the love and affection in her eyes mending some of the scars on his heart. Maybe on his own he wouldn't be able to get through this, but with her, he could.

"Come to bed," she said, pulling him closer.

He did as she requested, removing his dirty and sweaty clothes and sliding under the covers with her. He moved in close until their faces were only an inch apart, and she smiled half-heartedly, tangling her legs with his. She brought her hand up to rest on his chest and he covered it with his own, squeezing her fingers.

Her eyes were misty, but she found the strength to reassure him anyway. "We're going to be okay."

Chapter Twenty-Six

ALI

Nik looked so peaceful sleeping with one arm tucked around Ali's waist; she hated the idea of waking him. It was rare that either of them found solace in their dreams and she couldn't bring herself to pull him from his. Not when reality felt like a nightmare.

She carefully lifted his arm and scooted to the edge of the bed, placing her feet on the cool stone floor. She'd left her slippers nearby, and she slid her feet into them before heading to the bathroom.

Today marked two weeks since she'd lost her baby. Not that she was counting. She was just painstakingly aware of every minute that passed without the little life growing inside her. She subconsciously held her stomach while she showered and cleaned up.

Every morning was different than the last, and she never quite knew what to expect. Some days grief rendered her immobile, and others she felt a bit numb. Nik's mood was equally varied, though he rarely let his pain show. They were each pretending to be stronger than they were for the benefit of the other.

Ali kept waiting for the day when she'd feel something different, and today she may have encountered it.

Today, she felt resilient.

It was a far cry from cheerful or optimistic, but it was something—a miniscule amount of hope that there would be brighter days ahead and she could push through to find them.

When she finished detangling her hair, she stepped out of the bathroom to find Nik still lying in bed, his eyes half open.

"Morning, gorgeous," he said huskily.

"Good morning," she responded, edging closer to him. She brushed a hand against his cheek, and he leaned into it. "Care for some breakfast?"

Nik raised a brow. "Are you offering me breakfast in bed?"

Normally it was the other way around, Nik pushing down his own hurt so he could take care of her. She wanted to do something special for him while she had the energy.

"Yes. What would you like?"

He chose eggs and bacon, and Ali went to work in the kitchen. Before the pan started to sizzle, Nik was out of bed and jumping in the shower.

"The whole point of breakfast in bed is that you get to stay in bed," she shouted over the noise of running water. He shouted something back, but she couldn't make out the words.

By the time he finished, the eggs and bacon were both done and she scraped them onto two plates. After tossing on a pair of shorts, Nik climbed back into bed and waited for Ali to join him.

"Thank you," he said when she handed him his food.

"You're welcome."

"What's the occasion?"

Ali shrugged, not sure she could explain what she was feeling. "You've been taking such good care of me. I wanted to return the favor."

He nodded like that made all the sense in the world, then brought a bite of eggs to his mouth and moaned in satisfaction.

Ali rolled her eyes. "It's just eggs."

"Eggs made with love."

She paused, her fork halfway to her mouth. "That was one of the cheesiest things I've ever heard you say."

Nik chuckled. "You're right. They're still good though. Thank you again." He leaned across the bed to kiss her cheek, and the warmth of his lips lingered on her skin.

"I had something else in mind for today, too."

Nik didn't look up from his plate. "What's that?"

"I thought we could go for a hike." Her medic had advised against strenuous activity, but the walk through the woods she had in mind hardly classified as demanding. "I could use the fresh air, and there's somewhere I want to take you."

That got his attention. "Should I be concerned?"

She smiled, the first genuine one in two weeks. "No."

A half hour later, they were both dressed and heading out of the mountain. Ali had the strange feeling that people were staring at her as she led Nik to one of the trail paths, but she had to be imagining it. It was her own discomfort in her skin that had her on edge. From what she'd been told, the poisoning had been kept under wraps so as not to alarm the population of Berland. These people had no idea what had happened to her or why she hadn't come out of their studio home in weeks. They probably hadn't even noticed.

The trail Ali sought was hidden among overgrown bushes and weeds. If she hadn't hiked it so often, she wouldn't have known it was there. She pushed aside a branch and motioned for Nik to step forward. He eyed her suspiciously but did so.

After the initial portion of the trailhead, the path became more defined. Hidden under the canopy of trees and blocked from the sunlight, the vegetation hadn't had a chance to overtake the path.

"It's this way," Ali said, recognizing some landmarks, like the boulder twice the size of her that had been there long enough to be covered in moss. Or the giant tree that had been split down the center from a lightning storm a few months ago.

Nik followed closely behind, keeping his thoughts to himself. Ali had taken this path so many times on her own, and there were a few times she forgot that he was even with her until she heard the crunch of leaves or a twig splitting in half.

"Almost there," she said, and then she rounded a corner and the trail sloped upward. The last bit of the hike was the most strenuous, and her thighs burned, but she pushed forward. Then she found herself face to face with a tangled couple of trees.

Eli had dubbed it the 'Twisted Tree' and it was where he had constructed memorials for their deceased parents. She smiled at the pile of rocks commemorating her mother and placed a hand over her heart.

Hi, Mom.

Nik came to stand beside her, his eyes glued to the matching rock formations. "What is this place, Ali?"

Until now, it had only been a place for Eli and Ali. But it felt right to bring Nik here after what they'd been through. She bent down and collected a handful of rocks in various shapes and sizes, ensuring they were flat and would stack well.

"This is the Twisted Tree," she said. "That monument right there is for my mom and that one over there is for Eli's dad."

She began to stack the stones neatly next to her mother's until it rose a few inches off the ground. Then she kneeled in front of it and folded her hands in her lap. "And this is for our baby."

Nik came to kneel beside her, and she could feel him looking at her out of the corner of her eye.

"Do you think it's silly?" she asked quietly.

"Does it make you feel better?"

"I don't know," she answered truthfully. "But it might in the future."

One day, when the wounds weren't so fresh. Remembering the life that should've been hurt like hell right now, but one day she hoped she could come to this spot and find comfort.

"Then I don't think it's silly," Nik said.

They sat in silence for a while, and Ali searched for a sign. Some indication that her child was still here with them, even in spirit. The only sound was the chirping of birds chasing one another through the trees.

"What are you thinking about?" Ali asked when the silence became too much to bear.

"I was wondering where I'd be if I'd never met you."

The way he said it made her wonder if that was a bad thing. Their relationship hadn't been easy by any means, but she'd never trade this life for any other. Hopefully he felt the same.

"That sounds ominous."

Nik smirked and nudged her with his elbow. "I'm certain I would've been miserable without you. Every day with you is a day my life has more meaning, more love, more joy. You're the best thing that's ever happened to me."

Tears of joy, not sorrow, fell down Ali's cheeks, and Nik was quick to wipe them away with the pad of his thumb. "I'm sorry. I didn't mean to make you cry."

Ali wrapped her arms around Nik's neck, gently pressing her lips to his and catching him off guard. His taste mingled with salty tears and she kissed him even harder. When his initial surprise wore off, he kissed her back, inhaling deeply through his nose as he pulled her into his lap.

When they finally broke apart, Ali rested her forehead against Nik's. "I love you."

Ali told Nik stories of her mother and Eli's father, what her life had been like in Andus, and every childhood memory she could think of. Eventually, storm clouds rolled in and brought a chill wind to their mountain side memorial.

"Are you ready to head back?" Nik asked with his head tilted toward the sky. It was dark and looked as though rain might begin to fall at any moment.

"I suppose," Ali said, lifting her head from Nik's shoulder. Her heart ached to remain in this place where she felt hope and the promise of a brighter future. Going back to the mountain would bring back the loss and dread, but they'd be soaked to the bone if they didn't move soon.

Before they were halfway home, droplets of water began to sprinkle down on them, creating a peaceful hum as the drops hit the leaves overhead. They held hands as they walked down the path, neither of them in a hurry to get back. As long as the rain stayed light, they wouldn't be bothered.

Just as the central strip of town appeared in sight, a chorus of laughter erupted in a field to their right. Ali searched for the source of the noise and saw two young girls slipping and sliding in the mud.

Beside her, Nik laughed. "Glad to see the rain isn't stopping them from having fun."

Together they approached the girls, watching as they took turns running toward a muddy puddle and sliding through on their bums. Each time, they squealed with delight.

Nik's voice rose over the sound of the girls' laughter. "Shouldn't you two be somewhere else?"

They abruptly ceased all movement, and Julia turned to face Ali and Nik. "No," she lied easily. Her companion, Kaydence, stared at the ground with her hands behind her back.

There was no way their caretaker, Ms. Carpenter, would be okay with them playing alone in the middle of a field without supervision.

Nik tilted his head like he was thinking the same thing. "Do you know what happens to liars?" he asked, taking a step forward with his chin raised high.

Julia shook her head, and Kaydence looked nervously between Julia and Nik.

"They get chased by the swamp monster," he said so seriously that Ali had to hide her amusement. Nik took another slow step forward, and Julia giggled while Kaydence's mouth curved into a tentative smile.

"There's no such thing as a swamp monster," Julia stated confidently. "Monsters don't exist."

If only that were true. Unfortunately, the worst monsters were all too human.

"Hmm," Nik said, squinting his eyes and pointing over Julia's shoulder. "Then what's that?"

Both girls turned to see what he was pointing at and Nik pounced, scooping them both up around the waist. The girls laughed and hollered for him to put them down. Kaydence even swatted at his back and yelled, "Bad swamp monster!"

Ali laughed so hard her side ached, watching as Nik stomped around with the girls tucked under his arms, splashing mud everywhere. He dropped to his knees and gently lowered each of the girls into a puddle while they screamed and kicked their feet. Despite their pleas for him to stop, they were having just as much fun as he was.

When they finally broke free from his hold, they splashed water back at him and he guarded his face. He mockingly called for Ali. "Help! I'm under attack!"

Ali shook her head. "You got yourself into this one. You're on your own."

He looked back at her with shock and feigned betrayal. "You'd leave me to fend for myself?"

"Afraid so."

Nik pointed a finger at her and grinned. It was difficult not to smile in return at the devilish threat in his eyes. Like he was about to spring forward and wrap her up in his arms, too. It gave her chills.

But in his moment of distraction, Julia climbed on his back while Kaydence cupped water with her hands and dumped it over his head. He sputtered while the girls roared with the sound of victory.

Their laughter was contagious and healing. It made Ali feel alive again and reminded her the world was still full of joy amidst the heartache. While Nik and the girls carried on with their muddy mayhem, Ali found herself hopeful for what the future might bring.

Chapter Twenty-Seven

NIK

"THANKS AGAIN FOR RETURNING to duty today," Grace said to Nik as they walked through the center of town. She hadn't told him where they were going and he hadn't asked. Wherever she wanted to go was fine by him. He was just happy to have something to take his mind off of things.

Each day was a foggy haze and Nik was convinced the only way to clear the air was by returning to his routine. Those moments when he had nothing to keep him busy were the hardest to cope with. His only concern was leaving Ali alone, but she had mentioned grabbing dinner with Eli. It was a good sign that she was getting out of the house more often.

The sun was slowly sinking behind the peak of the tallest mountain, casting a warm glow over the shops lining the street. Some of the merchants were bringing in their goods and locking up for the evening while others finished up their last transactions. The only businesses to remain open this late on a weekday were the dining halls and taverns.

"Here we are," Grace said, turning onto a stone patio that led to the quietest tavern on the street. In fact, it was so quiet, Nik wondered if they had already closed for the evening too.

"Are you sure this is the right place?" He looked around at some of the more lively establishments, figuring Grace must be meeting someone at one of those places. Not this building with dark windows and a closed door. He couldn't even hear music on the other side.

But Grace pressed on, reaching for the handle and opening the door to a dark room. Nik rushed forward and pushed in front of her. Something about this didn't feel right. "I'll go first."

Grace didn't object but gestured toward the entrance. "After you."

As he took a few steps forward and waited for his eyes to adjust to the darkness, he asked, "What are we doing here? Are you meeting someone?"

A council member? Friends? What if Eamon or one of his followers had set her up? There were a hundred reasons to be suspicious, and Nik's senses were telling him to turn around and head straight back to the mountain.

Before Grace could answer, a dozen lanterns flickered on and a sea of bodies popped up from behind long wooden tables.

"Happy birthday!" they roared in unison.

Nik tensed, but once the initial shock wore off, he realized he was staring at Ali and their friends, who had somehow managed to throw him a surprise party. He stared at Ali, and she beamed back at him. She and Sam were the only ones who knew when his birthday was, but he'd assumed she'd forgotten with everything that was going on. He should've known she'd never forget him.

He shook his head and crossed the room to hug her. "I can't believe you didn't say anything."

"Then it wouldn't have been a surprise." She stood on her tiptoes and kissed his cheek, then his lips, pulling away much too quickly for his liking.

Before he could taste her lips again, Sam laid a heavy hand on his shoulder and drew his attention away.

"Happy birthday, man. Another year older and still none the wiser."

"Ha-ha," Nik replied. "Thank you for this."

"That's what friends are for."

Strange how just a year ago, Nik wasn't sure he had any friends at all. Sam had always been the closest thing to it, but life after Rysburg had only brought them closer. Behind Sam, Nik caught sight of Grace and Eli eyeing each other with a disgusting amount of lust. Across from them, Amaya and Heather were deep in conversation while Theo stared off in boredom.

These people had only known him for a handful of months, yet they had shown up for him. It was a feeling he wasn't used to, and he didn't know how to express his gratitude.

Despite his happiness, a small voice inside yelled at him to run. To protect himself because people he loved could become people he lost. His throat felt scratchy, and he rolled his head to the side, cracking his neck—a nervous tic.

Beside him, Sam seemed to sense it. "It's about time you realized your worth, Nik. Gone are the days when you get to push people away. You're stuck with us whether you like it or not."

Unable to speak, Nik merely nodded. He'd been alone for so long, but he was certain this reality was better than the past. Having people to celebrate and support him—especially when he and Ali had just suffered such a tremendous loss—was priceless.

He sought Ali again and found her carrying a two layered cake with a mix of berries decorating the top and circling the bottom. A single candle was lit on top of the cake, and it flickered restlessly when Ali placed the cake on the table. She began to sing and everyone else jumped in, wishing Nik a happy birthday.

"Make a wish," Ali said.

As he stared at his beautiful girlfriend and the friends who'd gathered to celebrate him, there wasn't much he could think of to wish for. There was only one tiny thing missing in their lives, and wishing wouldn't bring it back.

He thought for a few more seconds and then blew out the candle on top of the cake.

Everyone clapped and Sam popped in with a knife, cutting slices and placing them on small plates. He passed them out one by one and once the cake was all divvied up, they all took a seat at the table in the center of the tavern.

"Did you kick everyone else out?" Nik asked, looking around the empty tavern and registering that they were the only ones present. Not even a bartender behind the counter or a cook watching through the kitchen window.

"The owner is a family friend," Grace said. "It wasn't hard to convince him to let us rent out the place for the evening."

Nik took a bite of cake. It was rich with chocolate and a layer of fruit jam in the center. "Mm, that's delicious. Did you make this?"

Ali smiled. "I did, with some help. Do you like it? I wasn't sure how the angelfruit would taste with chocolate, but it was the easiest fruit to find."

Nik took another bite, this time ensuring he got a sufficient amount of fruit on his fork. "It's fucking amazing. Thank you, Ali."

After kissing her temple, he brushed her hair behind her ear. The cake was amazing, but the idea of her baking and socializing all day rather than staying home and drowning in sorrow was even more satisfying.

"So what did you wish for?" she asked before taking a bite. She'd always been a sucker for sweets and wasn't afraid to let it show. The sensual sound that came from her mouth made Nik's heart swell and something in his lower stomach flip, a sensation he hadn't felt in weeks.

He cleared his throat. "If I tell you then it won't come true."

She eyed him with disapproval. Like she didn't believe that in the slightest.

Once everyone had finished their cake, Theo and Heather cleared the dishes while Amaya and Grace retrieved glasses, wine, and a caramel-colored liquid in an unlabeled bottle.

"Who wants a birthday shot?" Grace asked with an obnoxious smile on her face.

"What is it?" Ali asked.

Grace shrugged. "House special."

Translation—*no one knows.*

In the end, everyone agreed to take a shot of the mystery liquor, and Grace poured a finger into each glass before passing them out.

"To Nik!" they all shouted—even Eli—and Nik huffed a laugh before downing his drink. It burned his throat and chest on the way down, but the smoky flavor was overall enjoyable. Much better than that fruity shit Ali and Eli preferred.

Ali shuddered next to him after only drinking half of hers, so Nik took the glass and drank the rest.

"Thank you," she mouthed.

"Another!" Theo exclaimed to a round of laughter.

While Theo poured another glass of liquor or wine for each member of their party, Ali scooted closer to Nik and wrapped an arm around his waist. He leaned into her, taking a moment to just stare into her eyes. So bright and full of love and light. Could she see that love reflected in his? Did she knew how much he loved her?

She beamed at him, and he was certain that she did.

"I got you something," she said.

Nik looked around at the room and back to Ali. "This was already more than enough, Ali."

"You deserve all of this and more. But I think you'll like what I got you."

"Is that so?"

A sly grin stretched across her lips and Nik could practically see the naughty thoughts scrolling through her mind. He couldn't decide if it was a good thing or a bad thing. They'd never been able to keep their hands off each other, but Ali also had a habit of masking her pain with sex, and he didn't want to enable her. They'd have to take it slowly until he was certain she wasn't using sex as a crutch.

"Can I get a hint?" he asked.

She leaned closer until her lips softly grazed the shell of his ear. "It's black and lacy."

He groaned and fought the desire to pull her out of the tavern and take her home immediately. Taking it slow would be easier said than done.

His throat bobbed with the effort to swallow and when Ali dragged a hand up his thigh, he gritted his teeth. "You have no idea what you do to me."

"I have *some* idea." Ali smirked and sat straight in her seat, taking joy in the suffering she inflicted. It made him love her even more.

"Clear the table," Amaya said, waving at those who were still seated and the glasses in front of them. "It's time for a game."

While Amaya and Theo pushed everyone into a line, Grace explained the rules of the game. It seemed simple enough. They took turns bouncing a coin into a glass. If they missed, they had to drink. If the coin landed in the glass, they got to choose someone else to take a drink.

Nik missed his first two shots, but on his third turn, he sank the coin into the glass with a clank. He looked around as he weighed his options. So far, Eli and Theo had both given him a drink. Ali had threatened to, but she'd missed all her shots and he felt pretty safe from her words of warning.

"Eli," he said, pointing his finger at his foe-turned-almost-friend.

Eli raised his glass and took a large swig of alcohol, swallowing with a wince.

As the game carried on, it became clear that everyone was hoping to get the birthday boy drunk. Half of the shots made resulted in another drink for Nik and he struggled to make his own shots after a few more rounds.

"You're trying to kill me, aren't you?" he slurred.

Next to him, Ali kept an arm around his waist, and he couldn't tell if the room was swaying or if she was. But she hadn't drunk nearly as much as he had, so it seemed like maybe she was trying to keep him upright. Except she was a good foot shorter than him and far less sturdy. He stumbled a few steps, and they both collided with a bench.

"Oops," he said, falling to his bottom and pulling Ali into his lap.

She grinned and pushed the hair back from his forehead. "It's quite amusing seeing you like this."

"Like what?"

"Usually I am the one who's had too much to drink. How can I give you your gift if you're too inebriated to enjoy it?"

"I'm never too drunk to enjoy you."

Ali's cheeks reddened, and she pushed his shoulder. Her playful touch only increased his desire for her. He leaned over and bit her neck gently.

"Nik!"

"You can't tell me you don't like it. I know you do."

Ali was the type who liked a little pain with her pleasure. Images of her bent over their bed with reddened handprints on her ass flashed across his mind. In fact, that would be the first thing he did when they got home.

Wait...*slowly*. They were taking things *slowly*.

"Hey, it's your turn," Theo yelled.

Standing affectionately close to him, Sam's arm disappeared and Nik had the impression that Sam's hand was tucked into Theo's back pocket. Nik squinted to make sure he was seeing correctly.

Sam knocked his hip against Theo's and said, "Leave them alone. It's his birthday. They can do whatever they want."

"Yeah, I don't think Nik needs another turn. We might actually kill him," Eli said, and Nik couldn't help but notice his dry tone. In another life, Eli might've wanted him dead. Now Nik knew it was just his terrible sense of humor.

"I think we should head home," Ali said, standing from her seat on Nik's lap. He missed her presence immediately and tried to pull her back to him, but a knock on the door distracted him.

Before anyone could reach the door, it swung open and a man with a plump belly and a gray beard rushed inside. His wide eyes and haunted expression were enough to sober anyone, and Nik immediately felt a sense of clarity and heightened awareness.

This man was not bringing good news.

"Miss Grace, you are needed back at the mountain. The trees...the fires are everywhere...it's...I've never seen anything like it."

Was it alcohol, or was the man in shock to the point of incoherence?

Grace's demeanor shifted from youthful friend to stoic governess in a matter of seconds. Eli put a hand against the small of her back while Heather began to collect glasses, cleaning the space with urgency.

"Go," she said. "I'll take care of all this."

"Thank you," Grace said. Then she and Eli headed out the door after the elderly man. Nik jumped to his feet and rushed after them. He heard Ali's hurried steps behind him, followed by another clamor he assumed belonged to Sam and Theo.

"Wait," he called after Grace. "I'm your guard."

She glanced back at him. "Enjoy your night off, Nik. I can handle this one without you."

Eli nodded from beside her, and Nik had to admit she was in better hands with Eli than him right now. Still, he couldn't let them go on their own into unknown danger.

While Grace, Eli, Theo, and Sam sprinted toward the mountain, Ali stayed beside Nik and walked at a brisk pace with the elderly man.

"What happened?" Ali asked.

"I...I'm still not certain. All I know is there's a fire blazing on top of the mountain."

"A wildfire?" Nik guessed.

The man shook his head. "That's not what people are saying. I wasn't there when it happened, but others saw it."

"Saw what?"

"An explosion. It was intentional."

Chapter Twenty-Eight

ALI

THE FIRE ON TOP of the mountain was visible the moment they stepped out of the tavern. Grace ran for the base of the mountain, finding her mother and a few other council members huddled together and talking in hushed, worried tones.

She squeezed into their circle and waited for her mother to acknowledge her.

"Mason, if you could work with the medics to ensure no one has been injured. I know they said no one was near, but I want to be absolutely positive. Clayton, what did you hear from the fire chief?"

"Yes, Lady Ellen. He said they've contained the fire so it shouldn't spread, but they're still working on putting out the remaining blaze."

"Good. Good," she murmured. "And Maggie, what is the damage?"

"It's still being assessed. Most is limited to the forest, but there are at least a few solar panels that are beyond repair."

Grace's mother massaged her temples before taking a deep breath. "Okay, keep me updated. Everyone else can just make sure the residents are taken care of. Answer their questions as best as you can without instilling fear. If anyone is without power, tell them to head to the cafeteria where Diane is managing resources."

After her last remark, the council members split off and headed in different directions. A few were immediately rushed by concerned civilians who wore terror on their faces. Grace watched the council members attempt to ease their worries, but it would take more than words and patience to undo the damage to their community.

"Grace," her mother said, catching her attention. "You brought company."

Eli, Theo, and Sam were gathered behind her, an entourage of personal support. With her mother, it was always a toss-up on whether that support would be needed.

But tonight her mother looked weak and tired. Like she'd been fighting these battles for more years than she could handle. Grace wasn't used to seeing her mother look so frail. It caught her off guard, and she forgot what her mother had even said.

"What happened, Mom?" Theo asked, taking a step forward to support their mother by the arm. Apparently, Grace wasn't the only one to recognize her exhaustion.

She massaged her temples again and actually winced in pain. "An explosion set fire to the mountain peak. It appears the solar panels were targeted, but we're still determining how many were lost."

"The rebels?" Grace inquired. She couldn't imagine who else could be responsible.

"Please don't start with this tonight. There will be a full investigation, but it isn't helpful to jump to conclusions."

Grace scoffed. As far as she was concerned, there was no jumping. Merely taking the carefully placed steppingstones that had been laid out over months. Her mother was in denial.

"She's right. It's obvious who is behind this," Eli added, and she was thankful he was there to back her up.

"No, it isn't. Unless you've gathered some evidence in the past five minutes that I'm unaware of."

Even in the low light of the moon and lanterns, Grace saw Eli roll his eyes. Luckily her mother wasn't paying attention or she would've had an additional reason to scold them all.

"We'll head up there," Theo said. "See what we can do to help."

Grace nodded, and beside her, Eli and Sam mimicked their agreement. They were all ready to aid in whatever way they could.

"You don't need to worry about it, Theo. In fact, all of you should get inside. It's under control tonight, but we'll need you well rested in the morning. I'm afraid to say I don't think the worst is over. We won't know how bad it truly is until daylight, when the damage is fully assessed."

"Don't be silly. We're not going home." Grace crossed her arms. Why dismiss them when they were able-bodied and ready to assist? She was the future Lady of Berland. There was no way she was leaving in the middle of another attack to go home and kick her feet up.

Her mother shook her head and almost...wobbled. "I need to sit down."

Theo put a hand behind her back and frowned. "I'll take you home then. Grace can handle herself." He tilted his head toward Grace, waiting for her to back him up.

"Yes. You look like you need the rest more than I do. I'll stay here and if there are any new developments, I will come find you."

Her mother nodded and allowed Theo to lead her back inside the cavernous entrance of the mountain.

Once her mother was out of earshot, Grace turned to Sam and Eli. "I don't know what's gotten into her lately."

"Hasn't she always been a little...doubtful of your abilities?" Sam asked.

"Yeah, but she's never blown me off entirely. And why does it look like she hasn't slept in days?"

Eli's brows pinched together while Sam shrugged, saying, "Maybe the stress is getting to her."

"I guess..." Grace frowned as she headed toward the trail that led up the side of the mountain. The men stayed quiet, but while she walked, several civilians rushed up to her to ask questions. Mostly about the state of the infrastructure and whether they were safe inside the mountain. She couldn't give them an answer for certain, so she had to resort to vague affirmations.

"There's no place safer than the mountain."

"We will recover from this."

"The people of Berland are resilient and capable of withstanding any-thing thrown our way."

Words that she mostly believed in, but while the threat of Eamon's rebellion loomed over their heads, she couldn't be one hundred percent certain.

The trail, which was usually quiet and peaceful, was full of men and women running by with barrels of water. They had an emergency water reserve at the top, but apparently it wasn't sufficient. Grace made a mental note to have the resources replaced first thing in the morning, just in case another incident occurred.

By the time they made it to the highest peak, red-tinged smoke filled the air, illuminated by the embers of a fire that was almost extinguished. She recognized the fire chief standing next to a field of black square metal structures, all strategically placed to receive the most sunlight through-out the day.

Eli and Sam both gaped, and she could tell they'd never seen anything like it before. Compared to everything else in their world, this was probably the most technologically advanced structure that existed. The solar panels had been built long ago to keep the mountain powered long after society collapsed. The black slates covered the side of the mountain like scales on a fish, and on the far side, she could just barely see in the moonlight where the shiny panels faded into a wooded area.

Grace approached the fire chief, who spoke animatedly to volunteers, pointing in various directions and nodding at their questions. Once he caught sight of her, he dismissed the volunteers and gave Grace his full attention. "Miss Grace. I wasn't aware you'd be joining us. As you can see, the fire is contained and almost extinguished."

"Thank you, Oliver. I have complete faith in you."

"I told you to call me Olly."

Oliver, or Olly, had been the fire chief for as long as Grace could remember, and was highly skilled at his job. It was important to keep wildfires at bay, but lately it seemed like he was dealing with more arson cases than nature running its course.

"Olly," she repeated and smiled. "Fill me in on the damage."

Olly showed Grace around while Eli and Sam followed in their footsteps. The explosion appeared to have gone off near the seventh and eighth sectors. All the solar panels were sectioned and given their own battery bank. At least, that was what she could recall from the tour she'd been given a few years ago. It had been a while since she'd taken any interest in this stuff.

While it was clear the target was meant to be the panels, the forest had caught the most damage, and Olly approximated that only twenty percent of the panels in sector seven and eight had been turned to ashes.

Grace sighed. The other part she remembered about her tour was that replacing these panels was nearly impossible. It wasn't like they could go out and buy new ones. And if they had been burned to a crisp, it was unlikely they'd be able to salvage them.

"Which parts of the mountain are powered by the seventh and eighth sectors?"

"Mostly second level housing," Olly began. "There are a few common areas affected—classrooms, utility spaces, that kind of thing—but the majority is residential."

Grace nodded. It didn't feel like a coincidence that the second level would take the most impact. It was, after all, filled with mostly newcomers, and Eamon and his rebels clearly had no qualms about sacrificing them in their latest attack. Her mother had scolded her for jumping to conclusions, but her first instinct had been correct. Her righteousness was quickly extinguished by pity for the ones who'd be displaced.

"How bad is it?" Eli asked once Olly was finished walking Grace through his report. Upon seeing her face, he grimaced and pulled her in for a hug. "We'll get through it."

We. There was something so comforting about having Eli at her side. She could only hope that he would still be around to support her after the third round of the Rite in just two days.

"Let's go," she said. There wasn't anything else that could be done up in the solar panel field, but perhaps Diane could use their help directing families to temporary homes.

Back at the base, much of the commotion had died down. The crowds had diminished to half of what they'd been when the explosion first took place. Grace could only assume that most had either gone home after learning there wasn't much they could do or moved to the cafeteria to have their needs addressed.

The orange light from the fire was gone, leaving only the moon and a rare lamp to lead the way home. Neither Eli nor Sam spoke while they walked. Instead, the sound of crickets chirping and gravel crunching under their feet accompanied her racing thoughts.

Inside the mountain, a line had formed, leading from the grand entrance and disappearing through the doors to the cafeteria. Grace walked by families with small children who could barely keep their eyes open, young couples who looked stressed and confused, an elderly man who leaned on a cane with a stoic expression—so many people still waiting to be helped.

Just before Grace entered the cafeteria, someone called out to her.

"Grace!" Ali was still supporting Nik's weight as they both stumbled forward. Despite the evening's events, she was glad they'd had a good time celebrating Nik's birthday. The two of them had needed a night of fun. As Ali came closer, she asked, "How can we help?"

Grace took one look at Nik with his bloodshot eyes and smiled. "Go home. Seriously. Enjoy the rest of your evening and make sure *that one* doesn't have a hangover in the morning." She tilted her chin toward Nik, and Ali held back a laugh.

"Okay. I'll check in with you in the morning. Be safe." Then Ali turned to Eli and added, "Take care of her."

He shook his head like Ali was his mother, reminding him to brush his teeth before bed. Of course he would take care of her, but it was heartwarming to be considered.

When Ali had first shown up in Berland, Grace hadn't been sure how she'd fit into her friendship with Eli. They'd been best friends all their lives and Grace had been worried that she'd be pushed out, but that hadn't happened at all. Ali had accepted her immediately and Grace couldn't be more grateful for her support.

Sam stepped forward, taking a spot next to Nik and opposite of Ali. He wrapped his arm behind Nik's back, taking some of the weight off of Ali. "I'll help you get him home."

Ali quietly thanked Sam while Nik grumbled that he didn't need help.

"He's gonna feel that in the morning," Eli said as they watched the group walk off toward their apartment. Grace felt the weight of his arm across her shoulders and leaned into him. He gestured with one hand toward the front of the line. "Shall we?"

Grace simply nodded.

At the front of the line, Diane and another volunteer were handling the crowd as efficiently and compassionately as they could. They stood behind a table with a tray of keys and scattered papers where a line had been stricken through half of the text.

Diane finished handing a mother and her toddler a key before she spotted Grace and Eli. "Hello, Miss Grace. Eli."

"Hi, Diane. How are things going here? Anything we can help with?"

Diane grabbed a pencil and drew a line through another section of text on the paper in front of her. Then she studied the list. "We're hanging in there. Still a lot of folks waiting and we're going through empty units pretty quickly." She gestured toward the paper in front of her, which Grace now recognized as the list of available housing. She mentally tried to tally the units that hadn't been crossed out and compared it to the line of people still waiting for a temporary apartment.

"Will we have enough?" she asked, furrowing her brow.

Diane bit her lip and leaned in closer. "I'm not sure. Do you have a plan if we don't?"

Grace understood the need for secrecy. If anyone realized they might not have a place to stay while power was restored, chaos would break out while people from the end of the line rushed forward to guarantee their space.

"Did my mother mention the possibility?" It seemed like something her mother would've considered and had a contingency plan for.

But Diane frowned and shook her head. "I think we underestimated how many people would be affected."

Great. And Grace hadn't seen her mother since before heading up the mountain.

Wasting no time, Grace pushed her sleeves up and stepped behind the table. "Let's cross that bridge when we come to it," she said, and hoped like hell that they wouldn't come to it.

With the help of Grace and Eli, the line went much faster as they helped pass out keys and directed people toward their temporary homes. Since the power was the only thing affected, they at least didn't have to worry about extra clothing or food or any other essential items. The people could move their belongings from their old home to the new one at their convenience.

By the time they handed out the last key, the line had dwindled to only two families—a young couple with a baby and a single father with his two kids.

Grace exchanged a look with Eli, and he immediately turned to the young couple. "You can stay at my place." Privately to Grace he said, "Assuming I can share your bed."

She smiled and nodded. "Of course."

On the other end of the table, the volunteer spoke up. "My place is available too. I can stay with my sister for now."

Grace thanked the woman and so did the single father.

With that, the two families left to gather some belongings, giving Eli and the volunteer time to grab their necessities, too.

Grace rubbed her tired eyes and yawned. It had to be well past midnight by now, and her body ached to crawl into bed. But first, she'd help Eli collect his things.

Grace addressed their small group. "Thank you both so much for helping today. And thank you for offering your home," she told the volunteer. "That was so generous of you."

Eli made that face again, like there wasn't a circumstance in which he'd consider *not* helping her.

Meanwhile, Diane reminded Grace that it was in the job description of a council member and the volunteer simply said, "You're welcome."

Eli and Grace made their way to his apartment and packed his clothes and hygiene items in a bag. His cupboard didn't have much food, but they added what little he had to another bag as well. One of the fortunate side effects of being a newcomer meant that he had little personal items to pack up, so it didn't take long at all before his home was cleared and ready for the other family to move in.

Eli carried the larger bags, and Grace helped by picking up one of the smaller ones. She opened the door once they made it to her home and dropped everything on the floor.

"Mom," she called into the quiet entryway.

No response.

She headed for the stairs, but just as she climbed the first two, Theo appeared at the top of the staircase.

"Theo?" she asked, tensing at the glassy look in his eyes. "What's wrong?"

"It's Mom."

Chapter Twenty-Nine

ELI

Eli had known that keeping Ellen's deteriorating health a secret would come back to bite him. If he'd known it would be so soon, he might've told Grace the second he'd realized something was wrong. Instead, he was forced to watch as Ellen explained to Grace that she didn't have much time left.

Eli felt like an outsider inside Ellen's bedroom. While Ellen lay peacefully in bed with her husband and two children surrounding her, Eli stood in the corner and listened as the medic confessed there was nothing that could be done for Ellen's condition. Their only option was to ensure that she was comfortable in her last days.

"How long exactly?" Ben asked in a strained voice. It appeared even he was taken by surprise by the news. Had Ellen really kept it from her husband?

Eli shifted with guilt, realizing that he was likely the only person who had known something was wrong with Ellen. And he hadn't spoken a word of it to Grace.

Grace...who now sat on the bed next to her mother with tear-filled eyes and pink, splotchy cheeks. As tumultuous as their relationship was, even Grace wasn't ready to let her mother go.

The medic looked nervously at Ellen, and she nodded. "There's no way of telling for certain. It could be a few days. Might be a few weeks." He cleared his throat before continuing, "The chances of Ellen surviving for more than a month are slim, but not impossible."

Ellen inhaled sharply but otherwise did not appear surprised by the statement. She reached for Grace's hand to her right and Theo's on her left. "Thank you," she said, dismissing the medic.

Eli felt pulled to follow the medic out of the room, but before he could move, Ellen said, "Eli, could you fetch me a glass of water?"

Gladly, he thought. "Yes. I'll be right back."

Hurrying down the stairs, Eli made his way into the kitchen. He took his time finding a glass and filling it with water, not looking forward to returning to the somber room upstairs. But ultimately, Ellen needing a drink trumped his need to avoid the mourning family he didn't belong to.

When he returned, Theo and Ben stood up to leave. Eli placed the cup on the stand beside Ellen's bed and headed toward the door, assuming Ellen needed her rest, but she stopped him before he could get too far.

"Eli, stay."

Grace, still holding her mother's hand, stared at Eli for the first time since entering Ellen's room. Her breath caught and Eli's heart hammered, still riddled with guilt that he hadn't told her sooner.

What difference would it have made? Ellen was sick either way. Grace would've faced this devastation regardless of how soon she'd found out.

His feeble attempts to ease his guilt were unsuccessful.

He pursed his lips and moved closer, sitting beside Grace on the edge of the bed.

"I was just about to share some advice with Grace before I go," Ellen said.

"Mom," Grace cried. "Don't—"

"It's the truth, honey. Don't be scared and don't worry about me. I've lived a good life with your father and you and your brother. I couldn't have asked for more."

Eli rubbed Grace's back as she sniffed and wiped her eyes with the sleeve of her shirt.

"I know we haven't always seen eye to eye, but don't ever doubt that I love you and only want what's best for you. I thought...I thought I was making the right decisions. I was afraid of what an open rebellion would mean for you, so I pacified people when I shouldn't have. I turned the other way and ignored signs I shouldn't have. I thought compromise and collaboration were the answers. I was determined to leave you with a stable society, to make things easy for you after I was gone, but I think...I think I was wrong.

"You're so smart and compassionate and driven. No matter what happens in the future, there isn't a doubt in my mind that you're going to be just fine without me."

Grace wiped her eyes with the back of her hand and let out a sob. "I'm not ready to do this without you."

Ellen smiled. "Yes, you are. Your friends will be your support system, and your brother...and Eli."

At this, Ellen nodded to Eli and for the first time, he felt like Ellen might've accepted a marriage between Grace and him. If only she'd been given more time.

"You'll take care of her?" she asked.

Eli cleared his throat, the emotions of the conversation hitting him harder than he expected. "Of course."

"Thank you."

He watched as Ellen relaxed into the mattress, her eyes gently fluttering closed, her chest steadily rising and falling as she fell asleep. After a moment, he rose from his seat. "Are you ready?" he asked Grace. It had been a long day, and he was beyond exhausted.

"Give me a minute," Grace said, not taking her eyes off her mother.

So Eli left her, grabbing his belongings, which were still abandoned by the door, and making his way to Grace's bedroom. He had little to unpack, but he dug through one of his bags until he found a pair of shorts to sleep in. Then he found his toothbrush and prepared for bed.

By the time he was finished, Grace still hadn't returned. He climbed into bed, plagued with the image of Grace crying at her mother's impending passing, wishing there was something he could do for her. He knew what it was like to lose a parent—hell, he'd lost both of his—and he hated that she had to go through it too.

When the door to Grace's bedroom finally creaked with movement, Eli's eyes shot open. He must've fallen asleep and wasn't sure for how long, but he sat up in bed and waited for Grace to join him.

First, she went into her bathroom and he heard the faucet and what sounded like clothing hitting the floor. When she emerged, she wore a thin silky tank top and matching shorts that clung to her curves. She wordlessly climbed into bed with him and sat staring at the far wall.

"Are you okay?" he asked.

"No," she said quietly. When she turned to face him, her eyes were puffy and pink, though she wasn't crying anymore.

Eli pulled her in for a hug. "I'm so sorry, Grace."

Her limp arms barely embraced him, but she leaned on his shoulder and he held her tighter. He'd summon strength for both of them.

"I feel like I lost out on so many years. So much time spent fighting with her over our differences in opinions and for what? In the end, none of it matters. She'll be gone and I'll be left with pain and regret."

Eli brushed her hair with his hand, soothing her while giving her the shoulder she so desperately needed to cry on.

"She loved me...in her own way. I suppose that has to be enough."

"I'm sorry she couldn't love you in the way you wanted. But I believe her when she said she wants the best for you."

"I know." She cried against his bare skin. "I just wish she'd been honest with me. I would've understood if she'd explained her perspective. I want a stable society too, even if I don't agree with what that looks like. If she'd told me the truth, we could've worked it out together."

There was so much pain in her voice. It trembled with each word, and he felt her chest expand with a heavy breath. Her emphasis on knowing the truth especially pulled at his heart.

If she'd known...if he'd told her months ago after the first round of the Rite that her mother was sick... would it have made a difference? Would she have had time to make things right and work together with her mother instead of against her?

"Shit," he muttered beneath his breath.

Grace heard him and tilted her head, still resting on his shoulder, but turned to see his face now. "What?"

"There's something I need to tell you."

She took another deep breath, preparing for another blow. And Eli hated that he was the one who wasn't going to serve it.

"A couple months ago, I ran into your mother down in the study and something happened."

Grace swallowed audibly before he continued.

"She had a dizzy spell and passed out. When she came around, she had me fetch her some medication. I wasn't sure how serious it was at the time, and I told her she needed to tell you—"

Grace suddenly sat up. "You knew?"

Slowly, Eli nodded. "I knew something was wrong, yes. I just didn't realize it was this bad. If I'd known...I would've told you, Grace. I never meant to keep it from you."

"But you did."

Eli felt as though his chest was being split open. Grace looked at him with hurt in her eyes. She didn't seem angry, just devastated that he'd known and hadn't shared with her. "I'm so sorry."

He tried to pull her in against him, but she sat back farther on the mattress, creating a divide between them that ripped Eli's heart out. His throat went dry as he searched for the right words. But the right words didn't exist. The right *time* did, and that time was two months in the past.

"I should've told you sooner," he choked out.

Grace nodded but remained speechless. So much grief. She'd been put through so much in the past few hours and she looked like she was nearing her breaking point. His ray of sunshine was losing her light, and he couldn't help but blame himself for failing her.

"Grace..."

She held a hand up and closed her eyes, breathing deeply. "I need some time."

The weight of the world landed on Eli's shoulders, and he slumped over, his heart breaking. He'd do anything to take it back. To go back in time and be honest with her. How could he fix this?

Grace shifted and pulled the blanket over her legs, settling in for the night.

"Do you want me to leave?" Eli asked, praying she'd say no but knowing he'd find another place to sleep if that's what she wanted.

She thought for a moment before answering. "No, you can stay."

But she turned on her side, away from him, and Eli knew the conversation was over for tonight. He'd have to try again tomorrow to make amends. And the day after that. And the day after that.

He'd work every day to show her how much he cared for her. He would never keep the truth from her again. She was the most important person in his life, and he didn't know if he could handle losing her.

His time with her was only beginning, and he was determined to spend many more years by her side, loving her and supporting her.

He clung to that future for dear life as he crawled under the covers beside her.

Even though he was so tired—physically, mentally and emotionally—it took Eli a long time to fall asleep. He was too focused on the woman beside him, the hurt that he was unable to alleviate, that he'd added onto instead. He was furious with himself. All he wanted to do was hold her and comfort her, but instead, he had to watch her suffer on her own.

At some point, fatigue finally got the best of him.

Hours later, when he woke, he immediately looked to his left to find Grace and plead for her forgiveness once again. Instead, he found an empty bed where she should've been.

Chapter Thirty

ALI

Despite having such a late night, Ali woke up the next morning alert and restless. Her legs twitched beneath the weight of her blanket, but she tried to calm her nervous energy, afraid she might wake Nik.

Nik…who was still passed out to her left. He slept on his stomach with one arm bent beneath his cheek and the other at an odd angle on his side. The sight almost made Ali laugh. She'd never seen Nik drunk before, and last night had been more entertaining than she would've guessed.

Until everything went south and another attack was carried out in Berland. She knew little about what had happened since she'd been taking care of Nik, but it seemed serious. As a council member, she knew she should report for duty early today, but her body rebelled.

Although her mind was racing with the energy of a full-grown mare, her heavy limbs requested that she stay in bed and take it easy. It was like her body and brain couldn't get on the same page. Ever since her loss, it had been hard to regulate her emotions and thoughts. She felt out of control.

Her heart began to ache, seemingly out of nowhere, but she was familiar with this course—the one that took her down a dark path where her chest felt like it was caving in and hope was out of reach. She pinched her eyes closed and breathed deeply, wishing for it to go away.

She wrapped her arms tightly around her chest, heart beating wildly. She hated how these bouts of overwhelming emotions hit her out of the blue sometimes. While she concentrated on her breathing, tears welled in the corners of her eyes, spilling down her cheeks.

She had every right to be emotional. After losing her child, no one could fault her for having hard days. But that didn't stop her from being angry with herself. She wanted to be stronger than this. She didn't want to lean on people or need anyone's help.

But it was inevitable.

She opened her eyes again, still clutching at her beating heart, though it began to slow. Her tears flowed freely though, and she turned to her side, curling into a ball.

The room went dark, and there was a buzzing in her ears. She felt as though she might be sick.

She was faintly aware of something... a hand touching her back, moving in slow circles.

"Ali, look at me," Nik said. She could hear the concern in his voice but couldn't bring herself to turn around and face him. In fact, her body felt entirely drained of energy and she couldn't move her limbs if she tried.

Nik's hand slipped under her shirt, and he continued to rub her back gently. Her vision was still clouded, but she sensed his body hovering close to her, waiting for her to look at him.

Another wave of nausea rolled over her, and she tensed. Taking slow, deep breaths, she felt the pressure ease from her head and stomach. With a small shiver, she realized she'd been sweating.

Nik's voice broke through the white noise humming in her ears. "Ali, are you with me?" His voice shook a little, and she wondered how long he'd been whispering in her ear, waiting for her to respond.

"Yes," she said softly. "I'm okay."

She was far from it, but if she said it enough, she figured she'd eventually be okay with it all. With losing her mom, almost losing Eli, losing her baby...

She licked her lips and tasted salty tears, numbly wiping them away. "Can you get me a glass of water?" she asked, needing a moment to collect herself.

"Of course," Nik said. The bed shifted from the loss of his weight.

Ali blinked away any remaining tears and used the blanket to dry her face. By the time Nik returned with her water, the tears were gone, though her cheeks still felt hot to the touch.

"Here you go," he said, handing her a mug of tea rather than the water she'd requested. He'd made the right call, as the steam helped clear her sinuses and soothe her inflamed chest.

"Thank you."

Nik climbed back into bed with her. She could sense him staring, but she waited, taking a few more sips of tea, before she turned to face him. Worry was etched over every facet of his face.

"I'm fine," she said, but the words fell flat.

"I've told you before, you don't need to mask your emotions with me. If anyone understands, it's me. Lean on me, sweetheart."

She knew he meant it figuratively, but she scooted closer and actually leaned on his shoulder, nestling against his warm body. "I'm a mess," she admitted. "One day I feel normal, or at least close to it, and the next I'm waking up in a cold sweat, unable to breathe. Is this what it will always feel like?"

Nik sighed. "I wish I knew."

"I feel weak. Like I should've been taking care of you today, after the night you had, but once again you're coddling me because I can't cope." More tears begin to form, which only made her angrier.

"You can't compare our ways of dealing with tragedy, Ali. You *are* strong, even if your strength looks different than mine. You're one of the strongest people I know—to go through so much and still be standing. I'm in awe of you."

Ali sniffled and gazed up into his eyes. If only she could see herself the way he did. Strong and resilient. Capable of taking on anything. Maybe one day she'd feel the kind of unwavering fortitude that she saw in him. "I hate that you're always the one taking care of me."

"I don't," he said, kissing the top of her head. "I want to take care of you for the rest of our lives. And one day, I'm going to take care of our babies too."

She smiled. "Babies? As in plural?"

"Yes, Ali. You and I are going to have lots of babies. We're going to have a family full of love. They'll have my charm and good looks, and they'll have your big heart and generosity."

Her smile turned into a short laugh. "Will they have your arrogance too?"

"One can only hope," he said without missing a beat.

Together, they snuggled back under the covers, Nik's arms wrapped around Ali in an embrace that she could only describe as protective and healing. It wasn't long before she fell back asleep, exhausted from the brief anxiety attack.

When Ali woke again, it was to an empty bed. She sat up slowly and looked around for Nik. When she didn't hear him moving about in the kitchen or hear the shower running, she got out of bed and wrapped a robe around her body.

"Nik?" she called. She rubbed her tired eyes and tried to figure out what time of day it was. Mid-afternoon, if she had to guess. She couldn't believe she'd slept that long, but her body must've needed it.

"Where are you?" she called again, looking inside the bathroom to find it empty. Maybe he'd gone out for a run. It was something he did whenever he needed to release his frustration and grief.

Settling on the belief that he'd be back soon, Ali found the mug of lukewarm tea next to the bed and went to make a fresh cup. While the kettle warmed on the stove, she rinsed out the old dregs until her mug was pristine again.

The door slowly creaked open and Ali spun around, catching sight of Nik stealthily returning home. When he noticed her watching, he stood straight and walked inside as if there was nothing abnormal about his entrance. "I thought you might still be asleep and didn't want to wake you," he offered as an explanation.

Ali nodded and returned her attention to the now whistling kettle. She removed it from the heat and was about to pour it over her loose-leaf tea when another voice captured her attention.

"I hope there's enough for all of us," Grace said.

Ali looked over her shoulder to find Grace along with Heather and Amaya standing at her door. Grace was holding a basket of fabric in every color, while Heather held a brown leather bag that appeared heavy. Amaya, however, held nothing but the pinky fingers of two little girls, Julia and Kaydence.

The small party entered the room, making the quaint kitchen feel even tinier. But Ali beamed, thrilled to see their home full of love. She bent down to the girls' level. "What are you doing here?"

Kaydence hid her smile behind a tiny hand while Julia rocked back and forth on her feet, peering around as though she'd just stepped into a magical portal. Her eyes roved the room, taking in every nook and cranny with a look of bewilderment. Ali forgot what it was like to enter one of these units for the first time, being amazed at the convenience and comfort hidden in simplicity. She wondered how different it was from their current lodging with Ms. Carpenter.

Grace spoke on their behalf. "We were just in the area, burdened by these extra dresses"—she jostled the basket of fabric in her hands—"and Heather's incessant need to fix people's hair. Thought maybe you'd like to join in on the fun."

Ali knew better than that. Nik had clearly sought them out to boost her mood. And after watching Kaydence eye the basket of dresses with curiosity, she was certain he knew just how to cheer her up. "Well, let's get started then."

Nik left the room, making some excuse about needing to find something, but Ali knew he really just wanted to get out of the crowded room of women. Julia and Kaydence eagerly ran toward the bed and hopped up, Julia bouncing a few extra times while Kaydence waited patiently.

Heather started first, pulling out all sorts of brushes and sprays and instruments from her leather bag. She brought over a chair from the dining area and gestured for Kaydence to have a seat. One look at the pair of scissors in Heather's hands and Kaydence frowned, her eyes growing wide.

"What kind of hairstyle would you like?" Heather asked sweetly, doing her best to ease Kaydence's fears. "We could cut it short to your shoulders, or I can just trim it and keep it *really* long like a princess."

"I wanna be a princess," Kaydence said confidently. She rushed from the bed to the chair in a flash, leaving the adults full of joy. The girls brought such light and happiness to the room. It was hard to be sad while they were around.

"I think I have the perfect dress for you, Kaydence. Ali, do you want to help me?" Grace set down her basket and Ali came to sit beside her, sorting through the pile of dresses she'd brought along. They were small—like Grace might've fit into them a decade ago—but they'd likely still hang off the girls' tiny frames. But as excited as they were, Ali didn't think they'd mind if the dresses didn't fit perfectly.

Julia and Kaydence oohed and aahed while Grace and Ali took turns holding up dresses. A pink one with a big poofy chiffon skirt. A pale blue one with thin straps and beaded detail. A yellow ombre one that faded into cream at the bottom. Each new dress elicited another excited squeal.

In the end, Kaydence settled on a pink dress with enough sparkles to make her shimmer in the light and Julia chose a more practical dress with casual blue cotton and pockets.

The girls were equally unique in their hairstyles. Heather gave Kaydence a simple trim and Ali braided her brown hair, tying it off with a pink bow to match her dress. Julia chose the short style that Heather had initially offered, chopping her blonde hair just above the shoulder. She wanted a braid too, but with the shorter length, Ali had to do two braided pigtails instead.

Once they finished their makeovers, the girls paraded around the room, putting on a fashion show for the adults. Their joy and bright smiles tugged at Ali's heartstrings in the best way. Instead of pain, she felt overwhelmed with delight.

"Your turn," Julia shrieked. Ali watched while Julia ruffled through dresses, tossing aside those that she found unworthy of Ali.

"I'm not sure any of those will fit me," Ali said. It seemed as though Grace had brought her smallest gowns to fit the girls, not the adults.

Grace kneeled beside Julia and searched through the discarded piles of dresses. "Actually, I think there is one or two that might be big enough for you. You're pretty slender and a bit shorter than me. Maybe one of these from a few years ago."

She held up a pale minty green dress that *almost* looked like it could fit Ali, but the waist was too structured and didn't have any stretch to it. Grace threw it in the basket and continued her search until she suddenly pulled a mess of fabric and waved it over her head. "Found it!"

Seconds later, a white gown with embroidered flowers was thrust into Ali's hands. Grace pulled Ali up from her seat before she had a chance to give the dress much scrutiny. Her body was flung forward from the force of Grace's gentle push, causing her to stumble into the bathroom.

It was silly, dressing up like a child, but the fabric felt like heaven in her fingers. Soft and slippery, though she wasn't quite certain of the material. Nothing like she'd ever tried before, that was for sure.

She stepped out of her clothes and pulled the dress over her head, shimmying to get it over her hips. The top had loose straps that hung off her shoulders, like a string of flowers wrapped around her upper arms. The front was modest, while the back had a set of laces that she would need help tightening to fit her figure.

And the bottom half...

The bottom half took her breath away with the most intricate details she'd ever seen. The flowers grew in number and size as they fell to the floor, and the bottom of the dress took up nearly half of the small bathroom. She wondered how she'd even fit through the door with so much fabric gathered around her lower half.

Prying the door open, she made enough room to waddle through. Once inside the bedroom, she was met with silence. "What? Does it look silly?"

Of course it did. It was a gown made for a princess. Someone like Grace, who was used to dressing up for balls and other extravagant events. Not someone like Ali, who was better suited in a pair of jeans and an oversized T-shirt.

Grace spoke first. "You look like—"

"You look like a bride," Kaydence said with rosy pink cheeks and a bright smile.

Julia nodded. "Can we come to the wedding?"

Ali snorted. "I'm not getting married."

The girls exchanged a look of disappointment, and Ali almost wished she could tell them differently. Maybe one day.

"It does suit you, though," Amaya said. "Like it was made for you."

"An updo would be better, but I agree." Heather pointed toward Ali's head, and Ali stifled a laugh. She knew Heather well enough now to know that she meant no ill will with her statement. She just couldn't help herself when it came to styling hair.

Ali looked back at the mirror visible through the bathroom door and pulled her hair up with one hand. Heather was right. An updo would better show off her shoulders and back.

"Let me," Heather said, clearly unable to help herself. With a few quick movements, Ali's hair was tucked up into an elegant bun low on her head. Then Heather tightened the straps on Ali's back, which pushed her breasts up unexpectedly.

Ali clutched her chest as she settled into the new form fitted bust. "Well... how do I look?"

Before anyone else could answer, the front door opened and Nik walked in carrying a box that Ali could only imagine held sweets based on the cinnamon sugar scent wafting in her direction. He paused and his eyes slowly roved from her face all the way down to her toes.

He let out a short breath and licked his lips, bringing heat to Ali's cheeks. "What did I interrupt?"

Behind her, Ali heard Julia and Kaydence giggling. "Ali is a bride."

His eyes widened, but they stayed locked on Ali. "Is she?"

The smirk on his lips caused more than just her face to heat. Her neck and chest turned warm, as did her stomach and the point between her thighs. She'd almost forgotten the power he held over her. She hadn't felt a desire like that since before the accident. Up until now, she hadn't been sure she'd ever feel it again.

Nik placed the box of heavenly goods on the table before inching toward Ali. Her skin prickled from the intensity of his gaze. It was as though he was undressing her with his eyes, able to see straight through the white fabric to her pink skin.

"And who is the groom?" he asked.

Ali was unable to contain her smile. Of course, if she were *actually* getting married, Nik would be her other half. The way he played into the girls' make-believe was amusing, and somehow sexy too. Or maybe that was the way he still hadn't taken his eyes off her.

"You can be!" Julia exclaimed.

He playfully brought a hand to his heart. "Me?"

The girls cheered, and even Amaya and Heather stifled a laugh. Grace grinned, though she stayed silent, eyes bouncing between the two of them.

"If you want to be," Kaydence told him.

He took a deep breath and another step closer to Ali, wrapping his arms around her waist and pressing his body into hers. She tilted her head up to meet his gaze. His smirk slowly faded, and he suddenly appeared very serious. His eyes locked on hers as though they could express more than words ever could.

"I *definitely* want to be."

Chapter Thirty-One

ELI

Eli waited for Grace to return, taking his time getting ready, showering and changing inside her empty bedroom. When he no longer had an excuse to stay, he left her room and headed for Ellen's, thinking perhaps Grace was visiting with her mother, but he only found a dimly lit room where Ellen slept quietly. Unfortunately, Grace wasn't in the dining room eating breakfast with her brother and father, either.

Theo looked up from a small leather-bound book when Eli entered the dining area, arms crossed in disappointment.

"Breakfast?" Theo asked, pointing to the empty chair next to him. "We've got anything you want—toast, bacon, eggs—"

"That's okay. I'm not hungry."

Ben quietly assessed him. "You've been training a lot for the Rite. You should eat. Take care of yourself. Can't ease up now when the final round is tomorrow."

Eli and Ben hadn't exchanged many words since his arrival in Berland. It didn't help that Grace's father was frequently out of town for trade and when he was home, he rarely spent time with anyone but his family.

But if things went according to plan, Eli would be part of this family soon. He shifted toward the empty chair and nodded to Ben. "Yeah, you're right. I suppose I can stay for a quick bite."

As he sat down, he couldn't help but stare at Grace's empty seat with a frown. While Ben called for a servant to bring Eli a plate—rattling off a variety of breakfast items that Eli knew he didn't have the appetite for—Theo leaned over and said, "Were you hoping to see Grace?"

Eli nodded again. "Have you seen her?"

"Only for a couple seconds. She left in a hurry early this morning."

"Did she say where she was going?"

Theo raised a brow. "Trouble in paradise?"

Eli scoffed. "Hardly. Just… a misunderstanding." The words felt bitter on his tongue. It was hardly a misunderstanding, but he really didn't want to get into it with Grace's brother about how he had known about their mother's health troubles all along. Something told him Theo wouldn't react very well, either.

"Well…whatever it is, she'll forget about it by the end of the day. Grace is forgiving like that." He returned his attention to the book in his hands and, with a quick glance, Eli could see that the pages were full of little drawings. Most of them were from nature—flowers, trees, the lake near the middle of town. A few were sketches of unrecognizable faces. Probably various folks around Berland.

"Do you mind?"

Eli realized he'd been caught staring at Theo's book. "Sorry," he said quickly.

Theo smiled and Eli sighed with relief, knowing he hadn't seriously offended him. He wished he could say the same for Grace.

"So, are you ready for tomorrow?" Ben asked once the servant had disappeared.

"I believe so," he answered truthfully. Physically, he'd never been in better shape. Mentally, he was ready to put the Rite behind him. To stop fighting for Grace's hand in marriage and finally call her his own, like he belonged to her. He could finally tell those assholes around town that stared at him like an undeserving outsider that they could all go to hell. Trevor was at the top of that list.

But emotionally, he was nervous. After last night's conversation with Grace, he wasn't sure where her head was at. What if they'd come all this way for things to fall apart at the finish line?

By the time the servant returned with Eli's breakfast, he was itching to get out of the room. Not just because he needed to find Grace, but he felt like he was silently being judged. Like he had the words 'liar' and 'traitor' written on his forehead, shining brightly for Theo and Ben to see. He was waiting for either of them to question his loyalty to Grace and whether he was worthy of her.

It was all in his head, of course. Theo spent the rest of breakfast enamored with his drawings, occasionally smiling, while Ben cleared his plate and made room for a folder stuffed with old parchment, which he perused and scribbled on without a word.

The silence was the most grating thing Eli had ever heard.

He ate as much of his food as he could, not wanting to appear ungrateful. Once he'd cleared an acceptable amount, he pushed back his chair—the noise drawing attention from the others in the room. "Thank you for breakfast," he said quickly to Ben. "But I need to get going."

"No need to thank us," Ben replied. "You're always welcome here."

His hospitality caught Eli off guard, and he could only mutter another 'thank you' before rushing out of the home.

Eli checked all of Grace's usual haunts: the cafeteria, the council chamber—at least the outside, since he couldn't get in the locked room—and stopped by a few of her favorite shops in town.

He even checked the barn where their horses were kept. Hers was still there, so she hadn't gone out for a ride. While he was in the barn, he couldn't resist the opportunity to say hello to Obsidian, the horse that Grace had gifted him.

The horse greeted him with a nuzzle to the bars when she saw him approaching.

"Hey, girl. Are you excited to see me?"

Obsidian huffed, and her nostrils moved as she sniffed his hands and torso.

"I didn't bring anything with me this time."

Perfect, he thought. Now his horse would also be upset with him.

He opened the stall gate and Obsidian trotted out, still sniffing around for a hidden snack. When she finally gave up, she shook her head and her long, black mane glistened in the light.

"What about a ride instead? I can take you up the mountain and grab the angelfruit that you like so much. Fresh off the tree. How does the sound?"

She stomped once, and Eli could only assume she was satisfied with his offer.

He quickly got his saddle in place and pulled himself up—a move that had gotten a lot easier since his first attempt with Grace—and steered her toward his favorite trail.

Thick leaves kept the sun at bay as they traveled up the trail, but some trees had started to turn yellow, the first sign that autumn was approaching. He could feel it in the air, too. It was crisp and cool rather than the suffocating heat that he'd grown used to.

Eli kept Obsidian moving, only stopping once to let her drink from a stream. It didn't take long to make it to their destination. Hopping down from his horse, Eli took the reins and tied them around a tree, ensuring the knot was secure.

Then he cautiously approached the Twisted Tree. Even the birds seemed to respect the sanctity of the tree, falling quiet as they watched Eli from above. He lowered to his knees in front of the small tower of stones he'd created for his father, noting that there was another tiny collection next to Ali's mother's. Flames engulfed his lungs and heart as he considered the innocent life those stones represented.

It wasn't fair. Ali didn't deserve what had happened to her, and neither did this child. He shuddered, knowing that Grace had likely been the true target. Would there ever come a day when they would all feel safe?

Everyone was on the same page as far as the primary suspect was concerned, but without any evidence, Eamon and his followers would face no consequences. The rebels continued to slip through their grasp, and Eli had no idea how to stop it. They covered their tracks well, and they had the power to silence anyone who might've stepped forward with information, like Noah and his knowledge of the explosives.

Eli returned his gaze and his thoughts to his dad. He whispered softly to the empty space, "I hope you're taking care of her."

He didn't know if Ali's child would've been a girl or not, but somehow it felt right.

"I hope you let her stay out late, eat too many sweets, and do all the things you never allowed me to do."

He grinned. If there was an afterlife, he was certain his dad and Ali's mom would be taking good care of the child, spoiling her rotten.

"I miss you, Dad. I could really use your advice right about now. I think I fucked up. You know the woman I told you about, Grace? I kept some information from her. I didn't mean to. I thought I was doing the right thing…"

Allowing time for Ellen to tell Grace the truth herself really had seemed like a good idea at the time, but in retrospect, Eli could see the error in his decision.

"I didn't know things were as bad as they were. If I had known her mother was *that* sick, I would've told Grace sooner. But it doesn't matter now. I fucked up and I need to know how to fix it. I feel like you would've had the perfect advice for me." He sighed and looked up at the sky. "But you're not here."

Eli stared blankly, unsure what he had expected coming here. Did he think the trees would share their wisdom? That the leaves would whisper words of encouragement?

A bird above him broke the silence with a loud screech, and Eli glared at the obnoxious bluejay. It squawked again, bobbing its head up and down like it was reprimanding him. He huffed a laugh, because the bird, crazy as it was, reminded him of his dad and the way he used to scold Eli for feeling sorry for himself.

He'd always tell Eli there was no sense in entertaining negative thoughts. "Shit happens," he would say. "And complaining about the smell won't change a thing."

Eli laughed harder as he envisioned his dad speaking those words to him. It wasn't the most helpful advice. It never gave him a solution to his problems, but it always made him laugh regardless.

Grace would've probably found him to be hilarious, too.

"You would've gotten along well."

It was difficult to picture his dad's face, though it hadn't been a year yet since he'd been murdered. His voice, too, grew more distorted with each passing day. Remembering his father was like a muscle that Eli had to train each day. He was terrified of the day he'd lose that ability completely.

As he rummaged through hazy memories of his father, one in particular began to take form. It was the day he'd had his first real fight with Ali. They had been barely teenagers, and Eli recalled Ali planning a picnic for them by the lake. She'd spent the entire day before preparing—baking biscuits and fresh jam.

But when the time came, Eli hadn't met her. Instead, he'd chosen to hang out with a couple of older guys who'd teased him about spending time with his *girlfriend,* a title he had detested back then. None of the other guys had been close to any of the girls their age, and Eli had begun to second guess his friendship with Ali. He'd thought there was something wrong with him, and that by hanging out with the guys, he'd fit in again.

It'd been a terrible decision to desert Ali, one that he'd regretted the moment she came back from the lake with red cheeks and fierce eyes. She'd tossed the basket of food at his feet and stomped away without a word, leaving Eli to clean up the mess.

Guilt had eaten at him for days. Eventually, his father had noticed that Eli was miserable and that Ali hadn't been hanging around. He'd sat him down at the kitchen table and slammed his palm on Eli's shoulder.

"What did you do?" he'd asked.

Eli had stared at him blank-faced.

His dad had laughed and sat down next to Eli. "You don't have to tell me. Do you want some advice, kid?"

"Sure."

"You know that saying—if you love someone, let them go?"

Eli had frowned and scoffed. What a stupid piece of advice that was. He didn't want to let Ali go. Besides, she was just a friend. He wasn't in love with her.

His dad had chucked. "Toss that out. You chase that girl and beg on your knees if you have to. Never, *never* give up on the people you love."

And so he wouldn't.

Chapter Thirty-Two

NIK

AFTER APPEARING UNANNOUNCED TO find Ali in a sexy white gown that hugged her body in all the right places, Nik couldn't wait for their party to wrap up and for everyone to go home. He practiced as much patience as he could while serving each guest a cupcake—vanilla with angelfruit filling. He'd thought dessert would be the perfect way to cheer Ali up, but he was craving something sweeter now.

His mouth watered as he forced his cupcake down, and he wished time would move faster.

On the bright side, Ali seemed to be in much better spirits than when he'd left earlier in the day—something that he hadn't been able to accomplish on his own. He'd had a hunch that a girls' day might be just what she needed and seeing her smiling again assured him they were going to be okay.

And then the way she looked at him after Julia and Kaydence insisted he be Ali's groom...that was a look he'd never forget. It filled him with nervous energy and compelled him to drop to one knee and beg her to spend the rest of their lives together.

Nik didn't spend a lot of time envisioning the future. He'd always been the kind to go with the flow, focused on surviving day to day. But lately he'd found himself thinking about what their future would look like.

Their future.

Not *his* future. Every scenario he envisioned featured Ali by his side. And if he was to trust the way she lit up by being described as a bride, her vision was identical to his. There was no Nik without Ali.

He was the first to finish his cupcake while everyone else chatted between bites. It felt like they took forever to finally devour their sweet treats.

"The girls are going to be wired when I take them home to Ms. Carpenter. I blame you for this," Grace said, pointing a finger accusingly at Nik.

He put his hands up and feigned innocence. "I don't know what you're talking about, and they'll back me up."

The young girls nodded emphatically. They knew they needed to be on his side if they wanted the delicious desserts to keep coming.

Grace shook her head. "Teaching them to lie already. That's going to bite you in the ass one day."

"You're probably right." One day, when he had kids of his own, karma would come to find him.

"I think it's time we headed out. Thank you so much for having us."

Ali stood and leaned in to hug Grace. "No, thank *you*. This is exactly what I needed."

They leaned back and Nik watched them exchange a look of appreciation for one another.

"Oh, before you go, I need to give you this dress back," Ali said, reaching for the intricate laces on the back of her gown.

"Don't worry about it," Grace said with a wave of her hand. "I'll get it from you tomorrow."

Nik thought he saw her give Ali a wink but couldn't quite tell from this angle.

"And ours?" Julia asked, twirling so the skirt of her dress rose in the air before falling softly to the floor.

"Those are yours to keep," Grace answered, and this time Nik definitely caught a wink.

The girls beamed with excitement over their fancy princess gowns. Amazing how such a small gesture of donating hand-me-downs could bring immeasurable joy to their faces.

After what felt like an eternity, Grace rounded up the girls while Heather and Amaya gathered their scattered belongings. Once they left, the room felt eerily quiet.

Nik cleared his throat as he approached Ali. That familiar pink blush returned to her cheeks when she caught him staring.

She spun, offering her back to him. "Can you help me with these?"

"What? Help you take it off?"

Ali smiled over her shoulder. "Yes..."

It hadn't even been a day since his promise to take things slowly and already he was breaking it. But she seemed like she was in a good headspace, at least for the moment.

Nik gently grazed her bare arms with his fingertips, brushing them over her shoulders and then down her back. He felt her shiver underneath his touch. He whispered against her neck, "What if I like you in this dress?"

She inhaled deeply. Her voice shook as she spoke. "I can't wear this forever."

"No," he said, continuing to run his fingers over her smooth skin, mesmerized by the tiny goosebumps that sprouted on her flesh. "But you could wear it for tonight."

Slowly, she turned around to face him, eyes glistening with curiosity. "What did you have in mind?"

Nik took a step forward, his chest colliding with hers. He licked his lips and watched with amusement as Ali's eyes tracked his tongue's movement.

Step by step, he gently backed her up until her knees hit the bed. She dropped to sit and Nik pressed forward between her thighs. The fabric of her dress restricted his movement a bit, but it didn't stop him from dropping to his knees before her.

Keeping his eyes on hers, he felt his way to the hem of her dress and slowly lifted the fabric, bunching it up around her thighs. With a sigh, she fell backwards, allowing Nik to push her skirt up further to her waist. He placed a soft kiss on her thin underwear and her back arched off the mattress.

God, the things he wanted to do to her.

Her breathing quickened as he trailed kisses along her inner thigh, across her belly, and over her panties, humming in approval when she rocked her hips in anticipation.

Fingers twisted in his hair, pulling gently—desperation to experience more of him. He was eager to give it to her, but he loved teasing her more.

Nik peppered a few more taunting kisses over her skin before he hooked his thumbs into the sides of her underwear and slowly pulled them down her legs. He dropped them to the floor and pushed her knees apart, hungry for the taste of her.

With his help, she hitched a leg up over his shoulder and dug her heel into his back. Nik dragged his tongue along her slit, barely grazing her clit before pulling back. Her eager panting had his cock throbbing in his jeans. Taking his time with her, he blew a warm breath against her sensitive clit and watched as she squirmed, her thigh tensing over his shoulder.

"Nik," she breathed.

It was a plea that he happily answered. He covered her clit with his mouth and caressed her with his tongue, digging his fingers into her hips. Then he moved one hand down to run his fingers along her entrance, groaning with pleasure when he discovered how wet she was.

He eased one finger inside her, rocking his hand back and forth. When he pressed a second finger inside, she whimpered and tugged on his hair again. The sound brought a smile to his face as he continued to devour her pussy.

With his fingers, he stroked her inner walls, applying just the right amount of pressure to that sweet spot that had her knees trembling. It wouldn't take much longer for her to find her release. She bucked against his face and fingers, muttering unintelligible words of praise.

When Nik sucked on her clit, he felt her pussy clench around his fingers. God, he wanted to feel that pulse around his cock. Ali cried his name, and he released her clit, licking his lips to remove what was left of her arousal. She tasted like heaven.

Ali pushed up onto her forearms, watching to see what Nik would do next.

"Do you know what I can't stop thinking about?" he asked, pulling his shirt off in one smooth motion. It fell to the floor, and he started to unfasten his pants. "The first thing that popped into my head when I came home to find you in this little dress?"

Ali shook her head, her eyes trailing down his body. He didn't know it was possible, but his cock hardened even further. He couldn't wait to drive his shaft inside her and feel her warmth surround him.

But there was one more thing he wanted first.

With his pants loosened, he pushed them down, underwear included, and climbed onto the bed, forcing Ali backward to make space for him. He hovered over her, despite her efforts to pull his body against hers.

"I was thinking…" he said, sliding his cock back and forth over her slit. "That I want to make you mine…forever."

Ali's eyes fluttered closed, clearly losing herself to the feeling of his length gliding along her clit. "I am yours."

"As my wife."

Her brown eyes shot open, and she made a choking sound. "Wh-what?"

"Will…" Nik kissed her clavicle, peeking out from beneath her dress. "You…" Another kiss on her neck. "Marry…" A kiss to her forehead. "Me?"

The last kiss he saved for her lips, but he didn't close the distance. Instead, he left the thinnest slice of air between them, waiting for her to answer.

She swallowed audibly. "Are you serious?"

"Deadly."

"Aren't you supposed to have a shiny ring?"

He smirked. "I knew I was forgetting something."

"Nik…"

Nik put his forehead to hers. "Marry me, Ali. Spend forever with me. Since the day you came into my life, you've changed me for the better. I can't imagine…I *refuse* to live a life without you. And I hope you feel the same way."

The pause before her answer was painful. For a second, Nik thought she might say no. That he'd overestimated her love for him.

But then she smiled. "Yes, I will marry you."

"You will?" Even he was caught off guard by the shock in his voice.

Ali chuckled. "Of course. I love you and I want to grow old with you. I want to have your babies and listen to you snore every night. I want you to bring me cupcakes when I'm sad and I'll massage your shoulders after a tough day. I want my life to be forever intertwined with yours."

It was enough to close the distance between them. Their lips clashed in a whirlwind of passion and pure bliss. Nik had never felt this level of joy, didn't know that this level of rapturous ecstasy existed.

Her lips opened for him and he slid his tongue inside, kissing her deeper than ever before, determined for her to feel his love. At the same time, he reached between their bodies and drove his cock into her, delighted by her gasp of pleasure.

Slowly, intentionally, he made love to her, ensuring that every second of this night would hold a permanent place in his memories. He never wanted to forget this moment, because life couldn't possibly get better than this.

⁂

Morning came far too soon. Considering they'd spent most of the night tangled in bed sheets, Nik easily could've slept for several more hours, but duty called.

Today was the day—the third and final round of the Rite would take place in just a few hours and Nik needed to escort Grace to the last competition.

To his surprise, he hoped that Eli would emerge victorious. He wasn't sure when he had started caring about Eli's happiness, but it had happened regardless. Grace and Eli deserved a joyous life together, just like he did with Ali.

Ali—his fiancée.

That thought brought a lazy grin to his face and gave him the energy to sit up and pull the sheets back. Beside him, Ali still slept with one arm tucked under her head and the other holding the sheet to her bare chest. The dress had come off at some point during the night. Though she was sleeping, her lips were curved in a half smile and it broke Nik's heart that he needed to wake her. If they didn't get moving soon, they'd be late.

He leaned over and kissed her temple, brushing back her messy blonde hair. "Ali, wake up."

She stirred, but after a deep sigh, she returned to her motionless state.

"Ali. You can't sleep all day."

She grumbled and turned away from him.

Nik chuckled. He knew a lost cause when he saw one. Leaving the bed and Ali behind, he padded to the kitchen and began cooking breakfast. The sizzling pan and smell of bacon would wake her soon enough. Perhaps he'd make pancakes too, with the angelfruit syrup she liked so much.

Nik had cooked half the bacon and was finishing the pancake batter when Ali emerged in one of his shirts that barely covered her ass.

"Smells good," she said, coming up behind him and wrapping her arms around his waist while he continued to prepare their breakfast.

"Only the best for you, love." With a flick of the wrist, Nik flipped a pancake skillfully.

"I could get used to this," Ali said, pressing her forehead between his shoulder blades. "Waking up to find my *husband* making breakfast."

Damn if that title didn't shoot straight to his groin, but they had things to do...places to be...

"I'm not your husband yet," he reminded her.

Her hands began to wander, lowering from his stomach to the elastic waistband of his shorts. He sucked in a sharp breath as her fingers delved below the fabric.

"Close enough," she said, wrapping a hand around his cock.

Fuck it. They were going to be late.

Chapter Thirty-Three

ALI

ALI RUSHED TO GET ready at record speed. She and Nik had gotten
a little too carried away with their insatiable need for one another, but
after last night, it was hard to remember the real world existed. That they
couldn't stay holed up in bed, basking in their bliss, using their hands
and lips to express every ounce of love they had for each other.

Once Nik had left, she hopped in the shower and rinsed as quickly as
she could. He'd left before her since he needed to meet Grace before the
final round of the Rite. Ali had the luxury of a few extra minutes that he
didn't, so she agreed to meet him at the starting point.

She quickly pulled on a pair of faded jeans and a light blue tank top.
Then she grabbed a gray sweater, just in case it was cold outside. The
weather had been unpredictable lately now that summer was coming to
an end.

After sliding on a pair of boots, she headed out the door and made her
way through the web of dark tunnels. They were easy to navigate now
after living in Berland for a few months.

The closer she got to the large entry chamber, the more people began to gather and prevent her hurried pace. They were all moving in the same direction, so she fell into step, feeling like cattle being herded.

They squeezed together near the exit archway, funneling into a smaller tunnel. Shoulder to shoulder, they marched forward. Once the darkness gave way to daylight, Ali inhaled deeply, thankful to feel fresh air on her skin again.

Unlike the previous rounds, this day couldn't have been more perfect. Not too hot and not a rain cloud in sight. The sun broke through a thin layer of wispy clouds and a breeze rustled the tall grass lining the dirt path. Gravel crunched beneath the stampede of people making their way to the third and final location.

Truthfully, Ali wasn't sure why they even bothered to gather so early in the day. The last round was a race—a trek down the mountain to retrieve a flag and then a grueling climb back up. Most of the final competition wouldn't be visible to the crowd, but they all made their way to the starting point regardless.

Along the side of the road, vendors were positioned outside of their shops, hoping to make last-minute sales with the crowd meandering by. One young woman had a dozen flower crowns hanging off her arm. She waved one above her head and tried to catch the eye of anyone who walked past.

On the other side of the road, Ali glimpsed a couple exchanging money with the man who ran the local pub. Several large barrels were stacked next to him, each with a small tap toward the bottom edge. After the bar owner took the couple's money, a waitress poured amber liquid from one barrel into two travel mugs and handed them off to the patrons. Ali considered checking to see if one of those barrels contained angelfruit wine, but before she could squeeze her way through the flowing steam of people, a hand gripped her shoulder.

"Eli!" she exclaimed, wrapping him in a hug. "How are you feeling? Are you nervous? Are you ready? I bet you can't wait for today to be done and over with, huh?"

He chuckled and then scratched his neck, nervous energy glistening in his eyes. "I am ready...yeah. I guess I'll just be happy to know one way or another how this all ends."

Ali didn't miss the flicker of doubt pass over his face, no matter how hard he tried to hide it. She gently squeezed his arm. "It's going to work out. I can feel it. After everything we've been through, you deserve to be happy. And Grace loves you. What kind of cruel world would we live in if you two don't get your happily ever after?"

Eli snorted. "This world is nothing if not cruel."

"Such a pessimist. You can't go into the competition with that attitude. Say it loud and proud, Eli. You're going to win the Rite."

"I'm going to win the Rite," he said with very little enthusiasm.

Ali frowned. "You can do better than that."

He sucked in a breath and pushed his shoulders back. "I am going to win the Rite."

"Much better."

He rolled his eyes, but Ali knew that deep down he appreciated her support and innate talent at easing tension. "I can't believe by the end of the day, I'll basically be committed to Grace for the rest of our lives, as her future husband and partner in governing. Not that I'm complaining. I love Grace, but it is such a drastic pivot from what I thought my life would be."

Ali noted the way he confidently stated his expected outcome of the Rite—that he *would* be declared the winner. But she also couldn't help but recall the events of the night before—when Nik had asked her to be his wife and they, too, had committed their lives to one another.

She hadn't expected the opportunity to come so quickly, but after her pregnancy, she didn't want to hide things from Eli ever again.

"Listen, I know now isn't the best time," she said with a slight wince. "I don't want to distract you from the task at hand, but I have something important I want to share."

Eli's brows rose with curiosity, and he nodded and waited for her to continue.

Ali figured the best approach was to spit it out and hope for the best. Eli and Nik got along much better than they used to. Surely, he'd be happy for her...right?

"Last night, Nik asked me to marry him...and I said yes."

Eli's brows rose, and he blinked once.

Then twice.

His lips parted slightly, then stretched into a grin that didn't quite reach his eyes. "Are you happy?"

She nodded and couldn't contain the smile that made her cheeks ache. "I am."

"Then I'm happy for you."

Ali could tell he meant it. Her shoulders relaxed, and she realized she'd been tensing them, waiting for his reaction. She didn't need his approval, but knowing she had it was a tremendous relief.

She wrapped him in another hug, squeezing more tightly than before. He grunted under her relentless hold before the weight of his arms pressed against her back. "I only want what's best for you, Ali," he said, one hand brushing the back of her head.

Pure, unadulterated bliss warmed her heart. There'd been a time when she wasn't sure their friendship would ever recover, and now here they were, both of them about to get everything they ever wanted.

She finally relinquished him. "Should we get going? Wouldn't want you to be late."

He nodded. "After you."

They fell back into the stream of Berlanders making their way to the starting point. Some wished Eli good luck while others avoided him, viewing him only with a sideways glance before picking up their pace.

It was clear the people had chosen favorites in this contest. Ali had even heard murmurs of gambling amongst some circles. She'd bet everything she had on Eli.

When they reached the entrance to the viewing area—a series of bleachers pointed toward the downward slope of the mountain with the customary stage set up in the center for Grace and her family—Eli turned to Ali.

"This is where I leave you," he said, eyes flickering toward the other three contestants gathered near the stage. Jae and Trevor were stretching while a man Ali learned was called Roman spoke to an officiant.

As she watched, Jae bent down to ensure his boot laces were tied in a knot, his light golden skin mostly hidden beneath a navy long sleeve shirt and denim pants tucked into his boots.

When he stood, Roman finished speaking with the officiant and came closer, offering a hand to Jae. They briefly exchanged what Ali could only imagine were words of encouragement and good sportsmanship. Then Roman pulled his medium-length blond hair back into a small bun, a few tendrils falling loose around his round face.

Meanwhile, Trevor kept his eyes on Eli as her friend made his way to the group of suitors. She held tight to her conviction that Eli *would* win the Rite. Not just for him, but for Grace as well. Ali couldn't imagine Grace being forced to wed Trevor.

Trevor's lips moved. Ali couldn't hear what he said, but judging by the way Eli tensed, it wasn't good. With his back to her, she couldn't tell what Eli said either, but Trevor just smiled wickedly.

Thank god this would all be over soon. Hopefully Trevor would get exactly what he deserved.

Ali waited patiently for the crowd to move so she could make her way to the covered stage where Grace and her friends and family had the privilege of sitting. She could already see Nik, Grace, and Theo waiting. The rest of Grace's friends and family were probably still on their way. It was slow moving as people scoured the bleachers for an empty seat, several giving up altogether and opting to stand near the bottom.

Before she could reach the raised platform, out of the corner of her eye, she spotted a man pushing his way against the crowd, moving in the opposite direction of where he should be. Eamon, with his ever-present scowl, looked like a man with something to hide. He did his best to fade into the sea of bodies, but as the one source of friction in the current, Ali's eyes were drawn to him.

Where was he going?

Ali glanced back at Nik, who chatted with Grace and Theo, then to Eamon again, slowly making his way away from the gathering. She took one more look at Nik, knowing she should say something, but Eamon was already disappearing from her view. If she didn't move quickly, she'd lose him completely.

A second later, her feet were moving in the opposite direction, pushing against the flow of traffic with as much kindness and gentleness as she could muster. Lots of disgruntled looks were thrown her way, and she did her best to apologize quickly and keep moving.

Eventually, she was able to break through the wall of bodies and spotted Eamon walking alone in the distance. She picked up her pace but stayed close to the edge of the path, where bushes and trees kept her hidden in their shade.

Luckily, Eamon didn't look back. Arrogant bastard.

Just before they hit the main strip of town, he took a right turn, avoiding the stragglers who hadn't yet made it to the start of the final round of the Rite. A small crowd was still gathered around the bartender, seemingly perfectly content to skip the Rite altogether to drink with friends.

Ali turned the same corner as Eamon, catching sight of him just before he darted to the left. She walked faster, doing her best to stay light on her feet and make as little noise as possible. As she left the row of shops behind, the din of town faded into rustling leaves and chirping crickets.

She was careful to check around corners before following Eamon. He was up to something, but she had to avoid being seen if she wanted to find out what it was.

Shops became sparse and soon she had nothing to hide behind. Eamon was leading her down a path around the base of the mountain. By the looks of the overgrown grass and weeds, it was rarely used. A dead twig snagged at her shirt, and she pushed it aside, double checking that Eamon hadn't heard.

She had no reason to worry, because he walked without a moment of hesitation. Just as she was wondering how to continue her hunt while keeping her distance, Eamon pushed through the bushes and slipped inside an opening in the mountain.

What the...

Ali moved closer, taking the same steps Eamon did through the brush. There, on the side of the mountain, was a sliver of an entrance. It was so small she'd have to scoot sideways to get through it. How had Eamon fit through there? If she hadn't seen him disappear with her own eyes, she never would've known the entrance existed.

Without knowing what was on the other side, she dreaded forcing herself into the tight space. But she hadn't come all this way for nothing.

She turned to the side and began to shuffle her way inside, following Eamon into the darkness.

It was cramped, but she focused on each step, counting her breaths to keep calm. Slowly, the light from outside began to fade and her heart raced, urging her to go back and leave this foolish quest behind.

Ali ignored the pounding in her chest, but she breathed a sigh of relief when a cool light grew from inside the cave. She prayed that whatever space waited for her at the end of this small tunnel was large enough to continue her pursuit of Eamon without being noticed.

As luck would have it, she cautiously moved into a chamber almost twice as large as her apartment. She looked around, jaw slack, as she took in the room before her.

Only two lamps overhead lit the chamber with a bluish haze, but it was enough to see clearly. Rows of raised wooden plant beds filled the entire room, each full of damp soil and dead tree trunks speckled with small red bumps. She listened for movement, unable to spot Eamon from her position. When she heard nothing, she moved closer to the nearest bed, leaning in to get a better look.

The red bulbs were like nothing she'd seen before. Smaller than her fingernail and bright red like a rose, they grew directly on the side of the tree stumps, though she didn't understand how that could be. How could any fruit grow from a dead plant?

She started to reach toward the unknown red bulbs. Moments before she plucked one from its place on the tree bark, a voice from behind startled her.

"I wouldn't do that if I were you."

Chapter Thirty-Four

GRACE

Grace combed her hair before dividing it into two sections, braiding each with nimble fingers. She'd been practicing doing her own hair before bed for months and had finally gotten the hang of it. Once the two plaits were tied off, she slipped into a pink nightgown and crawled into her enormous bed. It had recently been upgraded from her kiddie bed, and she couldn't wait to have her friends over to stay the night. They could all fit in one bed at the same time!

As she nestled into the blankets, her bedroom door cracked open and her mother peeked her head inside. "Are you ready?"

"Yep!" Grace replied with a grin.

The door swung wide open and her mother stepped inside, coming over to take a seat next to Grace in her gigantic new bed. Her mother held a book—the cover faded and bent in one corner. Like every other book her *mother had read to Grace, this one also had delicate pages, so Grace knew that only adults were allowed to hold the precious item.*

*Her mother gently opened the book and read the title—*Happily Ever After. *It was a tale of a princess in a faraway land with dragons and magic. The ones with princesses were Grace's favorite. She knew it wasn't exactly the same, but she saw herself in them. Knew that she and her family held importance in her town, even if she didn't fully understand why.*

She listened with undivided attention as her mother told the story of how the princess found herself in a predicament, betrayed by someone she thought she could trust and destined to spend the rest of her days inside the dragon's lair.

But a prince *came along, and he was able to vanquish the dragon using powerful magic. The princess was so thankful and impressed by his courage and charming smile. It was love at first sight. And when they shared a kiss, fireworks exploded overhead.*

Grace giggled at this part. She loved it when the story ended with a romantic kiss.

"And they lived happily ever after," her mother concluded the bedtime story. With a kiss to Grace's forehead, her mother tucked her in.

Grace sighed happily. "When I grow up, I'm going to find my prince."

"Is that so?"

"Yep. And we will be in love and throw a big wedding for everyone *in town and we'll have seven kids...and a puppy."*

Her mother chuckled. "Where are you going to find one of those?"

"I don't know." Grace shrugged. "Maybe I'll go on an adventure to find one. I'm going to have the most perfect, amazing life...like you and Daddy."

She yawned and pulled her thick blanket against her chest. Through heavy lids, she watched her mother nod and head toward the door. Before she left, she turned back to Grace one more time. "I believe you'll get everything you ever wanted, Gracie. If anyone will, it's you. I love you, sweetie."

"Love you too, Mommy."

*****

It was easy for Grace to hide her nerves. Playing the part of a perfect, stoic regent was something she had been doing for years. Ever since she'd learned the history of the matriarchy in Berland and the position she'd be expected to fill, she had left her own dreams behind and put on the mask that was required of her.

There'd been a time in her early teens when she'd rebelled. She had stayed out too late, hung out with people who were too old and too wild. She'd had her first sip of angelfruit wine in a dark back room with people who had been eager to steal her youth. One day she had stumbled upon Azalea's and that was one sinful habit she'd yet to give up. The one bit of freedom she clung to with white knuckles even as responsibility and propriety tugged her away.

Today it felt as though everything she'd been running from had finally caught up to her. For years, she'd been swimming against the current, desperately seeking ways to maintain her individuality before she fell into the role her mother had carefully curated for her.

But she couldn't fight the raging river forever.

Grace gazed at the crowd gathered to watch the spectacle that was her life. Like she was nothing more than an object of entertainment, a nameless figurehead who rarely crossed their mind unless a ball or celebration was involved.

But that wasn't entirely true.

As her eyes swept the crowd, she spotted the woman who had taught her for over ten years sitting next to her husband. He gave the woman a peck on the cheek, and she smiled.

Two rows down, Grace watched as the man who worked with her father shifted restlessly in his seat. After a back injury, he'd had to retire from traveling missions, but he still did paperwork for her father and had always come to their holiday dinners, bringing along a small gift for Grace and Theo every year until they became adults.

Three teenage boys climbed the bleacher steps, and she recognized them as the kids who'd shown up barefoot and broken, having lost all of their family and friends to a devastating mudslide in the mountains to the east. They were only a few years younger than she was and had spent their first few months in Berland clinging to her like a shadow until they finally felt safe. She smiled to see that, years later, they were still inseparable.

Grace continued to pick out friendly faces—Heather's parents who waved when they spotted her, the man who ran the general store, her doctor, the seamstress who frequently mended her vintage gowns. The list went on and on of all the people she talked to regularly. People who had made an impact in her life and those with whom she'd made an impact.

Suddenly, she didn't feel like such a stranger, such an untouchable recluse. This town was full of people she adored and admired. And one in particular that she was madly in love with, despite his imperfections.

Grace was too full of energy to sit in her assigned seat. Nik and Theo joined her on the platform, but they still waited for the remainder of their party. Her parents and friends would arrive any minute.

In the meantime, she searched for Eli, heart hammering when she caught a glimpse of him with the other suitors. He had his back to her, but she recognized his tall, lean frame. His broad shoulders stretched the fabric of his black cotton shirt, and she could see his muscles rippling underneath as he rolled his neck and swung his arms across his torso.

Immediately she felt a sense of longing for him—to touch him, hold his hand and hear the low rumble of his voice. It had only been two days since her world had collapsed, her mother's deteriorating health finally coming to light. A revelation that Eli had evidently known for months.

Emotions had been running high when Eli had made his confession. Fear of losing her mother, relief from her mother's acceptance, yearning for the way things could've been different if only Grace had known... She could've spent more time working together with her mother instead of feeling like she'd failed her at every turn. The weight on her chest was suffocating as she considered the alternative outcomes.

Eli turned around and for a moment they just stared at each other, each waiting for the other to move first. In the end, Grace did, stepping down from the platform and heading toward the group of suitors.

But Eli met her halfway, saving her the hassle of pretending like she wanted to speak to all of her suitors, when there was only one on her mind.

When they were standing face to face, Eli forcing a timid smile and Grace biting her cheek, they both started to speak at the same time.

"Are you—"

"I'm such a—"

"You first," they said simultaneously, then laughed nervously.

Grace swallowed and fought the urge to reach for his hand. Soon...very soon.

"I was upset when you didn't tell me about my mom," she began.

"I know," he said, shaking his head. "I don't know what I was thinking. I truly am sorry, Grace. And I hope you'll forgive me and give me the chance to prove that I'll never keep secrets from you again."

His brows pinched together, and she could see the hurt in his eyes. When she hurt, so did he.

"When I woke up in the morning and you were gone, I...I don't know...it *scared* me. The thought of losing you scares me. I'm so fucking in love with you, Grace. I'll do anything to earn your trust again."

Grace nodded. "I forgive you. And I believe you. I know you would never intentionally hurt me."

Eli breathed a sigh of relief.

"And I'm so fucking in love with you, too," she added with a grin.

He took a step closer, oblivious to the crowd surrounding them and his fellow suitors, who were no doubt eyeing him with envy. They all wished they could be as close to her as Eli was. And they would fight tooth and nail to beat him today.

Eli quickly glanced around before his cautious eyes returned to her. "When I win the Rite and make you my wife, I'm going to show you just how in love with you I truly am," he said, licking his lips and allowing his gaze to roam over her body.

Heat spread over her skin, but the long, thin green dress she wore hid her flush. Still, he watched her as if he could see the way his words affected her insides, turning her legs to jelly and her stomach into butterflies. His smile was just as cocky as it was charming.

"Good luck," she said, winking before she turned away. A gust of cool air blew through her hair and cooled her overheated body.

On her way back to the covered platform, she noticed more people had arrived. Heather and Amaya were both there in matching blue dresses, though the cut was slightly different—Heather's strapless while Amaya's had a halter top. Theo was now enamored in a conversation with Sam and Nik and at the center of the stage, her dad was flipping through a couple sheets of paper.

Climbing the steps onto the platform, she turned to her dad. "Where's Mom?"

He folded the papers and tucked them into his back pocket before meeting her gaze. "I'm so sorry, Grace. She wasn't up to it."

Grace nodded and stared straight ahead. She'd had little hope that her mother would be able to attend after spending the past few days in bed, but it still felt like a piece of her was missing. Finally reaching the finish line, a day that her mother had endlessly prepared her for, and not having her standing beside Grace felt like a punch to the gut.

And this was only the beginning. There would be many days to come, once in a lifetime experiences, that her mother wouldn't be there for. And she'd be further away than the bed where she rested now. She'd be out of reach.

Grace's eyes stung, but she blinked away the tears before anyone could see. The last thing she wanted to do was cause a scene. She could hear the gossip now.

Grace was so distraught at the thought of being auctioned off, she was crying!

Poor thing isn't ready for this kind of commitment. She's still a child!

She's so spoiled. She should be grateful for this opportunity.

Of course, none of them knew the real reason for her tears. Their family had decided to keep her mother's illness confidential until Grace made it through the Rite and married, fulfilling her prerequisites for becoming the next Lady of Berland.

The idea of a hasty wedding didn't terrify her as much as it should. As long as Eli won, she'd happily marry him tomorrow. She was certain no other person on earth could make her feel like he did—alive and full of hope for a brighter future, eager to fulfill the role she'd been groomed for with him at her side. She smiled as she pictured that life, bittersweet as it would be without her mother.

Beside her, her father cleared his throat, preparing to give a few opening remarks before the official start of the final round. A blanket of silence slowly fell over the crowd as neighbors shushed one another and waited patiently for her father to speak.

The suitors turned their attention to the stage as well, each of them eyeing Grace with desire and determination. She offered a warm smile to Jae and Roman but ignored Trevor's slimy smirk. Eli stood at the left end, standing tall with his arms behind his back. He winked, and she had to look away to hide her grin.

Finally, the bleachers full of onlookers quieted enough for her father to speak.

"Welcome," he roared, loud enough for the far ends of the crowd to hear. "Today is an exciting day!"

Grace's ears buzzed with the cheers of her people. The sounds, the sights, the tickle of loose hair on her neck and shoulders—her senses were overwhelmed with it all.

Before she knew it, the suitors were lining up, ready to begin their race down the mountain. Diane and Fox accompanied them, waiting to give the signal to start. Eamon was noticeably absent, considering his own son was about to compete. Grace looked around, expecting to find him on the sidelines or meandering through the crowd, perhaps busy chatting with one of his cronies.

But he was nowhere to be found.

She looked behind her. Most of her companions were enraptured with the proceedings, listening attentively to her father as he wrapped up his speech. Theo gave her a little thumbs up—a sign of solidarity.

When her eyes met Nik's, he frowned, as though he could sense something was wrong. He shifted towards her until he was close enough to whisper.

"What is it?"

"I don't know," she said quietly, shaking her head. Maybe it was nothing. "Eamon is missing."

Nik scratched the back of his neck and looked around. "You think he could be running late?"

"I doubt it. There's a lot riding on this final round. He's depending on Trevor to win so they can solidify their power and influence. There's nothing more important than this."

"Unless..." he hesitated.

"Unless he has something up his sleeve. Unless he's planning something while everyone else is away."

"Fuck," Nik said, running a hand through his hair. "What do you want me to do? I can stay here if you need me, but—"

"But you'd be more useful back at the mountain. See if you can find him. I want to know what he's up to."

Nik nodded and then looked to his left. His brows pinched together before he looked to his right. Panic bloomed on his face. "Where's Ali?"

Before Grace could respond, her father shouted, "Begin!"

Chapter Thirty-Five

ELI

ELI WAS SO OVERWHELMED by his thoughts and the roaring crowd that he barely heard Benjamin shout for them to begin. He caught movement out of the corner of his eye and, realizing the other suitors had started running, he darted forward to catch up. After a few long strides, the ground began to slope downward, and he felt the tug of gravity bringing him closer to his goal.

He stumbled forward, maintaining his balance with pure determination. The sound of the roaring crowd faded until he only heard the clamoring of footsteps.

Right now, the four suitors were running down the hill together, but soon they'd split off, finding their own path to the bottom of the mountain.

There were many routes that one could take, and Eli had practiced running almost all of them. One was a gentle slope but would take more time with its weaving path, and one followed the river but would require traversing a waterfall halfway there. And there were a hundred other ways in which the flag could be reached.

After five minutes passed, Jae was the first to split from the group, sliding between a row of trees and disappearing from view. The mountain turned steeper, and Eli had to slow his pace to keep from toppling over. When it flattened again on a small landing, two paths emerged. Roman took the left, while Eli and Trevor carried on to the right.

Eager to leave Trevor behind, Eli sped up, pumping his arms hard at his sides. Within seconds, he noticed Trevor was right next to him. He huffed in frustration and slowed down, thinking Trevor might run past. Instead, Trevor slowed to match his pace.

"What the fuck are you doing?" Eli demanded. He knew he shouldn't let his irritation get the best of him. It was what Trevor wanted, and the last thing Eli wanted to do was give Trevor the impression that he was under Eli's skin.

But he was. Eli was counting down the minutes until he could rid Trevor from his life for good. When he would give up his conquest for Grace and the power she offered. There was no guarantee the rebellion would be squashed entirely, but at least the traitors would have to come up with another plan to seize power. So far, their physical attacks hadn't been successful, and Trevor wouldn't be successful either. Not if Eli could help it.

"I don't know what you mean," Trevor said, flashing his white teeth.

"Stop following me."

Trevor huffed a laugh. "That's quite the assumption. I'm just following the path, same as you."

Eli rolled his eyes. He could split off at any moment, but that would mean enduring the weeds and thickets. Snakes and other wildlife inhabited the unkept areas of the mountain. He would've preferred to stick to the cleared path, but Trevor was making that option difficult.

A small opening appeared, wedged between two overgrown bushes. It was a far cry from a true trail, but it was also the best chance Eli had at creating distance between himself and Trevor. A ray of light broke through the treetops and illuminated the narrow path, almost like it was calling to Eli, assuring him that *this* was the way he was meant to go.

With a disgruntled look at Trevor, he turned sharply and abandoned his unwelcome companion.

"Really?" Trevor called after him, but Eli continued to trudge forward. "Terrible decision, my friend. I hope you enjoy the poison ivy and rattlesnakes!"

Without turning around, Eli lifted his hand and gave Trevor the middle finger over his shoulder. He heard a soft, sinister chuckle before Trevor's footsteps faded into nothing.

Eli would face a hundred poisonous creatures if it meant getting away from the most venomous of them all.

Fortunately, he didn't immediately run into any snakes or bears or coyotes. He didn't even run into a hungry vulture. His ankles stayed covered by his long jeans, and he kept his arms close to his body to avoid the encroaching foliage. Although he didn't touch a single leaf or vine, his skin still itched at the thought of attracting an angry, red rash.

The mountain continued to carry him forward and downward. As easy as it was to descend, he knew it would be a strenuous hike back up.

His pace quickened as the thought of reaching the flag consumed him, driving him onward as though he were being chased. Suitors were allowed to steal the flag on the return trip, but he didn't want to let it get to that point. No, the easiest way to win was to claim the flag first.

Sweat formed near his hairline and dripped down his neck, but he didn't falter. The peace of the forest was disturbed by his heavy breathing and the snapping twigs beneath his feet. This overgrown path would ultimately merge with another, wider path, but he wasn't certain how much farther he had to go.

He raced against time and only stumbled when he heard a piercing yell. The noise died out as quickly as it came and he paused, straining as he tried to determine what direction it had come from. And who, or what, it was.

Eli peered through the gaps between trees, searching for a sign of life, but the forest remained still. Even the leaves stopped swaying in the wind.

Then the shouting started again, more clearly than before.

Eli bolted off the path he'd been following and tore through the bramble and unruly tree branches that sliced at his cheeks and snagged on his clothing.

Another cry rang out just as Eli stumbled across a body lying on the ground, torso twisted so one arm was reaching for his ankle while the other propped him up. Though he faced the opposite direction, Eli only had to see the messy blond bun to know it was Roman. And his ankle...

His ankle was a mangled, bloody wreck caught between a metal hunting trap. Roman groaned in pain as Eli fell to his knees beside him.

"How did this happen?" Eli asked, inspecting the trap to figure out a way to release it.

Roman spoke through gritted teeth. "I didn't see it. It was covered in leaves."

Obviously he hadn't seen it. No one would voluntarily step on a hunting trap. But why was it even here? The metal wasn't brand new, nothing was in this world, but it didn't look weathered either. It had to have been placed intentionally. And if that was the case, why was it placed on a trail for a human, or suitor, to come across, rather than the woods where an animal would be caught?

"Hold still," Eli said, pulling the levers on each side of the trap to loosen the tension. The trap's teeth slowly relinquished their hold on Roman's ankle and blood gushed from the wound.

Roman hissed and pulled the pack off his back, throwing open the flap and retrieving a small roll of bandages. Eli offered to help, but Roman was stubborn, wrapping his ankle himself before tying it in a knot.

"Can you stand on it?" Eli asked as he rose from his knees and extended a hand to Roman.

"I think so." With a small grunt, Roman rose to his feet and only winced for a second before steeling himself. "Thanks."

Eli watched as Roman took a step forward, limping on his wounded leg. He took another step, breathing heavily, and then another.

"You're in no position to carry on. You should go back or wait until someone else can come to help."

"I can walk just fine," he spat, though Eli could tell his frustration lay with his injury, not Eli. To come this far and be taken out before the final round was halfway through? Eli understood his irritation. It was exactly why Eli wouldn't be staying to help him any further. It wasn't a life-threatening injury. Roman could sit and wait until the race was finished or crawl back to the top if he felt so inclined.

Roman went to take another step but stumbled and only stopped himself from falling by grabbing onto the nearest tree trunk. "Fuck," he muttered. Then he turned to lean his back against the tree, tilting his head back and squeezing his eyes closed. "Fuuuck."

"I can send someone to fetch you once I finish," Eli said, beginning to move again. He'd lost several vital minutes by stopping to help Roman and couldn't afford to lose any more.

"Thanks," Roman mumbled in a rather ungrateful tone. Again, Eli chalked it up to anger at the situation. There wasn't anything else Eli could do for him.

As he headed down the path, Roman called out to him once more. "Hey, Eli?"

"Yes?"

"Make sure you beat that motherfucker."

Eli's brows lifted in surprise. He didn't know much about Roman other than his mother worked in the cafeteria and his father had died several years ago. Occasionally, he helped his mother in the kitchens when she needed an extra hand or filled in when someone else was too ill to work their shift. Before this conversation, Eli guessed the two of them had exchanged less than ten words. But that sentence alone was enough for Eli to judge his character. He was a good man. One who was loyal to Grace and her family. One who knew exactly what was at stake if Trevor were to win.

They were on the same side of this fight.

Eli nodded and spoke with conviction. "I will."

After more reassurance that Roman would be okay without him, Eli finally left his newfound comrade behind. Running off to save Roman hadn't just cost him time; it had also turned him around. This wasn't the path he'd meant to travel, but he kept moving downward, waiting for a landmark to give him a hint as to where he was.

He found that hint in the worst of ways—a waterfall plunging off a cliff and down nearly three stories into the river below.

On one hand, he was closer than he'd realized to the point where the flag had been placed. On the other, the cliff extended for as long as his eyes could see, and the fastest way to his goal would be a steep climb down the side of the craggy rock.

Of all the paths that led to the flag, he would've chosen this one last. Roman had to be a madman to choose this route, or perhaps he hadn't realized that the only way down from here was to climb down slippery rock.

Eli took a tentative peek over the edge, swallowing hard when he caught of glimpse of the flat land below. It seemed so far away, and one wrong step would have him tumbling to his death.

He studied the path forged into the mountainside. It was clear that once upon a time, someone had chiseled into the stone and created small *steps* to make the climb easier. Those steps were only two inches wide at best and while at one point they may have been sharp and sturdy, now they were eroded and smoothed over by wind and water. It would be hard to get a good grip on them.

But he looked around him, at the stretch of earth that dropped off into the blue sky, and knew there was no other way.

First, he double checked his shoelaces, ensuring they wouldn't come undone during his descent. Then he crouched down to the ground and slowly eased his lower half down the mountain, feeling for those tiny steps and holding onto the cliff for dear life.

Carefully, he moved one limb at a time. Reaching to grab a piece of rock jutting out at an angle, lowering his leg to find a new foothold. His arms began to burn within seconds from the amount of strength it took to hold on. He shifted to place more weight on his feet and give his hands a break, fighting the urge to look down. It would only make him dizzy if he did.

His muscles felt as though they were on fire, but he continued to move slowly and carefully, double and triple checking each step and grip before he moved on to the next. His forearms began to cramp and his legs trembled, but he was only halfway down the cliff by his estimate.

Curiosity got the best of him, and he quickly glanced down to see how far he was from the bottom. A burst of air flew from his lungs, part disbelief and part relief to know that he was approximately twice his height away from the ground.

Impatience surged through his body, and he moved faster, desperate to reach solid ground and shake out his weary muscles. But his lack of attention cost him, and his foot slipped. His body collided with the rock and the impact loosened his grip, sending him tumbling backward. He reached toward the sky, grasping but finding nothing but empty air.

Fear was an emotion Eli knew intimately. The past year of his life had been one horrific event after another. But the fear of plummeting to his death was like nothing he'd ever felt before.

Time moved slowly and too quickly at the same time. It was enough to replay his life's most significant moments but too fast to catch his breath before his back slammed into the ground.

Eli grunted, lying still for a moment and blinking up at the bright blue sky. He was alive. He'd only fallen a few feet, and he was alive.

A shocked chuckle escaped his lips, and his body shook. Then he groaned from the pain coursing through his back. He slowly sat up. Everything was sore, but nothing was broken.

Thank fucking god.

He pulled himself off the ground and stretched out his arms and legs, still burning from the climb. Then he put his hands on his hips and stretched his back too, wincing at the twinge of pain. It would likely bruise, but he'd felt worse in the past, far worse.

Forcing his feet and pained muscles to move, Eli continued to follow the stream's path. The ground here had leveled out, making it easier to push forward despite his fall. The water beside him transitioned from raging rapids to a peaceful flow that glistened under the sun. The current moved quickly, however, and he used it to set his pace.

It couldn't be much longer now.

As if his thoughts had conjured it into existence, he glimpsed a small, red triangular piece of fabric waving in the light breeze. Attached to a wooden rod, the flag had been planted in the middle of a dried-out tree stump.

Eli released a sigh of relief and started running, slowly at first but then quickening to a sprint. The flag grew larger as he approached and he noticed the smaller details, like the frayed edges and the way some parts were more faded than others, like a muted rose color.

His lips curved into a smile. He was so close to having it all—to having Grace.

He reached out his hand and seconds before his fingers grazed the tattered fabric, something moved to his left. He didn't waste time turning toward the figure and instead focused on grabbing the flag and pulling it from the stump.

The feel of the fabric against his palm was like touching heaven. It sent him soaring, his body filled with indescribable bliss, while also keeping him grounded, taking in the significance of this moment.

His moment of revelry was short-lived, because less than a second later, greedy fingers clawed at his arms and hands, desperate to rip the flag out of his clutch.

Chapter Thirty-Six

ALI

"It's quite unexpected, running into you down here," Eamon said, stepping out from behind a particularly large tree trunk near the back of the room. His face was lit by the pale bluish light, casting shadows over his sharp features that left Ali's hair standing on end. It gave him an unearthly appearance, like a demon hiding in the depths of hell.

Ali didn't speak. There was no good reason for her to be here. It was obvious she'd followed him, but she didn't want to give him the satisfaction of admitting it.

"What is this place? What are these?" she asked, nodding to the odd red bulbs growing on the tree bark.

"You don't recognize them?" he asked, taking a step toward her. She countered his approach with a step to her right, shielding her body behind the closest planter. Eamon chuckled. "I suppose you wouldn't. They were crushed up into dust by the time you got your hands on them."

Ali watched him with unease. With each step he took, she retreated farther into the chamber. It was like a checkerboard with rows of planters that came up to her waist. Spaces between each planter made it so one could move freely between the rows, making it difficult for Ali to create a sufficient barrier to separate them. She did her best to keep at least two planters diagonally between them, but Eamon watched her like a predator toying with its prey. He knew the layout better than she did. He didn't even have to watch his step.

With the little distance that separated them, Ali watched as Eamon dragged his hand up a tree trunk, pausing to pry a few of the red buttons from the bark. He held them up in his palm, which Ali could see was covered in a black leather glove. "They're helberries. Do you know what those are?"

Yes. Those cursed fungi were the reason she'd lost her child. The reason she'd almost lost her own life. She backed away from the planter closest to her, only to bump into another behind her. The rows upon rows of helberries growing, waiting to take their next victim, pressed in around her and made the chamber feel smaller than it was. She hesitated to move an inch, just in case she accidentally brushed up against one.

"Hmm. I think you know exactly what they are."

"Y...You," she stammered. "You poisoned me." She'd always suspected it. Who else would be cruel enough to do such a thing? But there was no proof and she couldn't figure out a reason other than the fact that Eamon was a horrible human being. "Why?"

He shrugged. "Would you believe me if I said you were just a casualty of war? The poison was never meant for you. It was for your *friend.*" He spat the last word like it was bitter on his tongue.

"Grace?"

"Obviously."

Ali glared at him and carefully took another sidestep. She needed to come up with a plan to get out of here. Every minute inside the dark chamber forced her farther from the entrance. Eamon seemed to know that too, carefully wedging himself between her and the narrow tunnel that led out of the mountain and back to safety.

She needed *time* to come up with a plan. Maybe she could distract him somehow.

"Why did you want to poison Grace?" she asked, though she already knew the answer. Eamon and his rebellion were power hungry, and they'd do anything to end the line of succession. But if she could keep him talking, then she could use that time to figure out her next steps.

"Because she doesn't deserve to call herself the *Lady* of Berland." His voice dripped with contempt. "Her mother doesn't either. For years, we've been subjected to weak leadership. Allowing too many people in, draining our resources, and ignoring the concerns of those who've been in Berland the longest. Women like Grace and Ellen are too weak to lead."

Ali resisted the urge to scoff. It wasn't that Grace or Ellen were incapable of leading; they just didn't lead in a way that benefited Eamon above all else. His followers were foolish enough to think he'd reward them for their loyalty, but Eamon didn't care about them either. He only cared about himself.

"And you think you would make a better ruler?" she asked.

Eamon stepped around a planter. His hand moved to his right pocket.

Ali didn't want to find out what he was holding. She moved backward until another planter separated them, eyes flicking from side to side for something other than helberries.

To her right, she noticed a workbench littered with tools, a watering can, and red-stained protective clothing hanging on the wall. It wasn't much to work with, but there had to be something she could use to help her escape. Slowly, so she didn't alert Eamon to her intentions, she inched toward the wall.

"Of course I would be. I'd be strong—strong enough to make the tough choices like keeping outsiders *out*. And expanding our territory, giving more land and wealth to those who deserve it."

This time, Ali couldn't hide her snort. "That's your grand idea? To make enemies of everyone outside of these borders? To claim what isn't yours and antagonize neighboring communities who have helped build and maintain our trade routes? You'd start a war just to stroke your own ego."

Eamon took an angry step toward her, and his hand slid out of his pocket carrying a small white piece of fabric. It looked like a small sack full of some substance Ali couldn't see, but by the way the edges bulged, she assumed it was full of helberries. What was he going to do? Shove them down her throat? Toss them at her? She squatted lower just in case she needed to duck.

"I wouldn't expect a woman like you to understand. You're just as useless as Grace. And her mother and her mother before that. Too much of a pacifist, letting your emotions get in the way. Letting it blind you from seeing the future Berland could have. The future we *need*."

"The future you've painted is dark and lonely and destined to lead to ruin."

"What would you know?" Eamon spat.

"I watched it happen myself...in Rysburg. Foolish men who thought they could take what didn't belong to them, and in the end, it cost them everything. Just like it will cost you everything."

The longer she spoke, the angrier Eamon became. Ali could tell she was running out of time to stall him. He was tired of playing with his prey and was ready to be rid of her. He clearly didn't appreciate the truth she spoke.

Thankfully, the wall was just a few feet away now. But Eamon was inching closer every second. She slid her right foot across the uneven floor but stumbled when she came across a rather large jut in the surface. She recovered quickly, hoping her wobble was too subtle to notice, but as she studied Eamon, she knew she hadn't been that lucky.

His eyes were fixed on her lower half, like he could see through the planters to where her feet were sneaking toward the wall. He glanced in that direction, eyes squinted, and then back to her. His head cocked to the left. "Oh, Ali, do not delude yourself into thinking you'll be getting out of here alive. I may not have been successful the first time around, but your life ends today. It ends here."

He said the words so carelessly, and somehow, that made it worse. Her life was expendable to him. Just another casualty in his quest to overthrow the matriarchy. He didn't care about any of the lives he'd taken. The council members who had died in a fire, the hundreds who could've lost everything had his attempt to sabotage the solar panels been successful, whoever these helberries were meant for—none of them mattered.

Ali didn't matter. And her baby hadn't mattered.

An uncontrollable flame lit inside her, blazing across her skin and turning her vision red. She abandoned stealth and lunged for the wall and the bench that came up to her waist.

But Eamon was ready. He sprinted around the few planters that kept them apart.

Ali grabbed the first thing her fingers touched, and she prayed that she hadn't just gripped helberries with bare hands. When she raised her fist, she briefly glimpsed a jar filled with a jelly-like substance, which she threw at Eamon's face.

He held his arm up just in time to prevent the jar from colliding with his forehead, and the glass shattered, sending the slimy red substance all over his face and arm. It slowly dripped down and, for a moment, time stood still.

Ali watched as Eamon processed what she'd just done. His eyes went wide, and they both realized at the same time that Ali had just thrown some sort of helberry preserve and it had splattered all over Eamon's unprotected skin.

Eamon moved fast, but Ali acted faster. She reached behind her and grabbed the remaining three jars, sprinting to the side before he could get to her. When she felt she had enough distance, she spun back around and tossed another jar at his head.

He ducked, and the jar exploded on the corner of a planter, raining glass and poisonous goo to the floor. Eamon yelled in frustration and flung the sack he'd been holding in her direction. She stepped out of the way and the sack hit the wall behind her, bursting open with a cloudy powder.

Ali closed her eyes and mouth on instinct. She'd been wrong about its contents. Those little bumps weren't raw helberries. They must've been pellets containing the same type of powder she'd once been poisoned with. Stepping away from the cloud, she pulled the neck of her shirt up until it covered her mouth and nose. After a few steps, she dared open her eyes, only to find Eamon running toward her.

She threw a jar in his direction, but it slipped out of her fingers. Though she'd aimed for his nose, it fell short and landed on his upper thigh. The glass cracked but didn't split open until it hit the floor. Eamon lost his foothold in the slippery mess and reached out, grabbing one of the planters to keep himself upright.

In his moment of distraction, Ali saw the perfect opportunity. She took one step forward and threw her last jar at him with all her might. The container tumbled through the air and miraculously collided with Eamon's cheek, bursting open and covering his eyes and mouth.

He hollered and spat, but the more he tried to clear the jelly from his face, the worse it spread. His cheeks broke out in hives almost instantaneously and his right eye swelled shut. Little red streaks dotted his face where the shattered glass had sliced his skin.

Eamon's head whipped in her direction. He tried to feel his way toward her, fingers brushing the wooden edges of the planters while he walked between them.

Ali ran around the perimeter of the room while Eamon fumbled forward.

"Come back here, you bitch," he screamed. "I'll kill you!"

Ali ignored him, making her way to the little tunnel so she could escape. But she skidded in her tracks when her eyes caught on something shiny on the workbench. Shiny and *sharp*.

A pair of gardening shears at least six inches long were hanging by a nail on the cave wall. She looked between them and the exit, taking only a heartbeat to decide. Then she backtracked and headed for the shears, her heart beating wildly in her chest.

She didn't have time to second-guess herself. To consider what the consequences would be for what she was about to do. All she could think about was how much pain and suffering this one man had caused, and how she could end it with one grisly choice.

Eamon was still blindly fumbling around when Ali went quiet. In order for her plan to work, she needed to catch him off guard.

It took a minute for Eamon to realize he was the only one making a sound. He stopped moving and waited for her to make a noise.

But none came.

"Where'd you go, you little bitch?" he muttered.

Ali gave him no response. She tiptoed closer, working her way through the rows of helberries until she could position herself behind him.

"Don't tell me you ran," he sneered. "Like a pathetic *woman*. I'll bet you went to find that boyfriend of yours. Or maybe your friend Eli? I always thought you two were abnormally close. Does Grace know her beloved Eli is still in love with someone else?"

Ali ground her teeth, but not because of his comments regarding Eli. Their friendship had never been healthier, and Grace was completely aware of their history. They had nothing to hide.

But Ali *hated* the way he spoke, as if she was inferior. As if she was weak or fragile. She was stronger than he ever would be. He wouldn't have survived half of the things she'd been through. She gripped the shears tighter until the handle dug into her palm.

"Ali," he taunted, drawing out her name like an eerie song.

She was close now, close enough that she had to step into the same slippery sludge he'd gotten caught in. She shuffled her feet forward carefully until Eamon was within an arm's reach.

Ali raised the shears over her head, ready to plunge them into his back, right between his shoulder blades.

But just as she began to bring them down, Eamon spun around, baring his teeth like a wild animal. He opened his mouth, likely to spew more hatred and insults, but before he could utter another word, Ali drove the shears right into his chest.

Chapter Thirty-Seven

NIK

THE CENTER OF TOWN was mostly deserted, since almost everyone in
Berland was attending the final round of the Rite. But there were a few
places still open, serving drinks to those who didn't want to sit and wait
on the hard bleachers.

That was where Nik started. If Eamon was up to something shifty,
a hidden corner in a dimly lit pub would be a great place to conduct
business.

The first bar Nik came across was packed. People had to shout over
one another in order to have a conversation and more than one person
spilled a drink on him as he walked through the crowded hall. He wiped
off his arm with a disgusted snarl.

Forcing his way through the horde of people was a difficult task. By
the time he made it to the edge of the room, his cheeks were red with
irritation and the sweltering heat coming off the mass of bodies.

He moved from table to table, checking for any sign of Eamon or Ali,
but came up short. When he made it to the last table tucked inside an

alcove, he pinched the bridge of his nose and groaned. The gentleman and woman sitting in the booth gave him a look before the latter asked if he needed help.

Nik could just imagine how he appeared—like a drunken slop, with sweaty, flushed skin and wide eyes searching for Ali. He probably looked lost and confused.

"No, I'm all right. Thank you, though," he said over a round of laughter from the group next to him. Then he pushed his way back outside where he could breathe easy again.

The next two businesses he searched went almost identically to the first, though thankfully they were slightly less crowded. Both times, he found himself no closer to finding Ali or Eamon.

He headed toward the mountain at a slight jog, peeking inside various shops on his way but mostly finding them empty. Some of them were locked, and he didn't even get the chance to search inside. He shouted Ali's name and moved along when his call was met with silence.

Time slipped through his fingers. A feeling deep inside told him something was wrong. His heart pounded erratically, and he clutched his chest as his mind ran through every worst-case scenario.

What if she'd followed Eamon and found herself in trouble? Eamon was known to be violent and Nik didn't trust him alone with Ali for even one second. What if he tried to hurt her? Or worse...

What if Nik was too late?

Inside the entry chamber, he made his way toward their home. He didn't think she'd be there, especially if she'd been following Eamon, but a part of him hoped he had it all wrong. That she'd just forgotten something and had come home to grab it. That nothing was wrong at all.

The door flung open and Nik let it slam closed behind him.

"Ali," he called frantically. Although their home only consisted of a kitchenette, a small bedroom, and an attached bathroom, Nik checked the entire space twice as if Ali might pop up from a hidden corner.

But she never did. She wasn't at home.

Or the cafeteria.

Or the supply chamber.

Or the medic chamber.

He made one last attempt to find her in the wing that housed the council chamber but came up short there, too. Of course, he couldn't get into the locked chamber, so there was a chance she was inside, but when he called her name, she didn't respond. He had to force the image of her lying on the ground after being poisoned out of his mind.

Panic set in as Nik rushed back to the entry chamber. He wasn't sure where to look next. Maybe the horse stables? Or the lake? One thing was for certain—he couldn't wait idly while Ali was out there, possibly in danger.

His mind raced as he took the tunnel that led outside and back into the bright sun. He ran a hand through his disheveled hair, staring at the path while mentally making a list of all the places he could search.

He was so lost in his thought that when he looked up again and saw a blonde woman with red stains on her shirt and a haunted look on her face, he froze in disbelief.

"Ali?" he said softly, taking a tentative step forward. "What the hell happened?"

Ali's bottom lip trembled, and her hands alternated between clenched fists and outstretched fingers. She opened her mouth to speak but erupted in a fit of coughing. She doubled over, barely getting a breath in between each burst of angry air.

Nik closed the gap between them and wrapped a hand around her waist. He rubbed soothing circles onto her back with his other one. "Deep breaths, Ali."

But she continued to cough, and her cheeks went pale from the lack of oxygen. Without a second thought, he picked her up with one arm behind her knees and the other bracing her back.

Ali managed to get one deep inhale in before she struggled to breathe again. She grabbed the front of his shirt and looked at him with pleading eyes.

"Don't worry, love. I've got you." And then he ran as fast as he could to the medic chamber.

Ali wove in and out of consciousness on the way there, leaving Nik terrified that he would lose her this time. This situation was way too similar to the last time he'd ushered her to the medical chamber. The weight of her limp figure sent chills down his spine and made his feet feel heavy and numb at the same time.

After what felt like an eternity, Nik burst into the medical chamber, startling the young man at the front desk.

"Can I help you?" he asked.

"I need Meg," he choked out.

"What happened?"

Nik wanted to leap across the desk to strangle the man. "I. Need. Meg."

"She's in with someone else right now, but if you sit for a moment, I can go—"

"I will not *sit*." Nik's voice had risen an entire octave. In his arms, Ali made an unintelligible noise, and he thanked god for the confirmation that she was still alive.

"Maybe you should go get Meg," another voice broke in. Nik turned around to find Soren approaching the desk.

The young man at the desk looked alarmed by Nik's manic expression and his outburst, and irritated by the arrival of Soren, who was taking Nik's side. "One second."

Soren came closer, frowning as he took in the sight of Ali. "What hap—"

Nik shook his head, cutting Soren off. He could hardly speak through his fear and desperation.

It took closer to twenty seconds, but when the receptionist came back, Meg was at his side. She took one lock at Ali and her pleasant smile faded. She pointed down the hall. "Bring her here."

Nik gave a curt nod to Soren before following Meg.

She led Nik to an unfamiliar room, but it looked identical to the one before with its pristine counter tops and floor, abrasive white lighting, and sterile atmosphere. A plain wooden stool waited in the room's corner, but Nik refused to sit, even after he laid Ali gently on the bed. He stood with his hands laced behind his head while he waited for Meg to check Ali's vital signs.

"I found her in the street like this," he said. "She looked like she was in shock and then she just started coughing and couldn't stop."

"Her breathing is very faint," Meg confirmed. "Is this her blood?" She lifted Ali's shirt, searching for wounds, but her skin was untouched.

"I don't know," Nik said.

"It doesn't appear to be," Meg said, continuing her assessment. Her hand grazed Ali's neck. "What's this?"

A red rash had spread over her throat and extended past her shirt collar. He couldn't recall if it had been there when he'd found her. Everything had happened so quickly. "Is that—"

"Helberries." Meg stood and pulled out a drawer, sifting through until she found a vial, then punctured it with a needle to draw out its contents. "I'm not sure where your girlfriend keeps finding these things. I thought Grace was supposed to be handling this."

His *fiancé,* but he didn't bother correcting her.

Nik flinched when Meg brought the tip of the needle to Ali's arm. "What is that?"

Meg didn't take her eyes off of her steady hands. "I'm allowing you to stay because I don't need another lecture from Grace. If you'd like to keep it that way, I suggest you don't distract me while I'm working."

Nik pursed his lips, but he held his breath as the needle pierced Ali's skin. The liquid drained into her flesh and then Meg was pulling the needle back, applying pressure to the small puncture.

"How long does it take to work?" He couldn't help himself. He needed to know if she was going to be out for hours like she had been the first time. Waiting for her to wake up had been torture, but at least she'd be okay.

"It won't be as long as the last time. When you found her, she was still conscious, so I'm hopeful the toxin hasn't had as much time to course through her system. Perhaps an hour or two?"

Nik's shoulders relaxed and the heavy weight on his chest disappeared. An hour or two. He could survive that.

He pulled the stool closer to Ali's bed and finally took a seat, reaching out to hold her hand.

"I have to check on another patient. If you need anything, let Brady at the front desk know."

Nik nodded, and once Meg had left the room, he leaned in closer to Ali, kissing her cheek and brushing her hair back from her face. "You've got to stop doing this to me, babe."

A short time later, Brady came to check on them, bringing Nik a glass of water. "Can I get you anything else?"

"I'm fine, thank you."

While Nik waited, counting down the minutes until Ali woke, his mind wandered to the Rite. The race had to be half over by now. Was Eli winning?

He shook his head. How had he gotten to this place where he gave a shit about Eli?

It was just because Ali cared about him. Nik also considered Grace a friend and therefore wanted her to be happy as well.

It had nothing to do with a friendship blossoming between him and Eli. *That* was not possible.

At one point, he stood and began to pace near the foot of Ali's bed. Waiting was not his strong suit. He cracked his knuckles and stretched his arms above his head, then returned to the stool, tapping his foot and reaching for Ali's hand again.

He stroked the back of her hand with his thumb. "Come on, love," he said softly. "Wake up."

Her fingers curled around his hand ever so slightly. He thought he'd imagined it, but then it happened again, this time stronger.

"Nik," she rasped.

"Ali." Nik gingerly wrapped his arms around her and kissed her temple. He spoke her name with reverence. "Ali, I'm here."

She coughed, and he pulled back, giving her space to breathe. Then he found his untouched glass of water and offered it to her, watching as she took a few sips and then returned the cup to him.

"What happened?" she asked.

"I was hoping you could tell me."

"I remember walking out of the cave, and then you were there. But then...I was dizzy and everything was spinning..."

"What cave?"

She blinked a couple times, her eyes slowly clearing. "The cave with Eamon. I followed him from the Rite because I didn't trust him. I knew he wouldn't leave unless he had a good reason, and I wanted to know what that reason was.

"He led me back to the mountain, except we didn't come in through the main entry chamber. There was a trail and then he disappeared into a narrow tunnel and I followed him there too.

"It was like nothing I've ever seen before, Nik. The helberries...that's where they are. He's been growing them under the mountain like his own hellish conservatory. They were everywhere."

Her brows furrowed, and Nik wondered what was going on in her head. If she was recalling the image of the plant room. He needed to go there to see for himself—Grace, too—but that could wait until she was ready to return.

"What happened next? Where's Eamon now?" If the blood on her shirt wasn't hers, he had to assume it belonged to Eamon.

Ali looked down at her hands, wringing them in her lap. "I...I killed him."

She was oddly calm for having just killed a man, but then, this wasn't the first person she'd killed. Nik reached for her hands and held them still. "Whatever you did, I'm sure it was out of necessity."

She looked at him with glassy eyes and nodded. "It was. He would've killed me if I hadn't gotten to him first. There were jars full of a slimy solution—like helberry jam. I threw them at him and once they broke open...well, you can imagine how he reacted. The poison spread quickly, but it wasn't enough to take him out entirely. He nearly hit me with helberry powder but missed. I still inhaled quite a bit, though, which is how I suppose I wound up here." She looked around the room and took a steadying breath.

"You're safe now," he said, reassuring himself as much as her.

"For how long? I'm so tired of fighting. Of looking over our shoulders and waiting for another attack." A tear escaped and trailed down her cheek. "Eamon was right there in front of me. He couldn't see because the helberries had gotten in his eyes. I could've run. He could've survived with treatment like I did. But I grabbed a pair of shears and stabbed him in the chest. I watched him take his last breath. I killed him, Nik, and I don't regret it."

Nik reached up to wipe away her stray tear. "There's nothing to regret."

Chapter Thirty-Eight

ELI

ELI SHOVED AGAINST THE body that had come out of nowhere. He should've known it wouldn't be so easy to claim the flag as his own. At least two other competitors remained, and he still needed to make it back up the mountain.

Jae grunted as he attempted to pull the flag out of Eli's hands. His elbow landed hard against Eli's stomach. Eli folded in half but held tightly to the piece of fabric, refusing to let go of his key to ending up with Grace.

Eli reared his head back and collided with Jae's face. The crunching noise sounded as though he'd hit Jae's nose and possibly broken it. Jae groaned and his hold loosened just enough for Eli to break free.

Just as Eli had suspected, Jae was clutching his face. Blood trailed down his mouth and chin. He dropped his hand, wiping it against his pant leg.

Eli raised his hands. "Give it up, Jae. The flag is mine. Grace is mine. Even if you managed to rip the flag from my hands, she'd always be mine. She'll never love you."

Jae gritted his teeth. "You don't get it. I'm not in this for *love*. To those of us who have lived in Berland since we were children, this is every man's dream. Do you understand the respect and awe that comes with marrying Grace?"

"That's all she is to you?" Eli asked incredulously. "A stepping stool to bolster your ego?"

"Not all of us can marry for *love*. My parents have never been proud of me, always setting the highest standards and expecting me to fail. But *this*—this would be my greatest achievement."

Eli almost felt sorry for him. But as pitiful as Jae's reasons were, it wasn't enough for Eli to take it easy on him. "If you want this flag, you're going to have to pry it out of my cold, dead hands."

"That can be arranged," Jae said. He sprang forward to tackle Eli, but Eli was too fast. He leaped to the side and Jae stumbled a few steps before catching his balance.

Jae charged forward again, swinging his fist at Eli's head. He missed, hitting Eli's shoulder instead as he dove out of the way.

"Are you going to fight back or run away like a coward?"

Truthfully, Eli would've preferred to run. He had nothing against Jae, except that they were fighting for the same woman. He didn't want to hurt him.

Before Eli could respond, however, a third figure emerged from the trees, running toward them like a wild beast. Jae noticed a second too late, and it cost him dearly. Trevor plowed through him, sending them both flying to the ground. Trevor drew back his fist and struck Jae in the face again and again, alternating between his left and right. Jae never had a chance to block or defend himself. In a matter of seconds, his head lolled to one side, a bruise already forming over his right eye.

Eli stood slack-jawed as Trevor got to his feet, dragging his arms like his assault had left them feeling heavy and stiff. Then he turned to Eli. One look inside the endless black pits of his eyes and Eli knew he was out for blood.

"Looks like it's just you and me," he said.

Trevor didn't give Eli much time to weigh his options before he was charging toward him. Eli spun on his heel, running as fast as his legs could carry him. His arms pumped at his sides, the flag still held tightly in one fist.

The trail began to slope upward, and Eli had to work even harder to put distance between him and Trevor. His shoes slipped against the loose dirt and crumpled leaves, but he didn't let it slow him down.

Behind him, Trevor panted heavily. While he was undoubtedly stronger than Eli, Eli was faster and had more stamina. The third round was turning into a true race to the top, and Eli couldn't let Trevor catch him.

Weaving between the trees, Eli darted up the most direct path while Trevor nipped at his heels. His chest burned, aching for a break, for a deep inhale to satiate his desperate lungs, but stopping wasn't an option.

He heard what sounded like a branch snapping, followed by a loud, pained yell. Sparing a second to look over his shoulder, he was thrilled to find that Trevor had tripped and was now struggling to get back to his feet.

The sight gave Eli a renewed burst of energy, and he poured everything he had into the strenuous hike. He ran and climbed, hopping over fallen tree trunks and dodging overgrown thickets. When his legs finally demanded he slow down, he took another peek over his shoulder, unable to see Trevor at all.

He didn't allow himself to fall into a false sense of security. Trevor could be anywhere, waiting to pop out and attack him. Or maybe Eli had lost him in a moment of pure luck. Either way, he wouldn't take the chance to stop for a break.

Looking around, he tried to reorient himself. He'd been running carelessly in the direction he assumed would lead back to the starting point, but he hadn't taken the time to carefully assess his route like he had on the way down.

He was close to the river and the waterfall that fed into it. He could hear the steady hum of water running over the cliff side and cutting through the rocky terrain nearby.

Pausing for a moment, he listened closely for the sound of Trevor's footsteps, but heard nothing aside from the rushing water.

After hiking a few more minutes, Eli came across an old wooden sign. The image was almost entirely unreadable, but it didn't matter. Eli recognized it as the sign that pointed toward the top of the waterfall. If he took the path ahead, he wouldn't need to climb up the cliff side. His tired arms were grateful for the easier route.

Eli took the path at a jog, still expecting Trevor to pop out at any moment. He couldn't have fallen that far behind. Despite his absence, Eli couldn't shake the feeling that Trevor was playing games. That he was lurking in the shadows, waiting for the perfect moment to strike.

The thought gave him chills, and he sped into a run. While this route was less strenuous on his arms, it took longer than if he'd chosen to climb the rocks. This path serpentined up the mountain until it reached an old overlook next to the waterfall. The overlook was abandoned now, but the trail had survived the passing of time, marked by smooth stones.

It didn't take long for the waterfall to appear, and Eli breathed a sigh of relief. It wouldn't take much longer to reach the top of the mountain from here.

Just as his shoulders began to relax, a whistling noise sounded behind him.

Eli spun around, eyes roaming the tree line where he'd just emerged. It was eerily quiet as he kept still and searched for his nemesis.

Another whistle sounded farther to his left, and Eli craned his neck to find the source.

"Scared to come out and face me, Trevor?" he yelled into the shadows.

He waited. And waited.

He waited for so long that he almost thought his mind was playing tricks on him. That the whistling was all in his mind. Perhaps he was dehydrated or had been in the sun too long.

But then the whistling started again, and this time, Trevor strolled out from the woods with his hands in his pockets.

Eli tucked the flag deep into his back pocket. He had a hunch he'd be needing both hands to deal with Trevor.

"Nice to see you again, Eli."

"Wish I could say the same for you."

Trevor took a step toward Eli, who immediately positioned his body in a defensive stance. Trevor paused for a moment, and then his lips curved into a smile. Always playing games.

He started to whistle again, and the sound grated on Eli's ears.

"Whatever this is, let's get it over with," Eli snarled. "You can try to take this flag from my hands, but I'm telling you right now, it's never going to happen."

"I wouldn't be so certain," Trevor said, his arrogance as obnoxious as ever.

Rage surged from the soles of Eli's feet to the tips of his fingers. He was gripped by an urge he'd never felt before, the desire to wrap his fingers around Trevor's neck and squeeze until the smarmy smile fell from his face.

They stared each other down for several long seconds, and then, as if a barrier had been dropped between them, they charged forward at the same time.

Eli hit Trevor around his waist, pushing him back, while Trevor's fists landed against Eli's back and the side of his head. Everything blurred, and they tumbled to the ground. Eli wasn't even sure which way was up. All he knew was anger and violence.

He was so sick of battling for Grace, for his happiness, against the forces that sought to overthrow his partner and soul mate. All of his emotions poured out through his fists, and he beat and clawed unrelentingly at his opponent.

Trevor fought equally hard. A knee collided with Eli's rib, and it stole his breath. He responded by driving an elbow into Trevor's eye, and the man let out a blood-curdling scream. There was a solid chance that Eli had just blinded him.

Trevor did his best to push Eli off, but he struggled with only one eye. He reached toward Eli's face, doing his best to return the favor, but Eli held him off.

Moving as though he was possessed by the devil himself, Eli wrapped his hands around Trevor's neck, squeezing until Trevor's one good eye bulged. True terror took root, and for a moment Eli wondered if he had it in him...if it was possible for him to take this man's life.

Then he thought about all the times he'd threatened Grace's life, and he squeezed tighter, his thumbs digging into Trevor's throat. Trevor made a choking noise and his body went limp.

Eli jumped up immediately. He wiped his palms on his pants as though that would rid him of the ghost of Trevor's skin against his. Despite everything he tried, he could still feel Trevor struggling underneath his hands. Still felt the life leaving him.

It wasn't the first time he'd killed someone; he'd done it while defending Andus too. But it never got any easier. He wasn't built for taking lives.

He bent over with his hands on his knees, dry heaving with his eyes pinched closed.

He would have to go back to town and tell them what he'd done. Would they believe it was self-defense? Could Grace protect him from Trevor's father and his followers? Or would it just give Eamon more ammunition to use against Grace? Surely they'd call for him to be exiled, and then everything he'd done would've been for nothing.

The ground seemed to tilt underneath him, leaving him light-headed and dizzy. He tried his best to slow his breathing, and after a few deep inhales and controlled exhales, his head ceased its pounding.

Standing straight, he sucked in one more deep breath. He could handle this.

As he turned to find his path, a sudden movement caught his eye. On the ground, where Trevor *should've* been, was an empty spot.

Trevor was on his feet again...not dead.

Eli had little time to comprehend his mistake—Trevor had fooled him. He had been so caught up in his moral dilemma that he hadn't thought to make sure Trevor was *really* dead. Instead, Trevor had pretended just long enough for Eli to release him.

And now he was charging toward Eli once more, one eye still swollen shut while the other was red and angry.

Eli ducked as Trevor swung a fist at his head, but the man tackled him with the force of a crazed animal. The impact was so hard that Eli hit the ground and Trevor tumbled over the top of him. His momentum carried him forward, and he rolled until his body disappeared over the side of the cliff. His scream pierced the air, then faded until Eli couldn't hear anything but the water as it fell into the river below.

Eli lay there for a long moment, breathing hard. Everything hurt, but he forced himself to crawl over to the cliff's edge. Below, plumes of mist rose in the air, blurring the spot where the cascade ended. Farther out, the water rushed over a few uneven rocks before settling into a calm current.

Eli gripped the edge of the cliff. He waited, expecting Trevor to float into view at any moment. To swim to the shore and return for another round. But long moments passed, and Trevor was nowhere to be found.

Had he hit a rock on the way down? Was he caught under the rapids? Eli scanned the perimeter of the falls to make sure Trevor wasn't still clinging on to the side somehow.

But he was alone in the middle of these mountains. No one to witness what had just happened or accuse him of murder. No one to back up his claims of self-defense, either.

Finally, Eli caught sight of Trevor—floating in the water face down. His body was limp as it moved downstream, and this time, Eli was certain. There was no way Trevor could've survived the fall or the lack of oxygen as the force of the water held him under.

Trevor was well and truly dead.

Chapter Thirty-Nine

GRACE

GRACE'S NERVES ONLY INTENSIFIED at the start of the third and final round. Eli disappeared within seconds, Ali was missing, and Nik had run off to find her. Her mother was too sick to get out of bed. Half of her entourage was missing, and it was impossible to ignore their absence.

She knew it would take a while before any of the suitors made it back—hopefully Eli with the winning flag in his hand. Until then, she needed to find a way to keep herself distracted.

"How are things with Sam?" she asked her brother quietly.

His eyes quickly flicked toward Sam on the other side of the platform before returning to her. His throat bobbed as he swallowed.

"Oh, don't be shy, Theo. It's obvious there's something between the two of you."

"I'm not shy. I'm just not sure Sam is ready for people to know...about us."

Grace grinned. "But there is an '*us?*'"

Theo nodded silently.

"Good. I'm happy for you."

"Thank you," he said, rolling his eyes.

She peered out to where the ground began to slope and trees lined the edge of the clearing. A part of her knew that watching so intently wouldn't speed things up, but another part of her found it impossible to look away. If only she could see what was happening in the mysterious woods.

Theo's hand landed on her thigh, startling her. "Are you worried about him?"

She thought for a moment before responding, "I wish I could say I wasn't. He's smart and strong. There is no one better equipped for this Rite than Eli. But—"

"But what if something goes wrong?"

"Exactly. Anything could happen. It's agonizing waiting here with no hint of how things are going, just hoping that he's the first one to return."

Theo squeezed her thigh just above her knee, grounding her and stealing her from her sabotaging thoughts. "It's going to be okay."

"How do you know?"

He chuckled. "You're not supposed to ask that. Just trust me."

Her smile mirrored his. "All right then."

To the left of the platform, Grace watched Soren approach, a grim expression on his face. Their eyes met as he moved closer, and he looked nervous.

"Soren," she greeted him.

"Hello, Grace."

"What's wrong?"

"I had to stop by the medical chamber to pick up something for my dad. It's why I was late getting here."

Grace waved a hand. He was young and inexperienced, and still very adamant about proving his worth as a guard. He needed to relax a little. "Don't worry about that."

"That's not it. While I was there, I ran into Nik. Ali was passed out in his arms. I'm not sure what happened, but it didn't look good." When he saw Grace's eyes widen, he added, "She'll live. Meg seemed pretty sure of it. But I thought you'd want to know."

Grace sucked in a sharp breath and moved to stand, but Theo wrapped his hand around her arm.

"What are you doing?" he asked.

"I need to go see what happened. If there was another attack, I need to speak with Nik and make sure Ali is okay."

His serious expression made her hesitate. "You can't. Not yet, at least. People will get suspicious if you leave the Rite."

She frowned and looked out at the crowd. Most of them were chatting with their friends or finding ways to entertain themselves while they waited. Few, if any, were even looking her way. But would that change if she stood and left? Would it be that bad if they did notice?

"I can go," Soren said. "I can go back and see if there's been any update."

He looked distressed, like he just wanted to do a good job and impress Grace in whatever way possible and understood that informing her that one of her best friends was currently unconscious in the medical chamber wasn't the best way to do so.

"That would be great. Thank you, Soren."

He was about to leave when Grace stopped him.

"Soren?"

"Yes, ma'am?"

She spoke quietly, so no one aside from Theo and Soren could hear. "I have reason to believe that Eamon has something to do with this attack. He hasn't shown up to the Rite even though he's on the oversight committee. And when Nik left, he was concerned that Ali might've been searching for him."

"You think Eamon hurt her?"

It wouldn't be the first time, but Soren didn't know that. He hadn't been privy to most matters behind the scenes since he was only filling in for Nik. Grace hoped he was as trustworthy as she thought him to be.

"This is obviously sensitive information, Soren. Please find out what you can, but don't—"

"Don't speak a word of it. Got it."

"Thank you."

With a polite nod, Soren turned and headed back toward the mountain's entrance.

Grace's fingers tapped anxiously in her lap. Between Eli and Ali, her nerves had never been tested so severely. Her skin felt like it was too tight, her bones too rigid. Time moved slower than it ever had before, and she was seconds from pacing back and forth on the raised platform.

Voices grew louder throughout the crowd and Grace raised her head to find Roman limping out of the woods. She jumped to her feet, as did her brother and father.

When Roman passed the last tree, he took a tumble and fell to the ground. A collective gasp came from the crowd and two men sprinted forward to pick him up. Together they helped carry Roman until he was standing in front of Grace, a pained expression on his face.

Grace swallowed hard. She hated to admit that despite his obvious injuries, her primary concern was deciphering whether he held that red flag that signified he'd won the Rite. Her eyes raked over his body and studied his hands, open as they wrapped around his helpers' shoulders.

She breathed easier, knowing he hadn't brought the flag back with him.

"Roman." Her father said his name with a hint of curiosity.

When Roman's eyes met Grace's, there seemed to be an apology there. What was happening in those woods?

"I'm sorry, Grace. I injured my ankle in a rogue trap. I couldn't finish." He hung his head in shame.

Blood seeped through his pant leg, staining his jeans a deep crimson. Grace was impressed he'd even managed to get back to the starting point without help. "It's okay, Roman. You did your best."

His expression turned slightly less grim, although still disappointed.

Grace looked back and forth between the two men holding him up. "Can you take him to see the medic? Have that leg taken care of?"

They nodded and helped Roman hobble away.

"Are all Rites this exciting?" Amaya asked, beaming brightly until Heather elbowed her in the side.

"I have no idea," Grace muttered under her breath.

Once the crowd quieted down, Grace found herself in the same position as before—plagued by nerves and uncontrollable thoughts. Her mind wandered to Eli in the woods. Had he found the flag yet? What if he had also fallen injured with no one to help him?

Then her mind redirected to Ali. Had Meg revived her yet? Nik had to be going out of his mind. He had a tough exterior, but his soft spot for Ali was obvious to everyone who knew him. Hopefully by the time the Rite was over, all would be well back inside the mountain.

Grace's nerves settled into her stomach and she felt moments away from expelling her lunch all down the front of her dress. It must've shown in her face too, because Theo kept giving her sideways glances, and Heather repeatedly pushed a flask of water into her hands, saying she looked pale and unwell.

She tried to sip the water, but it just made her stomach feel as though there was a storm trapped inside, sloshing back and forth and making her even more queasy.

An undiscernible amount of time passed. She had no clue whether it had been an hour or twelve. The sun was partially hidden behind clouds, further complicating her perception of time.

No one else had emerged since Roman, and she wasn't sure if that was a good sign or not. Perhaps it meant they were still searching for the flag, or maybe Roman wasn't the only one to have fallen in his quest to win her heart.

Just when she didn't think she could take any more waiting, a shadow moved in the distance, lurking between the trees. As the figure drew closer, Grace squinted to try to make out who it was that was returning.

The man walked confidently, slow enough that he didn't seem to be worried about anyone chasing him. His build looked like Eli's, but Grace was so nervous, she didn't want to believe it was him until he was standing right before her.

Finally, he moved into the light, a small red piece of fabric in his hands, and Grace didn't have it in her to remain calm. She leaped to her feet and neither her brother nor her father had time to stop her before she raced across the clearing and flung her arms around Eli, kissing his cheek and running her fingers through his hair.

It didn't take long for the crowd to realize Eli held the flag. Cheers erupted all around them, but it was nothing compared to the way her heart burst with excitement. For them, the Rite was mostly entertainment, but for her, the Rite was her future.

And Eli had just secured his place in it.

Eli had *won*.

"You did it," she said against his ear. He squeezed her tightly, and she felt right at home in his arms. It dawned on her that this marked the end, but also the beginning. The end of an archaic tournament but the start of her life with Eli. The end of fear and doubt and the beginning of her legacy. It felt as though her life had just pivoted, a clear line drawn between *before* and *now*.

Before was dull and dreary. Now was bright and bursting with color.

Her lips found his, and they exchanged a series of quick, soft kisses before breaking apart. She pulled back enough to look him in the eyes and, although they were full of love and adoration, she also sensed that something else was on his mind.

"What's wrong?"

He shook his head and observed the crowd, most of them still on their feet and roaring loudly. "We should find somewhere private to speak."

It would be impossible to sneak away now. Not when the entire town was waiting for some type of speech, a declaration of the winner and the announcement that the Rite had officially ended.

Eli's eyes narrowed, and Grace followed his gaze, looking over her shoulder. The Rite's oversight committee was headed in their direction, led by her father. One member of the committee was noticeably missing.

"Where's Eamon?" Eli asked.

"He's..." Grace paused. Who knew where he was? Soren hadn't returned yet with an update, so she could only guess. But then another absence caught her attention. "Where's Trevor? And Jae?"

"Jae hasn't returned?" Eli asked.

Grace shook her head, wishing the committee would give them a few more minutes alone. But they were almost within earshot now.

Eli lowered his voice. "Jae will be fine. He was knocked out near the flag's point. Trevor, however..."

Her father cut in with a clap on Eli's back. "Well done, Eli. I didn't doubt you for a second."

Grace smiled. Even if her mother hadn't been supportive, her father only seemed to want what she wanted. For that, she would be eternally grateful.

"Thank you, sir."

"I thought I told you to call me Ben."

Eli let out a nervous laugh, still holding on to some piece of information that Grace was dying to hear.

Her father stepped to the side, allowing Diane and Fox space to join the conversation.

"Congratulations, Eli," Diane said, offering her hand to shake Eli's. "You've competed well and have proven your worthiness of Grace's hand in marriage."

"I'll second that," Fox added. "Well done, Eli."

Before Grace knew it, they were being pulled back to the platform, and the crowd was being silenced as her father prepared to make a speech.

Eli stood next to her, and she couldn't help but smile, feeling like she'd gotten everything she'd ever wanted. Nothing could bring her down from this high. Beside her, Eli broke into a smile. Whatever had happened with Trevor...it wasn't enough to spoil this moment.

Their moment.

Her father's voice was booming next to her as he waved a hand in their direction. "Everyone, please help me congratulate Grace, the next Lady of Berland and her consort, Eli!"

⚜ ⚜

Ali had everyone's undivided attention as she recanted her confrontation with Eamon.

"So Eamon is..."

"Dead," Ali said, nodding. "I'm sure of it."

Grace nodded and pondered for a moment. "We'll need to send someone to clean out his hideout. I can't believe he was growing helberries inside the mountain. If it's as bad as you described it, Ali, the casualties could've been endless. You saved many lives today."

Ali and Nik shared a smile, and Grace turned toward Eli. "And Trevor?"

"Also dead," Eli confessed. Attention turned to him as he told the story of what happened in the woods.

"Okay. Okay," Grace said, breathing deeply. It was a lot to process. Eamon and Trevor, the two men who'd spent so much time working to take her and her mother down, were now gone. It didn't feel real.

"What will we do now?" Nik asked. "How do we explain this?" He squeezed Ali's shoulder, concern etched between his brows.

"Ali and Eli both acted in self-defense. There isn't anything to explain. It's done. It's over."

"And Eamon's followers will accept that explanation?" Eli asked.

"They won't have a choice. None of the others have a claim to the title. Without a leader, their rebellion will fall apart."

"For now," Nik said.

"For now," Grace agreed. "And if or when another narcissist comes along and tries to take what is mine, we will deal with them. But today I will not let them take my joy. Today we celebrate—family, friends, community, and prosperity. We celebrate us."

Eli linked his hand with Grace's. "I like the sound of that." He paused for a moment, looking at each person in the room. "Us."

Epilogue

ALI

One year later...

Fingers gripped her thighs, spreading her legs apart while Nik's tongue flicked her clit. Ali gripped the soft white sheets with one hand and searched with the other for Nik's soft brown curls. When she gave his hair a tug, he hummed against her clit and her stomach twisted and flipped in desire for him.

Though his mouth was busy, there was a smile in his eyes as he looked up at her from between her legs. His fingers worked their magic inside her and before long, she was rocking her hips, desperate for more. He sucked and swirled his tongue, and when he added a third finger, she fell apart.

Her lips trembled, and her voice was shaky. "Fuck, fuck, I need you."

Nik licked his lips and crawled up her body, pressing a gentle kiss to her lips. "That's all you get for now."

The frustrated noise she made was the closest thing to pouting she'd ever done. She tried to wrap her legs around him and pull his body into hers, but he remained firm, propped up on his muscular arms. His eyes flicked down to her stomach and the small swell there, and she knew he wouldn't risk letting his weight crush her. Not for several more months.

He rolled off the bed and grabbed her by the hands, pulling her up into a seated position. She watched him, admiring his lean muscles and flushed cheeks, tracking him as he moved to the bathroom and disappeared to the sound of running water. It took her a little longer to follow, but eventually she joined him in the shower, relaxing under the warm waterfall and his soothing touch.

She could've stood there all day, feeling safe and adored in his embrace, but a knock at the door had her slipping out of the shower, quickly drying off and throwing on a pair of shorts and a button up top.

Ali pulled open the door and Grace rushed inside, carrying a long pearly-white gown and a bag that looked quite heavy. Ali grabbed the bag and dropped it on the dining table while Heather closed the door behind them.

Grace took one look at Ali and frowned. "Why is your hair wet? Didn't I tell you what time we'd be here? It's fine. Heather can take care of it."

Ali dragged her fingers through her tangled hair, feeling a bit self-conscious. She hadn't meant to lose track of time, but she couldn't resist Nik's charm.

Heather guided her into a chair and began to untangle her hair as gently as she could manage.

"Where are the girls?" Ali asked.

"They're with Amaya, grabbing some breakfast. They'll be here soon."

"I hope they behaved well."

Grace nodded. "Of course. They're absolute angels. We had a great time playing dress-up and Julia even put on a little concert for us."

"She did?" Ali laughed. Julia had recently discovered a love for singing and would perform for anyone who would sit long enough to listen. Kaydence had crafted a homemade tambourine so she could perform with her sister, too.

"Yes, they were absolute dolls. I'm happy to babysit anytime you and Nik need a break."

It had been ten months since Nik and Ali had adopted Julia and Kaydence, and this was the first night they hadn't stayed at home. Normally, they slept in their own bedroom across the hall from Nik and Ali.

When the council had decided to build a new housing development outside of the mountain, Nik and Ali were one of the first to sign up. She'd been sick of the dark depths and small spaces that had felt like a cage. And a small part of her had hoped the extra space would be needed for their family. She just hadn't realized how quickly their family would grow.

It had taken some time to develop the first plot of land and tap into plumbing and electricity, but now they were settled into their quaint three-bedroom home—the main bedroom, the girls' shared room, and a nursery for the baby currently growing in her belly.

Ali caressed her stomach while Grace pulled the dress off its hanger. "Let's get you dressed."

Before Grace could usher her back into the bedroom, Nik emerged in a pair of black slacks and a white button-down shirt.

Grace stopped in her tracks and snapped her fingers at him. "What are you doing here?"

Ali tried not to laugh at his dumbfounded expression.

"I live here."

"Yes, but you were supposed to meet the boys an hour ago. How do the two of you accomplish anything without someone here to keep you on track?"

Nik shrugged at the same time Ali did, and she could no longer hold back her snicker.

Grace pointed to the front door. "Get out."

He had just made it to the door when there was another knock. Nik pulled it open and two energetic girls burst through, giggling, and skipping around.

Ali's eyes met Amaya's, and she smiled. "I might've given them some chocolate pastries."

"I had two," Julia said as she bounced around the room. Kaydence showed a bit more restraint as she rocked back and forth on her heels.

Amaya held a wicker basket, which she placed on the counter. "I swear I saved some for the rest of us, too."

"Eat quickly because we have a lot of work to do," Grace said, pointing between the pastries and Ali's mess of a mane. "And you," she said, glaring at Nik. "It's time for you to leave."

He did, but not before grabbing a pastry out of the basket.

Eventually, the girls calmed down and hid away in their room, playing together quietly—or at least as quietly as two kids with a significant amount of sugar in their systems could.

The living room turned into a chamber of chaos as the women sorted through dresses and jewelry, laying out their outfits and deciding which shoes looked best. Heather set up a temporary salon to fix each of the girls' hair. Ali's was braided into a flowing cascade down her back, white and purple flowers weaved in to accent her blonde hair.

Ali didn't own a lot of jewelry, so Grace had brought an entire drawer for Ali to choose from. She chose a simple purple and gold bracelet that matched the amethyst necklace Nik had given her long ago.

Once Ali's hair was finished, Heather called the girls back into the living room. Knowing they would likely make a mess of any formal style, Heather did their hair in matching ponytails with a purple flower tucked behind their ears.

"Are you nervous?" Grace asked as she helped Ali clasp her jewelry behind her neck.

Ali reached for the purple rose Nik had given to her shortly after they'd met. "Not at all. I feel like this is right where I was meant to be. This is who I was meant to be all along."

She smiled, thinking of her soon-to-be husband and their two kids with one more on the way. Her new role in this stable society that offered sanctuary for those who needed it. She couldn't be more grateful for the life she'd been given. The life she'd created and forged through blood, sweat, and tears.

The sight of Julia scribbling on a piece of paper brought her out of her thoughts. She squinted, and when she recognized the writing, she jumped up.

"Wait," she said, bringing her hands up. Julia stopped with her pencil hovering over the sheet of paper. "Did you get that out of my bag?"

Julia bit her lip and nodded. She'd been told at least five times not to dig through Ali's work notes.

Ali reached her palm out and Julia stood, handing over the piece of paper with a guilty frown. "There's another note pad in the kitchen you can use to draw on."

She brightened quickly and skipped to replace the paper Ali had taken away.

Ali took a moment to read over the words written on the page, smiling as she considered their importance, and thankful that Julia's doodles hadn't destroyed too much of the text. It was still legible enough that she could rewrite it before work next week.

"What's that?" Grace asked, reading over her shoulder.

"The proposal to end the Rite. I know you said no working this weekend, but I just need to—"

Grace gently pried the piece of paper from Ali's fingers. Ali watched as her eyes traced the words, line by line. If she wasn't mistaken, Grace's eyes filled with mist.

She reached out to take the paper back, and Grace gave it willingly. Then she sniffed and straightened her spine. "It looks good. We can talk more about it next week, but I meant what I said. *No* working this weekend."

They exchanged a brief smile before Grace returned to command the room, directing everyone to finish getting dressed and proceeding to pass out bouquets of flowers—purple and white to match the ones in Ali's hair.

"Miss Grace, can we be the flower girls in your wedding too?" Julia asked.

Grace bent down to her level. "Of course you can. Now go put your shoes on."

Technically, Grace and Eli were already married. They'd held a small, intimate ceremony in their home the day after the Rite ended so Grace's mother could be there. Shortly after, Ellen had passed away. Even though they were officially married, Grace and Eli wanted to have a proper celebration in the future, on their own time and once they'd had the chance to enjoy life on their own terms. They weren't in a rush, even if Julia was.

When everyone aside from Ali was finally ready, Amaya, Heather, Julia, and Kaydence all left through the front door, leaving Grace and Ali alone.

Grace held up Ali's dress—a pearly white gown made of stretchy fabric, lace detail covering the bust and draping like vines down the skirt. It had thin straps and a small V-cut between her breasts where her necklace would lie.

Grace helped her step into the gown and zipped up the back. "Thank god you picked the stretchy fabric," she teased. It had been hard to pick the perfect dress when Ali wasn't sure how big she would get before the big day.

She turned around and Grace gave her an appraising once-over, clasping her hands under her chin and smiling. "You look perfect."

This time, Ali was the one with tears in her eyes. She was so grateful to call Grace her friend, and she proceeded to squeeze her tightly in a hug. "Thank you so much. For everything. Not just the wedding stuff, but...everything."

Grace held her and laughed softly. "That's what friends are for."

The door opened again and a tall man with short brown hair and a crooked smile walked in. Eli stuck his hands in his pockets while he waited for them to separate.

Grace gave Ali's arms one last squeeze, picked up her bouquet, and kissed Eli's cheek as she left the room.

"Are you ready?" Eli asked.

Ali nodded, but her words got stuck in her throat. She wrapped her hand around Eli's arm, and he led them outside.

Sunlight hit her face, and she paused to take in the scenery. The new houses had been built in a circle around a courtyard intended to be used as a communal gathering space. Stone paths led from house to house, coming together in the center, and lilac bushes grew in between. They filled the air with a heavenly scent, and Ali inhaled deeply through her nose, savoring the floral aroma.

The center of the courtyard had been set up with wooden benches facing a trellis archway. Nik stood underneath it, waiting for her. He smiled and tilted his head back in a sexy way that made her want to nip at his neck.

Eli bumped her with his elbow. "It's not too late to back out. If you want to run, just say the word."

Ali looked around at everything she'd worked so hard for, and as her eyes landed on Nik at the end of the aisle, she'd never felt more at peace.

"I'm not going anywhere," she said, smiling. "This is everything I ever wanted. This is my home."

Acknowledgements

Wow, I cannot believe my first ever series is now complete! What a journey this has been. I have grown so much as author since the day I first gave life to Ali, Eli and Nik, but they will always be my babies. This series made me question a lot and was basically one long experiment in self-publishing. I learned how to do some things better, and learned *not* to do a lot of other things. In some ways, it feels like I had my own character arc alongside these protagonists. We've been through it all!

Thank you so much to everyone, especially those who have been here from day one. You have no idea how much your support means to me. I couldn't have continued on without you in my corner. When things got hard, you were the reason I kept pushing onward! To my bookish besties, my author friends, my PA, my street team and ARC teams—I owe everything to you! Thank you, truly, from the bottom of my heart.

For a list of titles by Rachel Mays, please visit
www.authorrachelmays.com

351